BEHIND EVERY GREAT FORTUNE™

A NOVEL

THE OHEKA CHRONICLES

FRANK AMOROSO

simply francis publishing company
North Carolina

Behind Every Great Fortune™

Copyright © 2014 by Frank Amoroso. All Rights Reserved.

For information about this title or to order other books and/or electronic media, contact the publisher:

simply francis publishing company
P.O. Box 329, Wrightsville Beach, NC 28480
www.simplyfrancispublishing.com
simplyfrancispublishing@gmail.com

Library of Congress Control Number: 2013920671

ISBN: 978-1-63062-000-4 (paperback)
ISBN: 978-1-63062-001-1 (e-book)

Printed in the United States of America

Cover design by Menagerie Company
Interior design by 1106 Design

Historical photograph within the cover is used for editorial purposes only. No affiliation with or sponsorship by the individuals depicted in the photograph is claimed or suggested.

Publisher's Cataloging-in-Publication
(Provided by Quality Books, Inc.)

Amoroso, Frank L.
  Behind every great fortune : the Oheka chronicles / by Frank Amoroso.
   pages cm
   LCCN 2013920671
   ISBN 978-1-63062-000-4
   ISBN 978-1-63062-001-1

   1. Kahn, Otto H., 1867-1934--Fiction. 2. Investment bankers--Fiction. 3. Rasputin, Grigorii Efimovich, 1869-1916--Fiction. 4. Franz Ferdinand, Archduke of Austria, 1863-1914--Fiction. 5. Sanger, Margaret, 1879-1966--Fiction. 6. World War, 1914-1918--Fiction. 7. Oheka (Cold Spring Harbor, N.Y.)--Fiction. 8. Historical fiction. 9. Suspense fiction. 10. Biographical fiction.   I. Title.

PS3601.M668B44 2014   813'.6
                              QBI13-600300

Dedication

Behind Every Great Fortune™ is dedicated to the great woman who has stood behind me for better and for worse. This work and so much of what I am would not exist without the incessant love, encouragement and inspiration of my beloved wife, Rhonda.

Foreword

RECENTLY, I ATTENDED A CATERED affair at Oheka Castle in Huntington, New York on the fabled Gold Coast of Long Island. The magnificence of this facility prompted me to ask the host about its origins. He advised me that it was built by Otto Kahn in the early twentieth century. Beyond that simple fact, Mr. Kahn was a complete mystery. Curious about what I imagined was an interesting life, I began researching the life and times of Otto Kahn. Although Kahn's greatest claim to fame is his immortalization as the Monopoly® guy in the eponymous board game, Otto Kahn knew and interacted with many of the most famous and powerful people of his time. Luminaries like Teddy Roosevelt, Enrico Caruso, and Charlie Chaplin graced lavish affairs hosted by Kahn at Oheka.

I suppose that somewhere in the great beyond, the spirit of Otto Kahn sensed a disturbance in his repose. Perhaps Mr. Kahn followed the advice of Yannick Murphy, the author of *Signed, Mata Hari* who wrote:

If you want to be a good ghost, stay quiet for almost a century. Then, on the anniversary of your death, begin to haunt the dreams of a writer so that the writer tells your story the way it should be told.[1]

Behind Every Great Fortune™ is a novel of historical fiction that tells the story of Otto Kahn and Oheka Castle the way it should be told.

Most of the characters and events are based in fact. Throughout the book I have used the actual words of historical characters in order to provide verisimilitude. Statements of this sort have been italicized. The sources are compiled in end notes. *Behind Every Great Fortune*™ is based in what I call tenable fiction. The interaction between and among the characters provides a compelling story and answers many of the mysteries surrounding Otto Kahn and Oheka Castle. Kahn was one of many partners of venerable banking houses in the early twentieth century. Yet, he alone built a castle. Thus, the most compelling mystery surrounding Otto Kahn is: how did he amass his fortune? Add to this, rumors of blood, mayhem and unimaginable treasure that swirled around Oheka and you have the makings of an intriguing story.

It is generally recognized that the winners write history. Historical fiction, using creative, plausible alternatives, is the writer's antidote to that truism. As Gore Vidal, the noted writer of historical fiction, observed, *"History is nothing but gossip about the past, with the hope that it might be true."*[2]

Before entering the labyrinth of our protagonist's life, the reader should know that prior to writing this book I received a literary license to imagine, speculate and create scenarios that may or may not have occurred, but that are within the realm of possibility. Some of the characters are fictitious; others are used fictitiously. Lest anyone take offense, I reiterate that *Behind Every Great Fortune*™ is a work of historical fiction, with emphasis on the word fiction. The goal of any imagination, speculation or conjecture in this work is to entertain, titillate and provoke the reader.

With that said, enjoy this novel,

Frank Amoroso

1916
St. Petersburg, Russia

A THIN LAYER OF SNOW covered the rutted ice in the courtyard of the Yusopov Palace. Dim silver light from the crescent moon illuminated his path. The vision in his left eye faltered as he stumbled toward the exit that was his only hope to escape and survive. Stay upright, keep moving, he exhorted himself. A sticky clot congealed over his left eye and cheek, blood from the wounds inflicted by his assailants. He slipped again, his throbbing wrists breaking his fall.

Voices behind him hurled curses. Panic surged in his chest. The murderous princes were pounding the door to the courtyard. In a matter of seconds, they would break through the barrier he had toppled to block their pursuit. His only hope was to make it to the street. With his good eye he fixed on the street lamp ahead that stood like a beacon holding back the grave-like darkness that enveloped the courtyard.

His chest ached from the bullet lodged between his ribs. He felt his lifeblood flowing down his side, pasting his silk shirt to his skin. A wave of nausea swept over him. Bile and vomit hurled from his throat and splashed onto his boots. He suppressed the terror rising in his brain.

At last, he reached the gate. He threw his weight against it, and miraculously, it gave way. Behind him, splintering wood signaled the demise of his barricade. Loud voices and rapid footsteps crunching across the courtyard ice followed in hot pursuit. In moments they would be on him like wolves on a wounded bear. There was no doubt that they would finish their murderous task. Then, he saw his salvation in the form of headlights approaching. He staggered into the frozen street, waving like a drowning man.

The car stopped. He grinned madly and reached toward it. His head throbbed from the vicious beating he had endured. If he could only hang onto the side of the vehicle until he got away, he would survive. His assassins were at the gate. He had to get to the car. It was his last hope. He slipped and fell. He crawled until he reached the fender and lurched onto the running board. With his breath coming in short rasps, he steadied himself. The passenger window was opening. A sense of hope filled him.

He reached in and pulled himself up, straining to lift his weight even with the edge of the door. His eyes reached the level of the window opening. As he focused, he blinked uncomprehendingly at the barrel of a gun. He recognized the eyes of his enemy. The dim light of the moon reflected off the barrel of the Browning aimed at his forehead. Like a mortally wounded bear, trapped in a pit back in the forests of his native Siberia, he recognized the inevitability of his fate. With a moan, he whispered, "Lord help me." A dull chill radiated through his core, just as a flash erupted from the pistol and an ear-splitting crack thundered in the confined space of the vehicle. The smell of burnt powder and singed flesh filled the air. Then, blackness.

PART 1

The Early Years

1994

Cold Spring Harbor, New York

Stay your hand, leveler.

~ WALT WHITMAN, *TEAR DOWN*

ALTHOUGH THIS STORY BEGINS in a castle, it is not a fairy tale. In the last decade of the twentieth century, Oheka Castle was a decrepit shell of her former opulence, as forgotten as the man whose fortune built it. Almost a century earlier, Otto Kahn, the once-proclaimed 'King of New York,' had spent a Midas-like fortune constructing Oheka as a monument to his wealth and power. During his life, monarchs, ministers and presidents vied for his attention. He held the destinies of nations in his grip. Now, if Otto Kahn remained in the popular consciousness at all, it is only as the cartoonish icon of the classic American board game, *Monopoly*. And, yet, the secrets of Kahn and his fortune lay shrouded in Oheka waiting like a forgotten prisoner.

As Luke drove up the cypress-lined allée to Oheka Castle, darkness surrounded him. Unlike most castles he had visited in Europe, this castle was built in the twentieth century to modern specifications. He swung the car through the stone arch around the central fountain toward the

5

main entrance. The towering portico led into a large foyer that opened into a double staircase encircling the room and leading to the main floor. With his flashlight lighting the way, he navigated through the debris and fallen plaster. He thought of the memories these walls would reveal if they could talk.

Luke shivered as he passed the dark, windy tunnels on the lower level. He recalled with dread the bitterly cold nights while walking guard patrol when Oheka was a military academy. He would never forget the first time he had the graveyard shift in the lower quadrant. It was a cold, windy night in November and his route was the base of the castle along the outer perimeter in the woods by the ventilation shafts.

Tiny shards of sleet tore into his skin and mixed with his tears as he turned the northwest corner. It had been only six months since the fatal accident had taken his parents and his heart ached as he trudged along the gravel path. It had only been one week since his best friend had mysteriously disappeared. He had never felt so alone. There in the night, his aching was matched by a low, haunting moan. It echoed his despair and reverberated in his heart as he forced himself toward the sound. It grew louder and more plaintive. He shivered.

His reverie was broken when his client, Jed Spencer, clambered up behind him. Jed was more disheveled than usual from exploring the crumbling edifice.

"Isn't she grand?" he huffed. "You went to school here. You must know all the spooky legends about this place."

"Yeah, I'm sure you've heard about the infamous tarring and feathering of Charles Kelsey, whose mutilated body was found in the Oheka woods. The domestic staff at Oheka reported hearing dreadful moans and seeing dismembered body parts floating through the trees."

Jed winced as he associated the fate of the victim with the phrase "dead as Kelsey's nuts." Glad for the diversion, Luke related rumors of buried treasure that belonged to Sadie 'the Goat' Farrell, a pirate whose colorful name came from her penchant for headbutting those who resisted her. Sadie was betrayed and brutally murdered by a rival woman pirate who wore Sadie's ear in a locket around her neck as a trophy. According to local legend, Sadie's ghost draped in a Jolly Roger flag haunted the area around Oheka Castle searching for her severed ear.

"OK, enough with the spooks. You are creeping me out. Here's the plan. We have an option to purchase the entire estate for forty grand on the condition that we restore the main building of the Castle up to code by the year 2000."

Luke shook his head and said, "That raises a few questions. First, how much do you think it will cost to resuscitate this castle; the vandals have torn her up pretty bad? Second, what do you plan to do with it once it's restored? And, what's with the deadline?"

"I'll answer the last question first. Huntington will be celebrating its 350th anniversary in '03, and Supervisor Crouch envisions a sumptuous celebration in the Castle's grand ballroom. I know, I know, that's an ambitious schedule, but we can do it with the tax incentives he's offering."

"Yeah, but what do you do with it after the big party?" said Luke.

"We'll turn it into a Disneyland for brides. You know, destination weddings, recapturing the extravagance of the Gold Coast Robber Barons. In its heyday, this Castle was the playground of the rich and famous. You would not believe the guest list that old Otto Kahn entertained at this place."

"Whatever."

Little did Luke know that, with that dismissive word, he was about to enter the mists of history where he would encounter a web of intrigue and betrayal beyond his wildest imaginings.

2

1871

Mannheim, Germany

Gold conjures up a mist about a man more destructive of all his old senses and lulling to his feelings than the fumes of charcoal.

~ Charles Dickens, *Nicholas Nickleby*

"Otto, I need you to take this rag and polish the dinner bell, while I cook the latkes," said his mother. He looked at her swollen belly and felt a rush of excitement at the prospect of no longer being the youngest child in the family. When the new baby came, Otto would have someone to boss around just as his older siblings did. His fingers ached as he pressed the rag against the metal. He polished the brass surface until he could see the silly faces he was making to himself.

"Otto, get your coat. I want you to come with me to the Emporium."

The Festival of Lights was his favorite time of year. The city of Mannheim was a kaleidoscope of colors, reflecting off shiny surfaces intent on pushing back the darkness of winter. He shivered and looked skyward as if he could somehow halt the sunlight from waning. His mother reached for his hand and guided him into Jacob's Emporium where she was planning to buy some toys and confections for the children who would be celebrating the second night of Hanukkuh at their home.

"Now, Otto, I'm going to shop for some things. I want you to stay close to me. When we are finished I will take you to Schnitzer's Bakery for a special treat."

The young boy nodded, but he had different plans. He patted his pocket, which contained his treasure. As he trailed behind his mother, he spied the object of his yearning. Ever since he had seen the carved wooden cavalryman last month, he had dreamed of nothing else. The soldier was astride a bold charger and the two pieces bristled with armor and buckles. The horse was painted shiny black and it was skillfully carved capturing the musculature of the powerful haunches and depicting a finely detailed equine face that even had dots of red in the nostrils. There were hinges at the leg joints so the toy could be manipulated during the imaginary battles the boy would win. The handsome rider was wearing a Prussian blue uniform with red stripes down the pant legs and white sashes across his chest. He wore a black cylindrical helmet that had a white plume of real feather arising from a tiny gold medallion in front. Like the horse, the man had hinged joints so he could be moved and even removed from his steed to engage in hand-to-hand combat with the removable silver sword that hung in a scabbard at his side. Otto had already named the cavalryman Max, and the horse Shotzie.

While his mother was chatting with Mrs. Gruber, Otto saw his opportunity. He patted the coins in his pocket again and slipped away unobtrusively. At dinner the previous evening, he had been mesmerized by his Uncle Wilkin, who had performed magic with a gold coin. Otto could not understand how his uncle could make the coin disappear and then reappear, in of all places, Otto's ear. Wilkin even turned the coin into a silk scarf. Displaying great dexterity, he had rolled the coin over and through his fingers into his palm where it disappeared, only to reappear in the palm of his other hand. When Wilkin was through with his magic, he gave Otto not one, not two, but, three gold coins. Otto was elated for he knew that he could now purchase the cavalryman he coveted.

The Emporium was crowded with townsfolk bustling about shopping for gifts that would make their loved ones happy, or so, they hoped. His heart thumped in his tiny chest as he approached the sales counter, cradling his prize. His breathing was shallow and drops of perspiration beaded on his forehead; this was his first purchase ever. He steeled himself, remembering all the times he had watched his mother buy stuff. Just place it on the counter and slide the money across the counter and it was yours to bring home.

"Yes, what do you want, little man?" snapped Mr. Jacob, a large, barrel-chested brute of a man who loved his schnapps. Earlier, he had finished the last bottle from his stash. His mood was fouler than usual because he had dropped one of the glasses he was retrieving for Mrs. Mayer when that fat butcher, Jensen, had bumped him. Listening to Mrs. Mayer berate him for his drunken clumsiness while cleaning up the broken glass, had pushed him to the boiling point.

Otto placed the expensive toy on the counter. Jacob glowered at him. People on line behind him began to grumble impatiently. Oh, Otto remembered the money. He reached into his pocket and pulled out the three shiny coins and placed them on the smooth, wooden counter. Jacob's eyes narrowed fiercely.

"Look at what this stupid little Yid is trying to do," he said maliciously. Like a wolf taunting his prey, Jacob slowly and deliberately picked up one of the coins and put it toward his yellowed grin. A trembling started in Otto's leg and quickly engulfed his torso. Blood pounded in his ears and his eyes widened, as a hushed silence smothered the room. His eyes were riveted on the big vendor. A drop of foul saliva dripped onto Otto's hand. He pulled it back as if stung by acid. His teeth clenched his lower lip, almost piercing the skin.

The figure of the vendor loomed over Otto as Jacob waved the coin for all to see just like Uncle Wilkin had done. But Otto sensed none of his uncle's gaiety; only cold malevolence. Jacob chomped down on the coin. It crumbled metallically, revealing a soft chocolate interior. Otto stared dumbfounded.

"The Yid tried to pay with chocolate gelt!" roared Jacob, in a tone that made Otto flinch.

The remark pulsed through the crowd and almost every person in the shop laughed derisively. A bewildered Otto reddened, tears welled up in his eyes, his heart fluttered wildly in his chest. He felt like the canary in his neighbor's kitchen, when the cat climbed onto the windowsill near its cage — only Otto lacked wings to distance himself from his tormentor. In typical bully style, Jacob pressed his advantage with a barrage of insults. His thick hands clutched the sides of his work apron, and he pontificated in a stentorian voice as if from the pulpit. He made snide remarks denigrating Otto's ancestry and rained taunts on his head about the ludicrousness of chocolate money.

Suddenly, Otto's mother appeared, her eyes darting anxiously, searching for her son. With arms flailing like the wings of an agitated goose, she shoved her way through the crowd. When Jacob saw Emma Kahn coming to Otto's rescue, he directed his caustic barbs toward her.

"Fraülein Kahn, are you so ignorant that you teach your little nincompoop that chocolate gelt is the same as real gold? No wonder you Jews have been kicked out of every country you've ever been in. Teaching a boy to cheat is despicable. Take this sniveling, little weasel and get out of my store and don't come back," he said emphatically, growing bolder as Emma's shoulders drooped.

She dropped her purchases, knelt down and embraced Otto. When Otto saw his salvation, he lost all control and started bawling into his mother's shoulder. Uttering soothing words in his ear, she picked him up and fled out of the Emporium like they were fleeing from Lucifer himself.

3

May 15, 1891

Kyoto, Japan

Demoralize the enemy from within by surprise, terror, sabotage, assassination. This is the war of the future.

~ ADOLPH HITLER

"I HOPE THAT YOU ARE ENJOYING your first visit to Kyoto, Otto. It is quite remarkable," said Sir Edgar Speyer. "Now, this lovely young geisha is going to massage away my aches from all the traveling. I've heard that the baths in this *ryokan* are especially invigorating. I suggest that you partake in the hot spring water from the *onsen*. It will do you good."

Kahn looked at the venerable banker who was his boss and nodded. In his twenties, Otto was looking forward to some free time. As he entered the common baths wearing his new silk kimono, one of the attendants beckoned. As Otto skirted the steaming pool, he was jostled by a tall, muscular man who barged forward without regard to Otto. The blow knocked him off balance and he tumbled into the pool. Otto sputtered to the surface.

"You clumsy oaf! Now, look what you've done," a young man shouted imperiously.

"My good fellow, are you all right?" the man addressed Otto. The startled banker doggy-paddled to the edge of the pool.

"Someone is going to have to pay for this," Otto blurted.

"Please accept our apologies for the rude behavior of our guard. We are Tsarevich Nicholas of Russia. Our man here sometimes forgets that he is not at the *dacha* and that others have an equal right to passage. We will see to it that you are fully recompensed."

Unlike most of his Romanov relatives, Nicholas was relatively short and slender. His grandfather, Alexander II and his father, Alexander III, were huge men towering over six foot four inches and possessing prodigious strength. He had seen his father bend iron bars with his bare hands. Both men had outsized personalities suitable to autocratic rule. In contrast, Nicholas had a sensitive, introverted personality that was more suitable to a career as a scrivener than the absolute leader of one-sixth of the known world.

"Would you like to join us for some sake?" said Nicholas, gesturing toward an empty chair that the chastened guard had submissively placed adjacent to the young heir. Before Otto could demur on account of his drenched state, several attendants rushed at him with luxurious towels and a dry kimono. In a flash, with a golden cup of sake in his hand, he was ensconced next to the Tsarevich.

"Thank you, Your Excellency," Otto exclaimed, lifting his cup convivially. "Allow me to introduce myself. Otto Kahn," he said, bowing slightly. "I am a banker who is in Japan to work with the Imperial government on financing the modernization of their rail transport system."

"Most interesting, Herr Kahn. Perhaps, we can do business together some day."

"Perhaps."

It was the height of cherry blossom season in Kyoto. The young, American Naval officer stopped pedaling his bicycle for a moment to savor their beauty. He was short by Western standards, but he fit in comfortably with the local populace. He was wearing peasant garb, a simple, short black robe with straight sleeves and tied with an *obi* about the waist, over what he liked to call his pajama pants. He wore wooden sandals. The traditional clothing masked his trim, muscular physique. Over his black crew cut, he wore a wig of long, black hair tied in a pigtail and topped with a bamboo sun hat. Around his mouth, he had pasted a wispy moustache and goatee. His dark brown eyes narrowed as he watched the *jinrikisha* he was shadowing turn into a narrow alley.

His assignment was to gather intelligence about the twenty-three-year-old heir to the Russian throne, Nicholas Alexandrovich Romanov. Alexander III had sent Nicholas on a world tour to prepare his son for the responsibilities of leadership. The young heir was traveling in a squadron of Russian warships with his brother, Prince George; his cousin, also George; the Prince of Greece and several Russian nobles. The itinerary had taken them to Athens and Cairo, then East to Hong Kong, Saigon, Singapore and Bangkok.

Thus far, the trip had been uneventful and James "Strafe" Oliver was enjoying the challenge of blending into diverse cultures. His nickname came from his stint on the Navy boxing squad where he had exhibited a relentless, punishing, attacking style. His hand speed was legendary. It was so fast that he often landed ten blows before his opponent could try to retaliate. He also had a knack for disguises and languages that had served him well during his career in Naval Intelligence.

This afternoon Strafe was following the party of the future Tsar as it toured the ancient city of Kyoto, renowned for the beauty of its Buddhist temples and Shinto Shrines. Suddenly, a male voice shouting in distress drew Strafe's attention. He quickly thrust down on the pedals to close the gap between him and the Tsarevich.

Racing down the narrow street, he watched in horror as an assailant in a policeman's uniform struck Nicholas with a sword on the right side of his head. The attack was partially deflected by the collapsible sunscreen of the *jinrikisha* that was in the up position, shielding the victim from a direct blow.

"*What, what do you want?*" screamed Nicholas.[3]

Before a finishing blow could be struck, Nicholas bolted from the *jinrikisha* and ran for his life down the street. The assailant pursued the future Tsar with murderous determination. Strafe accelerated and within seconds was alongside the would-be assassin. Nicholas ducked into an alley and was flailing at clotheslines crisscrossing his path. The assailant used his sword to slash at the falling laundry. He was closing in on Nicholas, when Strafe leaped from his bicycle and broadsided the attacker. They tumbled to the ground and rolled to a stop. Both quickly, reflexively, sprang to their feet.

The stunned assailant faced Strafe with a confused look that turned into a malicious sneer as the attacker comprehended the situation. He brandished his sword at Strafe. Before the attacker could strike, Strafe wheeled and delivered a fierce kick to his kidneys. The assailant staggered. As he tried to regain his balance, Strafe was upon him with lightning speed, pummeling him with a barrage of punches. The weapon clanked harmlessly to the ground as the assailant crumpled onto the dirt alleyway.

Chest heaving, Strafe heard a clamor behind him and quickly mounted his bike and whisked past Nicholas, who was huddled in a recessed doorway cowering with his head down. With the clotheslines shielding his escape, Strafe heard someone thrashing the assailant and calling for 'Nikki.'

The news reports the next day told the story of how Prince George saved the Tsarevich by using a bamboo cane to beat the assailant, a xenophobic policeman named Tsuda Sanzo, into submission. Oliver's report was matter-of-fact about his role in thwarting the assassination attempt, noting that his cover had not been compromised.

1903

St. Petersburg, Russia

Oh, no, my dear; I'm really a very good man,
But I'm a very bad Wizard, I must admit.

~ L. FRANK BAUM, *WIZARD OF OZ*

THE WIND OFF THE Gulf of Finland had transformed St. Petersburg into a crystalline prison for the Tsarina. Ice formed on every surface and made it slick and murderous blue. The Russian name given to her was Alexandra Fyodorovna, but her given name was Alix Viktoria Helena Luise Beatrice of Hesse. She was raised in Germany under the tutelage of an English nanny. Her family called her Alix or "Sunny" due to her upbeat disposition. She was tall, with gentle blue eyes and golden hair that she wore in curlicues ringing her attractive round face.

Alix could handle the cold; it was the darkness that ravaged her psyche. During the long winter months it was dark when she awoke and dark again by mid-afternoon. She experienced unexplained fatigue and foreboding negativity.

As was common in the intertwined aristocracy of Europe at the time, Alix's pedigree covered a multitude of royal houses. She was the daughter of the Grand Duke of Hesse-Darmstadt, Germany and the granddaughter of Queen Victoria of England. Her godfather was Tsar Alexander III. Alix met her beloved Nikki at the wedding of her sister, Ella, to Grand Duke Sergei Alexandrovich, who was Nicholas' uncle. Her cousin, whom she called "Uncle Willy," was Kaiser Wilhelm II of Germany. Throughout her reign, she was haunted by malicious rumors of her loyalty to Germany that were propagated by a jealous, duplicitous court.

The Tsarina married Tsar Nicholas II in November 1894, just three weeks after the death of Alexander III. Most of the distinguished attendees at the funeral simply stayed over in St. Petersburg after the funeral, rather than make two trips to Russia. Alix remarked, *"My wedding was the continuation of the funeral, only I was dressed in white."*[4]

In the ensuing years, Alix gave birth to four daughters, Olga, Tatiana, Maria and Anastasia. The lack of a male heir weighed heavily on the Imperial couple. This unfortunate reality, along with Alix's weak Russian linguistic skills and her German roots, resulted in her ostracism by Russia's aristocracy. To avoid the hostile atmosphere, Alix moved the primary residence of the Imperial family away from the capital to the Alexander Palace in Tsarskoe Selo, about twenty miles outside of St. Petersburg.

She sensed that he lie awake next to her. She reached for him and wiggled over to him, absorbing his warmth as she intertwined her legs with his. "Oh, Nikki, you are my furnace. You burn so hot and keep me from freezing in this bloody winter."

"Don't worry, my *Duschka*, with Easter comes new life. And there is nothing like spring in Russia, when our Mother awakens from her slumber and bursts forth with brilliant light and green, leafy promises. Then, we know that all is good. Without the cold and the dark, we scarcely appreciate the warmth and the light."

"Nikki, you are such a romantic. I fear that you will be crushed by your duties."

"Don't worry. It is my destiny to guide the Motherland into the future. But I am torn. Yesterday, I wandered into the royal library and took up the journal of my great, great cousin Peter. He is such an inspiration. He believed that while our Mother is bountiful, we need to open her riches to new ways, western ways so that her sons will grow strong. My father, rest his soul, thought the opposite. He believed that the West was decadent and would corrupt the soul of Russia."

"Is it this dichotomy that keeps you awake?"

"We need to modernize, but how? I'm meeting today with that American banker about financing the railroad that will bring our Mother together. In my head, I know that he has the knowledge to help us develop a more efficient, transportation infrastructure. But, there is something about him . . . I can't put my finger on it. There is a coldness, a hunger, about him that makes me wary. He is originally from Germany; maybe you will have a better insight. Would you mind dropping by the Maple Room for tea with Mr. Kahn and help put my mind at rest?"

"Of course, my Nikki, of course."

Later that afternoon, a footman ushered Otto and Nicholas into the Maple Room. Otto's eyes widened and absorbed every exquisite detail of the lavish and spacious salon. The Romanovs certainly knew how to impress. Across the width was a substantial balcony constructed with curved maple. The Tsar explained that to make the wood sufficiently pliable for curving, the panels had been immersed in water for seven years. The wood shone with a marvelous luster of deep, matte gold that exuded a subtle opulence. Leaded-glass panels filled the curves of a maple wood beam that arched over the length of the balcony. A sinuous staircase of maple wood descended from the corner of the balcony to the main level. Delicate carvings of cabbage roses and vines adorned the wood panels.

Floor to ceiling windows ran the length of the main section of the room. The Tsar walked over to a corner where banquettes nestled, and gestured for Otto to sit. The floors were carpeted with a deep-pile wool rug dyed in the Tsar's teal-green. Two massive, bearskin rugs were spread over the carpets, so that, as Nicholas said, the room would have a touch of masculinity. The sharp teeth of the predators, now yellowed with age, reminded Otto of his mission.

Otto watched as Alix made her way into the room. She was much prettier in person than he expected from the unflattering images published in the press. She was wearing a high-necked, rose-colored dress and had her gold tresses piled fashionably on her head. A stunning hand-carved Cameo of white-on-blue layered agate with silhouettes of her four daughters graced the lace collar at her throat. The blue of the jewelry matched her eyes perfectly.

"Herr Kahn, I presume?" she queried in a soft voice. Otto rose to attention.

"Yes, Your Highness, it is indeed a great honor to meet you," he replied in his most courtly manner. There was something in her bearing that had caused him to revert to his native German.

"Likewise, I'm sure," said Alix, in German.

"You know, Your Highness, I grew up in Mannheim, just twenty-seven miles from your home in Darmstadt-Hesse. In fact, my cousin, Mordecai, was your mother's violin teacher."

"Is that so? My mother always lamented the day that her violin instructor left Darmstadt. Whatever happened to him?"

"He was invited to play for the Vienna Symphony Orchestra. It was the opportunity of a lifetime for him."

"I'm sure it was," said Alix. Her eyes betrayed a wistful resignation.

"Your Highness, allow me to present a few items that I picked up while in Mannheim last week," said Otto.

She genteelly opened the first box. It contained *The Secret Doctrine* by Madame Helena Petrovna Blavatsky and a zodiac birth chart for each of her children that had been prepared by the noted mystic. The Tsarina smiled with appreciation and held his gaze for a long moment as if to say, how could you know that this is something I will treasure.

"I have long admired the work of Madame Blavatsky. I was not aware her study of ancient religious wisdom had been published in German," she said, riffling through the pages slowly, pausing occasionally.

The second box contained a regional specialty, chocolate-covered pretzels. For the briefest instance, Alix's face sparkled like a child on her birthday.

"Thank you for the thoughtful gifts, Herr Kahn," she remarked.

Tea was served. Otto regaled the Tsar and the Tsarina with gossip from Mannheim and Berlin. Alix listened attentively to Otto's descriptions of the romances and dalliances of the German Imperial court.

"Forgive me for my forwardness, Your Highness, but I must admire your cameo broach. It is stunning."

Alix touched the jewelry distractedly and lowered her eyes. "It was a gift for my thirtieth birthday from my Uncle Willy. I mean, Kaiser Wilhelm," she corrected.

"Ah, yes, I have an Uncle Willy, too. But, he only gives me chocolate gelt," replied Otto jocularly. They all laughed at the self-deprecating contrast.

"Do you know where that beautiful piece was made?" asked Otto.

"Uncle Willy had it custom-made by the Nahe Gemstone Company, a family of artisans from Idar-Oberstein, who have been supplying exquisite jewelry to the Habsburgs for a century. They use secret, chemical-dying processes to capture the brilliant colors of the agate."

"I am familiar with that company because my firm has been financing the importation of agate from Brazil. They are the best in the world. True *artistes*."

"Herr Kahn, do you still have family in Mannheim?" asked Alix, changing the subject.

"Oh, yes. I have brothers and sisters who are engrossed in raising many nieces and nephews there."

The Tsarina asked, "And, do you have children yourself?"

"Ah, yes. I have two daughters, almost six and two years old. My wife is expecting our third child this summer. Everyone says that she is carrying like it's a boy. I certainly hope so, that would be grand."

As soon as the words left his mouth, he realized his mistake. There was an awkward silence.

"Excuse me, it is getting late. I mustn't overstay my welcome."

"Nonsense," replied Nicholas. "We enjoy seeing our Sunny laugh like she has this afternoon," patting his wife's knee.

"Thank you, Your Excellency. But I must return to my hotel. We have an early hunting date in the morning and I need my beauty rest," chuckled Otto. He rose and bowed *adieu* to the suddenly pensive Tsarina.

As Otto slogged through the Tsar's hunting preserve adjacent to the Tsarskoe Selo, his snowshoes crunched on the surface of the deep snow. Five yards ahead of him was Nicholas, the Supreme Leader of what he unfailingly referred to as Mother Russia. Their small party had just finished their hunt for the day and had bagged four wild turkeys, one red fox, three bucks, four does and six rabbits.

In a clearing ahead, he saw a small winter lodge where they intended to warm up and enjoy lunch. A thin stream of white smoke was driven from the rustic stone chimney by a brisk wind out of the northeast. The sun-dappled forest reminded Otto of the northern reaches of the Black Forest in Germany. He detected a wisp of venison stew and salivated. As Otto followed the Tsar into the lodge, the warm air fogged his vision momentarily.

He paused to admire the chiseled wood log walls that featured a veritable Noah's Ark of wild creatures that the Imperial taxidermist had crafted from the Tsar's kills. Otto looked into the dead, glass eyes of a black bear in a menacing pose that stood across from the entrance. It stood seven feet tall and its mouth was caught in a perpetual snarl complete with long, teeth that could sever a spinal cord with one horrifying snap. The bear's monstrous paws were the size of frying pans edged with three-inch-long claws designed to rip prey to shreds. It stood on powerful hindquarters that could propel the creature at astonishing speeds. Otto thought it ironic that such a majestic creature had been felled by a puny man with an 'iron thunderstick,' as the Tsar was fond of calling his rifle.

"Come, he is an impotent bear now. We must drink the cold away," said Nicholas, putting his arm around Otto and steering him toward the fire that snapped and crackled in the massive stone fireplace. Otto carefully avoided the hounds that were resting in front of the hearth and sat next to the Tsar.

"You made quite an impression on the Tsarina yesterday. She so enjoyed your news of the Prussian court. She gets homesick, you know."

"Don't we all," commented Otto.

"So, Otto, tell us what is exciting in that wonderful city of New York these days?"

"Well, Your Highness, I must share with you a clever theatrical production relating to monetary policy that is all the rage. It's called the '*Wizard of Oz*' and is playing to packed houses on Broadway."

"Tell us about it."

"The play appears to be a child's story, but it really is an allegory proselytizing in favor of bimetallism, the recognition of gold and silver in America's currency. Of course, as you know, we are governed by the gold standard, committing us to maintain a fixed exchange rate in relation to other countries on the gold standard. In the story, this young, naïve girl named Dorothy is whisked away by a cyclone to a strange world ruled by witches and a wizard. One of the witches tells her that the only way she can get home is to visit the Wizard by following the yellow brick road. She has various adventures on the road which is obviously the gold standard. The yellow brick road leads to Emerald City, which is only an illusion and represents paper money that only pretends to have value. Dorothy and her small party of misfits ask the Wizard for help, but he is a corrupt politician and he shrewdly manipulates them with empty promises to go kill the Wicked Witch of the West. The Witch represents the 'evil' trusts in the American West. To make a long story short, Dorothy eliminates the Witch by dissolving her with a bucket of water."

"That sounds quite fantastical, Otto."

"Oh, it is, but it gets better. When the heroes return to Oz to claim their reward, the Wizard reneges. They expose him as a media-manipulating fraud. He has no real power and must leave Oz the way he came, on a hot air balloon. Like many politicians, he floats away on a cloud of hot air." Both men laughed heartily.

"How does it end?"

"The Good Witch of the South, meaning the Southern United States, which voted for the silverite policy, miraculously arrives and tells Dorothy to click her silver slippers three times and she will be transported home again. She follows the instructions and arrives home to her family, safe and sound. Silver has saved the day."

"That's quite a fable. There's one thing about you Americans that we don't comprehend; how does your President allow such traitorous talk? The world understands only gold. The silver standard as the way home, indeed. It reminds us of the Peacock Clock in the Winter Palace, with that imperious bird flaunting its silver tail feathers at the viewer," Nicholas scoffed.

"I must admit that it is a little bit shocking; but I've grown to see my adopted country as unique because the people can laugh at these issues, rather than take to the barricades. It's quite clever and remarkable."

"Yes, quite remarkable . . . . Listen, we have business to discuss with you. Otto, we are planning to construct and modernize the Trans-Siberian Railway as part of our strategy to connect our resource-producing regions to trading opportunities in the Pacific. We will need significant capital to accomplish this goal and will be looking to your firm for assistance in placing bonds."

"Have you prepared a prospectus?"

"Count Vladimir Nikolayevich Kokovtsov, who is currently serving as Imperial Secretary, is working with Pyotr Bark to prepare a prospectus to secure an omnibus loan that will include financing the railway. You can deal with Herr Bark directly."

"Thank you. I am familiar with him. I will contact him when I return to St. Petersburg."

Sensing a rare moment of conviviality with the Tsar, Otto decided to broach a sensitive subject. "Your Excellency, pardon me for my forwardness, but I would like to discuss a matter of some delicacy if I may."

The Tsar regarded Otto with a wary look, then sighed, as if the warmth of the lodge and the toddy had melted away his usual Imperial frostiness. "Please feel free to raise whatever concern you may have," Nicholas replied.

"Your Highness, we are hearing rumors, just faint murmurs, mind you, that the press is going to report a shortfall of gold in the Imperial vault. If that is so, we can help."

"You know better than to believe rumors, Otto. In fact, we are planning to bring the press into the vault to see Mother Russia's gold. You're welcome to accompany the press. However, your remark intrigues me. How can you help with perceptions?"

Otto looked furtively over both shoulders, leaned over and whispered into the Tsar's ear. He nodded gravely. The ensuing silence was broken by a loud gong and the chief steward's announcement that lunch was ready.

Several weeks later, Otto found himself back in St. Petersburg on his way to meeting with a close collaborator, who would help solidify his influence with the Tsar and set in motion a chain of events that would have devastating consequences in the future. Otto's ally was R. B. "Hard" Scrapple, a railroad man and client. His shoulders and chest still bulged with a thickness that comes only from manual labor. Hard had worked in the iron mines outside of Harpers Ferry, West Virginia until he was nineteen. His nose bore the ridges of numerous breaks from charging face first into whatever situation came before him. Whether it was in the mines, on the athletic field or behind the barn, Hard was not a man to back down from anything or anyone.

R.B. was spared a life in the mines by virtue of the fact that his massive physique was matched by exceptional agility and foot speed. When he was recruited to play both quarterback and linebacker for the Virginia Tech Hokies, the scouting report stated that, "He's got it all. Heart like a lion, fearless and tough. Smarter than a miser's wife." And that was how R.B.

Scrapple began his legendary college football career. College was good for Hard the All American football star. He got educated, travelled, and, most significantly, he met Lucinda Gergens Loree, the prettiest young woman at WVU and daughter of Leonel Fresnel Loree, the owner of the Lehigh Valley Railway Company. After a whirlwind romance, R. B. and Lucinda married on the weekend of their college graduation.

A rugged individualist, R.B. Scrapple, established the Serpentine Rail Company to manufacture items necessary to operate a railroad. Starting with rails, switches, signals, Serpentine soon developed expertise in the manufacture of rolling stock and locomotives. R. B. was a veteran of two decades in the railroad iron business, learning from his father-in-law. The two men shared more than their connection to Lucinda; they were like a twin-headed hydra when it came to business acumen, and they were just as lethal.

Otto walked briskly as he passed the Alexander Column while crossing the cobblestone *Dvortsovaya Ploschad* (Palace Square) in front of the main gate of the Winter Palace. There were still vestiges of snow in the corners and where the sun rarely ventured. The rough surfaces of the cobblestones shone from the gray water that had not yet evaporated in the early spring sun. The red, polished Karelian-granite column crowned with a bronze sculpture of an angel holding a cross dominated the square. He listened appreciatively to the chimes of the Tower Clock on the reddish-brown South façade of the great building.

The Winter Palace was an impressive three-story structure in the Elizabethan Baroque style. It was located between the Palace Square and the Embankment on the Neva River. The 'Home of the Tsars' was finished in Tsar-green, trimmed in white. The Winter Palace was an elongated rectangle that stretched over two-hundred-and-fifty yards long and was almost one hundred yards tall. In actuality, it was a series of lesser palaces combined into one grand structure. There were over one thousand rooms within its confines. In one corner under a golden onion dome, stood the Grand Church that held cathedral status and was the site of three centuries of Romanov weddings. Also notable was the Hermitage that housed the world-class Imperial art collection.

With his usual sense of caution, Otto stopped and looked around the immense paved square. His gaze extended beyond the Column to the General Staff Arch on the opposite side of the square. The low angle of the sun in the late afternoon resulted in long shadows. Did he see a shadow furtively slip behind the General Staff Arch, or was it the product of an overactive imagination? All he saw now was a group of British tourists being led by a Russian guide toward Nevsky Prospekt, where they would undoubtedly partake in an *authentic* Russian dinner in front of a roaring fireplace.

Passing the massive iron gates, topped with the ubiquitous gilded Romanov eagle, Otto presented his credentials and invitation to the guard. Otto was escorted to Pyotr Bark's office. Bark was a slight man who wore a wide handlebar moustache that was upturned with copious quantities of wax. His eyes were close-set and gave him a slightly myopic look. His sandy brown hair was prematurely thinning, giving way to a high brow. As a result of an almost fatal ski accident when he was a teenager, Bark carried himself with a stiff-necked posture.

He was an international banker, who counted the dowager empress Marie Feodorovna, Tsar Nicholas' mother and the sister of Britain's Queen Alexandra, among his illustrious clients. Otto and Bark had first met in Berlin when they were both young men. Over the years, they had worked together on transactions and financings in London, St. Petersburg and New York, and as a result they shared a close, professional friendship. Pyotr advised that the shipment had arrived.

Pyotr led Otto past the Rotunda, the circular hall that separated the public areas from the private areas of the palace. They proceeded down a long hallway with vaulted ceilings painted smoke white. Otto slowed his pace, admiring the priceless paintings and huge classical urns carved of jade, Siberian jasper and malachite that flanked the corridor. Otto inhaled sharply as the massive Peacock Clock came into view. His jaw dropped at the sight of one of the largest automatons ever built.

Originally a gift to Catherine the Great in the late eighteenth century, the clock was more majestic than described by the Tsar. It stood almost nine feet tall and featured life-size, animated creatures made of gilded bronze, silver and glass. Most notable was the peacock perched on a tree. An owl representing night was enclosed in a sphere, and a cockerel representing day completed the main figures. All three of the birds were delicately formed with each feather perfectly molded. At that moment, the elaborate timepiece whirred into action. A melody of bells circling the owl filled the hall. The owl blinked and moved its head naturally. Next, the peacock spread its magnificent golden tail feathers, then, pivoted to display the silver-backed feathers. The head of the peacock arched and peered down regally. Otto reflected momentarily on the Tsar's disdain for the bird's impudence. To the right, a golden cockerel greeted the night with a mechanical crowing. The dial of the clock was a series of mushrooms that represented the hour and minutes. A delicate dragonfly hovered on the head of one of the mushrooms bearing Roman numerals. When the mechanical marvel completed its cycle, the creatures dutifully returned to their appointed positions.

Pyotr showed his badge to the two armed cadets posted at the lift in the east wing. After a curt nod from the guards, Pyotr and Otto entered the lift. Another soldier, wearing a revolver on his hip, pivoted the brass handle of the mechanism activating the descent to the Imperial Vault.

They stepped into the cold, dank, poorly-lit space. Pyotr led the way through the ceiling-high shelves that bore the gold of the realm, stacked bar upon bar. A dull, metallic gleam reflected off the gold adding a strange aura to the chamber. Three men along the far wall unpacked crates stenciled in bold black letters "SCRAPPLE METALS." The elder of the group separated himself and gave Otto a hearty handshake after removing a stiff leather glove.

"Otto, it's good to see you," said Hard, his voice echoing slightly off the metallic surfaces of the vault.

"Welcome to St. Petersburg," said Otto. "How was your journey?"

"It was good. The cargo made the trip without a glitch. Customs did not even crack open any of the crates. We're set to go."

"This is Pyotr Bark. Pyotr, my colleague, R.B. Scrapple."

"Nice to meet you, Pete. I'd like to chat, but right now I've got to help these fellows finish up. Wait right here. We'll be done quicker than a cougar chasing a rabbit off a cliff." Pyotr looked at Otto quizzically. Otto lifted one eyebrow and shrugged his shoulders.

Scrapple returned to the others who were passing gilded bars from the crates to an assistant standing on a ladder, stacking them horizontally near the top of the range. A dull, screeching sound accompanied the insertion of each bar onto the shelves. The stout oak shelves rose thirty feet and were divided into ranges, each wide enough to bear twenty gold bars. The oaken shelves were capped by wood panels elaborately carved with the Romanov eagle.

"We're almost finished. Sections Sixteen through Twenty have been replenished or filled."

"Excellent, no, Pyotr?" said Otto.

"Yes, the press will be impressed, very impressed."

Without warning, a bar slipped from the assistant's hand and clanged noisily on the concrete floor. A noticeable, dark-gray spot marred the gilding at the end of the bar.

"Jonathan, place this one in the last row facing the wall, OK? When you're done, you and Larry take the ladders and crates to the trucks and bring everything to the rail yard. You'll leave in the morning like we arranged," said Hard.

After surveying the vault with satisfaction, Pyotr led Otto and Hard to a small dining area near the Throne Salon. Pyotr showed Hard to a lavatory where he cleaned up. Otto admired the dramatic oil paintings of Russian naval victories that bedecked the walls. Images of cannons blazing across roiling, ink-colored seas launching fiery projectiles with deadly accuracy into doomed Turkish barks seemed to be the recurrent theme.

Pyotr walked to a cabinet and removed a Baccarat crystal liquor bottle containing a clear, yellow-tinged liquid. He poured the liqueur into Linne glasses. Otto delighted in the unique azure-colored crystal upper section of the glass attached to a clear, faceted stem. The three men toasted to a successful endeavor, clinked glasses and threw down the fiery spirit in one decisive gulp. Otto smacked his lips in appreciation.

"Now that's smooth. Pyotr do the honors again, please." A comfortable warmth spread through their chests as Pyotr refilled the glasses repeatedly. The companions were soon experiencing a familial conviviality.

"Hard, I must compliment you on the bars. They look exactly like the real thing. How did you do it?" asked Pyotr.

"It takes special equipment at the foundry. Gold bullion is cast from molds; the molten metal is poured into what we call nesting molds that are specially coated. The molds have the imprint of the Tsar's crest incorporated into them. The molds and their contents are slowly cooled. We invert the molds and stamp sequential numbers into the bottom surface before the gold sets completely. When the molds are cool, we send them to the tapper machine which removes the bottom of the mold, inverts the mold and gently taps out the finished bar. It then goes to the polisher which removes any burrs or nubs.

"With *these* bars, we followed the same process only substituted iron for gold. We shipped them to Stockholm where we have an electroplating facility. There, we immersed the bars in a tank holding a special solution and 'coated' the bars by running electricity through the solution. This enables the next and final step, the adherence of a thin layer of gold to the special coating. We pass the bars through the gold solution and zap them with electricity. *Voilá*, the iron bars are now gold-plated."

"My friend, Hard, is a virtual alchemist. He turns iron into gold."

"Fascinating," said Pyotr, who filled their glasses again. The inner door to the dining room opened and the wait staff emerged carrying *crepes suzette flambé*. The party watched as the burning liqueur on the desserts sputtered out leaving a faint citrus scent in the air.

"So, tell us how the Tsar got into this predicament," said Otto.

"He's got this habit of engaging the newspaper editors in a war of words. He has not grasped the fact that the world has changed since his father's reign and the Tsar is fair game to the cockroaches that pass for journalists these days. As far as they are concerned all that matters is how many papers they sell. The truth or the welfare of Mother Russia does not matter."

Bark waited until the server's door swung shut before continuing.

"Well, about a month ago, the *Russkoye Znamya* criticized the fiscal policies of the Tsar. The Tsar responded by challenging the newspaper editor to go to the vault and 'see for himself' the riches of the Empire. Tomorrow the press will get the opportunity to enter the vault."

"Interesting," replied Otto.

"You know, I often wonder about which is better to have. Money, power, or love? If you could only have one, which would be the best?"

Bark poured another round, then, gulped it down. "I have managed the finances of many aristocrats and I can tell you that they covet power. It leads to the other two."

"I may be old-fashioned, but I don't believe that you can buy love. I've been married for twenty years and my Lucinda means more to me than anything else. She would sacrifice her life for me and I for her. We could live happily on a desert island without money or power. Love gets my vote," said Hard.

The two men refilled their glasses and looked expectantly at Otto. He sipped his drink reflectively. Otto puckered his lips several times and gazed vacantly toward the ceiling.

"It seems to me that if you have gold, you can have whatever you want."

"Really, how can gold give you someone else's heart?" protested Hard.

"Hard, love is like the smoke from this cigar. While it is satisfying and you can see it, you cannot possess it. It is illusory," said Otto, drawing deeply on his cigar.

"That's what makes it so valuable. Love must be given freely. I'm surprised Otto. You have children and a loving wife, don't you?"

The truth was that his marriage to Addie had devolved into a passionless marriage of business convenience that ceased to matter as he achieved success. After the death of his father-in-law, Bram Wolff, the stern moral guidance that he provided was gone and Kahn was easily tempted by the compliant beauties that he encountered in the world of entertainment. Being Chairman of the Board of the Metropolitan Opera had its perks.

"Maybe if I experienced true love, I'd change."

Otto absently fingered his monocle that bore the legend, *"Auri Sacra Fames,"* shrugged and tilted his head.

"When I was a boy, I learned an indelible lesson about the value of gold. Since then, I have been motivated by the motto engraved here: *Auri Sacra Fames.* It means the sacred hunger for gold. The ancients knew."

"Otto, if I recall my high school Latin correctly, *Auri Sacra Fames* means 'the accursed hunger for gold,'" said Hard.

Otto smiled.

❧

5

1903

Siberia

When you are where wild bears live you learn to pay attention to the rhythm of the land and yourself.

~LINDA JO HUNTER, *LONESOME FOR BEARS:
A WOMAN'S JOURNEY IN THE TRACKS OF THE WILDERNESS*

A LOUD ROAR SHATTERED the silence as Grigory Yefimovich Rasputin walked along a ridge in the Ural Mountains. The itinerant traveler sprinted toward the sound. Baying and growling provided a counterpoint to the impassioned roar that Rasputin recognized as a bear in distress. The monk broke through a thicket of trees. Before him was a primal scene of survival. A large bear was surrounded by a pack of wolves whose snarls and growls filled the air. They circled warily, their heads lowered, black eyes riveted on their prey. White, foamy mucous sprayed from the bear's muzzle as he bellowed in warning, trying to ward off the multi-sided attack.

Suddenly, the largest wolf leapt onto the bear's back. The bear swatted vainly at the attacker and another wolf lunged onto his shoulder, chomping fiercely into the thick fur. Bright, red blood filled the jaws of the wolves, who slashed and tugged at the bear. The taste and faint coppery smell of the blood fueled their fury. Two more wolves circled the bear patiently, probing for an opening that would spare them the wrath of the bear's powerful claws.

The bear rose on its hind legs in an effort to dislodge the alpha male on his back. A wolf lunged at the bear's exposed midsection but was met squarely with a blow from the bear's paw. The blow launched the wolf into a tree with deadly force, shattering its back.

With all his strength, Rasputin clubbed the lead wolf across the back with his oaken staff. He felt vertebrae crunch. The staff bowed from the ferocity of the blow and cracked in two. The lead wolf fell motionless, his yellow-tinged eyes glassy.

A wolf hurled himself at Rasputin. Instinctively, he raised his arm. The wolf bit him powerfully. Claws ripped at Rasputin, who struggled to stay upright. Pain ran through him as the wolf clawed at him. Bracing himself, Rasputin swung his free arm in a blurry arc and viciously stabbed the ragged end of his staff into the wolf's unprotected belly. The spear-like shaft punctured the skin and plunged forcefully into the vital organs beneath the creature's ribcage. He could feel sinews and membranes rend as he drove the shaft deep into his attacker's gut. Warm blood drenched his arm as he twisted the shaft. Their eyes met; Rasputin watched as primal hate melted into confusion and then black stillness. The wolf crumpled, releasing his grip on Rasputin's arm. He dropped to his knees, gasping heavily.

The remaining wolf continued biting the bear furiously. When the wolf lifted his head to go for the bear's jugular, the bear dropped down and slashed the wolf's throat in one lightning-fast motion. The wolf's spurting blood ebbed, then stopped.

The bear stood to his full height and unleashed the roar of the victor. His jowls quivered as he shook his mighty head. Spit and blood flew from his magnificent body. The sound reverberated through the forest and mesmerized Rasputin.

With a jutting chin and eyes afire, the bear turned and looked down at the man. Rasputin bowed low, touching his face to the ground. He held his injured arm under his body, lest the smell of fresh blood incite the bear. The great head of the bear sniffed Rasputin and swirls of dust and hot breath blistered the side of Rasputin's face. His heart pumped wildly as he fought the urge to flee. The bear's nose, wet and bloody, nuzzled at Rasputin's ear. He remained prostrate, praying feverishly.

Rasputin had been traveling alone for the last seven months. He had left his home in Siberia in response to his dreams. In the mornings after his dreams, he knelt and trembled with the realization that he was being summoned, but where and toward what end? At those times, he sensed something at the edge of his consciousness — an image of a young boy with ursine features, shrouded in darkness with red pain hovering over him. Sometimes in the dream, Rasputin could see the shroud lift and the boy was surrounded by five ministering angels. Although the youngster was smiling in those dreams, there was profound sadness in his eyes as if he could envision the future. Often a mournful, masculine figure haunted the dreams. Rasputin experienced a hunger to protect and release the boy from the impending tragedy. The itinerant monk knew, in a precognitive way, that his destiny was connected to this young cub of a boy.

Rasputin had journeyed from his home in Pokrovskoye, Siberia to the Nikolay Monastery in Verkhoturye, a town known as the "Gates to Siberia" because of its strategic location between European Russia and Siberia. There, he studied under the *Starets* Makariy, a holy man who instructed him on the principles of asceticism and taught him ancient shamanic rituals. The young man devoted himself to understanding Nature's pharmacy and how to use various herbs, drugs and fungi for healing and spiritual transformation. When Makariy could teach him no more, Rasputin became a pilgrim.

"Take this valise on your journey, Brother Grigory. It contains crystals found at Tungushka that will help you perform healing miracles in the name of God."

During his journey, he traversed much rugged terrain alone, occasionally encountering a rural settlement where he would perform manual chores in return for a meager meal and a few days' shelter. For the most part he lived ascetically, alone with his thoughts about God and the meaning of his dreams. He felt at one with nature and often sensed the presence of ancestral spirits guiding and shielding him from harm.

His pilgrimage had taken him through Greece and Israel where he climbed Mount Nebo to view the beautiful panorama that Moses had seen when he arrived at the land of 'milk and honey' — the Jordan River valley and to the south the rest of Jordan extending over the Dead Sea and the Desert of Judah. He fell to his knees in awe at the terrain before him that had been the intersection of God and man throughout biblical history.

In his early thirties, he was strong and vigorous. He wore a coarse, roughly-cut tunic of dark, brown wool. His midsection was bound by a leather prayer rope known as a *lestovka*. He had an oversized head that appeared to sit directly on his thick, broad shoulders. His dark hair was long and tangled and pulled back in an untidy ponytail. His most distinctive feature was his eyes; they were deep-set and the color of the luminescent blue that shines through glacial ice. At an early age, he recognized the power of his stare which he used to bring animals under his sway. As he matured, he used the piercing, hypnotic quality of his gaze to captivate and to persuade those around him.

Now, his first priority was to treat his injured arm. His eyes alighted on his satchel that had been cast aside during the battle. His large, thick hands protruded from his sleeves like the lethal paws of a Siberian tiger. His fingers bore the gnarled evidence of hard, rustic manual labor. There was a fresh wound on the back of his hand. Wincing, he methodically cleansed the bleeding furrows where the wolf had raked him. Next, he studied the multiple punctures on his wounded forearm. Rasputin shuddered as if he were fighting off a chill Siberian wind. Slowly, his breathing steadied. He dabbed a cloth with liquid from a dark bottle and rinsed his wound clean. He dressed the wound applying an ointment and wrapping it tightly to staunch the bleeding.

He followed the trail of blood left by his mighty comrade in battle. After a short walk, he spied the bear sitting near a large cedar, licking his cuts. The bear raised his head and sniffed the air alertly. Rasputin approached with his hands outstretched, murmuring a soothing, ancient song. His eyes stared directly into the eyes of the animal. Cautiously, Rasputin knelt before the beast. The bear ever-so-slowly stretched before Rasputin with a low, rumble emanating from deep in his chest. Rasputin placed some leaves from his valise into his mouth and chewed while humming. He carefully placed his hand behind the bear's ear and rubbed it softly. The low rumble gradually faded. With his free hand, Rasputin removed a slimy wad of green goo from his mouth and applied it to the wound on the bear's neck. The bear started to rise, then relaxed.

Rasputin repeated the process with the shoulder wound, all the while humming melodically.

Pilgrims from all across Russia filled the road to Sarov. They were flocking to celebrate the canonization of St. Serafim that had been decreed by Tsar Nicholas. Peasants, Cossacks and gypsies jammed every road and byway to witness the sacred event and pay homage to the great ascetic who had lived in the Urals and had performed countless miracles of healing. Legend had it that he lived in a cave with his pet bear. The atmosphere on the roads and at the travel inns was festive and gay.

The Imperial family had traveled to tiny Sarov to dedicate a new church that would house the relics of the holy man. There were reports that the Tsar and the Tsarina had donated a cypress coffin decorated with scenes of the saint's life to hold his remains.

Rasputin walked among the thickening throng. He smiled and nodded to his co-pilgrims, happy to be surrounded by his fellow Russians. There were still several hours of sunlight remaining on this summer day when he recognized a coach in a clearing off the road. His heart lifted as he approached the small group that congregated beside the coach. His mentor, Father Makariy had just emerged from the confined cabin and was stretching stiffly. The young man quickened his pace and burst upon the old cleric with a playful bear hug. Expecting a joyous welcome, Rasputin was crestfallen as Makariy pushed and struggled to free himself.

"Unhand me, you fool!" he screeched, slapping at Rasputin's head.

"Father, it's me, Grigory, your favorite pupil."

The priest squinted his eyes and craned his head toward the younger man. Father Makariy was slight and gaunt after a life of deprivation and devotion to spiritual matters. His cloudy, gray eyes searched Rasputin's face for a long moment before a benevolent smile creased his wrinkled face.

"So it is, so it is, my son. You appear from nowhere like an over-exuberant puppy and almost scared an old man to death. Come, let us sit and talk. You can tell me of your travels."

They settled around a camp that was being set up by a tall, thin, young man wearing a clerical collar.

"Brother Grigory, this is Sergei Iliodor. He is a novice, studying under Archbishop Theopan, inspector of the St. Petersburg Theological Academy. He has been sent to assist me during my journey to the canonization."

The young man's brown hair was short and spiky. His full beard hid a weak chin and thin lips. He had the sunken cheeks and gaunt look of an ascetic. Above his soft, intelligent, brown eyes, his eyebrows were thick and almost connected above his long, narrow nose.

The three men spoke long into the night about Rasputin's pilgrimage to the Holy Land. Grigory explained that for the most part he lived ascetically, alone with his thoughts about how God had mysteriously chosen this often harsh, xeric land to intervene dramatically in the lives of ordinary men to reveal his plan of salvation. Throughout the discourse, Grigory frequently turned his eyes toward Iliodor, especially when elaborating on some mystical aspect of his experiences. He could see the admiration tinged with envy growing on the novice's face. When Rasputin related his encounter with the wolves and the bear, Iliodor's eyes widened like the roaring muzzle of the bear defending himself. When Grigory's tale reached the point where the bear nuzzled him, Iliodor's jaw dropped and he blinked several times.

Suddenly, Grigory froze, his eyes focused on some distant point. He peered intently and, then, smiled knowingly.

"What is it? Do you see something?" asked Iliodor, straining at the darkness.

"I have seen Princess Galitzine, the elderly Mistress of the Robes, carrying a male newborn dressed in gold lined with ermine on a golden pillow to the baptismal font in the Peterhof Chapel. Mother Russia will soon have her heir!"

A harsh sun punished the side of Nicholas' face. The pain from his scar nearly obliterated his equanimity. He felt nothing but animus toward Bishop Innocent of Tambov who abused his time at the rostrum by subjecting the assembled multitude to a two-hour dissertation on the cardinal virtues exemplified in the life of Saint Serafim. At the mention of his own name, Nicholas snapped back to attention.

"And so, it is in the context of courage — the ability to vanquish fear and uncertainty — that we see another one of St. Serafim's spiritual gifts at work. He crosses the centuries to share his gift of prophecy to our beloved Tsar, Nicholas II. It is my great honor to present this letter from St. Serafim to '. . . the fourth sovereign, who will come to Sarov.'" With a puffed chest and purposeful stride, the Bishop left the pulpit and bowed before Nicholas. Innocent presented to the Tsar a small velvet pillow bearing a rough-sewn leather cylinder.

Nicholas rubbed his cheek absently and accepted the object. Thousands of eyes focused on him. The air was redolent with the distinctly agrarian combination of wet earth, rotting manure and honeysuckle. The proceedings came to a halt with expectation as the Tsar fingered the mottled, tan case. He removed the top and withdrew a curled yellow scroll secured with a red ribbon.

With her eyes wide and transfixed on the scroll, Alix leaned over to Nicholas and whispered in his ear. He nodded, then, pulled at the ribbon. The scroll crackled slightly as it unfurled, seemingly anxious to reveal the saint's long hidden secrets. The Tsar's heart pounded. Blood coursed through his head, causing an insistent throb in the scar. A slight breeze rippled the edges of the ancient parchment.

Holding the missive at the top and bottom, Nicholas read it and re-read it. His shoulders slumped and he raised his eyes heavenward while mouthing words of gratitude. It simply could not be!

Alix nearly toppled from her seat, straining to read along. Tears welled in his eyes and a broad grin creased his tired face. Releasing the parchment to Alix, he rose triumphantly, chest out, arms raised. He shouted, "All Glory to God!" Then, he fell to his knees with the alacrity and clumsiness of a marionette whose strings had been severed. For several minutes he lay face-down, uttering words of thanks and praise.

The Tsarina read the document hastily and whooped a joyous cry. She dropped to her knees next to her husband. A chant of "All Glory to God!" bubbled up through the crowd. Unable to contain their joy, a deluge of tears rained down the faces of the royal couple. They stood, hand-in-hand, basking in the love and adoration of the crowd. Many remembered the religious frenzy of that bright, summer day as the zenith of the reign of Nicholas II.

6

1905
St. Petersburg, Russia

A starets takes your soul, your will, into his soul and will. In choosing a starets you renounce your own will and surrender it to him in perfect submission, absolute self-abnegation.

~ FYODOR DOSTOEVSKY, *THE BROTHERS KARAMAZOV*

"YOU MUST SECURE THE HAT with pins so it will not tilt or fall off. That would not do," commanded her mother, Nadezhda. Anya Alexandrovna Vyrubova's lustrous brown hair balked at being stuffed into the confines of the miter-shaped headdress. She was wearing a pointed *kokoshnik*, the traditional Russian female hat that matched her dress. Her mother fussed with, and tugged at, the lavender hat covered with tiny pearls until it rested securely on her daughter's head.

Anya was large-boned, yet had a refined bearing that came from generations of service in the Romanov court. Her round face and wide cheek bones were the perfect setting for her expressive eyes that were the deep blue of the Hope Diamond, as her mother liked to boast. She had full lips that curved upward into a naturally demure smile. The headdress matched the tall teenager's gown that was lavender satin with a swath of pearls in a filigree pattern down the front. Her ensemble was elegant and perfect for the theme of seventeenth century Muscovy that the Empress had decreed for the first ball after the birth of her son, Alexei, heir to the Romanov throne.

Anya's invitation had come with a diamond studded pin signifying the Empress' wish that Anya attend as a maid of honor. Her mother's chest swelled with pride at the royal recognition of her daughter. Nadezhda was the daughter of Field Marshal Mikhail Kutuzov and she was well aware of the fickleness of the court. The sight of her eldest daughter, who had clearly grown into a beautiful woman and had entered the inner circle of the Tsarina, caused Nadezhda to offer a prayer of gratitude and to sigh inwardly 'Where did the time go' as she wiped away a tear of joy.

Anya was the daughter of Aleksandr Taneyev, who was the Chief Steward to the Imperial Chancellery. When the Tsarina first came to St. Petersburg, she was shunned by the entrenched aristocracy who resented her. In her isolation, she gradually came to rely heavily on Anya's father. Alexandra grew to trust his counsel and judgment. Earlier in the year, when one of the Tsarevich's nursemaids fell ill, the Empress accepted the recommendation of her adviser to employ his daughter, Anya, as a replacement. The young girl had a shy, yet radiant, smile that endeared her especially to the Empress. In addition to her native language, Anya was fluent in English and German, both of which were valuable assets.

Although Anya was only a teenager, she was mature and had a gift when it came to calming children. Whenever the little "Sunbeam," as the Tsarina called Alexei, was inconsolable, which was often, only Anya out of all the nursemaids was able to settle him and get him to sleep. Anya was totally absorbed with the welfare of the ill-starred duo, Alix and the Tsarevich, and soon distinguished herself with her devotion. Many at the court were jealous of the growing intimacy between the Tsarina and Anya, who were often seen conversing earnestly or laughing freely at some private joke. The mean-spirited among them would refer to her as 'that cow' or mock her for being 'traditionally built.' Of course, with her ascension to royal favor, these pejoratives and worse were now only whispered behind her back.

Anya's stomach clenched as her carriage drove up to Catherine's Palace. The baroque Imperial residence had never looked better. It was ablaze with modern illumination, gas lights and electric globes glowed magically, giving the palace a golden, fairytale hue. She entered the Palace and climbed the regal staircase that led to the Grand Ballroom. Anya smiled appreciatively as she entered the ballroom that was all crystal, mirrors, gilded sconces and chandeliers.

She made her way over to the row of punch bowls that had been set up to serve the seven hundred guests. One of the stewards handed her a champagne punch in a lead crystal cup. She caught the eye of Princess Anastasia Pistolkors, the paramour of Grand Duke Nikolay Nikolayevich. Stana, as her intimates called her, and her sister, Militza, were daughters of King Nikola Njegos of Montenegro and were known as the Black Princesses. Stana valued Anya for her relationship with the Tsarina and soon the social climbers were chatting excitedly. Stana described her latest obsession with the holy man, Rasputin. When Anya expressed interest in the mystical teachings of the holy man, Stana invited her to a prayer meeting with the holy man or Starets, at *Znamenka*, the palace of her sister, Militza.

Not far behind Anya was Otto Kahn, resplendent in his silk and wool tuxedo. He surveyed the ballroom through his monocle. In the opposite corner of the ballroom, Otto saw the Yusopovs, Princess Zinaida Yusopov, Zina, to her friends, and her husband, Count Elston-Sumarokoff. They were among the richest, most favored families in Russia and one of the few non-Romanovs permitted to utilize the appellations prince and princess. The Yusopovs were longstanding clients of Otto's firm and he worked his way toward them.

"Good evening, Herr Kahn. It's so nice to see you," said a sultry voice from behind him as he felt a caressing puff in his ear. His monocle dropped in surprise. He turned around to see Princess Zina's young son, Felix Yusopov, dressed in full military uniform, grinning at him. Otto knew the boy from prior trips to St. Petersburg but had not seen him for several years.

The younger son of the Yusopov family had inherited his mother's good looks and some even said, derisively, her wardrobe. His delicate features and slender build lent credence to the rumors about his proclivities. His pale brown eyes twinkled seductively under his thin arching eyebrows, and behind long lashes that Otto could have sworn were enhanced with makeup. The prince's thin, shapely nose, bounded by high cheekbones that were ever so faintly rouged, was attractively proportioned to give him the look of a Parisian fashion model that might grace the pages of *Vogue*. Felix's lips were set in a coquettish smile; although Otto detected an innate cruelty in them. The young prince had perfect, smooth, white skin that was matched by his flawless white teeth. The only features that were not feminine were the thin pencil moustache and the way he wore his raven black hair in short military style. As the Prince spoke to him, Otto thought he noticed a drop of actor's glue glistening at the corner of the moustache. Felix linked his arm into Otto's elbow and steered him toward a doorway that led to one of the private areas off the main room.

Stationed at the doorway was a large, turbaned black man in white Araby trousers, a gold-embroidered teal military tunic and Turkish slippers who stood in sphinxlike silence scanning the assemblage for potential trouble. Unbeknownst to Otto and Felix, the guard was named Pasha Kelly who hailed from Elizabeth, New Jersey.

"I wasn't sure that you'd recognize me. I've been in London these last few years getting myself an education," Felix chuckled.

"Yes, so I've heard. London can be quite exhilarating for the adventurous. Where were your quarters?"

"I lived in Fitzrovia, near the writer Shaw. It is an ideal place for decadence, if you get my meaning."

"Ah, yes. That is a decidedly, how do you say . . . , Bohemian place."

"It is and I've heard that you are able to help Bohemian sons of clients with *Brighteye*."

"My aim is to satisfy by whatever currency necessary."

Otto had learned early in his career that in order to cement commercial relationships, it was sometimes necessary to satisfy certain appetites, whether sexual or pharmaceutical. This was particularly the case with nobility or old money, where degeneracy in subsequent generations seemed *de rigueur*. Consequently, Otto prided himself on being ready for any contingency. He reached into the left breast pocket of his tuxedo and removed a small tin containing a pure, white powder. He handed it to Felix with the quip, "One of the advantages of traveling in the Orient."

Felix accepted the tin hungrily, muttering a word of gratitude. As Felix meandered away through the crowd, Otto saw him signal his cousin, Prince Dmitry, toward the terrace door. A satisfied future client, thought Otto, in self-congratulation.

He joined Princess Zinaida and Count Elston at an elaborately decorated table. The Count's dashing military uniform of bright red with blue trim set off his mane of white hair and bushy walrus moustache. Zina was well-preserved for her fifty years. Her flawless alabaster complexion contrasted perfectly with her aquamarine eyes, full red lips and auburn hair that was swept up and topped by a stunning miter-shaped tiara studded with precious gems. The stylish turquoise silk gown she wore was so awash with pearls and baby diamonds that there was no doubt who was the richest woman at the ball.

Otto sipped champagne while enjoying the orchestra music.

"I've always been fascinated by the origins of centuries-old family wealth," said Otto. "There is usually some intriguing family legend as to how it all began. Princess, do the Yusopovs harbor any dark secrets?"

"You better hold on to your monocle, Otto, the story of the Yusopovs will take you on a wild ride. We trace our lineage to Khan Yusuf of the ancient Tatars. The Yusopovs were prominent in the Kazan Khanate, a medieval Tatar state. In the sixteenth century, the Kazan Khanate became extremely prosperous from trading furs and precious gems. However, they became so prosperous that their hubris led them to make a fatal mistake — they expanded their trade routes westward to Moscow. Initially, this was an excellent business decision and they flourished. However, they failed to anticipate the impact their prosperity would have on the Muscovite leader, Ivan the Severe or, as you Westerners call him, Ivan the Terrible. He observed the popularity of Kazan furs and jewels among the Muscovite elite and noted the wealth that the Kazans were accumulating. It was staggering, and soon Ivan obsessed over how he could acquire that wealth for himself.

"You must remember that this was almost three hundred and fifty years ago, so the leaders were not as sophisticated as they are today. They lived in an age where the dominant governmental philosophy was 'might makes right.' Today, of course, we are more civilized and would approach the problem using the tax code. By taxing the imports brought by the Kazans at a confiscatory rate, the same end of redistributing the Kazan's wealth could be achieved without resorting to military violence," Princess Zina said matter-of-factly. Otto refilled her flute and she continued.

"Ivan was a shrewd and practical man who realized that any military operation to subdue the Kazan Khanate would pose great difficulty due in large measure to distance and weather conditions. So, rather than make a frontal assault, Ivan took the son of Khan Yusuf into custody during one of the trading missions to Moscow and used him as leverage in enlisting the covert support of Khan Yusuf, who we affectionately refer to as 'Uncle Joe.'"

"I guess Ivan assumed that Uncle Joe possessed a certain filial affection," Otto joked.

"You're so right. Some fathers might relish the thought of telling their wives that 'regrettably the poor boy did not make it.' But Uncle Joe was not one of them; he truly loved his son," interjected the Count.

Zina continued, "Well, Uncle Joe realized that the situation presented an opportunity as well as a danger. He came up with a plan that he presented to Ivan who was impressed enough to give Uncle Joe one year to implement his plan. Junior would be well taken care of at court in the interim and actually might enjoy the year if it wasn't for the potential death sentence at the end.

"In any event, Uncle Joe held the position of what we would call the Minister of Mines. As such, he was in charge of mines and excavation in the kingdom. Therefore, he knew that there was a secret escape tunnel that ran from the castle under the city walls to a stand of trees to the north. He also knew that the royal treasury was below grade at the castle's east wall along the river about fifty yards away from the tunnel."

As Otto listened with rapt attetion, the Princess said, "Uncle Joe and a small group of confederates worked for many months, under cover of darkness, to construct a tunnel connecting the escape tunnel to the wall of the royal treasury. When everything was set, Uncle sent a messenger to Ivan and the Muscovy leader mobilized his army and marched on Kazan. Of course, the castle went on full alert, leaving the treasury guarded only by a skeleton crew.

"The treasure room was quite large and the din created by the war preparations above, masked the noise of Uncle Joe's men as they chipped away at the rear wall. When they broke through they systematically removed as much treasure as they could without disturbing the guard. They were able to remove about three quarters of it without detection. They resealed the wall and notified Ivan that he should press for negotiations."

Like any good storyteller, she allowed the suspense to build before continuing. In a conspirational tone, she narrated, "Moxammad, the leader of the Kazans, summoned his vassals to the castle at night to make loyalty payments to secure their allegiance. When Moxammad brought the Lords to the treasury to make the payments, he discovered the great perfidy. Seeing that most of the treasure in the treasury was no longer present, the Lords quickly abandoned Moxammad. Shortly thereafter, the city and the Kazan Khanate surrendered to Ivan without a fight. Ivan put every male in the city, even infant boys, to the sword. Moxammad went to his death without knowing what had happened, or who had betrayed him.

"Uncle Joe gave half of the pilfered treasure to Ivan who had no way of knowing that a large measure of the trove had been secreted by Uncle Joe for himself in a side tunnel that had been constructed and camouflaged before Uncle Joe revealed the location of the secret escape tunnel and the hiding place of the pilfered treasury to Ivan."

Zina relished the look on Otto's face as she concluded, "And that is the story of how Ivan became the first Tsar, or Caesar, in Russia and how the Yusopov family gained its fortune. For his part in the betrayal that resulted in Ivan's ascension, Khan Yusuf was granted dominion over vast tracts of land rich in minerals, lumber and profitable fur trade. Over the centuries, the family adroitly cultivated these assets into a fortune. So you see, Otto, behind every great fortune, lies a great crime."

Otto nodded and raised his flute in tribute.

"An important corollary to that principle is that a smart thief covers his tracks and has the 'victim' eliminated so there is no one left to complain," she added with an elapid-like smile.

The sun streamed through the ivory lace curtains into the main salon of *Znamenka*, the palace of Princess Militza Nikolaevna in the fashionable Petrodvortsovy District of Saint Petersburg. More a tribute to her naïveté than her punctuality, Anya was the first to arrive. She helped Stana as she fussed over the last-minute preparations. Stana regarded her friend curiously.

"How are you, Anya, after the dreadful Yusopov boy created such a scene at the Ball?"

"Did you see his eyes? Why he looked absolutely possessed. And his language. My goodness, such filth."

"What provoked him? I mean, one minute everything was fine and the next, he was raving and haranguing you. What happened?"

"I was standing at the dessert table minding my own business, when he rudely pushed past me. I said 'Don't be in such a hurry, *Korotyshka*.'"

"You called him a runt?"

"Yes, but in an endearing way. That was what his family and everyone in our school called him when we were growing up. I guess he took offense because he whirled at me with those satanic eyes and started spewing despicable epithets at me. I was mortified. It's a good thing that Lieutenant Vyrubova interceded on my behalf and dragged Felix away."

"M'lady," interrupted the maid, "Father Grigory is here. Shall I bring him in?"

"Yes, of course."

Dressed in a rude, threadbare suit, Rasputin entered the room hesitantly. After kissing Stana on both cheeks and bowing to Anya, he walked over to the groaning board, which was weighed down with delicacies. Sighing ravenously, he began to heap food onto a plate with his stout fingers. When he spied a platter of *selianka d'esturgeon,* Rasputin nodded agreeably toward Stana. She shrugged toward Anya as if to say, pay no attention to his earthiness.

Soon the salon was filled with devotees, mostly young women from the aristocratic families of St. Petersburg.

"Ladies, allow me to present my confessor, Father Putin."

"It's Rasputin, Grigory Rasputin," said the self-styled monk humbly. He thanked Stana for hosting the *soiree* and prayed to the Almighty for the proper words to inspire the group. He spoke about his humble upbringing in Siberia and how he had been a reprobate, drinking and carousing, bringing shame and rebuke to his family. How he had been accused of horse theft and other crimes. Finally, having brought great shame to his family, his father banished him.

"I was devastated and did not know where to turn. I had nothing but the clothes on my back. I was ignorant and rebellious. The Spirit must have guided me because I walked aimlessly for months until I stumbled into the monastery of the Monk Makariy near Mount Zhima, Lake Baikal. I labored during the day and listened to the Monk teach from the Bible at night.

"One night after a long day behind the plow, I collapsed bone-weary on my pallet. Suddenly, the Virgin Mary appeared on a luminous cloud. She was the most beautiful sight I had ever seen. Mother Mary implored me to quit drinking, smoking and to avoid eating meat. The Mother of God told me to stop wasting my life; that I was blessed with gifts beyond my limited *muhjik* understanding. The Father wanted to use me to heal and foretell. But, in my piggish self-indulgence, I disobeyed and dismayed the Father. When I awoke, I was imbued with a love and sense of purpose that flowed over and through me. I wept for hours."

Rasputin paused for emphasis and peered deeply into the eyes of every woman present as if he were penetrating their souls. His hypnotic stare was so powerful that Olga Nikolaevna swooned and the Black Princesses cried audibly. He related how he had walked from village to village healing and preaching until the Spirit moved him to bring his gifts to the broken and hurting people in the cities. Then, he raised his arms and motioned for them to bow their heads while he prayed over them.

Rasputin retired to a sitting room to receive his admirers. He sat on a small, green velvet divan in semi-darkness, counseling each of the women as if in the privacy of the confessional with the intimacy of a boudoir. He frequently touched, caressed and hugged them while administering his particular brand of salvation. Many of the women left his room flushed and excited. Others were pale and on the verge of fainting. Anya hung back shyly until the others had completed their personal sessions.

After a brief prayer, the monk unfastened his tunic, grasped both her hands and placed them on his naked chest over his heart. Anya started to pull away, but he gazed into her eyes hypnotically and she slumped forward. The beating of his heart echoed the beating of her heart that she felt thrumming in her ears. He whispered in soothing tones. She rested her head on his shoulder like a compliant child. A warm security enveloped her. Suddenly, his hands were cradling her face and his eyes were close to her eyes, entrancing her. She could feel his breath on her lips. He spoke softly, "You have met a young man, a Naval officer. Do not be fooled by him. He will change your life for evil. Run from him."

"I don't understand . . . ."

"Yes, Annushka, you do. Once again, I say, do not become involved with this man. He will only bring you grief. Now leave here my child," he whispered as his hands slid over her bodice with gentle pressure as he pushed her away.

Sept. 11, 1907
"Bay of Shtandart" Gulf of Finland

You come of age very quickly through shipwreck and disaster.

~ PHILIP DUNNE

ALIX AND ANYA WATCHED from their vantage point on the pebbly beach as Nikki tried to teach Alexei how to swim in the calm waters of a secluded bay in an area in the south of Finland known as the Finnish Skerries. The three-year-old Tsarevich chortled as he splashed between the Tsar and Vladimir Derevenko, a *diadka,* assigned to protect the young heir. The broad-chested young sailor had trim blond hair and a wide, friendly face. Alexei idolized the young Georgian like the older brother the Tsarevich would never have.

Using the Imperial Yacht *Shtandart* as their base, the royal family had vacationed every September at the tranquil islands off the Finnish coast at Horsoë. In this casual setting, Nicholas and Alix released the royal children from the strict protocols of the court and let the youngsters behave like normal children. One day, in a burst of jollity, the young Grand Duchess Anastasia was so enamored with this idyllic location that she dubbed it the

"Bay of *Shtandart*" and the nickname became part of the family's private lexicon.

The majestic *Shtandart* graced the horizon several hundred yards off shore. The *Shtandart* was unique by virtue of her size and the way in which she was outfitted. The Tsar's ship of state was named after the legendary ship of state of Peter the Great and was designed to Tsar Alexander II's specifications with the majesty of a tall ship and the power of a Navy cruiser. When launched out of Copenhagen in 1896 by the Danish shipbuilder Burmeister-Wain, she was the largest private vessel in the world. The *Shtandart* was the size of a first-rank cruiser, measuring over four hundred feet long and fifty feet wide. She was a graceful black-hulled yacht with three masts and two large white funnels to exhaust her powerful diesel engines. More than one maritime journalist had called the *Shtandart* a 'floating palace.'

After a picnic lunch of chilled shrimp remoulade and Waldorf salad under the welcoming shade of the blue-and white-striped canopy, the family prepared to return to the massive yacht. The Tsarina, the Grand Duchesses and Anya boarded the launch first, via portable steps placed at the prow of the beached vessel. Next, came Seaman Derevenko, cradling the Tsarevich carefully in his burly arms and gently entrusting him into the waiting arms of the Empress. Alexei happily played with several seashells that he had collected while foraging along the shore. Bringing up the rear was the Tsar and his fellow noblemen. Nicholas' chest welled up with emotion and gratitude for the blissful family time.

Back on the *Shtandart*, Nicholas and Alexei went directly to the bridge, while the others retired to other activities. With orders to 'hoist anchors' ringing through the chain of command, the perfunctory ease that had permeated the ship while the royal party was ashore, transformed into an efficient frenzy as the large vessel came to life. Nicholas spritely climbed the metal steps to the bridge where he was warmly greeted by Captain Tchaguin, the ship's commander. The Tsar fancied himself a knowledgeable sailor and enjoyed studying navigation charts. Within minutes, the two men gravitated toward the chart table where they huddled over the stacks of charts.

Seaman Derevenko carried Alexei in his arms over to the pilot, Chief Petty Officer Mats Aalto, who was standing before a large spoked wheel that he used to steer the large vessel through the islands, large and small, that dotted the area. The pilot was a stout fellow with sunburned skin, who wore a salt and pepper beard that gave him a look of ruddy distinction. His thick, stubby right hand cradled the king spoke of the steering wheel. CPO Aalto loved to entertain children with his uncanny ability to mimic bird calls. As the great yacht steamed ahead slowly, Aalto performed his avian repertoire of whistles, caws and parrot talk. Alexei enjoyed the auditory show giggling joyously.

Suddenly, Alexei lurched with his arms spread in a big hug toward the pilot. Derevenko almost lost his grip on the squirming child, but righted himself. Alexei stepped on the spoke at the three o'clock position for balance. In the same instant, Aalto, seeing the child in limbo, reached to catch him. The weight of the Tsarevich pushed the wheel to the right. Derevenko grabbed the boy under the arms to free him from the spinning spokes. Aalto re-established his grip and brought the king spoke back to the center position.

Unbeknownst to the sailors on the bridge, the slight course change caused by Alexei's pressure on the wheel aimed the ship toward an uncharted rock. Suddenly, an ear-piercing screech and crunching tremor rocked the ship. Derevenko was thrown toward the windshield. Twisting to his left, he shielded Alexei. Unfortunately, the boy's knee slammed into the binnacle. Immediately, Alexei howled in pain.

Shtandart's serene glide turned into a nightmare. Shouted reports that the cruiser was taking on water echoed across the ship. Sailors raced across the decks, alarms sounded and officers frantically directed emergency procedures. The great ship stalled and began to list leeward. Life boats were unleashed by the crew while others distributed life jackets. Below decks, watertight compartments were secured. Bilge pumps were activated.

The Tsarina appeared on the foredeck, like a mother duck followed by the Grand Duchesses in a row and calmly supervised their evacuation. Once the girls were safely on board with their bulky lifejackets, Alix turned her attention to make sure that Alexei was safe. She encountered Derevenko carrying the Tsarevich, who was sniffling with tears in his red-rimmed eyes. She directed the sailor to take Alexei on the lifeboat with his sisters.

Nicholas was on the deck peering over the side at the water line. He alternately looked at his watch and calculated the rate at which the ship was sinking. Fortunately, the watertight compartments held and the emergency measures taken by the expertly-trained crew saved the *Shtandart* from disaster and the crew from total humiliation.

The "Wreck of the *Shtandart*" was over-hyped in the ensuing media frenzy. Predictably, anything involving the royal family was front page news. Rumors of sabotage and attempted assassination were circulated by the media with the standard disclaimer that the source of the story had insisted on anonymity. The most outrageous of the reports in the tabloids centered on a conspiracy involving the Tsarina and 'foreign' agents to eliminate Nicholas and then appoint herself regent. Unreported was the ominous swelling of Alexei's leg.

The knock on her door startled Anya awake. Since the incident on the *Shtandart*, she had been keeping vigil with her mistress as Alexei's condition worsened. The dear boy was her favorite, an imp who loved to play tricks on the staff. Once he had hidden her peacock feather duster in the aviary. Oh, did the children laugh while she searched for it high and low. But over time, the episodes of bruising and bleeding drained the sparkle from his eyes. His eyes had become the eyes of an old man used to suffering.

Another knock. She peered through the crack in her door. "Who is it?" she whispered hoarsely.

"It's Father Grigory. The Princess Militza sent me. She thinks that I can help with the young Tsarevich."

"Come in, please."

He bowed slightly and raised his gaze to hers. As she closed the door, Anya cringed.

"Are you OK?" he murmured.

"It's nothing," she replied, arching her neck with a grimace.

"May I?" he asked gently.

Before she could respond, he rubbed his hands together vigorously and placed them softly on her shoulders and began humming in a singsong cadence. As if by a hidden current, her pain started to flow from her shoulders into his hands. His head was bowed, his eyes closed and his expression was one of studied innocence. His eyebrows knotted as the tightness and pain left her. He shook almost imperceptibly as his hands fell to his sides. She felt a lightness through her shoulders and neck as if she had been massaged by angels. Anya chuckled softly and searched his eyes for a sign. Rasputin blinked, swallowed hard and smiled at her. "God has blessed me with this gift and I must use it to help the Tsarevich."

Anya nodded and led him to a small anteroom outside the royal chambers. She signaled for him to stay. She approached the large, black Araby guard, who stepped aside and opened a carved gilded door. The Tsarina was half-reclining on Alexei's bed. Her red and swollen eyes lifted querulously. Anya motioned toward the anteroom. Alexandra wearily gathered herself and entered to the side room quietly.

"Your Highness, this man is a *Starets* — a healer from beyond the Urals."

"I don't understand, Anya."

"We Russians have always had special, mystical men of God who are blessed with the gift of healing. This man is one such healer. He can help the Tsarevich."

"Come forward. What is your name? Why are you here? What is your purpose?" whispered the Tsarina impatiently. Rasputin haltingly shuffled forward.

"Your Highness, my name is Grigory Rasputin from Pokrovskoe. I am blessed with a gift from heaven. A gift to heal. I can take your son's affliction into my body and heal him. I have been sent by Princess Militza. Here's a letter of introduction." He fumbled for the paper in his breast pocket, handing it to Anya.

Alexandra sat down with an exhausted sigh. She broke the Militza's seal and unfolded the letter. She gasped slightly as the missive described how Rasputin had the spiritual gifts of healing and prophecy. The holy monk had been traveling throughout the land healing and had developed a large following of devoted followers in St. Petersburg. The letter detailed the myriad acts of healing that Father Grigory had performed during his time in the capital. She perused the list of august persons that the holy man had touched. She recognized many prominent and noble names. The letter concluded, "Trust him with your life. He is truly a man sent from God." The words resonated her prayers to God to send a man to heal her son.

"Your Highness, Lady Anya has shared with me that you suffer from migraines. May I?" Father Grigory asked softly. He stood before her with his hands stretching toward her head. Looking into his shining eyes, she nodded. Rasputin knelt before her, vigorously rubbed his hands together and then placed his large hands on her temples and he began to murmur a soft incantation. Her eyes closed and she experienced a gradual release of pressure and pain flow from her head like a purging of bad vapors. In what seemed like an instant, her pain was replaced by a feeling of lightness and, dare she think it, joy. She heard Rasputin go silent and collapse back onto his haunches with an audible groan. Startled, she opened her eyes just in time to see a dark cloud flash over his countenance.

"Excuse me, Your Highness, I must rest." He went over to a chair and slumped wearily into its soft folds. He reached into his pocket and withdrew a small glass flask from which he took a long draught of the green elixir within. "It is a restorative that I must have after accepting another's pain." The Tsarina nodded understandingly.

"Can you, . . . will you, . . . heal Alexei? His affliction is so much greater."

"First, I must know the precise nature of his symptoms."

"Of course, Father. . . . Well, when he was born he was a beautiful baby. However, when he was six weeks old, I noticed blood coming from his belly-button. That was when I first began to fear that my Sunbeam had inherited the dread disease of my uncle. To this day, I cannot even say the word. During Alexei's first year, there were no problems with bleeding. He handled teething exceptionally well. Shortly after he began walking, I noticed that even the slightest bump left an ugly bruise. I was terrified that he had that horrible incurable blood disease."

"Fear not the word hemophilia, Your Highness. I have the power to help," said Rasputin with a soft, confident voice.

"The Tsar and I have brought the world's finest physicians to examine our precious Tsarevich. They have all given the diagnosis that Alexei suffers from this disease saying that it is untreatable. Father, I despair that my beautiful boy will never grow up. Never become Tsar. His cries when the hemorrhages come break my heart." Alix stopped, her eyes filled with tears. Grigory's heart went out to the suffering mother. There was no longer a chasm between ruler and subject. There was only believer and cleric. He touched her hand empathetically.

"Your Highness, it would be my privilege and honor to be a divine instrument of curing. It may take some time." Her tearful eyes looked up at him with disbelief that dissolved into expectant hope as she held his gaze.

"Yes, Father, whatever it takes. We must save the Tsarevich; he is our only heir. We are surrounded by vipers and wolves; we don't know who we can trust."

"Please, I must rest. Then, I will see the Tsarevich." With that he removed his jacket, folded it into a pillow and lay down. "Lady Anya, please have someone sent to my home to summon my daughter, Matryona, and have her bring my satchel. She'll know which one. Thank you."

"Surely, "said Anya, as she and the Tsarina left the anteroom. By the time the catch engaged in the latch, they heard the sonorous rumble of a person in deep sleep.

He awoke refreshed but not conscious of where he was. Then, he recalled his meeting with the Tsarina and Anya the night before and how he had virtually passed out from absorbing the malevolence from the women. The darkness of the inner room engulfed him and deprived his senses of the ability to gauge the time. He waited, anxious and afraid of being arrested for trespassing in the palace. He had arrived late at night and had no papers, nor any way to prove that he was there legitimately. Neither the Tsarina, nor Anya were anywhere in evidence, and he did not know where, or how to find them. He decided to bide his time and wait for them to come to him.

After an interminable wait, he heard the faint footfall of slippered feet approaching his haven. There was a soft tap on the door frame, and Anya entered carrying a tray of food and his valise. In hushed tones, she explained that the Tsarevich had spent a restless night due to pain and swelling in his right knee. The Tsarina had slept at his bedside and was now desperate for the Starets to heal her son.

He followed Anya to the Tsarevich's chamber where he saw the Tsarina, her torso prone on her son's bed with her lower body seated. He heard her soft murmuring that was punctuated by "Please, Lord . . . ." Anya crossed the room and gently stroked Alix's shoulder.

"The Starets is here, Your Highness," Anya whispered. The Tsarina lifted her head. Rasputin stared intensely into her puffy, teary eyes and assured her telepathically that Alexei would be healed. She slowly withdrew from her son, placing him in the hands of God and Rasputin.

The young heir was semi-conscious, moaning quietly like a distant wraith signaling its approach. Rasputin thrust out his chin in defiance as if to say not today, not while I'm here. He approached the bed and kneeled before Alexei, whispering a prayer over the Tsarevich while stroking his brow softly. Then, Rasputin gently folded back the covers and exposed Alexei's right side. The healer motioned to Anya for assistance. While Rasputin lifted the thin boy, Anya slid his nightshirt up to his waist. From his hip to his toes there was a dark, almost black, purple bruise that clashed dramatically with the porcelain whiteness of his abdomen. Alexei's eyes opened in pain, wildly searching the room for comfort. He caught Rasputin's piercing gaze and calmness washed over him.

Rasputin opened his valise and removed three velvet pouches, each scarlet in color and marked with black runes. Inside were clear crystals — one blood red, one transparent and the last, deep-smoke black. Rasputin briefly warmed the black crystal in his beefy hands while intoning a low prayer. He placed it on Alexei's hip. Next, he warmed the red crystal and praying quietly, placed it on Alexei's knee precisely at the site of the injury. He then took the clear crystal, rubbed it and placed it on Alexei's ankle. The healer slowly lifted the blanket and covered Alexei.

Rasputin turned to the women and gestured for them to join him at the bed. He opened his hands toward them and they reached for him, forming a circle over the Tsarevich. Rasputin led them in prayer and they responded to his petitions, "Lord, hear our prayers."

The prayers had a chanting quality and the threesome closed their eyes, lapsing into a meditative state. Rasputin was tireless and, by virtue of his will, they prayed for a long time with outstretched arms and tears etching their cheeks. The trance was broken when they heard Alexei say, "I'm hungry, Mama."

Alix's eyes bolted open. She glanced toward Rasputin quizzically. He nodded and lifted the covers with a theatrical flourish. They stared, awe-struck. The right leg was the same, normal, pink fleshy hue as the left leg. As Rasputin removed the crystals gingerly handling them with the velvet pouches, careful not to have his skin make contact with the crystals, Anya noticed that the crystals were all darkly clouded to the point of opacity. The healer smiled and humbly advised her that the fate of the Tsarevich and the Imperial dynasty was now *"irrevocably linked to him."*[5]

As he waited in the anteroom to the Tsar's office, the peasant was suddenly self-conscious. He had been cleaning a basement room in the church around the corner from his apartment, when the large, turbaned, black, man in the teal uniform of the Tsar's Imperial Guard approached him and handed him an envelope decorated with the Romanov crest. Rasputin wiped his grimy hands on his shirt front and accepted the ivory-colored missive. A cold panic spread down his spine as he realized that the courier expected him to read the contents of the envelope and respond. After an embarrassed delay, the uniformed man spoke.

"My name is Pasha. Would you prefer that I read the message to you?" Rasputin nodded in relief. Pasha announced," The Tsar requests the honor of your company this afternoon. Transportation provided. R.S.V.P. to courier. That means, tell me if you are available to visit the Tsar today."

Indeed, a coach-and-four from the Tsar's mews was standing at the street. Rasputin murmured, "Yes, I'll go." When Rasputin ignored the black man's suggestion that he might want to 'freshen up,' Pasha decided to ride in the front of the carriage with the driver, while Rasputin rode alone inside.

In the anteroom to the Tsar's office, the monk was apprehensive. Rasputin, a lowly peasant, was about to meet the supreme ruler of Mother Russia. He wished that he had taken the time to clean himself. He looked around furtively and spied a vase filled with fresh lilies. He sidled over to it and tilted it. Spilling an ample amount of water on his hands he rubbed his straggly hair in an ill-fated effort to instill some order to his unruly locks. Before he could obtain a second dousing, the secretary returned and gestured for him to follow.

Nicholas was wearing his commander's uniform and staring out the window while smoking a cigarette. He turned and offered Rasputin a chair. Pasha Kelly stood silently at attention off to the side. The Tsar slipped behind his ornately-carved desk and smiled at his guest. The side of Nicholas' face twitched ever-so-slightly where there was a faint residue of a scar. The Tsar wore a neatly-trimmed beard that had a space where the remnant of the scar continued. It gave the ruler a rugged, asymmetrical look of experience that would have been enhancing had it not been accompanied by the tic.

"We wanted to meet you in order to express our profound gratitude for your excellent services in healing the Tsarevich. My Alix told us that your healing was miraculous. We are most grateful."

"Your Highness, the Lord Almighty is responsible; I am just a humble instrument. I am glad to be able to channel my gift to help the Tsarevich."

"Father Grigory, it is our pleasure to display our gratitude with this token of appreciation," said the Tsar, handing Rasputin a small, wrapped gift.

"Thank you, Sir. I am unworthy of your generosity."

"Quite," said the Tsar wrinkling his nose as a whiff of Rasputin's body odor wafted across the desk. "Please open it now. We want to see if you like it."

Rasputin struggled with the ribbon and tore it with his teeth. Finally, he opened the box. Inside was a gold belt buckle decorated with the ubiquitous Romanov eagle standing on a vermilion enameled crown. Two diamonds filled the eagles' eyes. With obvious, almost child-like pleasure, Rasputin grinned broadly at the monarch, who nodded back paternally. Nicholas' right eyelid drooped as his cheek flinched as if he were reacting to a blow to the side of his head.

"Your Excellency, I can help you with that," stated Rasputin in a low voice.

"It is nothing we can't handle," replied Nicholas pulling himself up rigidly.

"Seriously, Your Imperial Highness. I have helped with similar injuries. My mother's brother was struck by a black bear across the face and suffered like Your Highness. I cured him with several treatments for the nerves and muscles."

Rasputin's stare bore into the Tsar's gray eyes. The monk walked to the windows and pulled the draperies closed. The Tsar held up a languid hand to signal Pasha that it was alright. In the darkened room, Father Grigory moved toward the Tsar. The holy man was humming a soothing melody and whispering assurances to the Tsar.

"May I, Your Imperial Highness?" asked Rasputin, gesturing with his hands that he was rubbing together vigorously. The Tsar nodded assent. While facing the Tsar and maintaining eye contact, Rasputin placed his hands on the sides of the Tsar's neck and applied slight upward pressure. Nicholas rested his head in the cradle of Rasputin's hands. After several minutes, the monk instructed the Tsar to move to the center of the room and lie down on the thick rug that filled the room. In a semi-trance, the Tsar rose and somnambulated to the center of the room where he lay supine over the Imperial eagle that graced the woven surface.

"Rest! Rest! Thy guardian angel has his arms around thee," Rasputin chanted softly as he knelt at Nicholas' head. The monk gently pulled the monarch's ears outward in an effort to release the pressure of his cranial bones. Then, rubbing his hands together vigorously, he covered the Tsar's face and prayed for healing. Rasputin sat back on his haunches and shuddered slightly as his body adjusted to the influx of negative energy. The Tsar's countenance was peaceful and he dozed.

While the Tsar napped, Rasputin prepared a potion from some yellow powder and gray crystalline grains that he combined with heated water drawn from a samovar that was bubbling in the corner. The contents of the cup effervesced, a faint layer of vapor hovered over the glass. The guard Pasha made the monk drink some of the potion before he himself took a sip. Aside from the bitterness, it was rather tasty. When the Tsar awoke, Rasputin administered the elixir. As the drink took effect, Nicholas appeared younger and bright-eyed. He smiled as he rolled his head, stretching his neck muscles.

"Your next appointment is here, Sire," announced the secretary, eying Rasputin disdainfully. "Shall I escort this (pause) gentleman out?"

"Er . . . no, we want him to stay," replied the Tsar waving toward the secretary dismissively.

Emanuel Nobel, heir to the Nobel fortune and the president of Branobel, the oil company that had developed the oil fields at Baku, Azerbaijan, entered. The Baku oilfields produced more than half of the world's oil. The great Italian explorer, Marco Polo described Baku as a place where there was "*. . . a spring from which gushes a stream of oil, in such abundance that a hundred ships may load there at once.*"[6] The area had been known through antiquity as the "Land of Fire" or the "Flaming Steppe," because of an abundance of natural gas that fueled never-ending fires in the area.

Emanuel's father, Ludwig, was an innovator who modernized methods of petroleum extraction, storage and transportation. He was the first to utilize metal tanks, develop pipelines powered by steam engines and use ocean-going tankers to transport oil long distances. The first oil tanker developed by Branobel was named the *Zoroaster* in honor of the holy man who founded the eponymous ancient religion of fire worship. Emanuel was the nephew of Alfred Nobel, the Swedish Russian who amassed a fortune based on his invention of dynamite, cordite, and gelignite, or blasting gelatin.

Now, in his late forties, Emanuel was one of the richest men in Russia. Although the sandy brown hair of his youth had long since faded to gray, he had a youthful stride and countenance. As was the custom, he wore a full beard. Fashionably dressed in a dark, pinstriped suit, he was the epitome of a rich, successful businessman. The only blemish to the picture was the left side of his face, which was discolored red and pocked with shiny, white scar tissue. Up close, a slight distortion of his left eye could be detected.

When Emanuel was six years old, he had been riding his bicycle past a building that his Uncle Alfred was using to formulate his new explosives. Suddenly, there was a blinding flash and explosion. Emanuel was knocked off his bike by the blast concussion. Stunned, he was splashed with a clump of fiery gel that clung to him and scorched him, leaving the side of his face badly burned. The boy screamed in agony and, mercifully lapsed into shock. The rapid arrival of the emergency workers saved his life and the vision in his left eye. Later, in the hospital, Emanuel learned that his grandfather and cousin had been killed in the blast. He was too young and too sedated to cry.

With the burden of his facial disfigurement, Emanuel became an extreme introvert and applied himself diligently to the family business. When he was thirty years old, his father died, leaving him in charge of the thriving, multi-dimensional, petroleum business centered in Baku.

When his father passed away, a French newspaper mistakenly reported the passing as the death of Ludwig's brother Alfred. The obituary condemned Alfred as a 'merchant of death' for inventing dynamite, calling it a faster way to kill people. When he read the piece, Alfred was mortified at the characterization of his life's work and resolved to create a more positive legacy. A short time later, Alfred revised his will, leaving the lion's share of his considerable estate to establish prestigious awards in Literature, Medicine, Physics, Chemistry and Peace to be awarded annually.

In 1897, Emanuel learned from one of his young designers named Anton Carlsund about a novel new engine. Designed by Rudolf Diesel, the engine had the potential to render the steam engine obsolete by utilizing high compression to deliver greater efficiency and lower fuel consumption. Recognizing that the perfection of the diesel engine would increase the demand for petroleum, Emanuel Nobel purchased a license to manufacture the Diesel engine in Russia. Nobel's engineers improved and refined the design, so that in a short time it replaced the steam engines that powered Branobel's fleet of oil tankers throughout the world. The result was a company that was dominant technologically and profitable beyond belief.

The Tsar first met Emanuel at the salon of Karl Fabergé, where both men were commissioning elaborate gifts. The two wealthy patrons shared a love of art, particularly the masterworks of Fabergé. Perhaps, it was the relative equality of wealth or that both labored under the reputations of their prodigious fathers. There may have been a natural affinity for one similarly afflicted. In any event, Nicholas and Emanuel shared a special relationship. Emanuel's eyes danced and twinkled, as he crossed the room to greet his friend. Rasputin tried not to stare as the two men embraced for what seemed like an extra moment.

"Nicholas, it is wonderful to see you my friend. You look so, . . . uh, refreshed."

"We owe it to our new friend here. Please meet Grigory Rasputin. He is a healer from Siberia."

"It is a pleasure to make your acquaintance, Sir," Emanuel responded, bowing slightly.

Rasputin returned the gesture with an awkward nod; then addressed the Tsar.

"Imperial Highness," he croaked, his voice momentarily lost. "I must take my leave. I . . . ."

"Of course, but only after you promise to apply your healing magic to our good friend as you treated us."

"Yes, Your Highness, of course," said Rasputin, as he bowed and shuffled toward the exit, visibly relieved. He was escorted from the palace by the black guard.

1907
St. Petersburg, Russia

No, this secret society is so secret that I'm
not even sure I'm a member.

~ Jarod Kintz, *I Should Have Renamed This*

S EVERAL DAYS LATER, Kahn was in St. Petersburg trying to deflect the north wind blowing off the Neva River that was penetrating his thin woolen overcoat. The wind reminded him of the gales coming off the Hudson River whistling through the streets of Manhattan in the dead of winter. He entered a discreet mansion in one of the wealthiest neighborhoods in the city. The 'club room' on the main floor was as quiet and secure as a mahogany-lined tomb. Dark, tinted windows encased the first floor and there was a rear entrance with an adjoining *porte cochere* where visitors could enter and depart without being observed.

Pyotr's *entre* with officials in the highest levels of the ruling classes enabled him to facilitate the meeting expeditiously. The first to arrive was Grand Duke Mikhail, the Tsar's younger brother and next in line to the throne after the fragile Tsarevich. Tall and lanky, he possessed the renowned Romanov good looks and natural grace. Kahn thought that with his attractive masculine features, rakishly thin moustache and regal bearing, Mikhail was certainly the ladies' man that he was reputed to be. Otto shook hands with the young man, who caught his gaze and pumped vigorously as if he were genuinely glad to meet Kahn.

"Herr Kahn, it is truly a pleasure to meet you. I've heard so much about you."

"Is that so?" replied Otto. "Who has been gossiping about me?" he joked.

"Actually, we have several mutual acquaintances. But I was with Prince Felix last night and he sang your praises at length," answered Mikhail.

Before Otto could pursue this discussion further, Mikhail's Imperial relatives entered the room. First to enter was Grand Duke Nikolay Nikolayevich, Mikhail's cousin by virtue of his father being the brother of Tsar Alexander III. Nikolay was in his early fifties and bore the Romanov stamp, tall and impressive with an elongated, oval face and an imperious bearing. He was considered a true Russian patriot with a flair for the dramatic. During the darkest days of the 1905 Rebellion after the humiliating defeat inflicted by Japan, the Prime Minister presented the Tsar with a choice of either accepting constitutional reforms or declaring a military dictatorship. The Tsar lacked the dominant personality and support within the military to become a dictator, so he implored Nikolay to assume the mantle of dictatorship. Nickolay was enlightened enough to see that the tide of history was against a military coup. According to family lore, when the Tsar insisted, Nikolay drew his service revolver and threatened to shoot himself if the Tsar failed to adopt the constitutional reforms proposed by the Prime Minister. Only Nikolay knew that the weapon was empty. The emotional ploy worked. Nicholas II relented and accepted the reforms, on the condition that Nikolay assume the responsibilities of commander-in-chief. Nikolay clicked his heels and bowed elegantly to Otto in greeting.

He was followed by his younger cousin, Grand Duke Kyril Vladimirovich. The gangly, young man shuffled into the room with the gait of a stiff wooden marionette. During the 1905 war, Kyril had been the first officer on the *Petropavlovsk*, a battleship that was destroyed in the battle for Port Arthur. A Navy rescue squad found Kyril clinging to the remnants of a lifeboat four hours after the ship sunk. A back injury prevented him from emulating Nikolay's courtly bow. When Otto shook the Grand Duke's gloved hand, he noticed the still-red burn scars on his neck. Kyril's eyes were dull from pain medication. As the Grand Dukes peered down at Otto, he felt a compulsion to rise up on his toes slightly.

Lubricated by vodka, the group settled into a comfortable conversational buzz. With each new drink, a toast was raised and the fiery liquid downed. Kyril was on his fourth glass when Bark committed a *faux pas* by raising his glass to the Tsar. Nikolay looked down his nose disdainfully at the Minister. That was nothing compared to the hostile rancor of Kyril. On finishing his drink, he hurled his glass ferociously against the stone fireplace where it shattered.

"How dare you toast that weasel!" Kyril screamed. "He has ruined my life by stripping me of my military rank just because I married the former wife of the bitch's brother. Nikki is just a spineless tool of Alexandra. He will pay dearly for the attacks against me and my dear wife Vicky."

Nikolay rushed over to Kyril and embraced him, whispering consoling words in his ear.

"You must excuse my cousin. He has been under significant stress, what with his war injuries, medication and the ardors of traveling." Kyril slumped awkwardly into a chair. The strained silence was broken only by the puttering efforts of the steward sweeping up the shards of glass.

The tension was alleviated by the arrival of General Nikolai Ivanov, a short fire plug of a man. His face bore the bone structure of his Mongolian ancestors, flat cheekbones across a broad face with shallow, horizontal eye sockets. He wore a cavalry officer's uniform that was festooned with medals, reflecting his illustrious career as a field officer in no less than four wars. Ivanov liked to perpetuate the myth that he was a direct descendant of Taras Bulba, the legendary Mongol warrior. The General's men loved him because he always led the charge and was oblivious to molten lead fired in his direction. It was his determined leadership that had repelled the assaults of the Japanese army at Port Arthur, thereby preventing a total annihilation of the Russian military.

"I see that you have started without me. Bartender, pour me a double."

"Gentlemen, it is my distinct pleasure to welcome you all to our private meeting of great national, strategic importance to Mother Russia. It is no secret that Russia is rebuilding its shattered military after the disappointing defeat at the hands of your enemy to the East. I am here today to help you eliminate a vulnerability that goes to the heart of Russia's security that has gone unnoticed to date."

The General glowered at Kahn. Only the strong pressure on his forearm from Grand Duke Nikolay restrained him from jumping out of his seat and throttling the banker for his insolence. Ivanov ground his jaws together so hard, it was a wonder that his teeth were not pulverized. Otto continued, shifting his posture slightly so that he was not subject to the General's stare.

"I make this assertion, not to upset you, but to alert you. It is beyond dispute that petroleum is, and, will be, the resource that will fuel the engines of military power in this new century. Mother Russia is blessed with an abundance of this precious commodity. However, have you ever stopped to realize that 97% of Russia's oil is produced and transported by one entity? Remarkably, one company, Branobel, controls Russia's extraction and transportation of the single most important resource, black gold. And, that company has a fleet of diesel vessels that is larger in number than the Imperial Navy. Branobel controls more tank cars and rolling stock than the Imperial Army. Even more remarkable is the fact that this company is owned by a foreigner, a Swede." Otto pronounced the last word as if it were an epithet, allowing it to linger in the air.

"You may be saying to yourselves that Kahn is mistaken. Emanuel Nobel and Branobel are Russian institutions. Emanuel has spent his entire life here. He's one of us, a true Russian. I ask you: what nation's passport does he carry? Where does he go every winter? And, most telling, where does he deposit the revenue from Branobel? The answer to all these questions is Sweden. Branobel's primary bank is Nya Bank in Stockholm.

"Don't mistake my comments. I know that Herr Nobel is a good and decent man. He is a friend of the Tsar. And I might add, he has great admiration for Russia. That said, is his loyalty to Russia subject to, how shall we say, compromise? Of course, it is. So what is the answer? Total elimination of Nobel's ownership? Absolutely not. Russia needs his expertise and capital. Is there another, better solution? Yes, it's right here."

Kahn paused while Minister Bark distributed a folder to each man. Otto waited for them to peer inside before recommencing.

"In your hands you hold the solution to reducing this glaring vulnerability. We call it the Russian General Oil Company. The purpose of the company is to extract and process petroleum from the Baku oil fields. Each of you will own 15% of the company. The remainder will be owned by a management group that will run the entire operation. You will bear no responsibility other than to collect royalties and profits. There is a strong likelihood that the profits will be so immense that you may have to devote considerable time in spending it all.

"In addition, we have purchased control over a shipping and distribution operation known as the Caspian-Black Sea Society or 'Mazut' for short. As with the extraction and processing company, each of you will own 15%. In return for these very valuable stock holdings, you will pledge to work tirelessly to obtain a concession for 20% of the Baku oil fields and distribution routes for your new companies. The end result will be greater security and control of this precious resource by Mother Russia and significant income for you personally."

As the guests considered the proposal, Bark ushered in the evening's entertainment; feminine delicacies that Bark had arranged, plus a few prepubescent boys to satisfy the General. This latter piece of intelligence had been provided by the unctuous monk, Iliodor. The girls had the same thing in common — they were exceptionally pretty and were scantily clothed, all wearing gold chain halter tops that revealed more than they covered and diaphanous harem bottoms *sans* undergarments. The boys carried fresh bottles of liquor and were similarly dressed in harem attire. While the guests adjusted to the visual delights, Otto and Pyotr provided them with pens to sign the contracts inside their individual binders. Once the documents were signed and safely stored, the bacchanalia began.

A few days later, Kahn was adjusting his monocle in preparation for an evening of ballet at the Mariinsky theater, when the summons came. The large black man, who Otto recognized from prior meetings with the Tsar, had appeared at his door and requested Otto to accompany him. His unyielding demeanor made it obvious that refusal was not an option. When the Supreme Leader summons you, you go. An uneasy feeling spread through his abdomen as he entered the anteroom to the Tsar's office in the Winter Palace.

After two hours of silent waiting, the door from the outer hallway opened and the black guard, gripping Pyotr Bark's elbow authoritatively, ushered him into the room. Before they could speak the door to the inner office opened and the guard gestured for them to enter.

Nicholas had his back toward them. The two men stood expectant. Bright moonlight filled the office. Otto adjusted to the new light level and noticed a figure sitting in the shadows of the far corner. It was a large man with long, dark hair and a full beard. Before his eyes could recognize him, his nose detected the mixed odors of manure, sweat, cabbage and garlic. Rasputin.

Nicholas pivoted smartly and stood between them in front of his desk. He folded his arms and glared at them. Pyotr lowered his eyes and hung his head. Otto thought he saw beads of moisture forming on the rims of the Minister's eyes. Kahn stared forward trying to quell his rising sense of foreboding. He inhaled slowly and unclenched his hands and rotated his wrists.

"What do you have to say for yourselves?" asked the Tsar in measured tones. Otto turned toward the Tsar and blinked uncomprehendingly. The Tsar harrumphed impatiently.

"Are you aware that Emanuel Nobel is our closest friend?"

With that utterance, Otto suddenly understood why they had been summoned. Nicholas reached onto his desk and thrust a sheaf of papers under their noses. Bark flinched and leaned backward to avoid being swiped by the onrushing papers.

"Do these documents look familiar?" the Tsar demanded.

"How dare you interfere in our internal affairs with such disrespectful arrogance," the Tsar shouted at Kahn and Bark.

Otto, concluding that the best defense is a good offense, said, "These contracts were entered pursuant to Your Highness' instructions to secure and modernize Russia's transportation network by whatever means necessary."

"What?" stammered Nicholas.

"Remember our meeting last year when Your Highness commissioned my firm to upgrade all aspects of the transportation system with special emphasis on natural resources? After detailed study, which we presented to Your Highness last spring, we identified security of petroleum delivery as an area of greatest vulnerability."

Otto was counting on the tendency of most of his clients to accept lengthy reports without ever studying the details. This reality permitted the insertion of exculpatory and contradictory material into reports for later, *post hoc* justification. The Tsar paused. Otto pressed the point.

"We analyzed the rail and shipping patterns of Branobel's petroleum operations and calculated the theoretical effect of a disruption in its operations. These contracts will help diffuse the potential of any disruption at Branobel."

The Tsar's eyebrows knitted, his jaw clenched. He searched their faces for signs of duplicity. Then, his passion evaporated and he moved behind his desk, gesturing for them to sit. As Kahn leaned forward to sit, he thought he saw Rasputin shake his head from side-to-side.

The Tsar raised the documents to eye level and furiously tore them to pieces.

"These measures are unnecessary. We oppose them and instruct you to do your jobs and stay away from Branobel! Emanuel is a true and loyal friend and you will not interfere with his interests in any way! Herr Kahn, your commission will terminate once you have completed the Trans-Siberian railway upgrade report. Understood?" Nicholas bellowed.

"I can't believe that I just got fired," said Otto with his head resting on the backs of his wrists. Bark gulped his drink loudly and said, "You fail to understand, Otto, the Tsar is extremely protective of his friends; he has so few. You may have lost your work, but you still have your life. Be thankful."

"How could he have gotten those documents? What does Iliodor say?"

"Iliodor was in the home of Grand Duke Nicholay, when he overheard the Grand Duke's wife conversing with the Tsarina about a new oil venture. Alexandra asked for the documents so that Rasputin could pray with Nicholas about the best interests of Mother Russia."

"That *muhjik* is dangerous. We must take care to neutralize him in the future," exclaimed Otto, pounding the table with his fist so hard that his glass upended, sending a splash of Putachieside scotch across the Persian carpet.

9

1994
Huntington, New York

Memory is the treasury and guardian of all things.

~ MARCUS TULLIUS CICERO

BACK IN HUNTINGTON, Luke continued his pursuit of the enigmatic Otto Kahn. He stood in the Huntington Building Department where he was greeted by Marge Sammis. She had been working there since Neil Armstrong walked in moon dust. A grandmother many times over, she had the demeanor of a kindly librarian, unless you crossed her. She was one of those remarkable people in every organization who work in relative obscurity and are the organization's silent backbone who not only remember its history, but know where to find it.

Luke told her that he and his partners were attempting to resurrect the castle and restore it to its original glory. Without a word, Marge walked to a row of file cabinets along the wall. She paused, bending to view the labels on the file drawers, eventually alighting on the proper drawer. She removed a thick extra-wide expansion wallet bearing the label "Oheka Castle" and handed it to him.

"You mean, restore it like it was during the Gilded Age?"

"Yes. We've heard that it was a splendid structure and that it was the site of many historic events."

"Oh, there are dozens of legends about that place. Rumor has it that Oheka inspired Scott Fitzgerald when he wrote the *Great Gatsby*. Celebrities from movies, sports and politics were regular visitors there. My grandmother, God rest her soul, when she was a young girl, worked in the kitchen there during her summer vacations. She told me of how on weekends, limousines would be lined up along the allée all the way to Jericho Turnpike. She once saw Douglas Fairbanks, Jr. kissing Sarah Bernhardt in the garden next to the kitchen. Grandmother turned beet-red whenever she told that story."

Luke opened the reddish-brown Redweld and leafed through a folder labeled "Correspondence 1913–1918." According to the *Long Islander*, in November of 1913, Otto Kahn purchased one-hundred acres of the 'old Walters Farm' and the farm of Henry A. Monfort consisting of two-hundred-and-fifty acres. Four months later, in March 1914, the paper reported an additional purchase of thirty-two contiguous acres from Robert W. Gibson.[7]

Otto completed the Castle in 1919. In its heyday, it was known as the finest country estate in America. Otto retained an expert in the newly-emerging discipline of landscape architecture, none other than Frederick Law Olmsted, Jr., the head of Olmstead Brothers noted for their visionary design of New York's Central Park. Oheka included fountains, formal estate gardens and reflecting pools reminiscent of the finest palaces in Europe. Oheka boasted its own golf course, designed by world renowned golf architect, Seth Raynor as a traditional links course, greenhouses, a nursery, stables and even a landing strip for aero planes. Oheka was the second largest private residence in the United States, surpassed in size only by the Biltmore in North Carolina. Oheka was over one hundred thousand square feet and had over one hundred and twenty-six rooms, all tastefully furnished.

The building was designed in the French Chateau style. It was reported that Kahn was fearful of fire because his New Jersey mansion had been partially destroyed by fire. He insisted that the walls be built with reinforced concrete. Even the moldings in the interior were made out of plaster and not the customary wood, in order to reduce susceptibility to fire.

Kahn insisted that the site be the highest on Long Island. He battled with the architects, Delano and Aldrich, over this. One of these battles was memorialized, in the diary of one of Delano's assistants.

"Listen, this site is perfect. The elevation is consistent and the borings are excellent. The glacial moraine gives us stability for the loads that the structures will impose," said Will Delano.

"I appreciate your opinion, but the plot is simply not high enough," replied Mr. Kahn.

"What do you mean not high enough?"

"I want to be able to see both the Long Island Sound and the Atlantic Ocean from the master suite."

Mr. Delano stopped himself before he blurted out 'Are you crazy?' After all, his architectural firm was based on serving the rich and powerful and he was used to their eccentricities. In the end, Delano's solution was as it has been since wealth was invented — charge the potentate dearly for his idiosyncrasies, but by all means give him what he wants.

"Look, in order to do that we will have to raise the level of the site by several hundred feet and expand the estate by fourfold to accommodate the slope. It will take millions of cubic tons of material to reach that elevation. The cost alone . . . ."

"I've told you time and time again, damn the cost. Plus, I've already secured over 400 contiguous acres. Just draw up the plans and let me know when I can move in."

When Delano presented Kahn with the calculations on the scope of the earth required, he commented half-facetiously that to move that much dirt Kahn would need his own railroad. Without blinking an eye, Kahn replied, "That's what I do, Mr. Delano, I build railroads."

And sure enough Kahn constructed his own railroad spur off the Long Island Railroad and used it to deliver fill from the excavation of the new extension of the BMT Broadway Line of the New York City subway. And, the City paid him to do it.

While Luke was engrossed in the file, Marge bustled into the room with her arms filled with yellow-edged blueprints, rolled into tubes. With a dusty thump, she released the pile onto the desk like an excavator bucket releasing a load of logs.

Just before closing, Marge came to the door and told him that he could leave the materials out and return in the morning. He was just about to call it a day when he noticed a notation on the blueprint held open before him by two coffee mugs. The entry referenced another drawing of an elevator shaft not far from the railroad siding. As he packed his bag for the day, he momentarily considered that no other primary source all afternoon had referenced an elevator shaft.

Tommy MacIntosh, the proprietor of Apple Environmental Services, was glad to be out in the field. The office and the constant grind of regulatory reports were the worst part of his business. He had studied geology in college because he loved rocks. It was that simple. The idea that humanity was standing on a gigantic rock with a molten center fascinated him. He was always amazed at the complexity of the geology where he lived.

Oheka Castle was perched on the Harbor Hill Moraine, a deposit of rock, gravel and debris left by retreating glaciers at the end of the Ice Age. Tommy Mac was attempting to verify the existence of an elevator shaft from the Castle to sea level using his portable, geologic ground-penetrating radar device. He crawled through a broken archway from the courtyard on the south side of the Castle and down the rickety stairs into the lower basement of the structure.

He turned the GPR unit on. What registered on the dial confused him. He had never seen such a blanket reading that prevented the device from probing beneath the concrete floor. Apparently, there was a significant mass of metal directly at his feet that was blocking the sonic waves from penetrating. He flicked the machine off and knitted his bushy eyebrows. His freckled face was marked by deep thought. *This old lady is not going to give up her secrets easily.*

"You're not going to believe it," Tommy declared to Luke the next day. He tossed his spiral-bound report across the desk.

"This friggin' place has as much steel rebar in its foundation as I've ever seen. And I've examined buildings like the Empire State Building and the World Trade Center. This "Castle" could probably withstand a direct hit from a jetliner and shrug it off.

"There is so much steel in there that I could not use ground-penetrating radar through the floor, so I decided to aim the device into the side of the hill."

"So, what'd you find, a moat?" asked Jed Spencer sarcastically.

"Secret treasure?" joshed Luke. "Maybe you found the tomb of Colonel Jasper, who supposedly died looking for the map of Blackbeard, the scourge of Long Island Sound, Aaargh!"

"Alright, if you both want to bust my *cohones*, you can try to figure out the report yourselves," said Tommy rising, as if to leave.

"OK, we'll stop breaking stones, but give it to us without the drama," chuckled Luke.

Tommy proceeded to tell them about a flat "structure" about twelve feet wide that descended like a tap-root at the northern side of the hill. "It goes from the lower level of the building down to sea level."

"What do you think it is?" asked Jed, leaning forward in his chair.

"Well," said Tommy. "I think it's the mystery elevator shaft."

"As a cadet here, I remember rumors of an elevator that went from the Castle down to the harbor," Luke offered. "But we were never able to find it. And then there was the disappearance of my buddy Chuck Williams. He was into some weird stuff — he used to go to a radical bar in Bohemia every weekend. They celebrated April 20th, Hitler's birthday, there. I think he got mixed up with some skinheads. Anyway, he disappeared one night and was never heard from again. The police investigated it as a missing person and concluded that Chuck probably split for Canada, given the Vietnam war and everything. I never bought that story. After graduation, we all dispersed in every direction. Chuck's disappearance always bugged me. . . . . Whew, I have not thought about that in a long, long time." His voice trailed off.

"OK, . . . er. That's a little heavy for me. I'm just a geologist. Look, I'm guessing, that this could be an old elevator shaft. It's definitely not a natural formation, and . . . ."

"And, what?" implored Jed.

"And, there's more. After I used the GPR to identify and plot this vertical structure from the only two sides I could access . . . The undergrowth is a real bitch down there, and the East and South sides are completely built up . . . I dragged out my old magnetometer to see if I could identify the structure as containing iron. It was hard to discern, but I think I detected a large box-like structure adjacent to the vertical column about halfway up."

"What do you mean 'hard to discern'? Either it's iron based or not," queried Jed.

"That's just it. The magnetic readings were weak, but the GPR definitely showed a boxy outline," Tommy stated, scratching his head.

"At first I expected it to be the machine room for the elevator. That would have made sense. But the readings were way too weak. If there was an elevator back in those days, it would have been powered by a machine room filled with iron. I found a concentration of iron at the base of the column. I'm guessing that the machine room is there. This other thing, I don't know . . . the magnetic readings are just too weak."

10

1911
New York City, New York

Here was a man who was both equipped and disposed to be the most considerable *Maecenas* in the history of our theatre.

~ Alexander Woollcott

HE WAS SITTING IN THE OFFICE of his East Side mansion, stewing over the latest loss suffered by the Highlanders. The newspaper account of the late-inning collapse by his favorite team left him in a dour mood that worsened as he checked his watch. Where was his 3 PM appointment? Kahn was punctual to a fault, and nothing aggravated him more than tardiness. It was a sign of weakness and disrespect. He was about to leave his study and prepare for the opera when the housemaid announced the arrival of his appointment.

His gaze was drawn to her eyes, aquamarine irises with flecks of gold that sparkled as she bowed slightly. Her diminutive stature was perfectly proportioned. She was fair with a sprinkling of freckles across her cute, slightly upturned nose that gave her a youthful look. She was wearing a sea-foam green bonnet that contained red tresses that peeked out in ringlets surrounding her face.

"Margaret Sanger, sir," she said, as she strode across the study with her hand outstretched. "I'm so sorry I'm late."

Her abrupt approach toward him and decidedly strong grip caused him to flinch ever so slightly. He was not accustomed to such forward behavior by women. A thought akin to, 'My Lord, I wonder what she would be like in bed' flashed through his mind. Like a flustered schoolboy, he muttered, "Please have a seat. You come well recommended. Mary Harriman, the widow of my late client, Ned Harriman, speaks highly of you. And T.R., er, President Roosevelt, says that you are a major force in the new birth control movement."

She surveyed the study, with its oak-paneled walls and bookcases. She gracefully walked to a sofa and sat down, spreading her skirt around her. She removed her bonnet, releasing her shoulder length hair from its restraints. No sooner had Otto sat down next to her, than the housemaid entered, carrying a silver tray with two Baccarat crystal glasses and a bottle of Lillet.

"Tell me, what brings you here?"

"I am a nurse by training and have seen the horrible tragedy of uncontrolled birth. I have followed the work of the Hereditary Commission and believe that I have a solution to many of the problems we face." Otto gave her a perplexed look.

"OK, let me start with some background. The Hereditary Commission was established by President Roosevelt in 1906 under the U.S. Department of Agriculture to do several things: catalogue this country's genetic heritage and, as Agriculture Secretary William Hayes put it, to conduct scientific research . . . , quote '*with the idea of encouraging the increase of families of good blood, and of discouraging the vicious elements in the cross-bred American civilization.*'[8] Unquote.

"That brings me to Mrs. Harriman. She donated land in Cold Spring Harbor to establish the Eugenics Research Association and the Eugenics Records Office. These entities are exploring ways to engineer human reproduction so that human imperfections and ailments could be scientifically eliminated, and that human strengths could be enhanced. They believe that there should be more children by the genetically superior."

"That makes sense," opined Otto.

"It does, but it only addresses half the problem. I believe that we have to go beyond that, and first stop the multiplication of the unfit. This appears the most important and greatest step towards race betterment. In other words, we can create a better race of humans by restricting the propagation of unfit persons. One way to achieve this has been promoted by Bertrand Russell. He proposes that the government establish a system of color-coded "procreation tickets" and impose penalties on those who procreated with those having a different-colored ticket.

"Through the work of brilliant scientists, there have been breakthroughs in human knowledge that are shattering centuries-old beliefs. Charles Darwin's theory of evolution and the pioneering work of Gregor Mendel are guiding us in understanding the potential of human development through natural selection and survival of the fittest. We are fast approaching the time where mankind will have the power to create a race of superior beings and rid ourselves of hereditary contagion," Margaret lectured.

Otto refilled their glasses and looked up attentively.

Margaret continued, "The science of Eugenics will overturn the superstitions of the past. The word was coined by Francis Galton, who is related to Darwin. It is derived from the Greek term for the elites of society, the 'well-born' or 'good birth.' The underlying assumption was that only the well-born deserved to exist. Modern Eugenics has a dual focus: first, to improve humans by using selective breeding as in animal husbandry and hybrid plant propagation; second, to prevent the birth of those considered inferior or unfit. This latter goal can be achieved through legislation mandating elimination, sterilization and quarantining of those with undesirable genes.

"It starts with pregnancy. Women have always considered pregnancy to be a random event. However, recent advances in understanding of human reproduction have made it apparent that the timing and frequency of pregnancy can be controlled. We call this new understanding 'birth control' and believe that the methods we are devising and publicizing will create a revolution in the lives of women. Through birth control we can create a race of thoroughbreds."

He was fascinated by her eyes that were perfect focal points to her slightly oval face. As she pontificated about the latest scientific theories, his gaze devoured the rest of her.

"You see, Mr. Kahn, Eugenics is the self-direction of human evolution. And as it progresses, we can institute a better world. Through the 'religion of birth control,' we can ease the financial load of caring for children destined to become a burden to themselves, to their family, and ultimately to the nation. It is within our power to create a world not burdened by the weak and dull-witted.

"Simultaneously, science can liberate human sexuality by unfettering the pleasure of sex from procreation. Just imagine a society where public funds are used to ensure the joy of sex without the specter of pregnancy. Think how grand that would be."

"Yes, quite," he added, intrigued by the turn of the topic.

"I am devoting my life to liberate women from the economic and cultural shackles of the past. I am an independent woman who believes that women have been exploited for too long, and we need to pursue happiness as best we can, with or without men. We are in the beginning of a new century that will no doubt throw off the yoke of oppression for millions. We are asking enlightened benefactors for donations to support this essential science. We are preparing a fundraising event and would like to count on you as a sponsor."

The President had told him that she was striking before he had journeyed to Africa on some damn fool adventure. Old T.R. was rarely wrong when it came to passionate women, he chuckled to himself. Of course, the self-proclaimed 'King of New York' and the President often shared passionate women with each other. Suddenly, Margaret's verbal torrent stopped and he felt an uncomfortable silence. When he refocused, she was gazing at him intently.

"Did I say something to amuse you, Mr. Kahn?"

"Oh. No, no, my dear. I was just reminded of something that T. R., er, President Roosevelt had mentioned to me about . . . well, that does not matter. Go on. And, please call me Otto."

Otto gestured with the bottle of Lillet and Margaret looked into his eyes and nodded demurely. The sun was sinking lower on the horizon and as he poured the liquor into their glasses, it turned brilliant gold by a ray of sunshine hitting the crystal at just the right angle. She saw it too. They both smiled at the perfectly-timed moment of beauty. Otto raised his glass with a wide grin; she joined him in an unspoken toast.

"Now tell me about you," said Otto sipping on his beverage. Margaret followed suit before answering.

"There's not much to tell, Otto. I was born in the Western Tier of New York in Corning. I am one of eleven children. After I graduated from college, my mother got sick and I went home to nurse her until she died. Later,

I studied nursing at several hospitals in the City. I am married, but it does not suit me. I have an arrangement with my husband that our marriage is open. He is free to bed whomever he wants and so am I. Now I am an independent woman, who is liberated and answers only to myself."

Otto gazed into her eyes, absorbed in her speaking, vaguely hearing what she was saying. Elegantly, she lifted her glass and tilted her head back to capture every drop. The soft whiteness of her exposed neck had the desired effect. Otto reached for her and stroked the side of her neck. She emitted a soft sound and pressed her head to his hand.

"I have something I'd like to show you," said Otto huskily. She followed as he took her hand and led her to the bookcase. He pressed under one of the shelves and the massive piece lifted slightly, then, began to slide out of view. Before them was a spiral staircase made of elaborate wrought iron with red carpeted steps.

"Come, we can watch the sunset from my private hideaway," he said, as he rose up the steps with Margaret following with a look of bemusement on her face. As they climbed, she heard the bookcase slide back into place behind her. The steps led to a sumptuous chamber, lined with silk, linen-colored wall coverings, a thick, Shiraz Persian of hues of teal, burgundy and cream graced the floor. Before them was a floor-to-ceiling window with a view of the sun setting over manicured gardens and orchards. Otto went into a side room and emerged with a chilled bottle of champagne and two flutes. Handing the crystal to her, he proceeded to twist the cork. There was a distinct pop as the cork flew from the bottle and some bubbly spurted in its wake.

July 4, 1912
Huntington, New York

Hallowed be the day, forever bright its
memory in the heart of the Nation.
Sing to it, poets;
shout to it, freemen;
celebrate it with bonfires, parades, and triumphant assemblies.

~ *Daily Alta California, 4 July 1855*

THEODORE ROOSEVELT surveyed the holiday crowd from the speaker's platform adjacent to the gazebo in Heckscher Park in the village of Huntington. The natural stonewall gazebo was festooned with red, white and blue bunting. Inside the gazebo, a small brass band was blasting out patriotic music. Throughout the grounds, food vendors prepared succulent treats, tricksters manned gaming booths sporting Teddy Bear prizes while jugglers, mimes and puppeteers enthralled the festive crowd.

While listening to a rendition of the Star-Spangled Banner by a local choral group, he stood in the shade waiting to present his Independence Day speech. As he fingered the lengthy manuscript of his remarks that was in the breast pocket of his suit, he reflected that the crowd was considerably smaller than the two-hundred-thousand person crowd he had addressed ten years earlier in Schenley Park, Pittsburgh. But, as he admitted to himself, times had changed. Then, he was the sitting President; now, he was the recently-scorned candidate for the Republican nomination for President. If T.R. was stunned and smarting from his unsuccessful bid to regain the Republican nomination at the national convention in Chicago two weeks earlier, it did not show. He had learned in politics that you could never let them see you sweat and that when one door closed another was waiting to be opened. You just had to find it.

"And I'm proud to present to you our native son, President Theodore Roosevelt!" shouted the mayor enthusiastically, breaking the speaker's reverie.

With consummate skill, the former President graciously acknowledged the welcoming cheers of the crowd. He toyed with the crowd's emotions with self-effacing remarks, and tales of heroism of Americans who had sacrificed their blood for freedom. He deftly wove into his speech the story of Nathan Hale, a young patriot spy in the Continental Army who landed at Huntington in 1776, on a spying mission for General George Washington. Hale was captured by the British military at a tavern in nearby Halesite. With the mention of Halesite, Teddy gestured toward the tribute rock dedi-cated to the Revolutionary War hero. As the former President described the drama, he whipped the crowd into a frenzy of patriotic fervor, intoning Hale's immortal words just before he was hanged, *"I regret that I have but one life to give for my country."*[9]

Teddy concluded by alluding to his plans to run for the Presidency, stating, "Anyone can give up, it's the easiest thing in the world to do. But to hold it together when everyone else would understand if you fell apart, that's true strength! And that's what it means to be American. We must wear our patriotism proudly in a dangerous world."

After the speech, the indomitable Roosevelt held court with a gaggle of reporters, seeking comment from the former President on his return from a stinging rebuke at the Republican National Convention. In his piercing voice, he answered reporters' questions about his plans and whether there was any truth to the rumors that he was planning to run for the Presidency as a third-party candidate. He coyly deflected these questions with vague generalizations and folksy anecdotes. The impromptu press conference reached a climax when a young mother thrust a bundle of joy into T.R.'s arms with the precision born of expert planning and asked the photographers to take a picture of her darling baby with the President. He broke into his toothy grin as the cameramen obliged. With that photo opportunity concluded, the President excused himself and climbed into his Columbia Electric Victoria Phaeton, and headed for his beloved Sagamore Hill that was a stone's throw away.

Otto sat in the shade of the veranda nursing a mint julep as the President's big blue and yellow convertible pulled into the driveway in a cloud of dust.

"I'm positively parched, James. Would you be so kind as to get me what our friend Otto is drinking?

"Otto, it's so good to see you! How have you been?"

"I've been well, Mr. President, thank you."

"Would you like to take a ride before we dine?"

"Why I'd be delighted. I brought my riding clothes just in case."

"Excellent. James, please tell the stable boy to prepare Manitou and Rain-in-the Face. Otto, let's go change. I'm dying to get out of this dreadful suit."

The clopping of the iron horseshoes resonated on the cobblestone path until the horses reached the soft earth of bridle path that led to Cold Spring Harbor. The harsh scraping gave way to a rhythmic thud as the beasts were given a little head. Sensing that the horses were chomping at the bit, T.R. coaxed Manitou to a gallop along the wooded trail. The former President at fifty-four, cut a dashing figure in his buckskin suit with its fringes flapping frantically. Otto imagined a younger Roosevelt charging up San Juan Hill in Cuba during the Spanish American War, saber waving wildly, as he exhorted his troops forward. The President had certainly lost none of his vigor.

The two riders raced through the woods enjoying the raw, animal power of the horses. As the muscular forelegs and haunches propelled them through the carefully-tended path, Otto was vitalized by the dynamic respiration of Rain-in-the-Face. The powerful inhalation followed by the equally powerful exhalation gave Otto a feeling of mastery over nature. An array of maples, oaks and pines lined the path that declined gradually to Long Island Sound. The riders emerged from the woods into sunlight so brilliant that it shorted out the retina, temporarily blinding them. When their eyes adjusted, they were treated to a breathtaking view of Cold Spring Harbor.

The area took its name from the numerous cold freshwater springs that flowed down the hilly terrain to the natural harbor. T.R. dismounted and led Manitou along a path through the fragmites to a stream that trickled and bubbled to the saltwater of the Sound. He squatted and reached his cupped hand into the clear, fresh water scooping up a handful to his mouth. He drank deeply with water dripping off his bushy moustache. He released a loud guffaw, "By Golly, that's delicious!" Otto followed suit. Both horses lapped up the water and shook their muzzles appreciatively.

Otto stood and canvassed the scene with binoculars that had been thoughtfully placed in his saddlebag. To the east, he saw a narrow line of buildings that comprised the village of Cold Spring Harbor. He marveled that just half a century ago, this was a bustling whaling port that had been immortalized by Herman Melville in his masterpiece, *Moby Dick*.

"Let's go, Otto. I have something to show you."

They wheeled their steeds away from the water and up the hill. The bridle path wound through the pristine forest until they reached the summit where they dismounted again. T.R. walked through the underbrush to an opening that presented a panoramic vista of the harbor and Long Island Sound beyond. Otto caught his breath at the exquisite attraction displayed before him. The sun was still high in the sky and glinted off the dark blue water. A gust of wind coming off the water carried the faint scent of salt that erased momentarily the aroma of horse and pine that hung about them. The sun reflected off T.R.'s spectacles as he surveyed the glorious scene.

"Guess what, Otto, I have it on good authority that this property is about to be put up for sale. If you are interested, I'd suggest that you move quickly."

"Mr. President, you do me great honor. This location is stunning. Please provide me with the name and address of the owner when we get back to Sagamore Hill. Just think, we could be neighbors."

"Precisely."

They sat on small boulders and observed the majesty before them for a few minutes before Otto broke the silence.

"Mr. President, I know that the results of the Chicago convention were a grave disappointment, particularly since you prevailed in almost every primary. The Republican Party will rue the day they rejected your candidacy."

"Sadly, the primaries were irrelevant. The antiquated selection system for the Presidential nomination leaves it up to the boys with cigars in the back room. I thought that many of those boys would rally to my side given my past relationships. By golly, was I wrong. Crafty Tafty corralled those boys like steers heading to the abattoir."

"Mr. President, we believe that it's not over. We believe that the people love you and, if given a chance, will flock to the polls in November to send you back to the White House where you belong. There is much unfinished business. Taft has been a huge disappointment, as you well know. Despite Taft's assurances to you, he has not been cooperative on many issues important to our friends. There are so many pressing issues that only your fine hand would navigate us through; the impending war in Europe requires that the U.S. have a skilled diplomat in the White House in order to steer a clear path away from the shedding of American blood, while strengthening our influence throughout the world."

Behind his spectacles, Theodore's eyes narrowed as he studied Otto. The former President was lost in thought. Otto could feel the impressive brain across from him, sorting through all the permutations with clockwork precision. T.R. nodded to himself and then said, "Timing has a lot to do with the outcome of a rain dance, Otto."

"Mr. President, we know that a third-party candidate has never been able to win the Presidency. However, there are three reasons why this situation is different. First, you. You have an amazing connection with the voters. Let's face it; you would be the only candidate with charisma. Taft is a ponderous bore who inspires no one, and Wilson is an austere bookworm who is as charming as that stuffed owl in your study. You, on the other hand, have a great gift; don't hide it under a bushel basket. Let it shine."

Otto could see T.R.'s chin lift ever so slightly.

"Second, you've held this office before. You are not some outlier trying to uproot the system. You are, as they say, mainstream, respectable, safe. Don't underestimate the people's concerns about the upcoming war. They want the firm hand of someone experienced in military and diplomatic matters. No one fits the bill like you do.

"Third, we know that a third party campaign will be expensive. Not to worry. We are prepared to provide the resources necessary to win. We will supply financial firepower the likes of which has never been seen in an

American election. We have several million dollars available immediately, with more in reserve. Mr. President, you know the volatility in Europe, the winds of war are rising. The country needs your leadership today more than ever. We hope that you will accept this call to duty."

"Otto, I'm truly flattered. We are living in perilous times. I shudder to think how Crafty, or the Professor would react to the coming carnage in Europe. Without firsthand experience with the horrors and futility of armed conflict, they might easily be suckered into committing American troops to the conflagration. The cost in blood and treasure would be inestimable," said Roosevelt ruefully, as if recalling the moans and cries of comrades fallen in battle. He was somewhere else. Otto watched intently as Roosevelt removed his glasses and pretended to wipe a speck of dust from his eye.

"Listen, Otto, I know that money matters, but so do butts in the trenches. Plus, time is short. Do we have enough time and personnel to make this happen?" he asked rhetorically.

"Might I quote a great American, Mr. President? As you said a couple of years ago in Paris, it is the man in the arena who counts. The man *'who knows great enthusiasms, the great devotions; who spends himself in a worthy cause; who at the best knows in the end the triumph of high achievement, and who at the worst, if he fails, at least fails while daring greatly, so that his place shall never be with those cold and timid souls who neither know victory nor defeat.'*[10] Your country needs you to dare greatly and be that man."

"Otto, don't you know that it's unfair to throw a man's words back at him?" the President jested.

"Let me mull it over. Discuss it with Edie. I'll advise you of my decision tomorrow."

Otto smiled to himself. The hook and bait had been swallowed. All that remained was to let it catch and reel in the prize.

July, 1912
London, England

More children from the fit, less from the unfit —
that is the chief issue of birth control.

~ MARGARET SANGER, *THE PIVOT OF CIVILIZATION*

THE UNION JACK FLAPPED in the brisk, summer breeze coming off
the Thames River, as the carriages arrived at the Hotel Cecil. Otto
took his key from the reception clerk, along with an invitation to attend
the Lord Mayor's reception after the inaugural banquet that evening. The
lobby teemed with porters and bellmen, straining to keep up with the crush
of leather trunks and suitcases that were being disgorged from scores of
vehicles clogging the courtyard entrance.

Over four hundred people from all over the world had registered to
attend the First International Eugenics Conference. London was the hotbed
of intellectual furor over the nascent science that had been nurtured from
the principles of natural selection and survival of the fittest of the prominent
British scientist, Charles Darwin. His cousin, Francis Galton, had taken
Darwin's theories, combined them with the work of the botanist, Gregor
Mendel, and synthesized the budding science of Eugenics. Galton was joined

by George Bernard Shaw, H.G. Wells, Ellis Havelock and scores of British intellectuals in igniting a firestorm of interest among German, French and other continental intellectuals that led to this conference. The politicians were quick to see in Eugenics the potential for profound societal change, guided, of course, by the ubiquitous hand of government.

He entered the impressive concourse that adjoined the ballrooms and salons that would be the location of the conference's ambitious schedule of lectures, meetings and scientific presentations. He smiled as he spied the lift that would take him to his suite. His heart raced in anticipation of seeing his lover, his beloved Magpie.

The three-room suite had a magnificent view of the Thames and Westminster Palace. Otto pushed open the curtains to take full advantage of the panorama of the most prosperous city on earth. There was a tray in the center of the main sitting room with a champagne *seau* filled with ice and a bottle of *Veuve Clicquot Ponsardin Champagne*. His heart leapt as he heard a gentle knock on the door. She was here.

Sanger was standing in the hallway, beaming. Her pale skin fairly glowed and her eyes were bright. Her auburn tresses were swept up in a French bun. He stood enraptured and speechless at her healthy radiance.

"May I come in?" she asked after a few silent moments.

"Oh, yes, of course. How silly of me."

Once he shut the door behind them, they embraced passionately. He rained kisses on her face and neck as he undid the buttons on her blouse. She giggled as he nuzzled the nape of her neck.

"Oh, my precious Magpie, I have missed you desperately."

"Wait. You haven't shown me the other rooms, . . . like the bedroom . . ." she whispered, her voice lowering suggestively.

Otto swept her into his arms and carried her into the bedroom where he bounced her onto the waiting four-poster. Breathless, they rapidly stripped away all apparel and . . . . Later, as he lay across the bed with his head resting on her swollen white belly, he could feel the life within her stirring.

"Oh, Otto, I thought you'd never get here. The last week without you has been dreadful."

"Yes, I know," he agreed. "The crossing was tedious, but I have a meeting later after the banquet with William Maxwell Aitken, a.k.a. Baron Beaverbrook, of the Liberal Unionist Party to go over the plans for my run for Parliament and I'm meeting tomorrow with the solicitors to finalize the purchase of St. Dunstan from the Earl of Londesborough. You will love it, Margaret. There's a . . . ," he started," I do believe that I've just been kicked in the ear by the little bubbie."

"Otto, is that clock correct? I did not realize it was so late. Oh dear, I must be going if I am to make it to the banquet. Sorry, love," she gently slid from under him.

The banquet hall was abuzz with animated conversation. Otto caught a whiff of her scent and smiled like an infatuated schoolboy. He had never felt such passion. He was preparing to throw off his loveless marriage and restart in London with his true love. His future life was virtually in place — a seat in Parliament, a new mansion and a marital union with a magnificent woman who was every bit his equal, intellectually and physically. He ambled through the throng, hearing snippets about the latest theories and break-throughs. Finally, he arrived at his assigned table where he shook hands with other bankers and financiers already seated. He scanned the ballroom for his Magpie. On the verge of disappointment, he spied her wending her way through the crowd. His chest swelled with joy as the crowd parted to let the radiant woman with child pass.

Major Leonard Darwin, the master of ceremonies, called the assemblage to order. Among the notables on the dais were Sir David Burnett, the Lord Mayor of London, a smarmy, little man with a buck-toothed grin and scheming eyes. Next, was Sir Rickman John Godlee, President of the Royal Academy of Surgeons, a tall distinguished-looking gentleman with thinning gray hair and well-scrubbed hands with long, strong fingers. Sir Winston Churchill, the First Lord of Admiralty was the last to be introduced. He stood and waved enthusiastically to his vocal supporters.

Former Prime Minister Arthur James Balfour gave the opening presentation, droning on about how the task of Eugenics was to improve the hereditary traits of each nation, thereby improving humanity.

"We have in our grasp the key to eradicating every blight that plagues mankind. Once we are able to decipher the mysteries of human development, we will be able to engineer a better humanity. It is imperative to protect this nascent science from charlatans and faddists who would distort and pervert

our mission. We can stop at nothing short of the betterment of our race. I encourage you all over the next week to share your scientific knowledge and techniques. As I look out at this distinguished multitude, I am confident that we are the ones the world has been waiting for. We have within our grasp the ability to negate those prophecies of ill for the future of civilization and usher in a brave new world where human potential is fully realized. Thank you and all the best during this illustrious Congress."[11]

When the opening ceremonies were done, Margaret took her leave, whispering salaciously to Otto not to linger with the boys too long because they had to continue their own welcoming party. Otto's eyes sparkled as he assured her that he would not tarry.

Otto took a long drag on his Macanudo and surveyed the private reception room. It was ornate, with gilded molding encasing murals of various scenes of London. He located his friend Max Aitken, who was standing off in the corner engaged in conversation with Andrew Bonar Law. A native of Canada, William "Max" Aitken made his fortune by building a monopoly in the cement industry. After certain alleged stock improprieties came to light, he moved to London. Now, Aitken owned several British newspapers and had recently been elected to Parliament. Both Aitken and Andrew Bonar Law were from New Brunswick and had successfully immigrated to London.

Otto swirled his cognac, took a long sniff, then a sip. When Otto met Aitken five years earlier, they had immediately developed a great affinity for each other, particularly as to monetary and political matters. Otto had asked if Max was short for Maximilian. With a buskerly grin, Aitken responded, "No, it's short for Max-a-many-millions!"

He was the same height as Otto and had the ready smile of a born salesman. Aitken had a ruddy complexion and sandy brown hair that swept from one side to the other to mask a receding hairline. His hazel brown eyes were alert and created the impression of a shared joke when he engaged in one-on-one conversation.

"How are my fellow colonials?" Otto joked as he joined them. Both men grinned broadly.

"You know Bonar, of course," said Aitken. "He is the brains behind our tariff reform strategy and has been working closely with Prime Minister

Asquith. You watch, someday he's going to be the first Prime Minister from the colonies."

"Yes, good to see you again," said Otto, shaking hands with the taller man. Bonar had a firm handshake, befitting a man who had grown up working in his family's ironworks business.

"How was your passage across the pond? I'm sure that the summer crossings are booked to the hilt in the wake of that horrible disaster in April," asked Bonar, alluding to the recent sinking of the *Titanic*.

"A horrible tragedy. I went to the memorial service for J.J. Astor at Trinity Church. Such a waste; he was only forty-five and his young wife was pregnant. But, to answer your question; yes, it was a packed voyage. It's good to be on *terra firma* in London. If I could finance the building of a trans-Atlantic railroad I would. I guess we'll have to wait until the aviators develop a way to make the crossing over the icebergs," said Otto. "Please don't let me interrupt. I'm anxious to hear the latest news."

"Bonar and I were just discussing the prospects of a merger between the Liberal Unionists and the Tories. I think it's going to happen. We've had some preliminary dialogue with Winston and he's receptive to it. I was telling Bonar about our plans for you to run for Parliament in Lancashire. He agrees that you would be perfect for that district."

"I'm quite committed; although I must admit that I'm concerned about some anti-Semitic newspaper articles that I've seen, challenging the possibility of my candidacy."

"Don't fret about that, Otto. When I unleash my ink barrels on them, they won't know where to hide. You are a guaranteed winner."

"Er, . . . Winnie, Sir Winston, please come join us," said Aitken, who reached out to a passing Churchill by tugging on the sleeve of his tuxedo.

"Gentlemen, it is good to see you. I can surely use a place to park my arse. Thanks."

With another round of drinks, the party engaged in animated conversation about the ludicrousness of the left-wing Liberal Party and how the merger between the Unionists and the Tories would spell the well-deserved death knell for the Libs. Winston regaled them with stories of the history of the Tories all the way back to the Royalists of the 1640s and how his namesake, the original Sir Winston, had shed Churchill blood in support of King Charles I.

The discussion turned to trade and, ultimately, matters of international relations. Otto asked Churchill how the Royal Navy was preparing for the looming war in Europe. "Winnie, after I get my affairs in London arranged, I'm going to St. Petersburg to meet with the Tsar to discuss military preparedness and development of Russia's railway infrastructure. Is there anything I can tell him regarding Britain's plans?"

"It's no secret that we have been studying the feasibility of transitioning to oil, rather than coal, to fuel the ships of the Royal Navy. The preliminary word is that it is lighter, more dependable and less labor intensive on-board. Suffice it to say, I would not be investing in Welsh coal mines. Ah, my glass is empty. Does anyone else want another?"

Aitken, who was in his cups, asked Winnie about his mother, Lady Randolph, the former Jennie Jerome. Winston replied, "She's fine. About to get a divorce. It seems that my stepfather has been openly cavorting with an actress; and that is something that mother cannot abide.

"You know, she was born in Brooklyn. Her father, my grandfather Lawrence, was quite a character. According to family lore, for a time he lived in upstate New York and he married a beautiful Iroquois woman. He was a notorious gambler and actually won the estate of President Martin Van Buren from his son John in a poker game. It was called Lindenwald. The noted American author, Washington Irving, penned *The Legend of Sleepy Hollow* while living at Lindenwald.

"I visited it once, nice place, but the locals think it's haunted. Some story about a butler who hanged himself and now his ghost roams the apple orchard. Now, here's a piece of American trivia for you. Lindenwald is located in a village called Kinderhook. A lovely Dutch village. When Van Buren ran for President, his supporters called him 'Old Kinderhook.' They developed the hand signal of circling their thumb and forefinger and calling him 'OK.' And that's the genesis of the sign of agreement known around the world. I'll bet that you did not know that."

"Otto, today's sessions were so exciting. I think this generation, this group of enlightened people, will eliminate suffering and save the world. It's so thrilling to be here and hear such brilliance. This morning, there was a lecture based on the work of Thomas Malthus, who warned over one hundred years ago that the world would soon be overpopulated, leading to horrible suffering. He condemned charities suggesting that poverty, deprivation and hunger could not be alleviated by charity. Malthus believed that charitable benevolence only exacerbated the suffering. Therefore, the only truly humane solution was population control, especially of certain groups of people."

Leafing through her program notes, Margaret continued, "According to Malthus' magnum opus, *An Essay on the Principle of Population,*

All children born, beyond what would be required to keep up the population to a desired level, must necessarily perish, unless room is made for them by the deaths of grown persons. We should facilitate, instead of foolishly and vainly endeavoring to impede, the operations of nature in producing this mortality.[12]

"Isn't that brilliant? It seems so logical that if we eliminate the unfit among us, then they will no longer suffer. Otto, you can't imagine the suffering that the physically unfit, the materially poor, the spiritually diseased, the racially inferior, and the mentally incompetent experience."

"My dear, Magpie, do you think I spend all my time in opulent salons and Studebaker limousines? Of course I see the suffering; after all, I live in New York City."

"Guess who sat next to me during the afternoon sessions? The writer, H.G. Wells. His friends call him Bertie. Otto, to be around such great minds is so exhilarating."

"Yes, quite," said Otto as he worked on the buttons of her dress.

"I'll take that off. You know that Bertie believes that only healthy and intelligent people should be allowed to procreate and that the unfit and feeble-minded should be sterilized. According to him, 'We want fewer and better children and we cannot make the social life and the world-peace we are determined to make, with the ill-bred, ill-trained swarms of inferior citizens that you inflict on us.' What do you think?"

"Seriously? I think that the crime rate would be reduced significantly if we provided free concerts for all the blokes. They would become so enchanted by music that their baser instincts would be tamed."

"Stop the mockery. I asked a serious question."

"If you must know, I think that as a fit and intelligent member of the species that I'd like to procreate right about now," whispered Otto as he removed his trousers and pulled her down onto the bed.

Margaret closed her eyes in contentment and she rested in the nook of Otto's shoulder. She was nearing full term and yet had never felt sexier. Otto certainly was a skillful and attentive lover. Just then she felt the "little bubbie" move and the outline of an elbow or knee appeared on her naked belly. Otto chuckled and commented that the little bubbie must be aroused, too. They both laughed. Otto rose and headed to the bathroom mumbling something about catching a train. She watched appreciatively as he disappeared behind the shiny white door.

When he returned, Otto was holding a box colored robin's egg blue. Margaret's eyes widened and her lips spread into a broad smile when she recognized the signature Tiffany blue.

"My dear Magpie, I can't tell you how much I love you. I never thought that such profound love was possible for me. I have been so driven by my desire for money that I failed to understand the satisfaction that only true love can bring. Since our first meeting, my life has been transformed. I think of you constantly — to the point of obsession. But a good obsession. I want to provide you with everything your heart desires. With our new baby on the way, I foresee a life of happily ever-after in London. Can you believe it? Me, a member of Parliament. You and our little bubbie, proper nobility. Oh, Margaret, I love you so!"

Otto thrust the box into her hands and bounced excitedly on the edge of the bed like a youngster at his own birthday party.

"Otto, you are such a romantic!" bubbled Margaret. Her dainty fingers untied the elegant white ribbon from the box. She paused expectantly before lifting the lid. Her pale skin reflected the signature Tiffany blue that gave her an ethereal radiance. A gasp of awe escaped her lips. She lifted up a necklace of sapphires from which dangled a medallion of Star Aqua the size of a robin's egg. Otto took it from her and gently placed it around her neck. The pigmentation of the gemstone complemented her eyes. Otto thought that he might burst from the joy he felt. She threw her arms around him and kissed him passionately.

"Otto, it's stunning. I've never owned something so . . . so, valuable. You shouldn't have," she lied.

"Oh, yes, I should. You are the love of my life and I want to show it. Unfortunately, my darling, I must catch my ride to make my connections to St. Petersburg. I have made arrangements for you to stay in this suite through the end of the conference. Please stay here. The bellman will be here in an hour to pick up my bags for shipping. I will miss you, my love. Until I return . . ." he said, bending over to kiss her on the lips.

After completing breakfast, she hurried down to the panel session on Criminology in the Grand Salon. The Conference had settled into a routine of two-hour panels focused on a particular theme, wrapped around lunch and culminating in a premier speaker before dinner. This day's theme was the role of Eugenics in reducing crime. She was particularly intrigued by the statistics presented to demonstrate a correlation between physical characteristics and felonious actions.

"Criminals are apes in our midst, marked by the anatomical stigmata of atavism."

Based on his twenty-five years in law enforcement, the Chief Constable from Leeds boasted that he could predict with a high degree of certainty those individuals who were "born to evil." These included gypsies, epileptics and people from Southern climes. He concluded that people of this sort were unable to reform and opined that it would be prudent for society "to eliminate them completely, even by death." If anyone blanched at this suggestion, it was not evident from the enthusiastic applause of the audience.

There was a palpable buzz in the Ballroom when Major Darwin ascended to the podium to introduce the keynote speaker, George Bernard Shaw. The noted Irish playwright was a master of irony and satire and was guaranteed to entertain with his outlandish statements.

Shaw began his remarks by reprising the statements about the "social purity" movement that he had made at a meeting of the Eugenics Education Society two years earlier. Expressing the need to eliminate the unfit, he did allow for the fact that if social purity had been in force when he was conceived, he probably would not be speaking to them this night. The audience laughed appreciatively at the self-deprecation.

Raising his glass in mock mimicry of Socrates' imbibing of hemlock, Shaw questioned the ineptitude of modern science in its lack of efficiency in dealing with the unfit. He directed his remarks to what he identified as a practical test for those on the fringes of society.

"You must all know half a dozen people at least who are no use in this world, who are more trouble than they are worth. Just put them there and

say 'Sir, or Madam, now will you be kind enough to justify your existence? If you can't justify your existence, if you're not pulling your weight in the social boat, if you're not producing as much as you consume or perhaps a little more, then, clearly, we cannot use the organizations of our society for the purpose of keeping you alive, because your life does not benefit us and it can't be of very much use to yourself.'

Ever the showman, Shaw paused for effect. When he sensed a general concurrence, he ended with a flourish.

"I appeal to the chemists to discover a humane gas that will kill instantly and painlessly. In short — a gentlemanly gas deadly by all means, but humane, not cruel."[13]

Over the ensuing days, the Conference settled into a humdrum of sessions that blurred into lifeless technicality. After one particularly boring presentation by a Belgian entomologist, Margaret sat alone, lost in thought at a small round table in the concourse sipping tea. A short, narrow-shouldered woman carrying a satchel weighed down with books and bound articles that jutted out haphazardly, approached her and asked if the seat at the table was available. Margaret indicated that she was welcome to join her.

"Thanks. I'm Emma Goldman. Pleased to meet you," she said, reaching out with her right hand. Margaret took her hand and gave it a firm shake. She was overjoyed to be sharing tea with the renowned anarchist author and driving force behind her favorite periodical, *Mother Earth*.

"I'm ..."

"Margaret Sanger. I know who you are. I've been observing you and your adulterous benefactor since you got here. Where is he? Oh, that's right, he's gone away on business, right?" groused her companion.

She was diminutive, with her salt and pepper hair worn in short waves off her forehead and closely cropped. Margaret thought of the first description of Goldman she had heard was that Goldman was 'physically imposing.' Margaret mused that this short, plain-looking woman in her forties, wearing wire-rimmed glasses with over-sized, round lenses was hardly imposing. However, after conversing with Goldman for a while, Margaret realized that the anarchist was imposing by virtue of her intellect and charisma that was based on Goldman's unusually large leonine head and her deep resonant voice that could fill a warehouse packed with workingmen. Margaret had heard that Goldman's vocabulary matched the crude language of her audience, giving her speeches special allure with the working classes. As Margaret learned quickly, Goldman was an unapologetic feminist, always championing the duty of women to be independent and control their own lives.

"My dear Margaret, I'm not sure you understand how incongruous and precarious your situation is," said Emma.

"How old are you? I'm guessing early twenties, right?"

"Actually, I'm twenty-three," responded Margaret somewhat indignantly.

"Let me share with you a story about how a woman can almost experience total degradation for her love of a man. Several decades ago when I was much younger, I was passionately in love with Sasha. We were inseparable spiritually and physically. Like me, he was a devoted anarchist. We even planned an assassination of a dirty capitalist to prove our point. But we lacked the money to accomplish our plot."

Margaret shifted forward in her seat, engrossed by this brash revolutionary.

Emma continued, her eyes sparkling, *"I woke up with a very clear idea of how I could raise the money for Sasha. I would go on the street. I lay wondering how such a notion could have come to me. I recollected Dostoyevsky's Crime and Punishment, which had made a profound impression on me, especially the character of Sonya, Marmeladov's daughter. She had become a prostitute in order to support her little brothers and sisters and to relieve her consumptive stepmother of worry. I envisioned Sonya as she lay on her cot, face to the wall, her shoulders twitching. I could almost feel the same way. Sensitive Sonya could sell her body; why not I? My cause was greater than hers . . . .*

"My main concern now was whether I could make myself attractive enough to men who seek out girls on the street. I stepped over to the mirror to inspect my body. I looked tired, but my complexion was good. I should need no make-up. My curly blond hair showed off well with my blue eyes. Too large in the hips for my age, I thought; I was just twenty-three. Well, I came from Jewish stock. Besides, I would wear a corset and I should look taller in high heels (I had never worn either before) . . . .

"I stood on the corner of Fourteenth Street and Fourth Avenue, near the bank building. The first man that invited me — I would go with him, I had decided. A tall, distinguished looking person, well dressed, came close.

"Let's have a drink, little girl," he said. His hair was white, he appeared to be about sixty, but his face was ruddy. "All right," I replied. He took my arm and led me to a wine house on Union Square which Most had often frequented with me. "Not here!" I almost screamed; "please, not here." I led him to the back entrance of a saloon on Thirteenth Street and Third Avenue. I had once been there in the afternoon for a glass of beer. It had been clean and quiet then.

"That night it was crowded, and with difficulty we secured a table. The man ordered drinks. My throat felt parched and I asked for a large glass of beer. Neither of us spoke. I was conscious of the man's scrutiny of my face and body. I felt myself growing resentful. Presently he asked: "You're a novice in the business, aren't you?" "Yes, this is my first time — but how did you know?" "I watched you as you passed me," he replied. He told me that he had noticed my haunted expression and my increased pace the moment a man came near me. He understood then that I was inexperienced; whatever might have been the reason that brought me to the street, he knew it was not mere looseness or love of excitement. "But thousands of girls are driven by economic necessity," I blurted out. He looked at me in surprise. "Where did you get that stuff?" I wanted to tell him all about the social question, about my ideas, who and what I was, but I checked myself. I must not disclose my identity: it would be too dreadful if he should learn that Emma Goldman, the anarchist, had been found soliciting on Fourteenth Street. What a juicy story it would make for the press!

"He said he was not interested in economic problems and did not care what the reason was for my actions. He only wanted to tell me that there was nothing in prostitution unless one had the knack for it. "You haven't got it, that's all there is to it," he assured me. He took out a ten-dollar bill and put it down before me. "Take this and go home," he said. "But why should you give me money if you don't want me to go with you?" I asked. "Well, just to cover the expenses you must have had to rig yourself out like that," he replied; "your dress is awfully nice, even if it does not go with those cheap shoes and stockings." I was too astounded for speech.

"I had met two categories of men: vulgarians and idealists. The former would never have let an opportunity pass to possess a woman and they would give her no other thought save sexual desire. The idealists stoutly defended the equality of the sexes, at least in theory, but the only men among them who practiced what they preached were the Russian and Jewish radicals. This

man, who had picked me up on the street and who was now with me in the back of a saloon, seemed an entirely new type. He interested me. He must be rich. But would a rich man give something for nothing? The manufacturer Garson came to my mind; he would not even give me a small raise in wages.

"Perhaps this man was one of those soul-savers I had read about, people who were always cleansing New York City of vice. I asked him. He laughed and said he was not a professional busybody. If he had thought that I really wanted to be on the street, he would not have cared. "Of course, I may be entirely mistaken," he added, "but I don't mind. Just now I am convinced that you are not intended to be a streetwalker, and that even if you do succeed, you will hate it afterwards." If he were not convinced of it, he would take me for his mistress. "For always?" I cried. "There you are!" he replied; "you are scared by the mere suggestion and yet you hope to succeed on the street. You're an awfully nice kid, but you're silly, inexperienced, childish." "I was twenty-three last month," I protested, resentful of being treated like a child. "You are an old lady," he said with a grin, "but even old folks can be babes in the woods. Look at me; I'm sixty one and I often do foolish things." "Like believing in my innocence, for instance," I retorted. The simplicity of his manner pleased me. I asked for his name and address so as to be able to return his ten dollars someday. But he refused to give them to me. He loved mysteries, he said. On the street he held my hand for a moment, and then we turned in opposite directions."[14]

"You were most fortunate to avoid the debasement of the streets," said Margaret.

"Yes, I was," replied Emma. "But, what about you? I was willing to debase myself for a man with a cause. Unfortunately, his cause led to his imprisonment for fourteen years. Where will your debasement lead?"

Margaret flinched as if Emma had slapped her in the face. "I beg your pardon. What in heaven do you mean, 'my debasement'?"

Emma clucked derisively and stared at Margaret's protruding abdomen.

"You are wrong," Margaret countered. "Otto is kind and generous."

Emma raised one eyebrow sarcastically.

"He is committed to the cause. He's committed to positive Eugenics. We are propagating the best of the gene pool," Margaret pleaded.

"Ha!" Emma laughed. "Don't delude yourself. Your sugar Daddy is a vulgarian, who will exploit you for sex and then leave you for the next pretty face. And you will be left to raise his little bastard. How do I know? When

I look at him, I see a capitalist." She spat out the last word with contempt, as if naming the most vile, despicable creature.

"I believe that capitalism is inimical to human liberty. As I wrote in *Anarchism and Other Essays* 'The only demand that property recognizes is its own gluttonous appetite for greater wealth, because wealth means power; the power to subdue, to crush, to exploit, the power to enslave, to outrage, to degrade.' And that is exactly what he is doing to you. You must escape before it is too late. Only you can demand your own independence of woman, your own right to support yourself; to live for yourself; to love whomever you please, or as many as you please. The choice is yours, only yours," Emma lectured.

Margaret felt a torrent of tears building. She covered her face and began to cry. A bypassing gentleman paused to offer assistance, but Emma shooed him away like a broody goose. After a few minutes of sorrowful weeping, Margaret regained her composure. She turned her reddened eyes toward Emma and, in a childlike voice, said, "I've been such a fool not to see it. Would you help teach me? My mother died when I was young and I'm afraid that I'm living my life in a rudderless fashion. Would you please help me, teach me . . . ?"

The older woman was beside her now, kneeling and hugging Margaret. "Yes, my dear, I will."

For the next several months, Emma was true to her word. She not only imparted her wisdom and philosophy to her willing disciple, but she helped Margaret through the last difficult months of her pregnancy.

1912

St. Petersburg, Russia

(Oil) enables nations to accumulate wealth, to fuel their economies, to produce and sell goods and services, to build, to buy, to move, to acquire and manufacture weapons, to win wars.

~ DANIEL YERGIN, *THE PRIZE*

SUMMER IN RUSSIA; it was a time of warmth and light. Otto felt the warmth in his bones as he passed the Alexander Column after leaving the Winter Palace. There were many new and exciting things awaiting him when he finished his business here and returned to London. A new love, a new baby and a new life. Yet, he felt an uneasy sense of foreboding. He tried to convince himself that it was merely the effect of all the travel, but the feeling lingered.

His meeting with the Tsar had gone well. With the success of the infrastructure modernization project, the unpleasantness of the past had dissipated. Due to Russia's increasing need for capital and the avaricious urgings of the Grand Dukes, the Tsar had softened to the idea of the Russian General Oil Company. Of course, he refused to dilute his friend's concession, but he did communicate tacit approval to the establishment of the Russian General Oil Corporation.

During his visit with Nicholas, they had chatted about the centenary celebration of Russia's defeat of Napoleon that was planned throughout the Empire. The Tsar had described his upcoming trip in September to Borodino to dedicate a new monument to the great victory there by Mother Russia over Napoleon. The Tsar had proudly pointed out the window of his private library to Alexander's Column. He had drawn Otto's attention to the plaque commemorating his great-grandfather's victory with the inscription *"To Alexander I from a grateful Russia,"* and to the bronze sculpture of the Angel of Victory that bore his predecessor's face, resting atop the column. Otto had noticed a flicker of wistful envy in the Tsar's face when he had spoken about his illustrious ancestor.

Otto shared with Nicholas the information he had gathered recently in London. The Tsar was so appreciative of the intelligence regarding the British Navy's conversion to petroleum that he summoned Radomir Putnik, the Commander-in-Chief, to hear from Otto directly. Otto embellished the information with details about diesel propulsion systems that were being developed in Britain and the United States. Having whetted their appetites, Otto confided that he had had secret meetings with William Butterworth, the new chairman of Deere & Company, about manufacturing large diesel engines for export. Otto promised to keep them apprised of any new developments.

And now he was off to pursue a mission of even greater consequence.

The skinny young man with spiky, brown hair and a full beard sat waiting for him in the caviar bar at the Hotel Astoria. Otto had chosen the Astoria due to its proximity to St. Petersburg's preeminent ballet theater, the Mariinsky, where he would be spending his evening enjoying the ballet. The walls of the caviar bar were tastefully clad with black onyx, bleached Swedish birch panels and shiny chrome accessories. Iliodor wore his clerical collar and a long black suit that was the fashion. He smiled wryly as Otto approached. Over his arm, Otto had a full-length black cape lined with red silk that flashed as Otto arranged it over the chair next to Iliodor.

"Good evening, my friend," greeted Otto.

"Good evening to you, Herr Kahn," the monk replied in a nasal tone. His narrow set brown eyes glistened earnestly.

"I'll be candid. When I first met Rasputin I became one of his staunchest supporters. I saw him heal countless invalids. It was astounding. Soon, however, the rumors of debauchery began to circulate. I tried to validate the rumors for the main purpose of discrediting them. Unfortunately, the more people I spoke to, the more vivid and pervasive Rasputin's depravity was revealed."

"How shameful," responded Otto, adopting his most appalled expression.

"I know. I was devastated. How could God grant the power of healing to such a depraved individual? It was then I decided that he was a demon, a spawn of the devil himself. I knew that I had to stop him. That's why I'm here," said the monk. He paused to pile capers, chopped onion, egg and lox atop toast. He smacked his lips, savoring each morsel.

Otto wondered where this conversation was leading. He had met Iliodor while on earlier visits to Russia and his sources told him that the young monk was considered a promising, though opportunistic scholar. Otto glanced at his Rolex. Iliodor took the hint and reached into his breast pocket. He removed an envelope that emitted the faint aroma of lilacs.

"He is called 'Starets' by some. That is a disgrace. He is a disgrace. Once I befriended him, he took me to his apartment. He boasted, showing me letters that he had received from important people thanking him for all sorts of fantastical things. One bore the letterhead of the Tsarina. So, when the Holy Fool went to the next room to get more wine, I pilfered that letter."

"Why should I be interested in a letter from the Tsarina to Rasputin?" questioned Otto.

"The monk is not your friend. He is constantly badgering the Tsar through his wife, not to spend money on railroads, on armaments, on oil; rather, he should spend money to reform the system that oppresses the peasants. The Tsar's answer is that they are mostly Jews, so he does not care. His obligation is to defend Mother Russia from the coming storm. Rasputin has great power over the royal couple because he has cured the Tsarevich. As long as his power thrives, you will have an opponent at the throne."

"I see," said Otto. "What does this letter say?"

"I will read you part of it. It is in her handwriting. *'I kiss your hands and lay my head upon your blessed shoulders. I feel so joyful then. Then all I want is to sleep, sleep for ever on your shoulder, in your embrace.'*[15]

Otto whistled softly. His mind raced with the possibilities. He knew that Alix was vulnerable; her standing in the court was suspect. The Romanovs had never accepted her, and Alexei's illness had driven her further into isolation.

"You are sure this was written by the Tsarina?"

"Absolutely, I have other letters in her hand that were sent to our church with specific donations for the poor. Here, compare these two," said Iliodor sliding two missives over to Otto. Kahn perused the letters and held them side by side, nodding approvingly.

"I am impressed and would be willing to contribute handsomely in return for these letters," said Otto quietly.

"Of course, my church is adamant about exposing this scandal and putting an end to it," replied the cleric passionately.

"I will deliver a draft for $5,000 tomorrow," replied Otto, folding the letters in preparation for putting them in the pocket of his tuxedo jacket.

"*Nyet*. I am taking great risk here. I can be defrocked or imprisoned if it is revealed that I was the source of these letters." Taking the letters from Otto's hand, the monk said, "I need assurances and $20,000 deposited in my private account before we have a deal."

"What assurances can I give you?"

"There has to be a burglary of his apartment first."

"OK, I will arrange that. Tell me where in the apartment the letters are kept. I will have the funds deposited in your account tomorrow." Iliodor released his grip on the letters.

Two days later, the lead story in newspapers across the globe alleged an illicit affair between the Tsarina and Rasputin. The discredited monk wisely fled to his home village of Pokrovskoe. Only Nicholas believed Alix's explanation that the sentiments expressed were those between cleric and congregant. The *camarilla* mocked her.

Kahn received $10,000 each from the *St. Petersburg Journal, The International Herald Tribune* and *The New York Times* for his secret disclosure of the letter. Was it Machiavelli who advised, "*La vendetta è un piatto che va mangiato freddo?*" Revenge is a dish best served cold.

Fall 1912
Maternity Ward

One tiny hand to guide and hold,
One tiny life to shape and mold;

~ John H. Gower

O TTO STROLLED INTO THE HOSPITAL with an extra spring in his step. His trips to Russia, Sweden and Spain over the course of the summer had been extremely successful. He knew how to exploit the rising tensions throughout the world. Invariably, governments were interested in financing infrastructure and weapons procurement. Otto's firm was in the enviable position of receiving fees for arranging financing. If the financing was successful, his firm would receive a percentage of the offering. If the financing went unsubscribed or under-subscribed, the firm would receive a minimum fee, or a fee based on time charges, whichever was greater. It was a win-win. In addition, his firm had begun to service workouts and consolidations when a default occurred. Coupled with deep-seated relationships, these arrangements gave his firm extraordinary power and influence. For the moment, his initiatives were progressing nicely. The Russian General Oil Corporation was in place and the Jekyll Island plans for the establishment of the Federal Reserve Bank were in motion. Rasputin had been hounded back to Siberia. 1912 was turning into an excellent year.

All this was suddenly beside the point as Otto approached the nursery where he would see his newborn son. Otto searched the crowded nursery for the little bassinet holding baby Roger. There he was, third from the right in the second row. His angelic, pink face peeked out from a Columbia blue blanket. He was fair and had no visible eyebrows and only slight wispy hair on his head. His little fingers clutched the edge of the blanket as his lips puckered rhythmically in his sleep. Otto placed his palm on the glass, smiled contentedly, and sighed.

After a few minutes of gazing at his son, Otto turned and walked down the hall to the patient rooms. He hid a huge bouquet of flowers behind him and entered her room. Her face brightened when she saw him. She held up her arms signaling her desire for a hug.

"Flowers for the beautiful mother," he exclaimed.

"Oh, Otto. Have you seen the little angel? Isn't he beautiful? He is the spitting image of my father. Otto, we are so blessed."

"Yes, you did good. He's an angel. Thank you. How are you feeling?"

"I'm fine. The delivery was easy. Dr. Frankel worked his magic and the next thing I knew I was in recovery with our new son. I can't wait for the *bris*. I'm glad you made it home in time."

"Addie, you know that I wouldn't miss it for anything in the world. The *Olympic* made excellent time and we arrived ahead of schedule."

"Otto, I'm so happy. I just wish my parents were here to enjoy their new grandson."

"You know that Bram and Lydia are watching little Roger from heaven, Addie. I've got to go take care of some business now. You rest up and I'll be back to take you home tomorrow. I love you." He bent over and kissed her on the forehead and left the hospital room. He breathed a huge sigh of relief. She did not know.

Otto contrasted the scene here at Roosevelt Hospital in New York City with the debacle one month earlier at the New Hospital in London. On returning to London from his business in Madrid, he received a message advising him that Margaret was at the New Hospital. He thought, how much like his Magpie to go to a hospital staffed entirely by female medical professionals.

He was so excited about the blessed event that he could not wait for the lift. Otto anxiously raced up the stairs to the nursery. He pressed his face against the nursery glass and searched for the little bundle of joy. In the front row, there was an infant screaming at the top of his lungs. Otto chuckled to himself as he saw the name plate — "Axel William Sanger." He bounded down the hallway toward her room. He was walking so fast in anticipation that he almost bowled over a short, fortyish woman in a black dress with a sour disposition who was exiting the room.

"Flowers for the beautiful mother," he exclaimed.

Rather than a jubilant smile, Margaret gave him a sullen glare. He had never seen her so downcast. He rushed to her bedside and gently held her hand. She recoiled. The flowers fell and splayed haphazardly across the floor.

"What's wrong?" he implored.

"I can't do this."

"What?"

"I can't be with you. I can't be with this baby."

"What? . . . Why?"

"My life is in New York, not London."

"I thought you loved London."

"I have realized how artificial all this is. I have realized that I am being used. I belong in New York where my mission in life is."

"I don't understand."

"You never will. You're not a woman."

"You're upset. Let's not make any rash decisions. We have plans."

"*You* have plans. *You're* going to run for Parliament. *You* bought the St. Dunstan mansion. *You, you, you* . . . . Well, *I* have a ticket on the next steamship to New York on Monday."

"What? . . . What about the baby?"

"He's all yours. I just can't . . . ." Sobs racked her body and she moaned as she hid her face in her slender hands. An officious nurse entered the room and, taking Otto by the elbow, guided him out of the room. The fallen bouquet crunched under their feet.

"She's extremely upset. She's had quite a time of it. Are you the husband?"

"I'm the father, yes."

"Well, she's been here for three days and has not stopped crying. She arrived here a bloody mess from the London Hospital. One of the male doctors there tried to give her a Caesarean section and botched it so badly that we thought we were going to lose her. But, thank God, she's strong and we got her in time. She's doing much better, but she needs plenty of rest. She wants nothing to do with the baby. She's had such a dreadful time that she cannot nurse, and she's so depressed that she can't stand to hold him. Dr. Mary has prescribed some medication for her; however, she refuses to take it. She needs to rest now. You must leave."

For the first time in years Otto was speechless. His mind raced. How could this be happening to him? He almost stumbled down the stairs. His gaze was blank and vacant. Dryness filled his throat. At the landing, Otto slumped on a step and placed his head in his hands, stunned.

Eventually, he rose and wandered out of the hospital. The rest of the day was a blur of faces as he walked aimlessly through the city. The chill that accompanied the setting sun matched the lightless void in his chest. Gradually, as the moon rose, inevitability and resentment spawned a hardness that began to close over his wounded heart.

He admonished himself for giving into sentimental love — it must have been simply animal attraction. Kahn turned his attention to practical issues. What would this do to his plans? How could he not have seen this coming? Now what should he do? She was unstable; she could cause a lot of pain if he did not handle this correctly. A baby could not just disappear. Or, could it?

When he returned to the hospital the next day, the officious nurse informed him that Margaret had been discharged and left with an older female relative who was taking her to another, specialized medical facility. No, she could not provide details, except to say that Mrs. Sanger left instructions that if anyone inquired about her to tell them that her decision was final.

"Oh, yes. She also said that the father would be by to pick up the baby. That's you, correct?"

"What!" screamed Aitken, "No, I won't calm down. You listen to me, Otto. I put my reputation on the line for you. I got you the nomination for Parliament. You can't just walk away. You've met with these people. They are counting on you. At this late date, if you withdraw, they will lose their representation. What a *shandra*!"

"It's *shandeh*, the word for shame is *shandeh*, not *shandra*."

"Who cares? It's a disgrace, no matter how you people say it!"

"I'm sorry, things have deteriorated too much. I must go back to New York."

"Otto, this is the opportunity of a lifetime. When Bonar becomes Prime Minister, as an MP you will be in line to become Minister of the Exchequer. Do you know what that would mean?"

"I understand, but I can't help it. Believe me, I wish things were different, but they are not. There's nothing you can say to change things. Thank you for all your help. I'm sorry; I've got to go."

Back in his hotel suite, Otto was crestfallen. His heart ached. This was the worst he had ever felt, even worse than the day he had been humiliated as a child by the shopkeeper. How could she do this to him; just when all his carefully drawn plans were coming to fruition? What a fool he was. His despair was interrupted by a phone ringing.

"Yes, it's Otto. Cousin Rolfe. Yes, thanks for returning my call so quickly. How are you? How's your lovely wife, Verena?"

"Good. Listen I have a situation of some delicacy and I need your help."

"Thank you. Well, I'll just come out with it. I've fathered a son and would like you to raise him."

"He was born ten days ago. He's perfectly healthy. He's beautiful."

"Yes, I'll pay for everything. I'll send you money each month and provide for his education, everything."

"When? As soon as possible. I'll handle all the adoption details."

Sept. 1912
Spala, Poland

**When I am dead, it will not hurt any more, will it, Mama? . . .
When I am dead, build me a little monument of stones in the woods.**

~ Tsarevich Alexei Nicolaievich

ALEXEI HAD TURNED EIGHT earlier that summer and had not had an attack of the dread disease for quite some time. The family had relaxed somewhat in their vigilance over his activities. The Tsarevich thrived with his newfound freedom and began to engage in playful antics like he was almost normal. Almost.

It was the centenary of Russia's great victory over Napoleon at Borodino in September 1812. Napoleon's army suffered significant casualties in this decisive battle that spelled the end of Napoleon's attempt to conquer Mother Russia. The celebrations had been spectacular. Little Alexei, in his miniature officer's uniform to match his father's, had enchanted the crowds with his marching and saluting.

After the grueling schedule of official ceremonies, Nicholas rewarded his family with a vacation at the royal hunting lodge in Spala, Russian Poland. It was not long before they settled into a routine at the Lodge.

Each morning Nicholas would go bike riding with the young grand duchesses, while Alexei would go sailing within eyesight of the main building accompanied by his guardian, the sailor Vladimir Derevenko. Alix and Anya would sit in rockers on the porch, embroidering and chatting about the books they were reading. It was truly an idyllic time for the royal family, but their tranquility was to be short-lived.

"You are becoming quite the sailor, my Alyosha," said Derevenko to the Tsarevich, using the pet name he used only when they were alone. They were in a small skiff tacking toward the middle of the lake. The stern of the boat's white hull bore in gold letters, the name *Vernyĭ Morskaya svin'ya,* the *Faithful Dolphin.* As a modest breeze propelled the small craft through the viridian water, the early autumn sky was clear and bright. Leaning against the gunnels and resting on his life jacket, Alexei dipped his hand into the rushing water. He giggled his infectious, high-pitched laugh.

"I love the water, Vladdy. When I grow up I want to be a sailor just like you."

"I think your parents may have other plans for you."

"I know, but they can't force me to be Tsar if I don't want to," whined Alexei. The young sailor looked at his charge wistfully.

"Be a good boy. We're going to swing her around and head over there," said Derevenko, pointing toward a small island. "We'll stop there and explore for buried treasure. Would you like that?"

"Very much so," replied Alexei, excitedly.

The sailor guided the skiff expertly into a cove on the lee side of the island and told the boy to stay seated as he secured the boat. Vladimir hurdled over the side and pulled the craft onto a sandy beach. As the sailor was tying the line to a tree, Alexei tried to emulate the sailor's hurtle and caught his inner thigh on the oar lock. He splashed awkwardly into the shallow water. Vladimir raced to the boy crying out, "Alyosha, are you alright?"

"I'm fine," replied the boy wiping the water out of his eyes. Vladimir was unable to detect any tears in Alexei's eyes, so the sailor continued securing the boat.

They explored the island for the next hour finding no treasure, except three shells and a hawk's feather. Sailing to the dock at the Lodge, Alexei was unusually quiet. As they walked up the slight rise toward the house they were greeted by Alix and Anya.

"So, how is my little *moryak* today? Did you find any pirates on the island?"

"No, Mama. But I found these," said Alexei softly, displaying the shells and feather. "Can I go inside? I don't feel good."

Just then, Nicholas and the girls arrived ringing their bicycle bells. Their mouths and cheeks were streaked purple from the berries they had eaten on their ride.

"Mama, Anya, look. We found the best berry patch. We picked berries for dessert. Look at our baskets." As the women gathered around the girls and their baskets of berries, Nicholas' smile waned as he noticed his son limping into the Lodge. He hastened to the boy's room and watched in horror as Alexei removed his trousers to reveal a purple bruise the size of an apple on his inner thigh.

He instructed the frightened boy to lie down.

"Alix, call Dr. Botkin immediately. Derevenko, come up here!" Nicholas thundered.

Great tension and consternation consumed the family over the next days. Alexei's bruise was spreading and the family physician was helpless to stop the hemorrhaging. The only remedy that seemed to help was to pack the injury with ice and keep the leg elevated. Dr. Botkin recommended summoning specialists from the capital.

There were torn blood vessels in the left thigh of the Tsarevich and the swelling and pain in his midsection was symptomatic of blood flowing into his abdominal cavity. The condition was worsening and the effusions of blood brought terrible suffering. Despite palliative efforts, Alexei was in severe pain and frequently awoke screaming, "Mama, help me!" Alexandra stayed with him day and night. She cried so much her once lovely eyes became puffy and bloodshot. She refused to eat and could not sleep during her son's ordeal.

In words dripping with anguish, Nicholas wrote to his mother, the Dowager Empress:

The days between the 6th and the 10th were the worst. The poor darling suffered intensely, the pains came in spasms and recurred every quarter of an hour. His high temperature made him delirious night and day; . . . he would sit up in bed and every movement brought the pain on again. He hardly slept at all, had not even the strength to cry, and kept repeating, 'Oh Lord, have mercy upon me.'[16]

Dr. Fedorov, the court surgeon and several specialists were brought to the Lodge under a cloak of secrecy, lest the potentially devastating news of serious injury to the heir become public. Alexandra's maternal heart ached as they evaluated her son. Dr. Fedorov was a short plump man, who smelled faintly of boiled beets. He had a salt-and-pepper goatee and gold, wire-rimmed glasses that gave his beefy face the look of the career academic that he was. As he addressed the Tsarina, his hand unconsciously punctuated each statement as if he were driving a nail into a coffin.

"I'm afraid that there's nothing more that we can do for him. We have consulted all the medical experts. We have even contacted the doctors in Germany who treated your uncle. They say there is no hope. Hemophilia is a rare disease that has no cure. When a patient starts to hemorrhage, his blood lacks the ability to coagulate. . . . I'm sorry."

The Tsarina's face was streaked with tears as she absorbed the weight of her son's death sentence. Her eyes scanned the faces of the royal physicians for a glimmer of hope. They averted their eyes. Dr. Botkin walked over and said softly, "I'm truly sorry, Your Highness. We should call a priest to administer the last rites to the boy. Alexei's life is in God's hands now."

Alexei rose slightly in his bed and asked his mother, "*When I am dead, it will not hurt any more, will it, Mama? . . .When I am dead, build me a little monument of stones in the woods.*"[17]

At a loss for words, she collapsed slowly back into her chair, guided by the strong arms of Anya. Alix gazed at the physician vacantly. She dabbed her eyes with her silk handkerchief and thought bitterly that all the Tsar's wealth was impotent in the face of God's will.

"Please leave us."

After they left, she knelt prayerfully at the side of her darling son's bed. He slept the unmoving sleep of the sedated. His chalky skin was mottled with virulent purple blotches; the hemorrhaging beneath his skin was spreading and there was nothing anyone could do to stop it. She refused to leave his chamber, darkened by thick drapery to keep out the light so painful to Alexei's eyes. She lapsed into a floating consciousness, not knowing whether it was day or night. Occasionally, Anya gave her some warm broth, exhorting her to drink it to maintain her strength.

The pain of his heir's affliction wore heavily on the Tsar. Nicholas joined her in this death vigil when he could bear it. After several days, he told Alexandra that she must leave Alexei and rest. She looked at him with such sadness that his heart ached. Her head shook from side to side.

"No, my place is here."

"Yes, I know."

The Tsar stood wearily and left the oppressive chamber. As he strode out of the room, his regal demeanor slowly returned. A slight downward slouch of his shoulders was the only sign of the enormous weight on his heart.

When alone, he wept. With reluctance, he summoned Count Vladimir Fredericks, Minister of the Imperial Court to compose a death announcement. Nicholas could not summon the strength to draft the words, "His Imperial Highness, the Tsarevich Alexei Nicolaievich, Sovereign Heir of the Russian Empire has died, this ___ day of Our Lord, October, 1912."

In her greatest despair, Alexandra knew that she would have to disobey her husband's direct order to save her precious son. She sat quietly and penned a missive, "My dear Rasputin . . . ."

It was snowing the day Rasputin arrived at the Spala Lodge. Dark, ominous clouds hung in the sky as frigid wind whipped the snow into looming drifts. Nicholas stood stolidly and silently by as the monk entered Alexei's room. Anya helped the monk remove his overcoat and took his worn, leather satchel. Father Grigory was wearing a rumpled, black peasant's coat and baggy trousers that he had worn during his non-stop travels from Siberia. He grasped the Tsarina's frail hands in his massive paws. He lifted her chin. Gazing into her eyes with his piercing stare, he said,

"God has seen your tears and heard your prayers. Don't worry. The Little One will not die."[18]

The healer knelt in prayer before the bed of the Tsarevich who was moaning softly, deliriously. At the soothing tone of the Starets' voice, the boy's restlessness abated. Soon, the heir's labored breathing settled into the cadence of Rasputin's prayers and the boy appeared to sleep. The monk motioned for his satchel. Anya brought it and he removed three crystals from velvet bags. While murmuring in prayer, he rubbed each of the crystals with his thick hands. Seeking affirmation from Alix, who nodded assent, he raised the thin wool blanket and then the boy's nightclothes. There was an ugly dark purple bruise radiating from the Tsarevich's groin down to his ankle and up to his ribcage. The boy was emaciated. His skin had a grayish death-hue and hung over his skeleton like a limp sail on a becalmed sailboat.

Rasputin increased the ardor of his prayers as he placed the crystals strategically on the ailing child's body and returned the covers. Kneeling beside the bed, Rasputin prayed fervently as in a trance, his eyes closed, his lips importuning God to perform a miracle. Rasputin stayed on his knees at Alexei's bedside for twenty-seven straight hours.

Finally, the delirium broke.

"Father Grigory, it *is* you. I dreamed that you came to me. You were carried here by two archangels and the three of you prayed over me. I'm so happy to see you."

Rasputin smiled wanly and then slumped to a fetal position alongside the bed, exhausted. Alexandra, who was half asleep in a chair next to the bed, lifted her head at the sound of her son's voice. Although groggy and sleep-deprived, she sobbed dry tears of relief. From a nearby couch, Anya stirred awake. She immediately ran to summon the Tsar and the sisters, who were asleep in an adjoining room. She almost tripped over Derevenko who stood vigil outside Alexei's door like a faithful (and fearful) puppy pining for his sick master. Within minutes the house was abuzz with joyful relief over the miracle.

The following morning the sun rose bright, with the clarity that follows a snowstorm. As the staff unshuttered the windows, the glare from the reflected sunlight penetrated the rooms of the Lodge, removing the gloom. All the members of the medical team, except Dr. Botkin, departed hurriedly, citing urgent business.

Over the next days, the hemorrhaging stopped, the swelling subsided and Alexei regained a healthy pallor. When he was strong enough to travel home, the Imperial family boarded a train to Tsarskoe Selo. To avoid jostling the fragile royal patient, the Tsar instructed the engineer to travel the entire distance at a speed of no more than fifteen miles per hour.

The Long Island Railroad train to Babylon click-clacked as Strafe stared at the headline, barely able to comprehend the words.

ASSASSIN SHOOTS ROOSEVELT,

Teddy quips, "It takes more than that to kill a bull moose."

Devouring the column rapidly, Strafe was alternately, horrified and relieved as he read the account of the deranged assassin's unsuccessful attempt on the former president's life. The would-be assassin claimed that the ghost of President McKinley had appeared to him in a dream and told him to avenge his (McKinley's) assassination by killing Roosevelt. Oliver's amazement grew as read about how Roosevelt, with a bullet lodged in his chest, courageously delivered his speech for eighty minutes to a crowd of 10,000 people jammed into the Milwaukee Civic Auditorium. At one point during the speech, a *Doubting Thomas* heckled the former president, crying out "Fake!" The Presidential candidate silenced the crowd by parting his coat to reveal his blood-soaked vest and shirt. Although full recovery was expected, his presidential campaign had been suspended.

The Naval officer owed his career to Roosevelt. Back in '04, then-Lt. Commander Oliver had been scapegoated for a collision that resulted in several dozen deaths, involving a ship under his command, the USS *Culgoa*. The incident resulted in a court-martial and Oliver suffered the humiliation of being "stripped of his sword." He was ultimately acquitted, "with honor," of any wrongdoing.

In an effort to make amends, the Navy brass held a ceremony returning his sword. To everyone's shock, Oliver took the sword, broke it over his knee and threw it overboard. He stormed off and resigned his commission. It was only after the intervention of President Roosevelt who personally pleaded with Oliver to return, that he relented and accepted assignment to the Office of Naval Intelligence.

As America's influence in the world grew, so did the role of ONI. Originally focused on gathering information on the strength and positions of foreign naval assets, it now extended to detecting and eliminating spies and saboteurs. At ONI, Oliver's career had blossomed. It helped to have friends in high places, and none was higher than Theodore Roosevelt.

Strafe was chagrined when Roosevelt left the presidency in 1908 to go off on a safari in Africa.

From the train Strafe made his way to the village of Bohemia where he was to meet his contact. Strafe was wearing clothing typical of a shipyard worker: overalls, coarse white sweater, a woven wool hat and pea coat. Thanks to his make-up artistry, a short, straggly beard adorned his ruddy face. The *Valhalla Pirate*, a local pub, was crowded with workmen, unwinding after a wearisome day in nearby boatyards.

"How are you this fine Tuesday, mate?" asked Jasper Brandtaucher, from his table in the corner that gave him a strategic view of the establishment.

"It's been a good day for a workingman to earn his beer," replied Oliver, acknowledging the 'all clear' signal.

A sturdy-looking waitress with the name Madge embroidered on her uniform took their order. As she headed toward the kitchen, a large man with blond hair grabbed her around the waist and pulled her toward him.

"Fraülein, gib mir einen Kuss!" he bellowed with boozy breath.

"I won't give you a kiss, Klaus. You will have to wait in line, just like the others," she replied, prying herself free. The already boisterous bar erupted in laughter. Klaus slapped her on the butt as she retreated hastily.

Jasper eyed the several tables of men wearing nondescript denim outfits.

"Those fellas are crew members of the U-19, the newest *Kraut* submarine. It's anchored offshore just beyond the reef. See that one with the red beard? He was bragging earlier that they have the first *Unterseeboot*, as they call it, with a diesel engine."

Strafe exhaled a low whistle. The implications of a vessel with extended range by virtue of diesel power were staggering.

"I'd be extremely interested in learning more details. See what you and Madge can find out," said Strafe, discreetly sliding some bills to Jasper's waiting hand.

PART 2
Prelude to the Great War

16

June 1914
St. Petersburg, Russia

The destinies of nations were his sport; the movement of armies
and the affairs of government his special delight. In the wake
of war this mysterious figure moved over tortured Europe.

~ MAX AITKEN, LORD BEAVERBROOK,
CONCERNING A CERTAIN ARMS DEALER

OTTO'S MIND WANDERED as he recalled his many trysts with his
Magpie. He sighed and brushed some moisture from his eye before it
graduated to a tear. The time since Margaret's abrupt evacuation from his
life had been hellish. No more would his heart race in anticipation of her
scent; no more playful nicknames; no more sunny smiles when he entered a
room; and, no more scintillating skin-on-skin embraces between silk sheets.
Rather than a feeling of exhilaration, he felt a dull ache when he thought of
Margaret. He wondered where she was now and what she was doing. Did
she miss him? Did she feel a void like he did? Cold filled him. The pain of
emptiness and betrayal subsided slightly in the long months without his
Magpie. The void in his life could only be filled by a plan of grand audacity.
Such a plan was taking shape; the more distinct it grew, the less he ached.

The wind whipping down the street outside the Hotel *Europa* formed a tiny whirlwind that encased Otto, blowing leaves and dust into his eyes. Blinking vigorously, Otto pondered the turn of events that would have been impossible to choreograph. It had meshed like the gears in the Peacock automaton in the Winter Palace. He had been meeting with Finance Minister Bark when a messenger delivered a wire from his firm in New York.

"Oh, dear," he had exclaimed. "I must leave as soon as possible."

"But, we have not concluded our business," Pyotr Bark replied.

"It is unavoidable. I must go to Stockholm to handle a matter of utmost urgency, then, catch the next ocean liner to New York. I know that there is one leaving next Monday. I must make the arrangements now if I am to make it back to New York in time."

Minister Bark rubbed his chin thoughtfully. "Perhaps, we can shorten your travel time and still accomplish our business, Otto. Wait here."

Otto tapped his foot rapidly under the mahogany table that was covered with charts and calculations. They had been working on the latest phase of the capital improvements for the Russian railway system that would be crucial in the event of war. Otto had prodded and cajoled the Tsar to spend prolifically over the last few years, but now war was imminent. The Tsar was in denial and hoped that war would not come before the following year.

By the time Bark re-entered the room, Kahn's nervous tapping had degenerated to worried pacing and watch checking. Otto looked expectantly at the younger man who was trying to suppress a grin.

"Pack your luggage, we leave tomorrow morning with the Tsar and the Tsarina on the Imperial Yacht *Shtandart*, heading to Stockholm. I've persuaded the Tsar of the urgency of our business and your travel needs. He has graciously allowed us to join the royal family on their annual sea-borne excursion to the Norwegian fjords. We will have a day and a half to complete our business."

"Marvelous, I will call the hotel and have them pack my baggage. We must continue with our work if we are to have final documents for the Tsar's approval by the time we get to Stockholm," said Otto.

The following morning, with mist shrouding the *Shtandart*, Otto led the porter along the Imperial Pier. The armed sailor at the guardhouse wore a navy blue uniform with stripes on the collar that were matched by the striped jersey he wore under his blouse. He had been most accommodating and they passed through security quickly. The wheels of the luggage-dolly thumped rhythmically over the thick boards as they approached the Imperial Yacht. A ray of sunlight pierced through the mist and illuminated the bowsprit.

It was difficult to awe Kahn. He had been close to the rich and powerful for all of his professional life. But the Imperial yacht overwhelmed him. Aside from its sheer size, that necessitated a crew of two hundred seventy five, the great yacht was opulently appointed in every respect imaginable. Otto suppressed a not inconsiderable twinge of envy.

On board, he gazed out over the brilliant blue waters of the Gulf of Finland and saw the Tsar approaching with Tsarevich Alexei in tow. Their daily routine while on board was to check the weather reports each morning. The young heir wore a junior sailor uniform complete with a round white hat with *Shtandart* on the ribbon encircling the hat. He walked with a cane and the Tsar moderated his gait so that his son could walk comfortably. Otto thought sadly that the Tsarevich symbolized the state of the dynasty, then he exhaled with the realization that destiny was devoid of sentiment.

"Good afternoon, Your Highness. As you know, I have great admiration for the fine art of shipbuilding. And, I must say that the *Shtandart* is truly unique. I've sailed on many 'ships of state,' and in my humble opinion the *Shtandart* is maritime perfection."

"Ah, Otto, you speak the truth. She is elegant, yet, powerful; graceful, yet, sturdy. The Dowager Empress would say that it's the Danish craftsmanship. *Entre nous*, we would say she is the best of Danish craftsmanship and Russian design. You know, of course, that our mother is Danish and that our Father created the specifications. Like our parents, the *Shtandart* is the perfect marriage of both," Nicholas beamed.

"The best part of being on the *Shtandart* is that the Tsarina and the children love her. Here they can be free — no kowtowing to the expectations and rigid protocol of the Imperial palaces. For me, it is wonderful to enjoy our family on placid waters away from the troubles of the land."

"Yes, I have never seen the Tsarina smile so brightly. Life on the *Shtandart* certainly agrees with her . . . and, if I may say so, with Your Highness as well."

"After you and Minister Bark complete your work on the documents, we can go below decks to our private study to finish our business before dinner. We'll meet you there at three. Make sure that Minister Bark is present."

After directing the steward to summon Minister Bark to the Tsar's private study, Otto went to his stateroom and retrieved his portfolio. He proceeded past the formal reception salon and down the mahogany-paneled hallway to the Tsar's private study. He passed several members of the crew; one was buffing the floors, while two others polished brass fittings and cleaned glass windows.

Otto had learned that punctuality was integral to business success. If you were not twenty minutes early, you were late. Not only was it a show of respect, it facilitated strategic choice of seating and allowed for observation of other participants as they entered. Information of that sort could prove useful during negotiations.

After knocking, Otto entered the private study. It was tastefully paneled with highly-polished wood, stained a gorgeous, reddish brown. A desk covered with supple mahogany-colored leather and matching chairs occupied the center of the room. To the side, away from the porthole, was a table covered with navigation charts held down by polished brass navigational instruments. As Otto looked around, he spied some of the Tsar's stationery on the desk. Just then, a steward entered.

"May I get you anything, sir?"

"Yes, I'd like some Vichy water."

Before the steward returned, Otto hurriedly moved several embossed sheets to the back of his portfolio. He sat down, half-facing the door, and waited for the Tsar and Bark, pretending to admire the nautical paintings on the walls.

"So, Your Excellency, there are several major recommendations that we see for the Imperial Railroad heading West and South. First, the acquisition of a considerable number of passenger cars is a top priority. Your rolling stock is acceptable for current use, but woefully inadequate for expanded use that might become necessary in the worst-case scenario of war with your cousin. Passenger cars are the best choice because they are easily convertible to troop carriers.

"Second, there is a decided absence of sidings and by-passes along the Oktyabrskaya Railway. We strongly suggest the construction of new siding every twenty miles in order to provide critical flexibility for troop or materiel movement. They allow for strategic delivery of essential shipments of men or munitions expeditiously without getting bogged down behind slow moving traffic. Just move it to the siding and by-pass any logjams.

"We can source the purchase and construction of the necessary improvements, as well as supply the latest switch technology that the U.S. government is using in Alaska, guaranteed to operate at extremely low temperatures."

Otto sensed a momentary cloud of annoyance in the Tsar's countenance at the mention of Alaska. Like the good salesman that he was, Kahn was not diverted from pushing to closure. He continued without missing a beat.

"We have a significant interest in *Compagnie Internationale des Wagons-Lits* that manufactures the rolling stock for the Orient Express. We could expedite any order placed by Your Highness. The luxury carriages are extraordinarily sturdy and would easily convert to troop carriers. If we are so fortunate as to be spared war, the carriages could be put into service on the Trans-Siberian Express.

"The entire program can be accomplished within the next two calendar years, with delivery of rolling stock, locomotives and advanced switches by the end of the year. The design and manufacture of rails, etc., could be completed by next summer with a significant premium. The figures are all set forth in the attachment to the contract that I have presented to Minister Bark. My firm is prepared to underwrite the financing at our usual fee, plus 100 basis points."

The Tsar flinched imperceptibly at the last statement. He glanced at Bark, who nodded and said, "Excuse us, Herr Kahn."

After he had compromised with Bark at seventy-five basis points above the usual fee, Otto stowed the signed and sealed documents. The next day, Otto disembarked in Stockholm. Boarding a waiting limousine, he headed directly to the Hotel Diplomat — named for its practice of renting grand apartments to foreign diplomats.

"How are we today, Herr Kahn?" asked the clerk at the reception desk

"Exceptionally well, thank you, Olsen."

"You have a visitor waiting for you, sir," he replied, handing Otto a business card and nodding in the direction of a chubby, little man nervously toying with the brim of his frayed bowler. His round face and pear-shaped physique bore the effects of too many blinis with sour cream. His skin was mottled and sweat punctuated his forehead. A worn, brown leather briefcase stuffed with papers rested at his feet.

"Ah, he's early," said Otto in recognition. "Send him to my suite in thirty minutes. I have some business to attend to first."

Precisely one half hour later there was a knock at the door.

"OK, I will be there at 6 P.M. for dinner, Your Excellency. We have much to discuss. I will see you later."

Otto hung up the phone and opened the door. The chubby little man stood before him.

"Herr Givatovzo, it is a pleasure to meet in person after our dealings with you at the Nya Bank. Do come in. How was your trip from Kiev?"

"Fine, thank you. I'd prefer if you call me Abram."

"Of course, Abram. Call me Otto."

The two men sat in Queen Anne armchairs facing each other across an exquisite antique coffee table bearing a silver Samovar and coffee service accompanied by a dish of pastries. Otto motioned toward the table and the younger man leaned forward and poured himself a cup of tea from the Samovar and put a *vareniki* oozing strawberries on a plate. He looked at Otto questioningly.

"No thanks," said Otto. "I've been spoiled on the *Shtandart* by the Tsar these last few days and I must curb my eating, or I just might burst at the seams. So tell me about your cousin and what he is doing."

"As you probably know, Leon has left Vienna and is in the Balkans writing for *Kievstaya Misl* under various pseudonyms. He has placed his brother-in-law, Lev Kamenev, to oversee the organization in St. Petersburg. Lev is a good man who will hold it together until Leon returns."

"His assignments are about to get much more interesting," said Kahn, cryptically.

Abram took another *vareniki* and sipped his tea.

"We are approaching historic times, where justice is achievable. You know, when I travel on the railroads, the terrain on either side of a national border is the same. Only the man-made structures and uniforms of the border guards vary. The coming war will provide the opportunity for a global governing body to fill the vacuum left after the silly governments exhaust themselves. Then, people of all lands will be able to live in peace. There will be a global currency that will eliminate trade wars and prosperity will follow as spring follows winter. We, the bankers, with our understanding and connections throughout the world, will be able to achieve this harmony because they will all be indebted to us."

Kahn continued. "Listen, we believe that the time for action is at hand. We want Trotsky to lead a special Russian unity conference in Brussels during the Second International in July. A divided movement will not succeed. There is too much at stake. The regime is rotten and teetering from the effects of three hundred years of tyranny and corruption. The Kaiser is preparing for war against his cousin, the Tsar, and that will bring Russia to the brink of collapse. A well-placed push by the revolutionaries and the government will come tumbling down just like Humpty Dumpty."

"Otto, there are two questions, the answers to which are critical to success in this endeavor. First, will the Kaiser support the effort?"

"We have it from the highest sources in Berlin that the Kaiser will be with you 100%. He has designs on Alsace Lorraine and sees his cousin as the only obstacle. He has no animosity toward the Russian people. He will provide funds to the movement through us and support the new government wholeheartedly. And what is your second question, Abram?"

"You know that Leon will do anything for the cause. He was there in '05 and will be on the barricades until the Romanovs have been eliminated. The problem is that Leon is getting older and is tired of living hand-to-mouth while he drags his family around the globe. He has four children, you know, and cannot provide for them on the meager earnings from his freelance writing.

"Revolution against the Tsar will not be inexpensive. I'm sure that Leon will cooperate, provided that he can see the means to achieve the goal," A pregnant pause. "In the past, revolutionaries have risked everything, only to fall short due to lack of monetary resources. I believe that I can persuade Leon for the sake of his family to bury the hatchet, as you Americans say, with Lenin, in return for certain financial assurances."

"I see," replied Otto, leaning forward.

"We are prepared to fund an account in his favor at the Nya Bank, if he will cooperate with Lenin. We will advance him expenses in the sum of $100,000 in preparation for his return to Petrograd when the time is propitious. There will also be money for the movement when the time is right. In the meantime, let me know his answer as soon as possible. Events are about to overtake us all. Those who are well-positioned will thrive regardless of the final outcome of any hostilities." Otto paused.

"Of course, should you succeed in convincing him, we would utilize your bank as the exchange agent for certain recently-concluded transactions with the Imperial Court."

"Thank you, Otto."

"You're welcome, Abram. Please take the remaining *vareniki* with you; otherwise they will be wasted."

The heavy-set man bundled the pastries into a napkin and stuffed it in his pocket.

"Abram, I suggest that you leave the hotel by the rear exit. I think I saw some unsavory characters in the lobby who may be surveilling us. Take care. Send an encrypted wire to me in New York with Leon's answer as soon as possible."

June 1914
Suitland, Maryland

It looked as if a night of dark intent was coming,
and not only a night, an age.
Someone had better be prepared for rage . . . .

~ Robert Frost

Kurt Chorney was a big boy who stood a foot taller than Strafe. Academy-trained, multilingual and just twenty-two years old, he fit the profile of the modern intelligence officer. As he waited to see Captain Oliver, Kurt reflected on the course of his life since he left the Naval Academy. Barely six months had passed since he had stood on the mound for the Academy baseball team in the championship game against West Point. He recalled vividly the surge of adrenaline he had felt facing the Army best hitter, Omar "the Cobra" Bradley with two out in the ninth inning, a one run lead, and a man on base. How his heart had sunk as the Cobra launched a long fly to right that was destined to clear the fence and win the game. Then, the incredulity he had felt when his right fielder, Sam Rice, made an unbelievably, acrobatic catch, propelling himself over the fence. Finally, jubilation when Sam reappeared holding the ball over his head triumphantly. His last memory of that day was watching Bradley, who was on his way to second, kick the dirt in dejected disappointment.

Immediately after the game, Chorney had been assigned to Naval Intelligence. The ink on his diploma was barely dry when he was sent into a powder keg situation in Mexico with a naval detachment tasked with defending the "honor" of the United States. Not only did his task force occupy the city of Vera Cruz, but Chorney had recovered a German codebook from a Mexican spy, surviving a knife fight in the process and falling in love with a fiery, Mexican *mujer hermosa*. That was a story for another day.

Chorney was ushered into a drab conference room with another officer. They snapped to attention as Captain Oliver entered the room. Oliver was a no-nonsense leader who had been promoted to Director of the Office of Naval Intelligence at the Naval Maritime Intelligence Center in January. During Chorney's rotations through NMIC over the last two summers, he had worked under Strafe and a mutual respect and admiration between the two men had developed. Kurt's palms were sweating in anticipation of his next assignment. He hoped that his linguistic skills would be brought to bear. He was fluent in Russian and German thanks to his Bavarian-born mother and Muscovite father.

"At ease, gentlemen. Please be seated."

Although orders regarding naval intelligence tended to be cryptic, the orders before Strafe were as ominous as they were terse. "Hazard extreme — Monocle, London — send two." His resources were stretched across the globe; his options were limited.

"We live in a dangerous world. Evil is afoot and war is inevitable. It's our job to keep Uncle Sam as far away from the explosion when it occurs, and it will occur within the next twelve months, regardless of what the pols are saying. This will be the worst conflagration ever, and we need to discover what our enemies and friends are doing before they even think about it. Yes, I said our friends because we cannot let our guard down to anyone. Two oceans have protected us in the past. But, now the world is shrinking and armament proliferation is rampant. Any two-bit dictator like Huerta in Mexico can obtain modern weapons. And where it used to take weeks or days to find out what was happening, now we get communications almost daily. All this makes it imperative that we accelerate our efforts. This is an opportunity for guys like you. You will be thrust into the fray immediately. I know that you are up to it."

Strafe continued, "Hank has been in London shadowing the Monocle."
"Who's that?" asked Kurt.

"The Monocle is Otto Kahn, a financier with Kuhn Loeb, an influential investment bank headquartered in New York. He lives in New York, but he's a German émigré by way of London. He holds British citizenship and a couple of years ago was lined up to run for Parliament and then backed out at the last minute. He married his boss' daughter. He's involved with a lot of dames, but until recently was hot and heavy with one who is in the forefront of the Eugenics and birth control movements. Her name is Margaret Sanger and, after having a baby, we think it was Otto's, she split for New York and they have not seen each other since.

"He runs in the most powerful circles, you know, New York, London, Berlin, and St. Petersburg. As a banker, he hobnobs with royalty and the ultra-rich. As the chairman of the Metropolitan Opera, he socializes with famous artists and entertainers. However, he is more than a celebrity banker. We believe that he is the *éminence grise* of various revolutionary groups. We haven't yet figured out what his endgame is; but, there are reports that he is ruthless — that he'll stop at nothing — bribery, drug-dealing, murder — to achieve his ends. Our job is to learn what he's up to and stop him before he harms the United States.

"The Monocle is returning to London. You and Hank will follow him and keep me posted on his activities. We've received intel from London regarding a possible threat of interest. There have been numerous meetings between the Monocle and Vaslav Nijinsky, the world-famous ballet dancer. One theory is that those rendezvous may be more than innocent business meetings between impresario and talent. It seems like events are speeding up and the Monocle is in the middle of them. There's a picture in the envelope. He's kind of a dandy. You know, spats, cane, top hat, cape and, of course, the ever-present monocle. Your orders are in this envelope. Remember to follow protocol and, most important, be safe. God speed."

Otto was back on a steamer heading from New York to London. The tranquil days of spring were about to erupt into the harrowing days of summer and war. He knew that once the war started, crisscrossing the ocean would become out of the question. It was imperative that he activate his plans to the greatest extent possible. The financings secured with the Tsar and the King of Sweden for railroads and factories for munitions, guns, tanks and aeroplanes were enough to ensure that 1914 would be the most profitable year ever. He could hardly imagine the profits that would roll in once the shooting and bombing started. Yes, he thought, the profits would flow faster than the blood of the tragic victims of the coming conflagration. At least that was his hope.

His thoughts turned to his other passion, the Metropolitan Opera. His urgent return to New York had been rewarded by a major coup. Otto replayed the scene in the Met boardroom. Normally, meetings of the Board of Directors of the Metropolitan Opera were staid affairs, devoted to reports of ticket receipts and estimates for repairs to the roof, or upgrading the inadequate staging at the Broadway facility. Kahn certainly knew how to tantalize. After extolling the artistic virtues of his latest signing, he revealed the name of the mystery star who would perform to packed crowds the next winter season. There was a palpable rush of excitement as Otto concluded his presentation with a grand flourish.

"Gentlemen, behold the signature of the one and only Vaslav Nijinsky, the world's greatest male *danseur*. His artistry, beauty and athleticism are legendary. Nijinsky's gravity-defying leaps are positively angelic. He has been lauded from continent to continent as the greatest ballet dancer ever born. And, he will be performing in our theatre just below us. Not only that, Anna Pavlova and the entire *Ballet Russe* will grace our stage for the season!" exclaimed Otto, his moustache straining to cover the expansive grin that filled his face.

"Imagine the accolades when Vaslav Nijinsky, graces the New York stage. Then, imagine the torrents of disapprobation that will inevitably follow his outlandish behavior. Prince Felix told me about Nijinsky's most recent transgression. He was fired from the Kirov Ballet at the insistence of the Dowager Empress for appearing on stage at the Mariinsky Theater without modesty trunks and feigning masturbation during his performance. The scandal sheets will revel in the daily drama over the love triangle with Nijinsky in the middle between his former lover and boss Sergei Daghiliev, and Vaslav's new bride, the volatile Hungarian Countess, Romola de Pulszky. Add to the mix, litigation between Vaslav and Sergei and the emotional fireworks about to detonate will surely generate patrons."

"Bravo, Otto, you have done us proud. Those supercilious Italians and insufferable Germans will be weeping tears of envy when they learn of your stellar lineup for the coming winter season!" fawned Madame Fay Leval-Barrie, the Met's leading benefactor.

Otto basked in the compliments, eyeing his former detractors with satisfaction.

"Our prestige is on the rise; the sky is the limit. I suspect that we will be joined by the President for opening night next autumn." He spoke with an air of confidence that left no doubt that this was a *fait accompli.*

As Otto settled into the soft couch in his suite at London's Savoy Hotel, he asked Nijinsky, "*Tatacaboy,* do you remember when we first met?"

"Of course, Paris, 1909. I was dancing with your favorite mistress, Anna Pavlova, in *Giselle.* We were all the rage," replied Nijinsky.

"And what did you say to me that night when we were at *Café Anglais* after your performance, Vaslav?"

"Well, I said that I would do anything to have money like you, Herr Kahn."

"And now you have lots of money thanks to our arrangements and the investments I have made for you, no? But you need more money to . . . how shall we say, . . . maintain your habits."

"You should not believe everything you hear," muttered Nijinsky.

"Well, to put it delicately, I hear from very reliable sources that Mme. Fourier is threatening to go to the *gendarmes* over the loss of her daughter's virginity. Oh, yes, and Lady Marriott is outraged that her stepson was sodo . . . , you have been quite indiscreet, my friend," said Otto, holding up his palm toward Nijinsky in a gesture of silence.

"There is a certain gentleman who has been . . . let's say . . . troublesome to some business I have been pursuing in Baku. This gentleman works for Branobel and he is working with the Imperial Government to monopolize the latest motor innovation. He is known to drink heavily when gambling. When he wins, he likes to celebrate with nubile, young things back at his hotel room at the Savoy. It just so happens that this evening I've been invited to a game of baccarat with our friend. I will keep him occupied until one hour after your performance. He's on the ninth floor, Suite 922, overlooking the Courtyard on the north facade. That should give you sufficient time to . . . shall we say, . . . prepare his nightcap."

"How much?" asked Vaslav.

"$50,000. $15,000 to go to each of the horrified mothers of your victims, and $20,000 for your retirement fund."

"Make it $60,000, $30,000 for the Fund."

"Done," said Otto extending his hand.

"Once this has been accomplished, I have another job for you. Here is an envelope that I would like you to deliver as part of your next mission. The Ferret will brief you on the details in Vienna and you will keep the existence of this envelope between you and me. When your mission for him has been concluded, hand this envelope to the person the Ferret sends you to. This is extremely confidential. Under no circumstances are you to reveal this to the Ferret or anyone else. Your remuneration for delivering this letter will be an additional $10,000."

Otto exhaled slowly, "So, we are square, *ja?* I will be gone in the morning. I'm going to St. Petersburg to work on some unfinished business. I will see you in New York for the fall debut of the *Ballet Russe*. I can hardly wait. In the meantime, good luck!"

"Lady Veronica, it is so good to see you. I hardly recognized you. You look exquisite this afternoon. Have you just returned from Baden-Baden?"

Otto sidled up to an attractive woman in her early thirties. She was wearing a magenta jacquard-patterned dress made of taffeta with ruffles at the neck and cuffs. Her high cheekbones were accentuated by the slightest hint of rouge that echoed the color of her dress. She gave Otto a slight push with her hand that bore a large amethyst ring next to a signet ring signifying her ancestral lineage.

"You *are* such a shameless flirt, but so . . . charming," she replied, her eyes flashing.

"As a gentleman, I am bound to the truth," he said gallantly. He grasped her hand and brought it to his lips ever so gently. A waiter walked by with a tray covered with chilled flutes of prosecco, each punctuated by a ruby red raspberry that appeared to be releasing tiny beads of effervescence. Otto deftly acquired two glasses and handed one to Lady Veronica in a theatrical flourish.

"Madame, we toast to youth and vintage wines, may they improve through the years."

"Otto, you are such a dear," she cooed.

Otto took her elbow and ushered her toward a bench in the corner of the rose garden. The crushed quartz gravel path left a sheen of pink dust on his patent leather wingtips. They sat and conversed privately. At one point, Otto handed Lady Veronica his handkerchief which she used to wipe a tear from her eyes. As she sniffled, Otto's voice softly said, "This is best put behind us. You know that a scandal would follow her for the rest of her young life. Nor would you want to deprive the world of the beauty that he creates every night. Although what he did is despicable, you must understand that he is Polish and, well, you know, they just don't have the same, how shall we say, refinement? To make amends and provide for your daughter's dowry, I will give you $5,000. What do you say?"

A shocked look overcame her face as she realized the direction the sympathetic conversation had taken. Her head shook silently from side to side. Her mind was a jumble of emotions. Her husband's illness and the crash of '07 had diminished their fortunes. She knew that an arrest of that vile creature would not help business; but $10,000 would eradicate their debts. Inhaling deeply, she composed herself and, with her wet eyes downcast, uttered, "$10,000."

With his most concerned look, Kahn said, "Your daughter will thank you for sparing her further ordeal. I'll have a draught for $10,000 delivered tomorrow."

As he entered the dining room of the Savoy Hotel, Kahn felt a slight dampness on the back of his neck that had resulted from his vigorous game of squash that afternoon with Baron Bruno von Schroder, a senior member of J. Henry Schroder Banking Company of London. In between volleys, they had had a productive discussion about the implementation of the new central bank in the United States and how it would handle the demands for capital in the coming hostilities.

"Mr. Kahn, it is so good to see you," said Andre, the *Captain d'table* at Savoy's River Restaurant. "Follow me, please."

The dining room was lavishly appointed in Cararra marble that was softened by bleached wood panels offset by rich, deep red mahogany coping. Arrangements of pure white calla lilies were interspersed through the dining area, creating an intoxicating aura. Kahn sat between a Swedish engineer named Anton Carlsund, and Prince Fahid Abdulla bin Tazl and his lovely escort, introduced only as Marla.

Otto engaged the Prince in a discussion about the status of railroad projects within the Ottoman Empire. The Prince bemoaned the Caliphate's difficulty in adjusting to modernity. Carlsund was a senior engineer for Ludwig Nobel Engineering Works. He was a large man in his fifties with a jowly face that reminded Otto of a basset hound. He had big hands that engulfed his crystal wine goblet. He quaffed copious amounts of expensive wine and turned to Kahn.

"Otto, the diesel engine will dominate this century."

"That may be, my dear fellow, but first the world has to deal with the nation state. Over the last half century, the idea of the nation state has proliferated around the globe, while trade and communications worldwide have increased exponentially. This has led to currency instability and crashes like in '07. Until we have a world currency, administered by a world government, there can be no peace."

"Excuse me Otto, with all due respect, the pound sterling is the world currency and, thus, it will always be," blurted Sir Basil Zahoroff, a burly fellow who was already drunk. Lady Nora Zahoroff gestured for him to lower his voice.

"You may be surprised, Basil, but there are powers rising across the globe, as we sit here, that like a genie in a bottle may be very difficult to contain once they have been unleashed."

"That sounds prophetic, Otto. Do you know something we don't?"

"No more than any other student of history trying to discern patterns in the vast mosaic of an emotional, often irrational, humankind. But, I see that we are boring our lovely lady guests and François has arrived with our *entrées*," said Otto, his voice dripping with honey and his eyes engaging the lovely Marla. She returned a smile appreciatively.

The meal was exquisite. Raising his glass Otto toasted, "To good food, good wine and most of all, to good friends." He clinked glasses with Marla who winked coquettishly. Otto filed that away for future reference. As he prepared to leave, Otto raised his wrist and mimed to Carlsund, "10 o'clock in the D'Oyly Carte Room." The affable Swede gave Otto a 'thumbs up.'

Kahn headed to the Lounge off the Thames Foyer for an *après* dinner drink with Lady Gwendolyn. He favored the Lounge because the open space was incongruously suitable for discrete conversations. He chose a table near the birdcage-like gazebo under the dome. From this vantage point he could survey the entire room.

"Wendy, would you share some Dom Perignon White Gold with me?"

"To what do I owe the honor?"

"Actually, I would like to discuss with you a matter of some delicacy involving an associate of mine."

"And who might that be?"

"I'm sure that you are aware that I have been trying to get the *Ballet Russe* to play New York for several years now . . . ."

"Don't tell me that you want to talk to me about that lecherous, little degenerate, Nijnsky," she interrupted, her voice rising with each word.

Otto glanced around at the admonishing stares of the guests passing through the Thames and thought this might not have been the best place for this conversation.

"Wendy, I understand. I have a young son, too. I would protect him with my life. How is the boy?" he asked hoping to divert the tone of the conversation.

She sobbed, "All I wanted was for Jake to learn ballet from a master. A private lesson, that's all. I made the mistake of leaving the room for a minute and the next thing I see is little Jake standing there with that monster's . . . thing out . . . . Oh, it was horrible"

"I know."

"Well, that pervert tried to explain that he was teaching Jake about the symbolism of ballet and the passion it inspires. I screamed for our man Kirby to come and throw the little creep out on his arse. Except, he was too quick and jumped away from Kirby's grasp and pirouetted out the door. It was despicable."

"You're absolutely right. Maybe I can make it up to you. How about if I get Anna Pavlova to tutor Jake? She's an angel and has taught the Tsarevich how to *en pointe*. I could have her visit you on Saturday. Let's say, 11 A.M. She could stay until 2. Then, she has to prepare to perform in Rimsky-Korsakov's *Le Coq d'Or* at His Majesty's Theater at eight."

Wendy hesitated. Otto knew it was time to reel her in. "Listen, you can use my tickets, my box is just off to the right of the stage, on Saturday as well. With dinner at the Ritz on my tab," he pleaded hopefully. She was lost in thought.

"This is their final performance before the troupe leaves London. I'll arrange for Anna to meet you and your guests backstage for a private photo shoot with Anna. The troupe photographer owes me a favor."

"OK, just promise me that the degenerate won't come anywhere near Jake or our party."

"You have my solemn guarantee. I will personally escort him out of the theater after the performance so that he will not even be on the premises when you go backstage. Miss Pavlova loves to teach the next generation. This will be a treat for her. And Wendy, thank you."

"No. *Thank you*, Otto."

From the roof of the Savoy Hotel, Vaslav could see Trafalgar Square and Buckingham Palace from one side and the Victoria Embankment and Westminster Abbey from the other side. London was slowly adapting to the electric light and the city was pleasantly lit. When he located the proper façade, he set down his duffel bag. He removed the theatrical harness and stepped into it. He adjusted it securely around his shoulders and crotch. The *Ballet Russe* had been innovating with the flying harness for quite some time. The custom-made leather straps had been contoured precisely for his physique to conceal the device under his costumes. He was used to heights and the idiosyncrasies of the device from his many performances in theaters around the world. To avoid a career-threatening injury or worse, his first rule was safety. After securing the rope around one of the brick chimneys and double-securing it to the iron handles set into the parapet for maintenance purposes, he clipped the end to the hook on his harness.

Double-checking his preparations, he slipped over the side. Deftly rappelling down the surface of the building, he was careful to stay in the shadows. The Savoy was the first hotel to be illuminated by electric lights, which was a mixed blessing. As long as he stayed in the shadows and away from lighted windows, he would be virtually invisible. He located the target room quickly.

The practice at the Savoy was to refresh the stale air in rooms by having the maids open the windows during the dinner hour. The Savoy was an innovator in protecting their customers from particulates emitted from smokestacks in the increasingly industrialized city, while at the same time protecting the expensive linens. To combat the growing scourge of soot and ash pollution, the maids inserted light screen filters into the open windows. When the maids returned to turn down the beds and deposit chocolate confectionaries embossed with the ubiquitous Savoy "S" on the fluffy pillows, the windows were closed and locked.

Nijinsky hung like a spider outside the window of Carlsund's suite peering in. When he was sure that it was unoccupied, he gracefully swung over to the window and lifted the sash so that he could enter. He placed the filter on the floor. Unhitching the harness, he opened his duffel bag and removed a syringe filled with white grains of digitalis that in ample dosage would slow the heart, causing death as if by heart attack.

Nijinsky crossed the room to the bar and injected the syringe into the cork of a bottle of merlot that rested on the counter. He removed the syringe and a sliver of cork from the needle; then he re-injected the syringe and pushed the white grains into the bottle.

Since he was ahead of schedule, he searched the room. Figuring that Carlsund would be too drunk to notice, Nijinsky riffled through the suite. He found engineering drawings for the next generation diesel engine and, as a bonus, lifted several hundred-pound notes from an open suitcase. He made his way back to the window, surveyed the scene for any anomalies and, seeing none, strapped on his harness. As he stepped up to the window sill, he heard raucous laughter of a man and a woman stumbling down the corridor.

Nijinsky swung out the window and began to pull himself to the roof when he remembered that he had forgotten to replace the filter. Realizing that the open window might be suspicious without the filter, he crouched outside the window and reached in with his free hand feeling around for the filter. His heart was racing as he heard fumbling and cursing at the door as the drunken guest and his consort struggled to get the door open. Just as Nijinsky pulled the filter into place, the door opened and Carlsund barged in.

A gust of wind rose up and dislodged the filter knocking it into the room. Carlsund froze, listened, then lurched over to the window and put his head and torso out searching for what, he did not know, but suddenly his antennae were aroused. After an interminable few moments, Tasha urged him to come back in and keep her warm. Since his antennae were not as strong as another part of him that was aroused, he complied.

Meanwhile, Nijinsky hung suspended above the open window, hugging the brick façade as motionless as if he were on stage after his final scene. Although his motionless pose was not followed by rousing applause, he felt the same satisfying rush of a performance well done.

The next morning the hotel lobby was abuzz with the news of the death by apparent heart attack of the affable Swedish engineer. Based on the temperature of the corpse, the hotel physician, Miles Cavendish, announced the cause of death to be from natural causes and estimated the time of death as probably between 5 and 6 AM. Tasha, the escort, was discreetly removed from the scene by hotel security and her presence was omitted from Dr. Cavendish's report. In keeping with Savoy Hotel efficiency, the suite was ready for occupancy later that afternoon.

1914
St. Petersburg, Russia

All saints were sinners once. God loves sinners.

~ Grigory Efimovich Rasputin

Rasputin left the Winter Palace feeling buoyant. The Tsarina's indiscreet letter was a forgotten memory and he was back in the Tsar's good graces. At the Tsar's insistence, he had treated the migraines of Emanuel Nobel. Despite their apparent differences, or, maybe because of them, Rasputin and Nobel had developed a mutual bond. Nobel was intrigued by Rasputin's mystical world view that was so different from his own analytical mind, and Rasputin was attracted to the wealthy and powerful.

Recently, Nobel had confided that he was upset over several setbacks. First, was the untimely death of one of his closest advisers. Emanuel suspected foul play, but there was no evidence to support his suspicion. Second, the Tsar had recognized the Russian General Oil Company. When Grigory heard that his new friend's rival had been put forth by Otto Kahn, he bristled. Rasputin despised the smug, little German, suspecting his complicity in various nefarious events. Although he could not identify any specifics, his intuition told him that Kahn was trouble.

At that afternoon's healing session with the Tsar, Rasputin had manipulated not only Nicholas' cranium, but his resolve on maintaining Branobel's concessions in Baku. Almost as if under post-hypnotic suggestion, the Tsar informed Minister Bark that he had reconsidered the role of the Russian General Oil Company and decided to rescind its concessions until further notice. When informed of the Tsar's reversal concerning the Russian General Oil Company and Branobel, Minister Bark dreaded the prospect of informing Kahn of how the peasant had thwarted his plans.

Rasputin was in a celebratory mood when he met his devotees for, what he liked to call, 'collective healing.' His group entered *The Mad Monk* vodka den, a curiously Russian establishment, greeting Ivan the proprietor with a cacophony of raucous shouts and salutations mingled with a few expletives. As they wove their way through the dark warren of rooms to one near the rear exit, Rasputin clamped his heavy paw on the shoulder of his companion, Nadya, and held her close. The partiers doffed their outerwear and shuffled onto benches encircling a broad, flat center table that would soon be overladen with bowls of smoked sturgeon, salt herring, *priazhenie* (shallow fried stuffed meat buns), sausages, sour cucumbers and gunmetal gray Beluga caviar, supplemented with baskets of dense black bread and a condiment caddy with jars of pungent white horseradish, *chrein*, bright horseradish purple with beets, sour cream and Brassica nigra, black mustard.

But first, the drink. Ivan's wife, Olga, trundled in with four bottles of good Russian vodka and, for the less adventurous, a bottle of Medovukha, a sweet, low-alcohol drink, made with fermented-honey and various spices. *Cmonkas*, Russian 100 ml glasses, were passed around the table and quickly filled. She knew that when Father Grigory came to *The Mad Monk,* he and his companions were capable of consuming enormous quantities of food and drink.

The walls of the room were lined with weathered pine and lit by smoky oil lamps that were set low. Rasputin passed around the clean white plates to his group and began to pile food onto his dish. He thrust a stiff, white napkin into the collar of his emerald-green, silk poet shirt, gulped down a glass of vodka and shoveled a steaming *priazhenie* into his mouth. He wore several gold rings studded with precious stones that had been gifts from his numerous wealthy and influential followers. Over the last few years, his reputation for healing and prophecy had grown immensely. He could be witty and charming, especially with the ladies. He owed much of his ascendant prestige to the Black Princesses, Stana and Militza.

This evening's frivolities had been organized by Stana, who invited her friends Ekaterina, Sonja and Enya. Sonja had brought her younger brother, Ilya, a gangly engineering student from the University. Stana, a social climber who was in her mid-thirties, fancied herself a confidante of the Tsarina. In actuality, her influence was waning in direct proportion to the rise of Anya Vyrubova's influence with Alexandra. Stana was thin, raven-haired and had a petite china-doll quality with dark, delicate features and luminous brown eyes. She exuded the look of a pampered noblewoman, cultured and refined. Her expensive, brocade blouse in a green and yellow harlequin pattern, was open at the throat revealing a green velvet choker that held a large gold crucifix outlined with sparkling diamonds. She brushed crumbs off her black, wool ankle-length skirt and brandished a vodka bottle, splashing the clear liquid into the empty cmonka of her sister, Militza.

The elder sister, in her mid-forties, wore heavy pancake make-up to mask a poor complexion that was damaged in childhood by measles and acne. What she lacked in looks compared to her sister, she made up in intelligence. Though her features were coarser and her appearance frumpier than Stana's, Militza had a quick, powerful, analytical mind that beamed through her dark eyes. Her gaze matched Rasputin's in intensity and hypnotic quality. With a hint of bemusement on her face, she sat watching the holy man manipulate the gathering. She thought to herself that Stana and her friends had no idea of the power that Rasputin possessed.

As she sipped her vodka, Militza regarded the remaining guests. The gypsies, Mischa and Zimran, were, well, gypsies, quick to seize an opportunity for free food, drink and merriment. Nadya, on the other hand, was an interesting specimen. Rasputin had mentioned that she was a French baroness, who had travelled to St. Petersburg to experience it before the outbreak of, what the instigators were calling 'the war to end all wars.' She claimed to be a recent widow and was slightly past being young. Nevertheless, she had captivating dark, green eyes and an attractive come-hither smile that no doubt had enticed Rasputin when he met her earlier in the day at St. Isaac's Cathedral. Her Bohemian-style clothing, with its sashes, bangles and scarves, was belied by the luxurious quality of the fabrics and tailoring.

Despite her attempt to look plebian, this was a woman who came from money, thought Militza, as one who knew.

Nadya wore her long, blue-black hair straight, with bangs that rested just above her carefully manicured eyebrows. She had tawny skin and the gaunt cheeks of a professional dancer. Her tall, willowy figure had curves in the right places. Rasputin fondled her hip possessively when he wasn't gesticulating wildly or gorging on Olga's feast. She reciprocated by placing her free hand in his lap.

Rasputin rose to his feet and proposed a toast. He rambled on about the 'winds of war' that threatened to engulf civilization. He expressed his fear that a war among European nations would leave Russia grievously wounded. He recounted how past wars had wreaked devastation on the people, but if war came again, no one, not even the nobility — especially not the nobility — would escape without sorrow and death. Uttering an obscure Siberian proverb, he concluded, "The week that Russia suffers best, is the week that Russia suffers most."

Seeing Olga pass the room on her way to the kitchen, Nadya took the opportunity to follow her. Militza saw them converse briefly and Nadya continue to the lady's water closet. When she returned she was carrying a *panchachilam*, a five-pipe hookah, whose base was filled with an amber liquid. Nadya placed the vessel in the center of the table and then placed a rough cube of resinous, brown, silver-flecked material in each of the five marble bowls. Olga was right behind her with a cast iron container and tongs. She placed a slightly, concave metal screen over each bowl that she deftly filled with a burning coal. Militza looked at her watch and announced that it was time for her to leave; otherwise, she would never be on time for her appointment the next day.

"Don't go now, sister, the party is just beginning," implored Stana.

"I must go. Pyotr is waiting for me and I have a very important meeting first thing. Sorry."

Goodbyes and air kisses were exchanged as Militza departed.

While the group partook of the hookah, Olga cleared the table and replenished the food with an assortment of confections. Russian tea cakes, beze cookies, *blinchiki* and *oladi* served with a variety of jams and creams were laid out on the table along with more vodka. After the desserts were washed down with the fiery liquor and the group indulged more on the pipes, a blue, dreamy haze engulfed them.

In a scratchy voice, Stana asked Rasputin to relate his experiences. He started with his life as a peasant boy of nine or ten when his sister, Maria, drowned in front of him and later how his older brother, Dmitry, fell into the same icy river and Rasputin had rescued him, only to watch him succumb to a painful death due to pneumonia. Rasputin wept as he related how these events turned him into an angry, rebellious child who drank, fought and stole, until he had brought so much shame to his family that his father disowned him.

The Starets told how for years he wandered aimlessly over the steppes, going from settlement to settlement until he reached the monastery of Verkhoturye where he encountered Makariy. There, he learned a form of asceticism that resonated with his tortured soul. He explained the dual nature of man, spirit and flesh, and how, only by practicing "holy passionlessness," could one achieve union with God. Only by debasing and exhausting the flesh was it possible to experience the Divine through repentance.

Rasputin related how he joined a communal group called the *Novyi Vek* (People of the New Age). The *Novyi Vek* alternated between living chaste, holy lives, "in the Spirit," and unlimited debauchery. With the haze of alcohol and hashish floating through her head, Nadya asked him to elaborate on the meaning of 'holy passionlessness.'

"It is better to show, than to explain," said Rasputin, his eyes glowing maniacally.

"Olga, Show us to the Lower Room. We go to debasement!"

Olga led them down a narrow hallway to the stairs down. She lit a fire in a large, stone fireplace that dominated the far wall. Within minutes a roaring fire crackled, hissed and emitted a rush of firefly sparks up the wide chimney. Searing warmth enveloped the chamber.

From his satchel, Father Grigory carefully removed a prayer rug that had been given to him by Shamir of Tunguska. With reverence, he unrolled the rectangular rug in the center of the room, illuminated by the primal fire. The surface of the symmetrically knotted carpet was thick, woolen pile. The field consisted of a pattern of squares depicting fantastical garden scenes of blossoming trees and elegant floral bouquets. The wide border was decorated with elaborate lotus meanders and spiraling vines of wisteria racemes.

Mischa, the gypsy, followed down the worn, wooden steps, her thick-soled leather boots thumping noisily. At forty, she carried a few too many pounds from celebrating life's many joys. Her face was a study in olive and black — her skin serving as the field for her prominent black eyes under thick black eyebrows and a whisper of fuzz shading her upper lip. Tuning her balalaika, she assumed the practiced smile of a seasoned entertainer.

Her younger brother, Zimran, descended the steep stairs with a bulky accordion case that jounced off his knee. He had a portly build and was wearing coarse, black pants and a burgundy-red shirt under a black leather vest that looked like it had not been buttoned since the turn of the century.

Stana, Nadya and the others followed, carrying more vodka and glasses. Mischa sang a slow, plaintive song about the plight of her people as they search for a homeland. Next, was a heart-rending song about two lovers from different clans who experienced the torture of love unrequited. As she continued with melancholy songs, Rasputin prayed for grace and the presence of the Spirit so they could achieve spiritual ecstasy through *radeniya*, rituals. Clapping their hands and clacking their tongues, the gypsies quickened the tempo.

As if on cue, Rasputin rose to dance. The others followed his lead and they all gyrated to the pagan beat. As the tempo quickened, the dancers followed and alternately hugged the nearest dancer, or twirled them frantically. The fire roared and the heat increased. Soon articles of clothing were shed and more vodka was consumed. Nadya pulled several tablets from her pocket and after inserting one in her mouth, kissed Rasputin, easing the tablet into his mouth. His eyes widened momentarily. He washed it down with a swig of vodka. Nadya danced with renewed fervor and gyrated sensuously. She repeated the kiss with each of the group. In the center of the room, Rasputin stood like a maypole, shirtless, arms outstretched.

The flames grew higher and the scene took on the aura of the Garden of Innocence, with spirits circling the flame of temptation. The music pounded a Romani cadence. The light of the blaze reflected off their glistening bodies that shone with sweat and passion. The gypsies accelerated the beat. Rasputin began whirling like a dervish, spinning and spinning with an unexpected gracefulness, as if transformed into an ancient spirit. The others mimicked his frenzy and soon the room was a blur of bodies, spinning and pulsing to the wild music. They danced before him in a never-ending circle, lifting and twirling as they cavorted with and around him. Shouts of joy and delirium punctuated the air; more clothes were stripped to allow the flesh to breath. Ilya and Ekaterina fell to a heap and began copulating. Grigory and Nadya were next, desperately caressing and kissing each other. Stana and Sonja and Enya groped and slithered among the naked bodies as the group became one pulsating orgasmic mass. And the gypsies played.

Later, it was quiet except for rhythmic breathing. The fire had burned to a heap of embers, emitting a comforting orange glow. He stifled a chill by pulling the prayer rug over him. He felt the pulse in his temples and the blood coursing through his head. His eyes were bloodshot, pupils dilated as they opened to see the world on its side. With the scratchy fibers of the prayer rug rubbing against his ear, he succumbed to Morpheus. Exhausted, repentance would have to wait.

1914

Tsarskoe Selo, Russia

Don't pray when it rains if you don't pray when the sun shines.

~ SATCHEL PAIGE

So THAT SHE COULD BE AT the Tsarina's beck-and-call, day or night, Anya lived in a cottage right outside the walls of the Tsar's village where the Tsarina and her family lived. Anya had proven to be a steadfast friend and loyal aide to the children. Like a momma grizzly defending her cubs, Anya protected them from officious intermeddlers and fawning sycophants. More than once, she had brandished a broomstick to ward away the unwelcome or the malicious. In return, the Empress rewarded her with unimaginable access and candor. Over the last several years, Anya had risen to such a position of trust that she was included in every family vacation.

Alix frequently visited Anya's modest home to avoid the intense scrutiny of the Court. The bond between the women was cemented by their passion for mystical writings. They shared ancient books about legendary Slavic mystics, who guided Russian leaders through wars, plagues and heresies. Alix was particularly intrigued by *dvoeverie* (double faith) that posited

144

that the original religious beliefs of the Slavic people were subsumed into Christianity. She thought this would help her to understand her people.

When Father Grigory thumped the heavy brass knocker on Anya's door, he was greeted by Anya's younger sister Sana, Alexandra Pistolkors *nee* Taneyev. Rasputin had heard Sana described as Anya's clone *"with the little porcelain face."*[19] He marveled at the accuracy of that description. Her delicate round face was a miniature version of Anya's to the point where considering their faces alone, they could have been identical twins. Aside from that, however, Sana was the polar opposite of Anya. She had a completely different frame than Anya. If Anya was a cow, Sana was a fawn. If Anya was tall, Sana was diminutive. If Anya was laconic, Sana was gregarious. If Anya was naïve, Sana was savvy. If Anya was reserved and stolid, Sana was flamboyant and flighty.

"Ah, Father Grigory, I was hoping that you would arrive before I left. Please come in."

She ushered him over to the sofa and sat next to him. The furnishings were simple and inexpensive, much like the furnishings in Rasputin's home in rural Pokrovskoe. He could hear Anya bustling in the kitchen. She was probably preparing tea and the small sardine and onion sandwiches on pumpernickel that she knew were his favorite. Rasputin thought affectionately that Anya truly had a servant's heart just like Martha and that Sana was like Mary, the other sister in the Gospel of Luke.

"I have a friend who desperately needs your help. She was in love with a young man who recently met his demise. It seems that this young man was unfaithful to her and had taken a lover behind her back. Unfortunately for him, his lover was married to a military officer who challenged him to a duel and killed him. Now, she is so distraught that she wants to go to a nunnery. Her mother is beside herself. Would you counsel my friend, please?"

Although Sana had omitted names, Rasputin was familiar with all the identities, save one. It had been the scandal of the season. Nikolai Yusopov, the oldest son and heir to the largest fortune in Russia, had been caught *in flagrante delicto* with Countess Marina Heiden, who was married to Count Mantifel of the Imperial Horse Guards. To avenge his honor, the Count shot and killed Nikolai. There were rumors that Nikolai's younger brother, Felix, deliberately refused to intercede to save his brother from certain death. Felix had reportedly told friends that, *"The thought of becoming one of the richest people in Russia intoxicated me."*[20]

Based on Sana's remarks, what had escaped public knowledge was that simultaneously with his affair with the Countess, Nikolai had been involved with another woman. She was the person whose identity was unknown to Rasputin. The monk was quickly learning that the Russian aristocracy was rife with infidelity, depravity and corruption. He never ceased to be amazed at the depth of St. Petersburg's human cesspool.

"Of course, I would be most willing to lend my meager talents to the service of your friend," the monk replied.

"Excellent," said Sana. "I will arrange a dinner for tomorrow evening. Are you available?"

"I will make myself available. Would you be so kind as to tell me the young woman's name?"

"Oh, right. How silly of me. My friend is Maria Golovina. We call her 'Munya.' She is the niece of Olga Alexandrovich, who as you may know is the wife of Grand Duke Pavel, the uncle to the Tsar. As it happens in this incestuous city, I'm married to Olga's son Alexander. Munya and I have become close friends since my wedding.

"Father, I really appreciate this. Munya is in such a state that I fear for her. I will call you when I have made the arrangements for tomorrow. Thanks. I've got to run. Until tomorrow," Sana said as she rushed out the door.

Father Grigory turned to Anya with a shrug as if to say, all in a day's work for a busy cleric. While Rasputin and Anya prayed together, the Tsarina's carriage pulled up to Anya's house.

The attendant gracefully extended his white-gloved hand to assist the Tsarina as she disembarked.

Anya rushed to the door, her face beaming with surprise and joy. Alexandra smiled and reached to accept Anya's hands. They exchanged double air-kisses, European style, and proceeded into the house arms entwined. Father Grigory bowed in his clumsy peasant manner. Alix gestured that it was permissible to be seated. The Tsarina handed Anya a present that Anya unwrapped as quickly as a child on Christmas morning. When she saw that it was *The Secret Doctrine* by Madame Blavatsky, the celebrated Russian author and mystic, Anya gushed with gratitude.

"How is your little Sunbeam, Your Highness?" Father Grigory asked.

Seated on an armchair, the Empress faced Rasputin with her hands in her lap toying with a lace handkerchief bearing her monogram in fine, teal thread and embroidered along the edges in a red filigree pattern. Her face was devoid of make-up and her blonde tresses were tucked under a brightly patterned silk scarf. There were shadows under her blue eyes, evidencing another night of little sleep.

"He's fine, thank you, Father. Last night during his evening prayers, he asked God to keep you strong."

"Tell him thanks and that I will visit him soon, Your Highness permitting."

"Of course, just make arrangements through Anya. You are always welcome."

The Starets sensed Alix's anxiety; yet, if it was not the Tsarevich, what was it? He suggested that they engage in communal meditation. Anya drew the heavy drapes together and lit several saffron-colored candles that suffused the room in a tawny light. Meanwhile, Rasputin removed an enameled tin and weathered brass thurible from his satchel. From the tin, he piously spooned a brown viscous concoction of finely-ground frankincense, eucalyptus oil, aloe and various aromatics into the thurible. He placed a lit coal inside and fragrant smoke curled out of the thurible. Father Grigory swung it in cadence with his harmonic humming. The tiny brass bells attached to the censer tinkled metallically, providing a counterpoint to the monk's chant.

They knelt in a circle and leaned their heads forward until their fore-heads touched. With their eyes closed, Father Grigory muttered prayers of peace and serenity. He reminded them of the words of the Savior, who promised that wherever two or more believers are gathered, He is present. The monk beseeched them to unburden their souls so that Jesus could take up their load. There was a lengthy period of silence with each participant lost in her own thoughts.

Finally, Alix spoke. Her voice choking with emotion, she begged the Lord to protect her daughter, Olga, and eradicate evil from her betrothed, Prince Dmitry. The distraught mother implored the Lord to give Dmitry the strength to resist the temptations of impure relations with other males. That prayer hung in the air like a menacing thundercloud on a humid, crackling-hot summer afternoon.

As they prayed, Rasputin reminded himself that Olga, the oldest daughter of Nicholas and Alexandra, had recently betrothed Prince Dmitry Pavlovich, who, as the son of the Tsar's uncle, was Nicholas' first cousin. Dmitry was close friends with Felix Yusopov. Rasputin's head throbbed as he tried to sort out all the relationships. However, the one constant, the one whose web was the center of all this human tragedy and duplicity was Prince Felix.

As he left the Golovina mansion on the Winter Canal, Rasputin concluded that the evening had gone well. He had dined with the Golovinas. Munya's father was the Imperial Chamberlain, in charge of managing the royal household. Her mother, Lyubov Valerianovna, was a gracious hostess and doting mother. Munya had been a delightful dinner companion. Her flaxen hair fell limply onto her prominent forehead. Her irises were sky blue, rimmed with a distinctive, darker blue. In her demeanor, he detected an inordinate willingness to please. He surmised how she could be easily manipulated by a philanderer like Nikolai Yusopov.

Rasputin and Munya had retired to a drafty sitting room. They faced each other on a silk brocade divan and prayed for God's grace. She confessed her despair at Nikolai's death and her recurrent dreams of lying on his cold gravestone in the snow while surrounded by snarling wolves. Munya related another dream in which she was running through the fog toward the duelists only to arrive too late as Nikolai is shot at point blank range. In that dream, he dies in her arms, as his life faded. His last words were, "Munya, I never knew . . . ." She was haunted by her unrequited love. Through her tears, she explained to Rasputin that she had lost her will to live and wanted to spend her life locked away in a convent.

The monk consoled her by advising that tragedy comes to everyone and that life must go on. He counseled her that one may serve God anywhere and that it was not God's will for her to make such a drastic change. God had a plan for her life and she should not be so arrogant as to deny God's plan. She questioned him about God's plan for Nikolai and the monk responded that God had a plan for each person. He explained that Nikolai's plan was not the same as her plan, just as her plan was not Rasputin's plan. He counseled her to move past Nikolai and live the plan that God had made uniquely for her. Munya nodded silently.

Rasputin had a great thirst when he left the Golovina house so he took a cab to *Troika,* a nightclub where he hoped to encounter some of his dissolute friends. The doorman gave him an impudent look as he opened the large oak door. Father Grigory took no notice; he was too busy adjusting from Father Grigory, the holy man, to Grishka, the fool.

The club was crowded and noisy. He found himself a spot along the bar and ordered a mug of *Sibirskaja Korona,* Siberian Crown beer. While he surveyed the crowd, the band returned to the stage and began playing a spirited *mazurka.* Several couples moved to the dance floor and began gyrating to the music.

At a table in the far corner, he spied Prince Dmitry Pavlovich, seated with an attractive, dark-haired young woman. Dmitry was a handsome young aristocrat with the typical Romanov condescension born of a life of privilege. His long, sandy brown hair was combed straight back. He had a pleasing aquiline nose between wide-set, ocean-blue eyes. His thin, pencil moustache was a complement to his fair eyebrows and lashes, giving him a slightly epicene look. He wore a navy blue sports jacket with gold buttons that was exquisitely tailored to highlight his wiry, athletic physique. A white shirt with paisley cravat, pleated black slacks and black patent leather half-boots completed his cosmopolitan look.

Dmitry was the son of Grand Duke Pavel Alexandrovich, the Tsar's uncle. His mother had lapsed into a coma while giving him life, dying soon after. The old man had scandalized the hardly pristine Romanovs by notoriously cavorting around the capital with a married woman, Olga Valerianovna Pistolkors. The scandal was not so much that he impregnated her while his wife was in a coma and they shamelessly flaunted their relationship, but, rather, that she was of common birth. The Romanovs could marry their close relatives and have blatant extramarital affairs of every ilk; but openly having sexual relations with a commoner was beyond the pale. The Romanovs were so outraged by the Grand Duke's behavior that the Tsar banished the couple and their bastard child, Vladimir, to Paris. The young Dmitry was taken in by his uncle, Grand Duke Sergei. Unfortunately, Sergei was murdered while the lad was still a teenager. After Sergei's death, Nicholas and Alexandra raised Dmitry. Now, he was engaged to their daughter, the Grand Duchess Olga, and his relationship with the decadent Felix Yusopov boy was a matter of grave concern.

In a dim corner of the *Troika,* Prince Dmitry sat with his arm around a ravishing, young thing, who showered obvious affection on the handsome nobleman. She wore the stylish make-up of a wealthy dilettante that highlighted her fine features and shapely cheekbones. As Rasputin watched, she placed her hand on Dmitry's cheek, drawing his face toward hers and passionately kissed him while his hands explored her body. Their jaws widened as the kiss progressed and Rasputin felt a tingle in his groin. He found himself openly staring at the erotic embrace. When they came up for air, she adjusted the bodice of her strapless, black gown. Rasputin could have sworn that he caught a wink and impish smile aimed directly at him. He gulped down his beer and ordered a bottle of vodka and three cmonkas. He poured himself a shot, downed it, refilled his glass and drank another.

He watched as Dmitry's companion excused herself and headed to the ladies room carrying a small, bejeweled clutch. With lascivious eyes, he followed her shapely figure as she sashayed toward him. She was of medium build with narrow hips and attractive breasts tugging at the fabric, as if straining to be free. Her cherry-red lipstick was smeared slightly and her light brown eyes sparkled flirtatiously, as she came next to him. His eyes bore yearningly into hers and she winked at him, again, tittering coyly. Then, she was past him, entering the crowded hallway to the restrooms.

On several of his visits to Tsarkoe Selo, Rasputin had met Dmitry and they had conversed about sundry military matters. Rasputin decided to act on this opportunity. Rounding up his bottle and glasses, he walked toward Prince Dmitry. The Prince saw him and gave him a welcoming smile, gesturing at an empty chair for Rasputin to join him. The monk sat down and offered the Prince a drink. They raised their glasses to Mother Russia and tossed back healthy shots. A man at the adjacent table repeated the toast and they downed some more vodka. Rasputin bellowed to a passing waiter to bring another bottle.

Rasputin turned to Dmitry and stared deeply into his blue eyes. Rasputin told him of his meeting with the Tsarina who had expressed her concern over the rumors of Dmitry's homosexual escapades. Rasputin asked him to consider the reputation of his betrothed and the sensibilities of the royal couple. Dmitry nodded seriously as his eyes lifted to follow his companion as she neared their table. Rasputin felt a familiar rush below his stomach and gulped down another vodka.

"Grishka, this is Felicia, my dear, dear friend. Felicia, this is Grigory Rasputin, who we affectionately call Grishka," said Dmitry, clapping playfully on Rasputin's shoulder. They all laughed.

"It's a pleasure to meet you, Grishka," Felicia giggled in a honey-soaked voice.

Grishka half rose, wobbling slightly, as Felicia sat down between him and Dmitry. Dmitry poured drinks for all and proceeded to explain that Rasputin was the Tsarina's confessor and had shared with Dmitry her concern about his "mistakes in grammar." This was the nobility's code phrase for homosexual activity that was to be used in polite company. Felicia's eyes widened in shock and she exclaimed to Rasputin, "Tell the Tsarina that she doesn't have to worry about this one, he's all male." Saying this, she dropped her hand into Dmitry's lap and gave him a succulent kiss on the lips.

The man in the table adjacent to them gave out an encouraging cheer for the duration of the lengthy kiss. Rasputin sat with some embarrassment at the public display of passion. At last the kiss ended. Prince Dmitry took a deep breath and stood. He adjusted his trousers and headed for the men's room, muttering his excuses. Felicia turned to Grishka baby, as she called him. She poured more vodka and toasted to his health. Her lashes fluttered seductively, as she leaned toward him and whispered, "I've never made love to a peasant before. What's it like?"

Rasputin grabbed her by the wrist and said, "Let's dance, my Little One."

She willingly complied and frolicked around the floor with him to the beat of a folk dance. The tempo slowed for the next ballad and Felicia draped herself against him moving her hips suggestively. Her hand brushed against the buttons of his trousers and he was aroused. She whispered for him to follow her into the corner so she could take care of him. Almost blind with lust, he walked behind her fondling her taut *derriere*. Face to face now, he cupped her breasts.

"The suns are real, the darkness is fake," she whispered. In the dim light, she fumbled with his front buttons. His hand squirmed up her dress and he stopped, startled. Her eyes laughed as they met his, now panicked, saucer-like, in amazed comprehension. She reached over her head and yanked off her wig, giggling maniacally.

"You ignorant *muhjik*! Can't you tell Felix from Felicia?"

Rasputin was mortified. With his right hand he slapped Prince Felix hard across the jaw. Suddenly, the drunk from the next table grabbed Rasputin from behind and lost his balance. They both tumbled to the floor.

Rasputin watched as Felix hurried away, catching Dmitry by the arm, and exiting the nightclub, guffawing uncontrollably.

1914
St. Petersburg, Russia

I have been a stranger in a strange land.

~ EXODUS 2:22

SINCE HIS MEETING was not until 10 PM, Chorney spent his first day in St. Petersburg strolling around the city, marveling at its architecture. He was glad he was wearing the garb of a Russian factory worker with a tunic-style shirt and a peaked cap that enabled him to blend in with the locals. After the confines of the steamer, he relished the idea of walking around the center of this impressive city.

He used the golden spire atop the iconic Admiralty building as his reference point. The original building had been constructed in 1704 during the reign of Peter the Great. It started as a fortified shipyard and evolved into its present use, the home of the Ministry of the Navy and a Naval Museum. Radiating out from the front of the Admiralty like the spikes of Neptune's trident, were three of the grand boulevards of the city, the Nevsky Prospekt, the Gorokhovaya Utilsa and Vosnesensky Prospekt.

At the base of the Admiralty tower was a majestic arch that was bounded by Alexandrovsky Garden, named after the slain Tsar Alexander

II. Chorney was relaxed as he ambled across the sun-dappled paths lined by abundant flower beds. His gaze was attracted to the gilded cupola atop a colonnade of red granite that marked St. Isaac's Cathedral. The cathedral had been the seat of the Russian Orthodox Church for the last half century. He entered the portico of solid, red, granite columns and made his way to the stairway that led to the base of the dome. His legs rebelled mildly as he double-timed up the three-hundred steps to the observation level. There, he admired the panorama, mentally marking landmarks that might serve him in the future.

He headed toward Griboyedova Canal, one of the many canals that gave the city the moniker "The Venice of the North." The city had been built on marshland and islands in the delta of the Neva River where it enters the Gulf of Finland. After driving out the Kingdom of Sweden, Peter the Great recognized the strategic importance of the site and established St. Petersburg in 1704. It had been the capital of Russia for over two centuries.

As Chorney turned left at the canal, he spotted the Church of the Savior on the Spilled Blood in the distance. It was built to memorialize the location of the mortal attack on Tsar Alexander II in 1881. Its gilded and enameled domes glittered in the afternoon light. The domes rested on Estonian marble colonnades much like Fabergé eggs on display perches. Some were gilded, while others were fantastical enameled domes that were brightly colored and spiral-shaped with brilliant white studs tracking the upward curves. The central steeple was topped with an elegant sky-blue and white spiral bulb beneath a gold cross.

Chorney imagined himself as a knight approaching a colorful, mystical castle on a quest for the Grail. Entering this unique house of worship, he was entranced by the colors coming from the intricately detailed mosaics and painted icons of biblical scenes that adorned every surface of the majestic, yet, sepulchral interior.

His growling stomach reminded him that he had not eaten all day. He glanced at his watch and saw that it was almost eight PM. There was still bright sunshine streaming into the church as if it were midday. He had been warned about the 'White Nights,' but had never experienced the odd sensation of sunshine day and night. He decided to get some food at the nearby Yeliseyevsky Delicatessen and Emporium and eat his dinner in the park designated for his meeting.

Chorney sat on a bench adjacent to the *Bronze Horseman* and spread out his repast on his lap. Smacking his lips, he dug into the luscious food and devoured it. Kurt savored the bucolic scene before him. The park was filled with families with children picnicking, couples relaxing on blankets and vendors pushing carts loaded with pickles and *pelmeni* and all manner of dumplings.

The young officer was lost in thought when he was engulfed in a shadow. A large, black man stood before him. He had a massive chest that tapered to a trim waist. His broad neck supported a regal head befitting an African prince that was his ancestor. The man asked whether Kurt knew the tram schedule. On cue, Chorney responded with a question as to whether the inquiry referred to the electric tram or the horse-drawn tram. A meaty, black hand reached for him. He rose and grasped the proffered hand.

"Pasha Kelly."

"Kurt Chorney, nice to meet you."

"I see that you are becoming infatuated with this fair city. The same thing happened to me. I came here ten years ago with a team that secretly delivered the U.S. submarine *Fulton* to the Imperial Russian Navy. I loved St. Petersburg so much that I inquired to the brass about opportunities here. I was trained by ONI, learned Russian, and agreed to go undercover with a job on the Imperial family's security force. We are required to wear ridiculous Araby uniforms; but, other than that, the work is good. We work primarily on ceremonial occasions, you know, balls and state dinners. The thing of it is, the parasitic aristocracy here is so arrogant that they think of us as big, dumb statues. That works to our advantage. You would not believe the things we see and hear. Which brings me to the subject of our meeting: The Monocle."

Chorney applied spirit gum and set the moustache in place. He adjusted his wire-rimmed glasses and fedora. A brown, herringbone suit made him look like a university professor. Holding a dog-eared copy of Dostoyevsky's *Crime and Punishment*, Chorney ambled across the hotel lobby toward the breakfast café. Spotting the Monocle at a table near the window, Kurt asked the *maître d'hôtel* for a nearby table. A leafy fern shielded him from direct view by his prey.

Otto was joined by a thin, young man in a tightly-fitted velvet jacket and sharkskin pants. His black hair was plastered back. Despite a powdery attempt to conceal it, a red bruise, shaped faintly like a handprint, showed on his left cheek. Otto stood to welcome his guest and Kurt overheard concern and sympathy in the older man's voice. Trying not to appear conspicuous, Chorney leaned back, pretending to read his book.

The younger man was animated in his speech and repeated that, ". . . he must be eliminated. I will not abide this humiliation."

Kahn reached across the table and pressed the Prince's hand, cautioning the younger man to view the problem dispassionately. Timing was critical. There was no room for error.

"Listen, Otto, this is my country. I know how to get things done. I have my own plan."

Felix continued, "Munya has told us that the fool is planning to return home to Siberia later this week. We have an operative who will engage a 'friend' to get rid of him once and for all."

"I don't need to know the details, but, I do need to know when, and where."

"I don't think either of us wants to know details. Suffice it to say that the *camarilla* will achieve a final solution before the end of June."

"Felix, there are things in the works that are dependent on success here. If the monk lives, he will persuade the Tsar to avoid war regardless of the provocation. This would be very expensive advice. We must make sure he is not around to give it."

"Trust me, there is no need to worry," Felix replied earnestly. "On the subject of finances, we could use a contribution of, . . . say, ten thousand rubles to guarantee success."

"I will make the arrangements, but my clients will want assurances."

"They will have them."

"There are other plans in play. Don't miss the target here."

"I won't," Felix vowed, his hand gently kneading his cheek.

Strafe put down his tuna on rye and stared at the two documents on his desk. Events were outpacing his ability to respond. He instinctively resented being in reactive mode. He much preferred being the initiator of actions; at least then he had some semblance of control. Chewing absently, he perused the report from Hank Bitterman. Based on his surveillance in London, there was reason to believe that something significant was afoot. There had been numerous meetings between the Monocle and Vaslav Nijinsky. Were those meetings innocent business meetings between impresario and talent, or something more nefarious? The "apparent" heart attack death of the Swedish businessman, coinciding with his high-stakes baccarat game with the Monocle, raised Oliver's suspicions. He would have to rely on the Brits to investigate and let him know about the death.

Feeling a migraine forming behind his right eye, Oliver opened a translation of an encrypted cable from Chorney in St. Petersburg. It recounted the breakfast conversation between the Monocle and Prince Yusopov. He was intrigued by the reference to "other plans in play" and felt vindicated in his decision to send Bitterman after Nijinsky. Bitterman had gone dark after arriving in Vienna and Strafe was worried.

He had a decision to make with respect to Chorney. Should he have the young officer follow Yusopov or Rasputin? He weighed different alternatives in his mind and concluded that Yusopov would not be so brazen as to act directly. If so, then Chorney would be in a better position if he followed the potential target. At least Kurt might observe a threat unfolding and be in position to act. Besides, *Okhrana* agents were watching Prince Felix. On balance, he concluded that their interests would be better served by having Chorney follow the Monk than by staying in St. Petersburg where ONI already had a presence. Strafe knew that Chorney would be challenged by the lack of reliable communications and constraints on his ability to blend in with the locals in the rural Siberian village of Pokrovskoe, but Oliver had limited options and a lot of faith in the young officer.

1914
Sarajevo

More than any other time in history, mankind faces a crossroads. One path leads to despair and utter hopelessness. The other, to total extinction. Let us pray we have the wisdom to choose correctly.

~ WOODY ALLEN, COMEDIAN AND WRITER.

THE GENTLEMAN DISEMBARKED from the London train and quietly scanned the departures board at Gare de Lyon station in Paris. His gaze settled on the track number for the train heading to Vienna. Although short, he carried himself with an erect, confident posture that created the impression of height beyond the reality. His bearing befit his affluent attire. His suit was impeccably tailored, with fashionably creased trousers that broke slightly above his white leather spats. Custom-made half boots, concealing a lift were polished to a high sheen. Nimbly handling a fashionable walnut cane, he strode through the concourse as if it were his personal garden.

A porter wheeling a large trunk of the sort used by theatrical troupes followed him closely. At track 19, he approached a conductor who instinctively snapped to attention to receive a distinguished personage. The porter presented tickets for passage in a sleeper car attached to a night train to Vienna, and the conductor obsequiously led the way.

The big train quickly picked up velocity as it left the urban environs of Paris and was soon gliding through the countryside heading toward the German border. The sky was a brilliant blue and formed a mottled umbrella over the emerald green of the new growth of the spring. An occasional split-wooden fence came into view. Numerous dairy cow herds dotted the landscape as if in homage to the reliance on butter and cream based sauces in their cuisine.

He whiled away the twenty-nine-hour trip by sleeping and exercising in his stateroom. As the train pulled into Vienna's *Westbahnhof* Station, he spotted his contact on the platform wearing a black trench coat and black fedora. He approached the man in black and asked, "I'm looking for Joseph Legend, do you know where I can find him?"

"He works at the Volksoper Wien on Wahringer Strausse. I can bring him to you tomorrow at 10 AM."

"Good, I'm staying at the Hotel Sacher. Here's my card."

Satisfied with the coded conversation, he departed for his hotel. Although it was after midnight, the clerk at the hotel greeted him in a cheery, professional manner.

"Welcome, Herr Steinnekker. Your suite is ready, and here is a message for you," he said, sliding an envelope across the green marble surface of the reception counter. Steinnekker opened it and smiled appreciatively. His host thought of everything.

"Our records reflect that you will be staying one night and your luggage is to be stored for several weeks and then you will return and stay in our Suite Royale until sometime in the fall. Please wire us if there is any adjustment in your plans. Have a good stay, Sir."

Within twenty minutes he was reclining on a bench in the hotel steam room enjoying the eucalyptus-scented humidity that suffused the white-and cobalt-tiled area. A slim, blond youth with delicate features entered through the hissing mist. He was wearing only a leather belt that held a jar of aromatic oil. For the next hour he did Vaslav's bidding with eager hands and lips.

"I trust your accommodations were satisfactory," said the pale, thin man in the anteroom of his suite.

"Most definitely. You, scoot," he whispered to the young consort, "Out through the maid's entrance. *Schnell.*" The thin man paid no attention to the blond boy skulking out the rear entrance of the suite.

Vaslav emerged from the bedroom in a plush terrycloth robe with a large, stylized "S" embroidered on the left chest. His hair was tousled and his eyes bloodshot.

"I have instructions for you to take to the Black Hand in Sarajevo."

"It is good to see you too, Maximillian," he said absently. Maximillian was Max Warburg, the chief of the Kaiser's intelligence service and, more important, the brother of Paul Warburg, a former senior partner at Otto's bank, and currently chair of the Federal Reserve Bank. Max wore a three-piece, charcoal pinstriped suit that made him look like the banker he was. His face was thin, with a smartly-trimmed moustache that helped to hide slightly buckteeth. A prominent cleft creased his rather weak chin. He wore gold wire-rimmed glasses that were too small for his face, giving him a decidedly feminine appearance. Max's hands, pink and delicate, fluttered to open a large manila envelope and withdraw a map that he unfolded on the dining area table.

"You will have to memorize the route of the Archduke," he said, while tracing his finger along the surface of the map.

"He and his wife Sophie will be departing from here on the 27th of June. They will proceed to Sarajevo. The Archduke will inspect the airfield at 1030 hours, then proceed along this road through the city, attend a reception with the fool of a mayor, and then proceed to the municipal museum before travelling to field headquarters at the base of the mountains. The royal party will be in an open Gräf & Stift tourer. According to our sources, the road into the city is wide open, but they might be travelling too fast for a clean shot. Perhaps a diversion on the road to slow them down would work. However, the Archduke's security detail is meticulous about time and will divert if there is the slightest alteration in their schedule. The best opportunity will be in the city where the narrow streets and sharp angles will require the convoy to slow down. Once the royals are in the headquarters' compound they will be unassailable. The Black Hand commander on the ground will have to make the necessary tactical decisions. Your job is to transmit this crucial routing and timing information."

They reviewed the map and Steinnekker made notes about security measures. Max checked his watch and warned, "You are completely solo on this mission. You will destroy your notes. Once this plan goes operational, the border will be extremely hot. If you are compromised in any way, we cannot, and will not, help you."

"Understood," replied Steinnekker, jeering and giving Max a mock salute. Max glowered and snatched the notes from Steinnekker's hands and stuffed them in his pocket. The German folded the map and offered his right hand.

"Here are five thousand marks. Another ten thousand marks will be deposited in your account when the mission is successful. Good luck."

As the train slowed to a stop at the Central Train Station in Belgrade, he yanked his rucksack from the overhead rack. He was short of stature and his bland face was marked by a thick, dark moustache that spilled over his upper lip. There was a faded red bump of a scar across his left cheek just below his eye, the residue of a failure to react quickly enough to a beer bottle that was thrown at him by a disgruntled lover. His black working-man's cap was pulled low over his eyes and he hunched his shoulders as he shuffled off the train.

The "White City" as Belgrade was called, was on the Pannonian Basin nestled in the foothills of the Balkan Mountains. On a rise in the middle of the city was the Old Fortress. The Roman General Flavius had picked this spot overlooking the confluence of the Danube and Sava Rivers to defend the West from the marauding hordes from the East. For centuries, this area known as the Kingdom of Serbia had been the doormat of Europe, suffering innumerable attacks and devastation as armies whipsawed back and forth across its pivotal terrain. The Turks and Habsburgs had treated this land as their private battleground for as long as anyone could remember. The recent "annexation" of Bosnia-Herzegovina by the Austro-Hungarian Empire in 1908 had left the long-suffering populace bitter and as volatile as undiluted nitroglycerin.

He left the train station and walked about fifteen minutes to Republic Square where he found a boarding house on *Narodnog fronta*. After letting a room, he walked to the cafe *Zlatna Moruna* around the corner. It was early evening and he was hungry. He was in the midst of enjoying a dish of *moussaka,* when a stranger pulled up a chair and said, "You should try the *locovaca* with that."

The stranger, a young man not quite twenty, was wearing the typical dress of a university student: a dark, brown suit and a vest covering a grimy white shirt with an ill-fitting collar. His straight black hair barely covered his ears and surrounded a handsome face with a somewhat prominent nose. He was clean-shaven and had an air of daring about him. It was if he had just outwitted the local constable and was calmly waiting for him to burst into the café with a look of frustrated exasperation.

"I'm sorry, do I know you?"

"You would if you came here often. My name is 'Rilo.'"

"Excuse me, but I'm new in town. Perhaps you can help me. I'm looking for Dragutin. Do you know him?"

"Dragutin lives nearby. I can take you to him."

He put some money on the table and stood up. The young man led the way out of the café and down the cobblestone street. After walking several blocks, they turned left into a residential area. The street was narrower. At the next corner, 'Rilo turned down a side street and he followed. Suddenly, everything went dark. A bag was over his head and he was lifted on to a wagon and covered with a woolen blanket that smelled of wet horse. His hands were tied behind his back and his wallet was taken. As he began to protest, 'Rilo menaced, "Be quiet and you won't get hurt."

After twenty minutes of what seemed like a meandering drive, the wagon stopped and gruff hands pushed him down steps into a damp room that smelled of fish. The bag was removed and he found himself standing before a man in a chair. He squinted in the dim light trying to recover his vision when a deep voice with a heavy accent said, "Don't you know that Dragutin is dead?"

"Yes, he died as a free Serbian and my friends wish to see him again."

"And these friends of yours, they have a message for Dragutin?"

"Yes, but I must see the way of Black George first."

"First John, chapter 3 verse 18," the man replied.

The man in the chair nodded at the smaller man's rendition of the secret litany, and an older man came out of the shadows. The man was clearly the commander of the group. He was tall and heavyset with a large head. His skin was weathered and bore scars around both eyes that were the result of systematic beatings he had received at the hands of the Austrians when he had been arrested for leading a resistance group opposing the annexation of his homeland. He wore leather gloves over hands that had been disfigured by his captors. His hazel eyes shone with fevered intensity. With a deft slash of a razor-sharp stiletto, the rope binding Vaslav's hands fell to the floor.

"Yes, he has given us the way and it will be through Sarajevo on June 28th. Do you have a map?" asked the small man.

"Did you say June 28th? This is perfect. That is a day of Serbian patriotic celebration. We call it Vidovdan to remember the 1389 Battle of Kosovo when a Serb knight, Milos Obilic, killed the Ottoman Sultan Murad I. He was the only Sultan ever killed in battle. When we kill the Austrian invader on this June 28th, we will be remembered for all of time!"

A map was produced and the short man detailed the route of the royal party through the various stops and presented precise times for each portion of the itinerary. As they reviewed the details of the itinerary, a plan began to develop. The route would be lined with armed patriots equipped with bombs and firearms. They would attack the motorcade as it passed their positions.

"The *Narodna Odbrana* and the Black Hand are in your debt. Tell your friends that Dragutin will be there on June 28th."

Before he departed, Steinnekker handed the leader an envelope. Dragan opened it and smiled upon reading it. It was on the letterhead of the Tsar and contained long, sought-after assurances.

Bitterman followed the short gentleman to the Sacher Hotel in Vienna. The shorter man had utilized an artful disguise while traveling from London through Paris and on to Vienna. However, Hank was highly trained in surveillance and was not fooled by the disguises. Like a bloodhound on the trail of a stag, Bitterman maintained contact with his target, codename Puck.

Bitterman maintained surveillance of Puck, disguised as a working-man, as he boarded the train to Belgrade. Hank took the downtime during the train ride to prepare a report to Strafe that included a negative the size of a large period in the masthead of the stationery that bore an encoded message. The negative showed Puck with a short, thin operative who he did not recognize but thought bore a resemblance to one of the Monocle's partners. Bitterman posted the report when he arrived in Belgrade and followed Puck to a boarding house in a working-class neighborhood. Puck dropped off his belongings and headed to a nearby café. Hank followed at a discreet distance. The neighborhood consisted of brick tenements, three or four stories high. The summertime sun was beginning to disappear and the widely-spaced gas lamps flickered wanly as they unsuccessfully attempted to replace the daylight.

Since the establishment was too small for him to enter without drawing unwanted attention, Bitterman positioned himself across from the café so that he could maintain visual contact with Puck. The smells of savory, baked casseroles wafting from the café made his stomach growl, but he sensed that the purpose of his surveillance was about to materialize. His heart quickened as he observed a young man approach Puck and begin conversing with him. The two men left the restaurant. Bitterman waited as they headed down the block before following. In the dusky twilight, he saw them slip into an alleyway. He continued cautiously.

As Bitterman approached the corner, he was assaulted from the front and behind. Rough hands thrust his face into the corner of the brick building. A bloody gash opened on his cheekbone as a knee rammed into his stomach. Windless and bleary-eyed, Bitterman lost consciousness and crumpled to the ground. His senseless body was heaved into a manure wagon and covered with a canvas tarp.

When he regained consciousness, his right eye was swollen shut. His head throbbed and judging from the nausea, he figured that he had a concussion. Assessing the rest of the damage, he knew that his cheek bone was fractured, along with at least two ribs. A clot of blood caked his cheek. His hands were tied together and pulled above his head with a chain that went through an iron ring embedded in the coarse stone ceiling and attached to a winch on the wall behind him. The elevation of his hands made it difficult to breathe. Fortunately, the chain was somewhat slack and he could stand flatfooted and shift his weight from one foot to the other. He shuddered as he realized that he was in some sort of medieval dungeon. He had been stripped to his skivvies and he shivered in the cold, dank cell. Taking stock of his situation, Hank realized that he was in need of serious medical attention, he was securely shackled in an extremely vulnerable position and he was hungry and thirsty.

Voices speaking a language that he did not understand echoed in the hallway outside his cell. As the voices neared, he saw three men plus Puck cross before his cell. They stopped and spoke, pointing in his direction.

"*Nein. Nein*," grunted Puck, indicating that he had no connection with the prisoner. The group turned and departed, their noisy laughter bouncing off the damp stone walls. A feeling of hopelessness began to settle on the young officer as he tried to stave off shock. To distract himself, he replayed his favorite football game in his head.

As a young defensive back on the Notre Dame Fightin' Irish, he was thrust into a game against the University of Pittsburgh when Josh Anderson, the senior who started ahead of him, broke an ankle. The Fightin' Irish were undefeated to that point and were locked into a scoreless tie on the road at Forbes Field. Suddenly, the fans roared to life as the Irish quarterback heaved a thirty-three yard pass to end Knute Rockne. The big end rumbled downfield and was tackled before reaching the end zone. The Pitt defense stiffened and Notre Dame tried a field goal. The ball split the goalposts for three points. With time running down, Pitt moved the ball up the field to Notre Dame's twenty yard line. On the last play of the game, Pitt attempted a field goal. The snap was perfect, the placement was perfect and the kick was right on target. As the pigskin lifted off the ground, Bitterman leaped onto the back of defensive tackle, Alphonse Bledsoe, and launched himself skyward. His outstretched fingertips collided with the ball as it headed toward the goal posts. Bitterman and the ball thumped to the ground as the final gun fired to signal the end of the game.

Icy cold water splashed him back to his dismal reality. He tilted his head back to capture as much moisture as he could. A sullen young man with a cigarette dangling from his liver-colored lips shouted at Hank in a Slavic language. Nedeljko Čabrinović was a Bosnian Serb who had been recruited by the Black Hand. He was a zealot who hated the Teutonic race and the centuries of humiliation it had inflicted on his people. The captor scanned the fetid cell. Grunting maliciously, he reached over and pulled a slug from the mossy wall. Hank's good eye stared in unbelieving terror as the guard inserted the creature into Bitterman's left nostril where it sat inert. Just when he thought it could not get worse, a match flared. The guard placed the flame on the slug's tail. Wriggling desperately the creature took refuge in Hank's sinus cavity leaving behind a trail of slime.

Bitterman gagged and felt a wave of nausea rising in his chest. He coughed up yellow bile that splashed on to his tormentor's boots. A sharp, right backhand smashed into the side of Hank's face, sending a paroxysm of pain through his fractured cheek bone. The young Naval officer slumped and hung limply from his wrists. He began to hyperventilate as he struggled to get his feet under him.

Bitterman saw an older man enter the cell. He had a military bearing and for the first time since he had been shanghaied, Hank felt a glimmer of hope.

"Excuse my young friend's lack of manners. I am Captain Dragan. You are military?"

"I am Hank Bitterman, an American citizen," whispered Hank.

"Mr. Hank Bitterman, what are you doing in my city?" Dragan asked in a thick accent.

Bitterman refused to answer, except to say, "My name is Hank Bitterman. I am an American citizen. I would like to see the American Consul, Sir."

"Mr. Hank Bitterman, you act like military. I think you are military. You are not in a military uniform so you must be spy. Who are you spying on, Mr. Hank Bitterman?"

"My name is Hank Bitterman. I am an American citizen. I would like to see the American Consul, Sir."

"Mr. Hank Bitterman, you do not comprehend the precariousness of your situation. I would like to know what you are doing in my city, spying on my friends. If you refuse to tell me, I will have my crude friend use, how do you say in English? More enhanced methods of persuasion."

"My name is Hank Bitterman. I am an American citizen. I would like to see the American Consul, Sir."

Dragan sighed and signaled to Čabrinović to tighten the chain attached to Bitterman's wrists. As he passed the American, Čabrinović thrust his forearm viciously into Bitterman's side. The Serb grabbed the chain and tugged on it with so much force that his feet lifted off the floor. The tug of the chain was so violent that it caused the fractured rib on Hank's left side to snap. He convulsed in pain and began coughing blood. His eyelids fluttered and moments later Bitterman hung limply by his wrists, unconscious.

Dragan sprinted over to the winch and released the chain. Hank collapsed to the floor as the chain slipped through the ring and rained down on his fallen body. Dragan ordered Čabrinović to go get blankets and medical supplies. Bitterman's breathing was labored and shallow. Suddenly, the cell was quiet. Dragan took off the glove on his right hand and put two mangled fingers on the fallen man's neck. There was no pulse.

June 29, 1914
Sarajevo

This mess is so big and so deep and so tall
we cannot pick it up, there is no way at all.

~ Dr. Seuss

The Sarajevo Daily Journal, June 29, 1914

Dateline: Sarajevo:

"Austria's Archduke Franz Ferdinand Assassinated in Sarajevo by Serbian Student"

    It was sunny and warm yesterday on this fateful Sunday morning, but horrific events were to rock the City of Sarajevo. Archduke Franz Ferdinand, the Crown Prince to the Austria-Hungarian throne, and his wife Sophie, the Duchess of Hohenberg, were gunned down in broad daylight by a radical Serbian student apparently in protest over the annexation of Bosnia-Herzegovina by Austria-Hungary. The fifty one year old Archduke was the nephew of Emperor Franz Josef. His succession to the throne was assured when the Emperor's only son, Crown Prince Rudolf, committed suicide twenty-five years ago, and Ferdinand's father and next in line, Carl Ludwig, passed away some eighteen years ago, leaving Franz Ferdinand as the Crown Prince.

The Imperial couple was slain as they were visiting Sarajevo at the invitation of regional governor, General Oskar Potoirek, to inspect army manoeuvres being held outside the city. The Archduke had been recently named the Inspector General of Austrian-Hungarian forces. The presence of a unit of the Austrian army in Bosnia-Herzegovina has been an ongoing source of discontent among segments of the local populace who favor union with Serbia. Heightening the tension was the fact that June 28th is Vidovan, a holiday that celebrates the Battle of Kosovo, 1389. The air in Sarajevo on this day was crackling with nationalist fervor.

The Archduke, the Governor, the Mayor and other dignitaries were travelling in a motorcade across the city when a series of tragic events occurred. After an early morning review of the soldiers at Philipovic army camp, the Archduke's motorcade entered the city. The streets were lined with cheering people, who hailed the Imperial Party with flowers and flags. The heir to the Austro-Hungarian crown wore the dress uniform of a cavalry officer consisting of a pale, blue tunic with a high collar adorned with three stars and black trousers with red stripes along the seams. His waist was wrapped with a Bauchband, a broad gold-braided sash, and he wore a black patent leather cap decorated with pale-green feathers. His handsome face was adorned with a broad, handlebar moustache. The Archduchess was wearing a black coat with a fur collar. Draping her neck was a white silk scarf. A white hat with a large flower on the brim graced her head. A sheer veil covered her pretty face.

Not realizing the imminent danger they were in, he and his wife, who was with child, rode in the back seat of a 1911 Gräf & Stift Double Phaeton. The Habsburg banner, with its multi-colored, crowned double-eagle emblem on a yellow field, was attached to the front bumper of the third car in the line and proudly proclaimed the Imperial couple. They waved enthusiastically to the crowd. As the procession moved along the Appel Quay there were a few shouts of *Zivio!* ('Long may he live!').

As the motorcade wended its way through the city on its way to City Hall, a young terrorist hurled a grenade at the Archduke. The chauffeur of the Archduke's vehicle must have sensed the object heading toward the car because onlookers said that the car accelerated at that instant. The Archduke saw the grenade as it was heading toward the Archduchess and deflected it with his right arm. It bounced off the folded canvas top of the Archduke's car and exploded under the automobile following. Twelve spectators were injured in that explosion. One of those injured was General Potiorek's chief adjutant, Lieutenant Colonel Eric von Merizzi, who suffered a head wound from shrapnel and was hospitalized.

The police immediately apprehended the perpetrator, Nedeljko Čabrinović, after he tried to escape by jumping into the river. At this time of year the Miljacka River was only a few inches deep and he was immediately taken into custody. As he was spirited into a police van, he supposedly boasted, "I am a Serb hero."

Despite the grenade attack, the Archduke insisted on attending the reception at City Hall with city officials to show that he would not be intimidated. Those attending the reception noted that the Archduke's remarks stressed the historic friendship between Austria and the Serb peoples and that a few malcontents could not undermine this relationship. He mentioned the growing bellicosity of the Ottoman regime toward Serbia and pledged to work tirelessly to defend Serbia. His remarks were well-received. While at the City Hall reception, the Archduke decided to change his plans in order to visit Lieutenant Colonel Merizzi in Sarajevo hospital. Unfortunately, the revised itinerary was not communicated to the driver of the Archduke's car. This task ordinarily would have been performed by Lt. Colonel Merizzi who, due to his hospitalization, was no longer with the Imperial Party.

This critical failure of communication turned deadly when the motorcade mistakenly turned off the Appel Quay, a wide avenue that runs along the River Miljacka, onto the narrower Franz Joseph Street. The driver was instructed to back up and return to Appel Quay. At that precise moment, the assassin emerged from Moritz Schiller's grocery store on Franz Joseph Street only to find his prey within five feet of him. He seized the opportunity, pulled a revolver and fired point blank at the Archduke and Archduchess. The attack was so swift, deadly and unexpected, that neither the municipal police, nor the Archduke's armed military escort, were able to prevent it. At the time of the attack, the Duchess was holding a bouquet of roses that the Mayor's wife had presented at City Hall.

A bullet pierced the Duchess' abdomen and she began to bleed internally. The Archduke was shot in the neck. According to Count Franz von Harrach, who was in the front seat of the Archduke's car, the Archduke pleaded, "Sophie, Sophie, don't die. Stay alive for the children!" The Archduke was bleeding profusely from his throat. The car containing the mortally-wounded Imperial couple sped across the Lateiner Bridge en route to the Governor's Residence, where both the Archduke and his wife were pronounced dead on arrival.

The assailant, a student named Gavrilo Princip, was apprehended at the scene by municipal police and bystanders. There are unconfirmed reports that he unsuccessfully tried to take his own life by poison. He was immediately wrestled to the ground and disarmed by officers. A Browning FN semi-automatic pistol was used by the assassin. Reportedly, three rounds remained in the seven-round magazine

Sgt. Milan Pedroiavec of the Polizia Sarajevo reported that the crowd lining the streets that morning was generally festive, cheering the motorcade as it passed. The mood in the streets changed dramatically after the grenade attack on the convoy earlier in the day. There are conflicting reports regarding the route of the motorcade after the royal couple left City Hall, but it is known that while the Archduke's tourer was stopped on Franz Joseph Street, the assassin suddenly burst from the crowd and started firing. The military attaché declined to comment until further investigation. Investigating Judge Leo Pfeffer who has been assigned to conduct the investigation could not be reached for comment.

Little is known of the assassin, a 19 year old student named Gavrilo Princip. He is believed to be a member of the Narodna Odbrana or the "People's Defense", a radical nationalist group that has been linked to a secret society of Serbian military officers, known as "Unity or Death" and nicknamed the Black Hand. Several other students have been taken into custody and are being interrogated by the authorities.

Mayor Fehim Effendi Curcic, who was in the lead car of the Archduke's motorcade, was visibly shaken by the assassination of the Imperial couple. His office issued a statement to the effect that a great man had been senselessly killed and that his plans for peace and prosperity for the region were now in the hands of God. The Mayor asked for prayers

for the deceased and for the leaders in Vienna and Belgrade that wisdom and mercy prevail.

Kahn folded the newspaper and exhaled quietly. June 28th would go down in history as a momentous and enriching day.

June 1914
Pokrovskoe, Siberia

War is the statesman's game, the priest's delight,
the lawyer's jest, the hired assassin's trade.

~ PERCY BYSSHE SHELLEY

KURT SAT IN THE DINING CAR of the Trans-Siberian Railroad reading *Crime and Punishment* in Russian. It was good practice and helped him adjust his brain to thinking in Russian. A split-second hesitation in a verbal encounter while his mind translated Russian to English back to Russian could be fatal. He was wearing peasant garb, a faded blue tunic open at the neck, loose cotton trousers and black leather boots. His rolled-up sleeves revealed his thick forearms. He wore a bushy, Imperial-style moustache that was firmly attached to his upper lip. The appliance in his mouth that he wore to disguise his perfect white teeth with discolored, crooked bridgework cut into his gums. His uncombed, blond hair flowed over his collar onto his neck and gave him the rough appearance of a peasant farmer from Eastern Siberia.

The train rattled ponderously over the steppes. They had traveled fifteen hundred miles from St. Petersburg to the Ural Mountains. After crossing the mountains, the train headed toward the Toura River where he would disembark and wait for a river boat to take him to Rasputin's native village.

He focused on the loud peasant in the front of the car. Rasputin's face was one of the most recognizable in the Empire. His long, dark hair was parted in the middle and tied back in a ponytail. He wore a full beard that was greasy and unkempt. The monk was surrounded by a group of young peasant girls, who were cackling and giggling as Rasputin held court. Three bottles of vodka, two of which were empty, adorned a luggage shelf near Rasputin's seat. He quaffed a full glass of the clear liquor and paraded up and down the aisle mimicking a rigid martinet drunkenly reviewing his troops. The passengers watching the parody were laughing raucously. The exception to the jollity was a dour man in a brown suit, who watched the spectacle with disdain. Kurt pegged him as secret police. Whether that made him friend or foe Chorney was not sure.

Even the conductor, a kindly-looking older gentleman with a white handlebar moustache and a blue hat atop his bald head, was smiling at Rasputin's antics. The conductor ambled through the car with practiced balance. As he came even with Kurt, the conductor discreetly placed a folded piece of paper on Kurt's table. He continued to read his book, then nonchalantly slid the paper to the open book and positioned it in the center fold. The paper contained two digits: 4D. Chorney surmised that this meant compartment D in the fourth railway car.

Someone broke out a harmonica and started playing a lively tune. A young man near the door drummed along with his hands thumping the wood-paneled wall. Rasputin grabbed the arm of one of the peasant girls and started dancing spasmodically in the aisle. Foot stomping and hand clapping followed. After viewing the scene before him, Chorney concluded that the monk was not in danger. Kurt placed some rubles on the table and left the car.

Chorney carefully entered the next coach and saw a man beckoning him from one of the compartments. The tall, gaunt man was in his mid-forties and was wearing a gray cassock encircled at the waist with a thick chain of brown, wooden beads from which hung a large, steel-gray cross. His spiky brown hair was held in place by a gray beanie embroidered with purple thread in a repetitive olive vine pattern. There was a plain, leather covered Bible on the bench in the compartment. Chorney pointed to himself with a doubtful look on his face. The cleric nodded insistently and disappeared into the compartment. Kurt followed and looked at the man quizzically.

"I am the monk, Iliodor," he whispered in English. "Your colleague, how do you call him, Strafe Oliver knows me. He calls my code the Marmot."

Kurt looked at him uncomprehendingly and responded in Russian that he spoke no English. Iliodor cocked his head and grinned.

"OK. I understand," he said in Russian. "Just listen to me."

Chorney shrugged and turned to leave. The thin man placed his hand on Chorney's shoulder and hissed, "I am going to Pokrovskoe under orders from Prince Yusopov. I am supposed to hire someone to kill that filth."

Chorney stopped and digested the last sentence. He turned and looked deeply into the cleric's eyes. At that moment, there was a whistle from the locomotive and the train slowed noticeably. Kurt headed toward his compartment to secure his belongings. The train wheezed into Tyumen with a loud burst of steam. Chorney pondered the encounter and chided himself on the ease with which the cleric had penetrated his disguise. His confidence was shaken; doubt racked his brain. The cleric's words were certainly a mixed message.

Most of the train passengers bled into the city streets. A handful, including Rasputin, several peasant women, the dour man in the brown suit and three of the revelers, dragged their luggage to the dock on the Toura River. Chorney nonchalantly joined the group as they boarded the riverboat heading down river to Pokrovskoe. Kurt thought he saw the cleric through the dust climb into a dirty black motorcar. Rasputin sat on his suitcase and began a rambling diatribe about the horrors of war and the grief that would ensue if Mother Russia was drawn into any European armed conflict.

Kurt stood off to the side and mentally reviewed the intel he had about Pokrovskoe. It was a small village that had been founded in 1642 as a fort to protect the Muscovy trade routes. The area was predominantly agricultural and was known for its grain and cattle. The rural settlement was dominated by a large, central church of St. Nicholas, white with a gilded dome. Along Pokrovskoe's two main avenues were the wooden houses of the wealthy landowners and businessmen. The structures were surprisingly commodious and were ornately decorated with painted or carved beams and window frames. Although it had a population of only several thousand, Kurt hoped to find accommodations that would preserve his anonymity. He decided that he would follow the grumpy, little man in the brown suit.

It was still broad daylight when the river boat stopped at Pokrovskoe. Rasputin's wife, Praskovia, and his four children met him at the dock. Their delight at seeing their father turned to squeals of pleasure when he produced four candies from his bag and gave one to each. His wife gave him a mock look of disapproval as her eyes shone with love. As she turned toward the wagon, Rasputin hugged her from behind, grinding his pelvis into her rear conspicuously. She turned to admonish him for his crude behavior. Her ire turned to delight when he started pulling brilliantly-colored, silk scarves from his sleeve. The strand must have reached fifteen feet before he entwined her in a silk web and planted a noisy kiss on her lips. She laughed coquettishly and the happy family boarded an ordinary wagon and proceeded down the main street. Rasputin sat in the front with the two youngest on his lap, giggling and squirming in their father's arms. The older two daughters, knelt behind him hugging and kissing him. Chorney absorbed the scene with chagrin at the incongruity of the "mad monk of St. Petersburg" and the doting peasant father and husband.

When Kurt turned around, he found himself alone on the street. The man in the brown suit had disappeared. Kurt spied what appeared to be a boardinghouse down the block and walked toward it. Fortunately, he was able to secure a room. After unpacking, he scouted out the only restaurant that was still open and ordered fish *Solyanka*, a local stew. It was so delicious that he almost licked the plate clean. He reconnoitered the village, figuring that everyone, including Rasputin, would be attending church services the following day, which was Sunday.

Chorney spent a sleepless night. The incessant sunlight interfered with his sleep. The charm and novelty of the fabled White Nights had certainly worn off. He was beginning to crave the darkness of night so that he could regain the circadian rhythms that allowed the body to rest properly. This is unnatural, he thought. It made the sleep deprivation training he endured in survival school seem like a vacation with Rip Van Winkle.

He was alone without support in a strange environment, his cover had been compromised, and he knew for certain that his mission was deadly serious. Rasputin was definitely an assassination target. Kurt bemoaned the fact that he was *incommunicado*. Even if there was a telegraph office in this backwater village, it would be closed on Sunday.

What if Rasputin stayed in Pokrovskoe for the entire summer? Why wouldn't he? Here, he was surrounded by an ostensibly loving family that survived by farming. Obviously, he would be needed to work the farm. In contrast, in St. Petersburg, he was an alien surrounded by vipers. Chorney could only take things one step at a time. And right now, he had to make sure he was at the church early enough to scope it out, but not too early to arouse suspicion.

The Church of St. Nicholas had been rebuilt some twenty years earlier and probably had not seen a paint brush since then. White flakes of paint, half peeling were interspersed on the façade that, in the center, contained a brilliant stone mosaic of St. Nicholas kneeling among some children. Early arrivals congregated on a large welcoming cobblestone deck in front of stately doors shaped like a fat howitzer shell.

After skirting the entrance and circumnavigating the building, Chorney entered the church through a side door. The interior lacked the grandiosity of the churches in the capital. Icons depicting scenes from the Bible and the life of St. Nicholas decorated the plain, whitewashed walls. A stained-glass rose window graced the wall above a simple marble altar. An abundance of lighted candles in red glass holders flanked the altar.

As Chorney moved to a pew near the rear, a quiet buzz permeated the church. So far, he had failed to locate the Marmot, Iliodor's code name, or brown suit. He did notice two tough-looking peasants loitering near the rear prayer alcove. One was squat and powerfully built. There was a dirty, stubble of growth on his face and his eyes wore a mocking expression of one who has disdain for believers. He was wearing a gold loop in his left ear. The taller one had a lean and hungry look, like that of a caged wolf. His restless, dark eyes darted constantly around the crowd. He had sallow skin and a wide nose that had absorbed more than a few direct hits. They looked familiar and Chorney thought that he recognized them from the train station in Tyumin. He couldn't be sure. Otherwise, the assemblage appeared to be a polyglot of peasants and burghers typical of rural, Eastern Russia. A sea of broad, flat cheeks and round faces with ruddy complexions.

There was a balcony across the rear of the church where a pipe organ and vacant music racks stood. Kurt saw no sign of an organist or any choir members present. Just then, he thought he detected movement in the balcony. A burst of noise distracted him as the congregation responded to the entrance of the local celebrity, Grigory Eflimovich Rasputin. There he stood, savoring the moment. Kurt thought how satisfying this moment must be for the former reprobate who had been banished only to return triumphant.

He was wearing his Sunday best — a dazzling white poet shirt and blousy black cotton trousers held up with a broad leather belt clasped with a gold buckle bearing the Romanov eagle. A silk scarf bearing the Imperial seal on a field of teal was draped over his heart and pinned in place under his left arm. His wife wore a cornflower blue jumper, her tanned arms bare. Trailing behind the beaming couple were the four children all freshly scrubbed. The family walked to the front of the church, shaking hands with friends and well-wishers as they went. When Chorney looked back to the balcony, the shadow in the corner was gone. The crowd settled back into their seats and Kurt spied the brown suit as he lingered for an extra beat, scanning the crowd.

The priest, assisted by altar boys, seemed to relish the full house and milked the service for all it was worth. The homily was particularly lengthy and emphatic. Kurt felt himself drifting off several times. At other times he incurred the wrathful stare of the woman behind him whenever he peered over his shoulder into the balcony. At long last the service ended and Chorney quickly slipped out of his pew and exited to a strategic position outside. He bumped into a short, stout woman, who wore a faded red blouse and frayed kerchief on her head. She smelled like a farm animal and had wisps of straw on her clothing as if she had spent the night in a stable. When she grunted maliciously at him, he noticed that her nose was horribly disfigured. It was as if her left nostril had been eroded by acid and a smooth purple and brown lump of scar tissue had replaced it. Her black, beady eyes warned him away.

Chorney was glad to be out in the sunshine again and took a position on the deck to the left of the entrance where he could observe the departing crowd. When Rasputin finally emerged from the church, he was like an opera star, surrounded by people clamoring for his affection. Chorney stiffened to attention when he watched the two toughs approach Rasputin from behind. As Kurt moved forward, they grabbed Rasputin and lifted him. Before Kurt could react, he heard Rasputin scream in recognition of his old buddies from his wild days. He hugged and kissed them profusely.

Just then Kurt felt something bounce off his shoulder. He stared at a pebble and then upward. There was the Marmot. He nodded and pointed.

Standing by herself, off to the side by the street was the little woman with half-a-nose. Chorney looked at her and then back at the Marmot, who nodded solemnly.

Rasputin began slowly making his way toward his wagon. He was between Chorney and the woman, who started to move toward Rasputin muttering incoherently. Kurt bumped into Rasputin's buddies as he tried to rush to Rasputin. One of them knocked him off-balance and he staggered. As he righted himself, he saw a silver flash and the woman lunged toward Rasputin. Her knife struck Rasputin in the midsection and bounced off his bulky belt buckle. Confused, she slashed at him again; this time cutting him deeply below the belt. Rasputin immediately buckled in pain. Time seemed to slow. Kurt yelled, "NOOOO!"

As the crazy woman prepared to strike again, Rasputin ran for his life. His right hand was pressed desperately against his lower abdomen. The short woman gave chase, screeching dementedly something to the effect that "I will kill the Anti-Christ!"

The crowd was frozen, stunned by the ferocity of the attack and the volume of blood that had splashed onto the cobblestones. Already in motion, Chorney was the first to react. He sprinted after the assassin. Rasputin staggered to a nearby building and collapsed in pain, howling for help. The half-nosed woman slowed and gathered herself for the kill. Chorney blasted into her at full speed, knocking her into the brick wall. She bounced off and rotated toward him still grasping the knife. She menaced at Chorney with the knife as she side-stepped toward Rasputin, who was lying helpless, holding his intestines in place with his bloody hand. Rasputin was ashen from the loss of blood. Kurt recognized that the monk was going into shock and knew that he must take this demented woman out before she could finish off Rasputin.

Chorney spied a piece of pole near Rasputin's leg. If he could get to it, his chances would improve tremendously. He feinted aggressively toward his left. She reacted by jabbing ferociously. But she jabbed at air because Kurt had spun and placed himself between her and Rasputin. A deranged look came over her face and she charged screeching curses at the top of her lungs. She was slashing viciously with the knife. It sliced through the space between them. Kurt knew that he had one chance. He dived into a roll, deftly picked up the pole and sprang to his feet. He gripped the pole like a baseball bat and knocked her over the centerfield wall. The wood smashed into her lower back with a sickening thud and she lifted off the ground. She flew like a ragdoll. She crash-landed, face down . . . motionless.

Rasputin's wife and daughters raced to him and were moaning in anguish while he lay slumped against the wall, bleeding. The two buddies pushed through the crowd, half-dragging, half-pulling a man holding a doctor's case. He began tending to Rasputin, giving him medicine to ease the pain while he tried to stop the hemorrhaging. Chorney scanned the crowd and saw the Marmot. Their eyes met and the cleric slowly nodded. Then, he was gone.

Chorney was about to return to his room, when he was approached by a policeman who directed Kurt to follow him. The officer on duty at the police station was in his early fifties. Ivan Birankovsky was built of sturdy peasant stock, thick through the chest and short of stature. His broad face was clean-shaven and marked by a scar that was the result of a scimitar that slashed him before he could duck during the Siege of Plevna in the Russo-Turkish War. After service in the Tsar's infantry, he entered law enforcement. It so happened that he was the older brother of Kyril, Rasputin's boyhood friend, the one with the gypsy earring. Fortunately for Chorney, Kyril had explained to his brother Chorney's brave defense of Rasputin in subduing the assailant.

Despite the eyewitness recommendation, Ivan was skeptical of Chorney's cover story. The policeman retained Chorney's identification papers and admonished him to stay in Pokrovskoe until further notice. Knowing that any objection would be futile and appreciating the possibility of incarceration as a material witness, Kurt readily agreed, putting on a cheerful, 'of course, Sir' face.

Strafe considered the reports in front of him with dismay. Events in Sarajevo and Pokrovskoe proved that it was the right decision to pursue the intelligence leads with agents Bitterman and Chorney. But he was worried sick over the lack of communication from either agent. The world was spiraling out of control into a conflagration that threatened to consume

Europe and perhaps beyond. Reports from Russia seemed to indicate that Chorney was alive and well; just stuck *incommunicado* in a backwater village. The description of the attack on Rasputin and the manner in which the assailant was subdued sounded like Chorney.

Strafe was more concerned about Bitterman, who had been silent since he arrived in Vienna. He had alerted associates in Germany for any information about Bitterman. As yet, there was none. If Strafe did not hear anything on Bitterman in the next two weeks, the Director would have to perform the dreaded duty of notifying the next of kin. He prayed that it would not come to that, but in his heart-of-hearts he feared the worst.

On a macro level, Strafe was alarmed by the ominous congruence of date and time of the two events. He had calculated the time zone differences between Sarajevo where the Archduke was assassinated and Pokrovskoe and the attempt on Rasputin's life and came to the chilling conclusion that the attacks on Rasputin and the Archduke Ferdinand were virtually simultaneous.

Was it coincidence or the work of evil genius, he pondered rhetorically. If it were the latter, the world was in for one hellacious time. There would be much destruction, bloodshed and pain. He had already received a request from Assistant Secretary of the Navy, Franklin D. Roosevelt, for ONI's analysis of probable scenarios in light of the attacks. In preparing his draft analysis, Strafe had reviewed all of the intelligence reports compiled in 1914. He weighed the probabilities until his brain hurt. No matter how he balanced the assessments, he was having trouble envisioning a scenario that ended well.

Back in Pokrovskoe, Chorney was considering his options when there was a knock at his door. He rose and opened the door. Standing before him, dressed in a simple print frock that fell to her mid-calf above her *lapti* bast shoes, was one of Rasputin's daughters.

"Hello, sir. I'm sorry to disturb you. My name is Matryona; I am the daughter of Father Grigory. My mother instructed me to ask you to come to the hospital."

Chorney regarded the tall young teener before him. Chorney thought that he was talking with a feminine, albeit much more refined, version of her father. She was an attractive girl with alabaster skin that stretched pleasantly over broad cheekbones. Her square chin was nicely balanced by her clear, open forehead. She had her father's eyes, dark, deep-set and riveting. He could tell from the tone of her arms that she was strong; yet, from her gracefulness, he imagined that she could be a dancer. Although she was slightly self-conscious, he could tell that she had a certain level of maturity that only came from considerable experience in adult situations.

"Of course. How is your father?" he said with concern.

"He is strong and with God's help, he will pull through. I am so thankful that you were there when this terrible thing happened. Otherwise, I dread to think . . ." she said, choking up.

Her eyes filled with tears and Chorney saw the brave façade vanish and the scared little girl appear. She turned away from Chorney and sniffled as she wiped her eyes with a lace handkerchief that emerged from her waistband.

"I'm sorry," she sobbed. "My father is such a rock; it's hard to imagine being without him."

"Tell me about yourself," he said, not-too-subtly changing the subject.

"I was born here. But last year before I was fifteen, Father brought me with my younger sister, Varvara, to St. Petersburg so that we could attend Steblin-Kamensky private preparatory school. He wants the best for us; he wants us to be 'little ladies.' At first, St. Petersburg was awkward for us. It was such a big, modern city. We weren't used to all the activity. But now, after two years in school, we love it. The girls are so nice and the teachers are so smart. Father has been wonderful. And he knows so many important people; there is always something exciting happening."

She led him into the small, rural hospital. In the summer heat, the smell of disinfectant was almost overpowering. The tiled floor creaked drily as they walked down the hallway. The floor sent a blurry glare to his face and, through narrowed eyes, he noticed a uniformed policeman standing outside a room at the far end of hall. The officer eyed him warily. At that moment, Rasputin's wife emerged from the room and greeted them warmly. She rushed to Chorney and hugged him tightly, murmuring "*Spasiba, spasiba.*"

"*Pozhaluysta*, You're welcome," responded Kurt.

"Marochka, my darling, please bring Mr. Chorney to see Papa. I'm going to get some food. Papa is hungry. He hates the hospital food. That's a good sign. I won't be long."

Chorney entered the room and observed Rasputin lying on his back in a hospital bed with his head slightly raised. The monk was alert and gestured for Kurt to approach closer. Rasputin was pale and his brows were deeply furrowed. His famous, hypnotic eyes were dull from pain and medication.

Through his dry, cracked lips Rasputin whispered, "Forgive me if I do not recall much of what happened after I was stabbed, I am told that you saved my life. *Spasiba!*"

"*Pozhaluysta.*"

Matryona sat on the corner of the bed and took her father's hand in hers. Chorney looked around awkwardly. He spied a chair and sat down next to the bed. Spread on the bed was a newspaper. Matryona picked it up and began reading aloud about the horrific events in Sarajevo and the assassination of Archduke Ferdinand and the ultimatum that the Austro-Hungarian Empire had issued. As she read about the futile efforts of diplomats, Chorney noticed tears coming from her father's eyes.

"Nikki will be coerced by the *camarilla* into mobilizing the army and that will force a war. Russia will bleed much blood. If only I were there, I would advise him and the Tsarina against mobilization. If only . . . . Listen to what I have just written to the Tsar," he said, lifting a handwritten message. "'*A threatening cloud hangs over Russia: misfortune, much woe, no ray of hope, a sea of tears immeasurable, and of blood? There are no words: an indescribable horror. I know that all want war from you, and the loyal [wish it] without realizing that it is for the sake of destruction. You are the Tsar, the father of the nation. Do not permit the mad to triumph and destroy themselves and the nation. Everything drowns in great bloodshed.*'"[21]

Suddenly, Rasputin peered at him through red, puffy eyes, "I have sent a score of telegrams begging him not to mobilize. I have tried to make a phone call to warn him not to fight over the Balkans, just like I did last year. I have always told him that to protect Mother Russia, we must not be needlessly drawn into other people's battles. But, I do not get through to him. If only I were there, I would convince him to use diplomacy, not guns. I would convince *batiushka Tsar* and *matiushka Tsarina* ('Father-Tsar' and 'Mother-Tsarina') to seek peace, not war. But," he sighed wearily, "I am here in a hospital, helpless and near death."

"Don't talk like that, Father. You must stay strong in order to grow healthy again."

"Yes, my Marochka, you are right."

"Well, my friend, I'm glad we met. May the Lord protect you and keep you safe," said Rasputin, raising his right hand in benediction. He winced from the exertion and slumped back. Chorney whispered farewell and departed.

When he exited the hospital, Chorney was confronted by a young policeman in uniform who nervously asked him to follow to the police station. Captain Birankovsky smiling broadly ushered Chorney past the sergeant's desk into his office. Waiting there was a rotund, little man in a cheap, black suit. He had a puffy, pink, round face set off by a large, bulbous nose above a walrus moustache.

"Have a seat, Mr. Chorney," said Captain Birankovsky. "I'd like to introduce Vadim Stepinac. He is the prosecutor for this district. He has some good news for you."

"Nice to meet you, Mr. Chorney. I understand that you have acted bravely in the matter of the attack on Grigory Rasputin. For that we thank you. I have interviewed the assailant, Khioniya Kuzminichna Guseva. She is a citizen of Syzran', Simbirsk province. She is thirty-three-years old and freely, need I say, proudly admits that she tried to kill Rasputin. There are reports that she is a prostitute who lost part of her nose due to syphilis. However, she denies these allegations. She claims that her nose was 'damaged by medicines.' My office has received instructions to commit her to an asylum for the insane in Krasnoyarski. Apparently, there is a desire to circumvent the notoriety and distraction of a trial. No one has come to her defense and she has consented to commitment to avoid the possibility of execution. Since there will be no trial, your testimony is not necessary and I have instructed Captain Birankovsky to return your papers and allow you to go on your way as you choose."

July, 1914
Vienna, Austria

If he has a conscience he will suffer for his mistake.
That will be punishment as well as the prison.

~ FYODOR DOSTOEVSKY, *CRIME AND PUNISHMENT*

VASLAV SAT IN A PLUSH ARMCHAIR in the lobby of the Sacher Hotel reading the headlines in Vienna's newspaper, the *Reichspost*. He was dressed in gray, pin striped trousers and a forest-green smoking jacket. He wore a yellow cravat with an open-collared tartan plaid Oxford shirt. He was the picture of an affluent man of leisure. In actuality, he was becoming restless due to inactivity. He missed the rigors of the stage and performing nightly. Soon, he reminded himself, this respite would be over and he would be in New York City performing nightly at the Metropolitan Opera House with the *Ballet Russe*.

The headlines proclaimed Austria's ultimatum issued to Serbia was purposely designed to infringe on Serbia's sovereignty and humiliate the smaller country. Although the demands were designed to be rejected, it was reported that Serbian Foreign Minister, Nikola Pachitch, was prepared to advise Austrian Ambassador Giesl that Serbia would acquiesce.

Unbeknownst to Pachitch, the Austrian Ambassador had already arranged to depart Belgrade in anticipation of an attack by the Austrians.

The paper reported that Russia was aligned with its fellow Slavs in Serbia and that the Tsar had appealed to his cousin, Kaiser Wilhelm, in the hope of averting war. Nicholas wrote, ". . . *An ignoble war has been declared on a weak country. . . . Soon I shall be overwhelmed by pressure brought upon me . . . to take extreme measures which will lead to war. To try and avoid such a calamity as a European war, I beg you in the name of our old friendship to do what you can to stop your allies from going too far.*"[22]

Unfortunately, the momentum for war had grown too strong. The dominoes that would precipitate a European war were all lined up. Germany believed that it was in the position now to defeat France and Russia, both of whom had engaged in a policy of encircling Germany with hostile states. If Russia mobilized to defend Serbia, that would constitute an act of war against Austria-Hungary, then Germany would declare war against Russia. Then by treaty, Britain and France would come to Russia's defense against Germany and Austria-Hungary.

All that was needed was for the first domino to be tipped. That was provided by the Kaiser who, despite Serbia's capitulation, encouraged Austria-Hungary to occupy Serbia because ". . . *the Serbs are Orientals, therefore liars, tricksters, and masters of evasion . . . .*"[23] Thus, according to the Kaiser, it was necessary for Austria to occupy Belgrade to ensure that the Serbs would live up to their capitulation. At 11:00 AM on July 28th, Austria declared war on Serbia and unleashed a ferocious bombing attack on Belgrade.

Vaslav was about to go to lunch when he felt a heavy hand on his shoulder.

"Herr Nijnsky, please come with us quietly," said an unsmiling man wearing a black trench coat and matching fedora pulled down menacingly over his eyes. Another large individual in similar garb stood in front of Nijinsky with his right hand resting threateningly inside his suit jacket. Nijinsky had lived in autocratic countries throughout most of his life and instantly recognized the trademark invitation of the secret police.

"Of course, may I ask where we are heading?"

"We'll ask the questions. Just come with us."

Nijinsky put down his newspaper. The two policemen towered over the ballet dancer. Playfully, Vaslav hooked his arms in theirs and with a devilish smile, he minced his steps through the hotel lobby, proclaiming, "Oh, we certainly are going to have fun. I can't wait to see you naked."

The cops cringed and the taller one even blushed as the hotel patrons glared at the unlikely threesome. Outside, they thrust Vaslav brusquely into the rear of a waiting vehicle. They drove to a nondescript warehouse building near the River Danube.

"OK, wise guy, now it's our turn to have some fun. Get out."

The officers surrounded him and ushered him by his elbows into the building. His feet barely touched the ground as he was brought to a small windowless office in the back of the building dimly illuminated by a single gas lamp. Inside the room, there were several chairs and an old wooden desk.

"*Guten morgen*, Herr Nijinsky. Thank you for taking the time to join us," said a man seated behind the desk.

"I am Colonel Heinreich Schnell of the Imperial Home Guard. We have certain questions about your recent activities. You are registered at the Sacher as Hans Steinnekker. Explain."

"It's quite innocent, Sir. As you may be aware, I have some celebrity as a dancer. I use that identity to ensure my privacy. You know how invasive some devotees of ballet can be. Why just last week, I was dining when . . . ."

"Silence! Our reports say that you arrived in Vienna in June then you disappeared until late June when you re-registered at the Sacher Hotel. Where were you during that time?"

"I was hiking by myself in the mountains. I needed some time alone away from everyone who makes demands on me."

"Where is your family?"

"With my in-laws."

"Why aren't you staying with them?"

"You obviously have not met my mother-in-law, or you would not have asked that question." He heard Fritz stifle a chuckle behind him.

"What did you do in Sarajevo?"

"I have never been to Sarajevo."

"That's not what our sources say."

"Well, your sources are incorrect."

"We believe you are lying and will insist that you relinquish your passport and accompany us."

"Am I being charged with any crime? How long will this detention last? I'm scheduled to travel to America for a tour shortly. Who is your superior?"

"Fritz and Wolfgang will escort you back to your hotel where you will provide them with your papers. You will take what you need and leave quietly with them."

Seeing limited options, Vaslav asked for permission to send a telegram from the hotel. The officer consented. At the reception desk, Friedrich Werner took the telegram order and watched as the diminutive guest parodied the militaristic attitude of the arresting officers. The dancer would surely pay a heavy price for humiliating men such as those goons. When the outer hotel door closed behind the officers, the pace of the lobby returned to normal. The momentary disruption was over and the whispered conversations dissipated with the same alacrity as foul smell on a windy day. Werner also knew that he was presented with an opportunity to ingratiate himself to an important figure. Without delay, Werner telephoned news of the abduction to the German who had met Vaslav in June.

Meanwhile on Wall Street in New York City, Otto Kahn was listening to Jacob Schiff report the Firm's results for the last quarter, when Kahn's secretary handed him a telegram. All the partners were in the conference room eagerly anticipating a banner report. Otto discreetly reviewed the cable that informed him of the arrest of Nijinsky in Austria accompanied by a desperate plea for help. Kahn's mind began racing with the implications of the arrest and his potential exposure should Vaslav decide to confess. Otto's heart was palpitating as he rose to slip out of the room without being noticed. A chill sweat overwhelmed him. Suddenly, he was floating above the room with his appendages flailing as he tried to flee.

When Jacob saw Otto rise, the chairman interrupted his speech and adroitly redirected his remarks, saying, "We could not have reached this unprecedented level of achievement and profitability without the masterful efforts of Otto. Come on up here, Otto."

With a deer-in-the-headlights look, Otto had no choice but to approach the podium. He gave Jacob a worried glance and addressed the partners with feigned confidence.

"It has long been the policy of Kuhn Loeb to develop our business by bringing honest dealing to our clients. We do not boast about our successes but rather depend on the value of our reputation. We have a golden reputation that is based on our sound advice and integrity. The outbreak of war in Europe may well produce record profits for K & L. We must never forget our guiding principle — our clients' needs come first. We must put aside our selfish interests and work doubly hard to advance our clients' interests. I could elaborate on our efforts on behalf of the Tsar and the Kaiser and our absolute obligation to serve their best interests independently, despite their current antagonism toward each other; but I have received an urgent telegram that I must attend to. So I will leave you to enjoy the rest of Jacob's report."

He stuffed the telegram into his jacket pocket and rapidly departed the startled audience. As he bustled by, Otto ordered his secretary to get Secretary of State Lansing on the phone. Otto threw his jacket onto the chair and opened his collar, pulling down his tie. Helga announced, "I have Secretary Lansing on the line, Sir."

Otto took a deep breath to compose himself, then calmly said, "Robert, how are you on this glorious fall afternoon?"

"Otto, I'm up to my eyebrows in alligators. The world is exploding. What can I do for you?"

"I need your assistance with a matter of some delicacy. You may have heard of Vaslav Nijinsky, the premier ballet dancer in the world. Well, he is a personal friend and we have arranged for him to tour New York and Washington this fall. However, he has just been arrested by the Austrian authorities in Vienna. I must get him released. Much is depending on it."

There was silence on the other end and Otto thought he heard Lansing whispering something about expecting the fiercest war in history to stop so a ballerina could go perform in New York.

"OK, Otto, I'll send a cable to the Austrian Foreign Minister in the morning. Please wire me any details you may have as soon as possible. Is there anything else I can do for you?"

"No, no, thank you so much. And please send me a copy, thanks."

"Helga, get in here with your steno pad," bellowed Otto. His secretary's rear end had barely hit the chair, when Otto began spewing instructions for cables to be sent to George Bakhmeteff, the Russian Ambassador in Washington, David Rowland Francis, the American Ambassador in Petrograd, and Max Warburg in Germany. The gist of the messages was the same: Please help obtain the release of premier ballet dancer, Vaslav Nijnsky, from custody of Austrian officials in Vienna. It is imperative for

Nijinsky to be present in New York as soon as possible to advance the cause of culture and civilization during these horrible times.

As Helga hustled off, Otto poured a glass of scotch and fumbled ice as he tried to put it into the glass; his hands were shaking violently. As the ice spun on the floor, he gulped down the entire contents of the glass. Should he call his lawyer? No, bringing in legal counsel would be premature. The situation was a long way from the necessity to refute specific charges. Should he call the arms dealer, Basil Zaharoff? The shadowy 'Merchant of Death' certainly had connections in the capitals of Europe that could be of assistance. However, Austria was one of Zaharoff's largest clients and he would be hesitant to intervene in such an emotionally-charged situation. Zaharoff was a close friend of Emperor Franz Joseph and would probably betray Otto's confidence, if Otto tried to enlist his help to silence Nijinsky.

The image of his cousin Rolfe floated into his head. Rolfe was in Vienna and Otto had heard rumors that he had a sadistic edge. The last time Otto's son, Axel, had visited the United States, he had voiced incoherent complaints and petulantly refused to board the steamship back to Germany. Otto had dismissed the child's remonstrances as the rantings of a three-year-old who was frightened by travel. Perhaps, Rolfe could be enlisted to silence the dancer. Otto stopped — this is insane. Slow down, take stock. Don't panic. Have another drink.

He cradled his forehead with the heels of his hands; then, the image of King Alfonso of Spain entered his consciousness. He was the perfect person. His mother, Christa, was the daughter of the Archduke Karl of Austria and sister of the Austrian Emperor. Alfonso told him last summer that he was dreading a European war because he had relatives in every royal court. Kahn drank more scotch and concluded that Alfonso would relish the opportunity to play the grand statesman here, especially, since it could be presented as a purely artistic mission. Tell him that the Habsburgs are embarrassing his family by arresting a ballet dancer. Otto composed a wire to him along with an alert to his firm's man in Madrid to impress the King and his mother with the urgency of this request.

Time was running out. How long could Nijinsky withstand torture at the hands of the enraged Austrians? The amber liquor splashed over the edge of his glass as he refilled it and took a large gulp. A feeling of warmth permeated his chest. His anxiety was fading into a more pernicious feeling of self-pity. Another gulp.

Kahn felt an urge to weep. He had not done so since the rejection by Sanger. He had hardened his heart after the shock of Margaret's abandonment. Yet, this situation was more threatening. It was not just his heart at stake; his entire life would be destroyed if Nijinsky cracked.

Then, he thought of another woman of considerable persuasive skill and influence. Kahn feverishly penned a personal handwritten plea to Parisian Countess Elisabeth Regina Greffulhe, a woman renowned for her beauty and connections with European aristocracy. Otto's relationship with the Countess was of the most intimate sort and his letter was filled with terms of endearment and promises of liaisons during his next visit to Paris. He paused to envision her stunning face with eyes like *"the dark purple brown-tinged petals of a rarely seen pansy."*[24] One of her friends had shared this description with him at a gala the Countess had hosted at her salon on *Rue d'Astorg* and it had remained with him.

Drafting the letter to the Countess, was cathartic. He pleaded with life-and-death urgency for her to use whatever measures at her disposal to secure the release of Vaslav. She knew Vaslav well. He had endeared himself with an impromptu dance at one of her parties that had captivated her guests and was still a topic of awe among Parisian society. Otto concluded the letter "Faithfully Yours."

As Otto sealed the letter, he thought, "Who am I kidding? The last time I was with the Countess, she slapped me across the face so hard that my monocle ended up in Lady Cheshire's bisque." His shoulders slumped as he rubbed his eyes, defeated. As if it were independent of his body, his hand pulled open the desk drawer. The sound of a metal object sliding across the smooth wood was the only noise he heard above the thumping of his heart. A malevolent form with a pearl handle beckoned him. The best solutions are often the most obvious.

"Wake up, *schwein!*" the burly guard screamed as he flung a bucket of cold water in his face. Vaslav sputtered as the water dripped down his chest. He was hanging by manacles with his feet barely able to touch the floor. His wrists were bloody and raw from bearing his weight. He had been in this dungeon for days. He had lost count. By incessant light and dousings with ice water, Nijinsky had been kept awake since he was arrested in Vienna.

His windowless cell was cold and dank; he could feel congestion building in his chest and lungs.

Across from his cell were two other cells. A pathetic figure of a human occupied each cell. Their faces were unrecognizable due to multiple beatings that had been inflicted while Vaslav was forced to observe. His cellmates were naked and shackled by the wrists and hung in the same fashion as he was. Vaslav recognized the two prisoners from his meeting in Belgrade several months earlier. In the cell to his left was Nedeljko Čabrinović, the grenade thrower, and to his right was Gavrilo Princip, the gunman who murdered the Archduke and his wife. Despite repeated, brutal beatings by the inquisitors, neither of the assassins was able to identify Vaslav, or connect him with the conspiracy to kill the Archduke Ferdinand.

As he shivered, he could feel delirium beginning to take hold of his mind. Vaslav realized that his life would probably end here in this miserable cell. He looked at the other prisoners; they were whimpering hopelessly. Vaslav felt profound sorrow that these young men, the flower of their generation, had been driven in desperation to murder their political oppressors. He felt profound shame at his own callous disregard for life and the acts of evil he had perpetrated. He compared the noble motives of the Serb assassins with his own base motives. He began to weep. Self-loathing possessed him; his soul screamed denunciation of his life. He hallucinated events of his own youth. How his father had abandoned him to a sadistic dance master. He tried to shut the images from his mind. The degradations and humiliations that he endured as a young student flooded into his consciousness. He recalled the pain and inability to walk due to tissues rent by abuse.

As he watched the inquisitor return to the cells across from him, Vaslav saw the face of his dance master. He turned toward Vaslav grinning diabolically as he placed a red-hot poker onto Gavrilo's chest. Vaslav winced in pain and lost consciousness. A guard immediately doused him with ice water and whacked him across the backs of his legs, screaming curses at him. Vaslav gazed at the guard absently, seeing only an unfocused image before him. Vaslav envisioned a score of demons stabbing at him with hot pokers. He saw the faces of his victims with their faces bloated and maudlin-purple, contorted in the pain of death, floating around him. Their eyes, haunted with hate, bore into his eyes as if searching for his soul to extinguish. Vaslav shook his head in an effort to rid his mind of the spirits attacking him. He failed and the vision continued to bore into his being. "Stop, stop," he screamed.

His plea was met with another bucket of ice water. He briefly returned to his senses. Squeezing his eyelids to remove the water, he watched as the inquisitor held a burning torch to Gavrilo's legs. The smell of burning flesh filled the confined area. Vaslav began retching in despair and disgust. He saw the image of the Angel Gabriel with his head bowed standing behind the assassin.

Gavrilo screamed, *"My life is already ebbing away. I suggest that you nail me to a cross and burn me alive. My flaming body will be a torch to light my people on their path to freedom."*[25]

1914
Berlin, Germany

By the pricking of my thumbs
Something wicked this way comes.

~ William Shakespeare, *Macbeth*

I N A NONDESCRIPT BUILDING near the theater district of Berlin, Max Warburg sat in his office completing encoded instructions to his Dutch asset. The sign on the door said 'Torweg Booking Agents,' but it was the operational center for his worldwide network of agents and operatives. It was behind this rather shabby, unassuming façade that espionage, sabotage and assassination efforts were coordinated. He had risen through the ranks by utilizing the skills he had honed as the head of international initiatives for M.M. Warburg Banking House in Hamburg. Now, with the onset of the Great War, he was working around the clock trying to keep up with situations throughout the world.

His requests for additional personnel had gone unfulfilled, essentially because qualified young men were flocking to military careers, especially the new-fangled aviation corps. He could not really blame them for wanting the glory of the battlefield. In contrast, his work was by definition clandestine, unglamorous and unheralded.

Max had recently attended a secret meeting with the high military command and a brilliant young American named Edward Bernays about how to win the war through effective use of propaganda and hero management. Bernays was in Germany visiting his famous cousin, Dr. Sigmund Freud. Bernays presented an innovative theory that a government could benefit from romanticizing heroes by using techniques of embellishment and fabrication in order to create heroes that the public would idolize as larger than life. Throughout history, heroes had been proclaimed after the victory was won. Bernays believed that this was a missed opportunity; modern communications made it possible to elevate heroes before and during the war. This would be a powerful galvanizing force in a society. This approach entailed a full-fledged media blitz to elevate a particular individual or group to hero status in the minds of the everyday man.

Using survey techniques that Bernays had developed at Columbia University, Max's group had identified and recruited a young cavalry reconnaissance officer from a prominent aristocratic family. The good-looking youngster had distinguished himself at military cadet school at an early age and been singled out to personify the new aviator corps. His name was Manfred Albrecht von Richthofen. At Bernays' suggestion, the air corps painted von Richthofen's plane red and Bernays dubbed him the Red Baron. Soon, the press began to bestow accolades on the Red Baron and popular songs were being written about the aviator's exploits.

Warburg turned his attention to the report on his desk from the Dutch operative, Agent H-21, whom he had recruited while she was peddling sexual favors to German military officials. She was an exotic dancer of Dutch descent who had been raised in the Far East. Since the Netherlands was not entangled in the alliances of the major European powers, she was able to travel freely throughout Europe. She plied her trade as an exotic dancer, reputedly steeped in the mysteries of the Hindu god Siva and adept in erotica. In addition to her professional dancing engagements, she was the highest paid courtesan on the continent.

On his desk lay blank sheets of paper. To avoid compromise or detection, H-21 utilized invisible ink for her reports. She diluted a common disinfectant that doubled as her contraceptive fluid and used it as her ink. Max removed the lampshade from his desk lamp and held the first sheet over the light bulb. Gradually, a string of brown letters appeared on the paper. When he had completed the process for each of the pages, he labeled and dated the report. Then, he settled in his chair to peruse the papers carefully.

With interest, he read about the exploits of Grigory Rasputin, the "mad monk" who reputedly held great sway with Tsar Nicholas and the Tsarina. The agent's salacious account of a Khylst "ceremony" in the basement of a vodka den held potential as possible blackmail material. In his master journal, Max entered cryptic notes about future actions cross-referenced to H-21's report. He was almost finished when his phone rang. It was the clerk at the Sacher Hotel.

In the aftermath of the call, Max Warburg was lost in thought. One of his operatives had been arrested in Vienna by the Austrian Imperial Guard. Max felt his stomach constrict as he mentally reviewed his interactions with Nijnsky. He probed the events carefully to detect whether his fingerprints could be found on anything. He had travelled *incognito* and used cash for all transactions. He had taken care to wear lifts in his shoes, various hats, dental appliances and facial hair that would make identification difficult. Despite being satisfied his meeting in Vienna had been invisible, he began to weave an elaborate web of distortions and misinformation about any connection he might have with the renowned dancer. He made a mental note to make sure that Nijinsky's young, blond consort met with an unfortunate fatal accident.

He was in the process of fabricating a report about a June trip to Rome in case anyone claimed that he met Nijinsky in Vienna when the phone jingled for his attention. It was Otto Kahn.

"Max, it's Otto. Is it safe to talk?"

"*Nein*, emergency protocol seven. I'll be waiting," said Max as he slammed down the receiver. His career, his life, was in the hands of a rank amateur he thought with disgust. Warburg decided that he would activate the eradicator. The only question was whether he could complete the mission to eliminate Kahn before he bungled things so irrevocably that Max would be doomed. He formulated a telegram to his New York operative with instructions to terminate Otto with extreme prejudice, preferably by making it look like an accident.

In his New York office, Otto considered his options. They were frightfully limited. Max had instructed him to communicate only by encrypted telegram to a dummy address in Berlin. Now was not the time to panic.

Using his codebook, he drafted a telegram detailing the steps he had taken on learning of Vaslav's arrest. Otto concluded the cable with a frantic plea that Warburg send an assassin to eliminate Nijinsky immediately. Otto's message must have crossed Max Warburg's along the Transatlantic Cable.

The following day, Otto was in his office when Helga interrupted him to advise that Rudolph Hecht was there to make his monthly report. In the venerable, nepotistic tradition of Kuhn Loeb, Otto had hired his cousin to assist with his burgeoning international clientele. Otto welcomed the thin young man into his office.

"Rudolph, sit. Give me some good news. The dog days of summer this year are depressing me."

"Well, Otto, our collections for the last month are at the highest level of the year. They are 40% higher year-over-year. The payments to the Romanov account have doubled. Otto, are you OK?"

Otto regarded Hecht as if the young man had just appeared out of thin air. Kahn had been distracted by the sight of a telegram protruding from Hecht's shirt pocket. Otto's attention had drifted to his concerns about Nijinsky.

"Excuse me, Rudolph. Something reminded me of a dear friend who is caught up in those unfortunate events in Europe. I must attend to some urgent affairs. We'll continue later."

"That is fine. Just one more thing. Can you give me a ride to the office in the morning? There is a personal matter I need to go over alone with you."

"Of course. Are things alright between you and Marjorie?"

"Oh, yes," said a suddenly flustered Hecht. "I must see you alone . . . for some advice."

"7:30 AM, sharp," concluded Otto. As Hecht departed he stole a furtive glance at Kahn, almost bumping into the coffee cart as he hurried away. Otto chided himself for not thinking of his old friend sooner. He spent the afternoon crafting a handwritten note to the former president with a modest request for his assistance.

His day had been a futile waste of time; he absent-mindedly flipped through one report after another without accomplishing a single stitch of work. Only the list of his assets he prepared in the event of a disaster gave him any satisfaction. It was afternoon when there was a knock at Otto's office door. He forced a worried smile as Jacob Schiff and Paul Warburg entered.

"You look like you did not get a wink of sleep last night. We came to see if we could be of any assistance," said Jacob.

"Yes, I thought we might take you out for an early dinner tonight at Delmonico's to celebrate my new job," suggested Paul. Weeks earlier, pursuant to an appointment by President Wilson, the diminutive banker had begun working on the first Board of Governors of the New York Federal Reserve Bank.

"Come on, Otto, say yes. You've worried enough for today. Vienna is asleep. Let's put that behind us for now," insisted Jacob.

"Look, Otto, I have something to show you before we go out," said Paul. Warburg reached into his breast pocket and produced an envelope containing several telegrams. He riffled through them and produced one.

"'MY DEAR WARBURG STOP CONGRATULATIONS ON BIRTH OF FEDERAL RESERVE BANK STOP WE HOPE THAT YOUR CREATURE GROWS AND PROSPERS STOP YOUR DEVOTED SERVANT WOODROW.' Who uses words like that? This will definitely make it into my memoirs."

The three men laughed as they walked the short distance to the restaurant where they were welcomed by Giovanni Delmonico. Using an age-old practice that had served his family well, he fawned over his prominent customers, greeting them warmly and asking about the health of their family members by name.

Seated in their usual private table in the corner, the trio settled in for an exquisite meal. After salad, Otto excused himself, professing distress caused by the events of the day. Jacob took the opportunity to visit his old friend, Elihu Root, the former Secretary of State who was sitting on the other side of the dining room with a group of lawyers. Scanning the room furtively, Paul Warburg reached across the table and took Otto's wine glass. He placed it below the edge of the table and poured some white powder into the glass, stirring the contents surreptitiously.

When Otto returned to the table, he had a slight layer of sweat on his brow.

"Otto, are you feeling OK?" asked Paul.

"Actually, I'm feeling a little flushed. It must be the heat in here," replied Kahn. He reached for his water glass and gulped down the contents. He slumped back in his chair, fanning himself with his napkin. Schiff returned just as the waiter served the sizzling specialty of the house, Delmonico steaks topped with herb butter.

"Gentlemen, let's celebrate. I know that there may be some clouds on the horizon. We will stand together and prevail. Who knows, the storm clouds may blow away and never strike? We should enjoy the good things. I am commencing a new position as governor of the New York Fed which is the fruition of all of our efforts going back to Jekyll Island and before. So please raise your glasses and drink to the new order," toasted Paul Warburg. Jacob and Otto lifted their wine glasses, replying, "Here, here!"

Just as their glasses reached their lips, Giovanni rushed over excitedly, calling for Mr. Kahn's attention. Giovanni was waving a telegram above his head as he bustled across the room. Otto froze. Paul glared malevolently at the interrupter. Jacob nearly choked, coughing roughly.

"Mr. Kahn," said a contrite Giovanni, "excuse my interruption. I was told that this message was extremely urgent and to bring it to you immediately." Otto took the missive anxiously. As he read the contents, a broad smile stretched across his face. Raising his glass, Otto beamed, "Gentlemen, our Viennese troubles are over. We will have the *premier danseur* in New York within weeks. Our dear friend, Vaslav Nijinsky, has been released! Let's drink to life! *L'chaim.*"

Paul blanched; then, in an act of sheer desperation, leapt at Otto swinging his arms frantically in an effort to swat the glass from Kahn's upraised hand. Otto instinctively pulled back and bumped into Giovanni. The banker and the restaurateur toppled to the floor. The wine glass dislodged from Otto's hand and hit the floor, shattering as if it had been struck by a wrecking ball. Otto stared at Warburg incredulously; Paul shrugged stupidly and wiped creamed spinach from his cheek.

Earlier in the evening, just past midnight in Germany, Max Warburg was in his office trying to stave off his own sense of foreboding. He was jarred to attention by the harsh ring of his phone. He answered and listened to an authoritative voice on the other end. Max's countenance brightened as he listened to Chancellor Theobald von Bethmann-Hollweg provide him with instructions from the Kaiser himself. The monarch directed Max to contact

Colonel Schnell of the Austrian Imperial Guard in Vienna and secure the transfer of Vaslav Nijinsky to German custody forthwith. Upon securing Nijinsky, Max was to give him a *laisser passer,* diplomatic travel pass, and transport him to Bern, Switzerland.

Several hundred miles away, Colonel Heinrich Schnell received an urgent cable from the Minister-President, Count Karl von Stürgkh, advising him that the Emperor demanded the release of Vaslav Nijinsky. The Colonel was surprised that anyone even knew that Nijinsky was in his custody and immediately telephoned the Count. Schnell advised von Sturgkh that his men were on the verge of breaking Nijinsky and discovering who was behind the assassination of Archduke Franz Ferdinand.

The Count was adamant that the order must be obeyed without hesitation. Sensing Schnells' resistance, Von Sturgkh launched into a sarcastic tirade that the Empire was in the middle of a conflagration of global proportions that did not include abusing ballet dancers. He mentioned that the Emperor's sister, Christa, had berated him for embarrassing the family by torturing the world's foremost ballet dancer, and insisted that he be released. There was to be no delay; the Colonel was to release Nijinsky immediately. Schnell knew that he was fighting a lost cause and agreed to implement the order as quickly as possible. He promised that he would have the dancer back in his room at the Sacher Hotel by the next day.

Max Warburg watched as the burly Austrians carefully lifted the delirious dancer from the gurney and placed him on the goose feather mattress in his hotel room. He appeared diminished by his ordeal and his head lolled back and forth while he muttered incoherently. Max gave his counterpart a nod of commiseration that the Colonel acknowledged with his steely eyes.

"Your dancer must have friends in the highest of places."

"Apparently."

As Max's physician was providing Vaslav with a strong sedative, Vaslav shrieked, *"God said to me, 'Go home and tell your wife that you are mad.'"*[26]

1994
Cold Spring Harbor, New York

If gold rusts, what can iron do?

~ GEOFFREY CHAUCER, *CANTERBURY TALES*

OHEKA CASTLE YIELDED HER secrets reluctantly. The search for the elusive elevator shaft proved tedious. Since the partners knew that the actual structure would vary from the available drawings, they decided to proceed cautiously, by hand. Tommy directed Jason the mason as he chipped away at the basement wall. He complained that the tough stone kept dulling his blades. Just as they were about to break for the day, the large chisel struck a glancing blow and they heard a tumble of stones falling into empty space. Luke could see the others were smiling behind the bandanas that covered their mouths and noses. A rush of stale air blew into the basement causing them to cough.

"Let's go get the equipment from the truck while Jason clears a hole," said Tommy excitedly.

Luke, Tommy and Jed climbed out of the basement into the fading afternoon sunlight.

"You know, guys," said Jed, "We're excited about getting into the shaft, but there's not enough time today."

"You're right," replied Tommy. "But I have a surprise in my bag of tricks." He reached behind the driver's seat of his pickup truck and removed a gray plastic case. They returned to the basement. Tommy opened the case and withdrew a black snake-like object.

"This is Ralphie the snake. He can peer into tight spots and around corners. Let's see what we can see."

Tommy snaked Ralphie through the hole and ran it down the shaft. The device was equipped with a headlight and was attached to a small screen that showed what the snake-camera was viewing. The engineer manipulated Ralphie so that the lens pivoted 360 degrees to reveal a cobweb-streaked cavity with rusted rails running vertically that they recognized as an elevator shaft.

"How far can he go? Take him down as far as you can," insisted Jed. More of the same came into view as Ralphie reached the end of his length. The three friends released a collective sigh of disappointment that was at the same time charged with anticipation.

The next morning they were in the basement bright and early. Before them was a door-sized opening crisscrossed by caution tape. Tommy hooked up a tripod attached to a winch wound with thick wire. He lowered a string of utility lights down the shaft. They all peered down when Tommy flipped the switch, brightly illuminating the long, dark shaft.

"Looks like we found it," said Tommy.

"Somebody sure went to a lot of trouble to hide it. Makes you wonder why," Jed offered.

"Yeah, I can't wait to see where it leads," exclaimed Luke as he pulled on a bosun's seat while Jed attached a secure line to the axle of Tommy's truck. Luke covered his wavy hair with a hard hat fixed with a miner's lamp. He gave them a 'thumbs up' as he entered the shaft. He slowly rappelled down the side of the shaft as Tommy worked the winch. When he was halfway down, he gave the hold signal. Before him was a pair of doors. He reached into his tool belt for a small crowbar. Bracing his legs, Luke wedged the bar into the crack between the doors and pried. Sweat poured down his face as he strained against decades of rust and grime. The doors gradually levered open. He peered in.

"What do you see?" questioned Jed anxiously. Luke looked up. He savored their helplessness and shrugged. Jed threw a small pebble at him that ricocheted off his helmet.

"OK, OK, there's a room with a sarcophagus inside," he laughed. "No, really, there's a medium-sized room that looks like it's from Mars. It's covered red with rust. It looks like an iron bunker." Luke removed a camera from his backpack and snapped some pictures.

He signaled Tommy to lower him further. His stomach jumped as he saw the red eyes of a rat scurrying across the rotted fabric of an Eastern Military Academy uniform. He signaled for Tommy to lower him closer. He was startled to see a skeleton. Could it possibly be . . . ?

After retrieving the remains, the police took several days to collect evidence from the shaft. The chief inspector said that it would probably take several weeks to determine the identity and cause of death of the 'victim of the secret shaft' as the local papers had reported the grisly discovery.

Luke and his team waited impatiently to obtain clearance to re-enter the shaft. Although the coroner had not yet issued his report, the authorities green-lighted continuation of their exploration. Finally, after weeks of inactivity, Luke was back in the bosun's chair being lowered into the shaft. His objective was to explore the Iron Bunker. His heart was heavy because he had intuited that the body in the shaft was his high school friend, who had disappeared so long ago. The thought that his demise might be the result of foul play unnerved Luke. On the other hand, he and his group were on the verge of a once-in-a-lifetime experience. He knew that the Iron Bunker was another step closer to Otto; but how to decipher this puzzle piece?

He felt a little claustrophobic in the tiny room. It was roughly one hundred square feet with seven-foot-high ceilings. The metal room was cold and almost unbearable due to the pervasive rust. The bunker was well preserved, having been constructed out of metal almost a century ago. The worst aspect of spending time in the iron bunker was the faint grit of rust that caused a slight metallic catch in the back of his throat. When he sat at the metal desk on the metal chair, he imagined being in some odd torture chamber in an *Indiana Jones* movie where the walls and ceiling slowly moved together threatening to crush the occupants, usually Jones and his romantic interest. Given the fact that Indiana's typical romantic interest was a scantily–clad, foreign-born beauty who he had converted to his side, Luke figured that there were worse ways to die. Anyway, Jones was always resourceful enough to escape. Now, it was Luke's turn to be resourceful.

The task before him was daunting. The only way to solve the puzzle was to transport himself into the mind of a German-born, master international banker from the early twentieth century. One certainty was that Otto was a man of many secrets. He kept secrets from his wife and family, secrets from his clients, secrets from his partners. What other secrets have you been hiding, Otto?

Luke surveyed the room disconsolately. He had tapped, scraped and analyzed every square inch of the room hoping to find some clue, some hidden trigger to the room's secrets — all to no avail. There must be a gear-infested, cantilevered mechanism to unlock and activate. Luke envisioned a door to the treasure room opening slowly, with creaking, grinding, ponderous efficiency, to reveal secret treasure. Luke chided himself for watching too many *Indiana Jones* movies. In the real world, centuries-old mechanisms decay and rust. He was reminded of some principle of thermodynamics that he learned in school; something to the effect that, over time things tend to degenerate toward maximum disorder. Alright, so he should stop looking here for a magical Rube Goldberg machine to spring into action. If not here, where?

He exhaled deeply in exasperation. As he inhaled, some dust caught the back of his throat causing him to cough. I've got to get out of here, he thought. That's it, that's it. Otto would not stay in this creepy room either. The secret must be embedded in more luxurious surroundings. Where? Then it came to him. Otto loved secret rooms in his mansions so he could engage in amorous trysts. What if there was a secret room in Oheka — hidden in plain view?

Luke rushed out of the iron bunker and made his way back to the Castle. All he had to do was to channel the old boy and locate the secret room. Easier said than done. The castle had been open to vagrants and vandals for over a decade. What chance was there that a secret room had eluded such curious denizens? Luke deflated slightly at the thought. OK, let's be analytical, he chided himself.

He decided to focus on the public areas of the castle first — areas where the spider could bring the fly for culmination of the seduction. From his knowledge of the castle, he went to the "Charlie Chaplin" pub. The cavernous room was in shambles with plaster littering the floor and boards and broken furniture strewn everywhere. The framework of the bar still stood opposite the entrance to the room. Luke looked inside, outside and around the room for walls that were extra-thick or where there were unexplained gaps. Nothing.

Luke's mind was racing as he sifted through the detritus of the decrepit castle. Otto might not have had a secret room off the pub where presumably the company was likely to be lively. Maybe, just maybe, the secret lair would be somewhere else. Perhaps the library . . . a place where there may have been more formal gatherings and, therefore, a place where a discreet escape was arguably more needed.

Off to the library he went, carefully avoiding the boards with rusty nails sticking up waiting to inflict a puncture wound. He walked down the hall with his beam of light guiding the way. The library was lined with solid concrete shelves that had been painted to emulate wood. The paint and concrete had not fared well. The wall was chipped and gouged almost beyond recognition. The room was so large that it had been used by the military academy for the student library and study center.

The late afternoon sun filtered into the library in streams of dust motes that danced and glittered. Luke surveyed the scene, and wondered 'where are you hiding, Otto?' The obvious choice for a latch to a secret room was the fireplace. Luke scrutinized, pushed, pulled and yanked in every way imaginable. There was no play or movement anywhere near the fireplace. Luke walked over to catty-corner shelves in the corners and pushed, prodded and yanked every conceivable surface to no avail.

Shadows formed in the two niches on the inner walls and a thought formed in Luke's mind. He envisioned the room as it would have been when Otto was on the prowl for illicit romance. The niches would have contained statues or vases — things with some heft. Luke scanned the room for something compact and weighty. His eyes settled on a piece of andiron. He lugged it over to each of the niches and pressed down. What was he missing? Then he had a flash of inspiration; Otto would not have pushed down; he would have pushed back or to the side. He walked to the niche that was situated on the outside corner of the building. Placing the heavy metal piece on the shelf of the niche, he pushed it to the rear, nothing. He pushed to the right, nothing. Last chance, to the left. Click. A small panel along the molding cracked open. Bingo.

Luke hastily pried it open and found an old-fashioned switch with double buttons. Inhaling sharply, he pushed the buttons excitedly. Nothing.

Of course, he chided himself, there was no electricity. Now what? His heart was thumping. I can't believe this; he berated himself for not anticipating an electrical switch. It never works that way in the movies, he chuckled.

Hasta mañana.

Luke could hardly sleep. With his mind racing, he came to a realization. Assuming they would find a secret room, they should approach it like Howard Carter approaching the tomb of Tutankhamen. They needed to use modern archaeological methods and recording systems. He would contact Tricia Amare first thing in the morning. She was a professor of antiquities who Tommy had engaged to work through the issues relating to the Indian burial grounds that had been unearthed at one of Jed's developments in the Hamptons a few years ago. Her attention to detail, recordkeeping, photography and insight were invaluable in winning over the opposition groups and, more important, the New York State Department of Environmental Conservation. This decision settled his mind and he fell into a deep, restful sleep.

It took much of the morning to marshal everything needed for their project. Tommy gathered a portable generator, crowbars and a jackhammer. Tricia would be there after completing her teaching schedule. She would bring the commercial-grade video camera, Nikon SLR, and her laptop to inventory items with her customized spreadsheet program. Jed was bringing elevation drawings and whatever blueprints and sketches he had been able to garner from the granddaughter of Chester Holmes Aldrich, one of the senior architects of Oheka.

The team assembled in the library in mid-afternoon. Tommy reported that he had found the appropriate connections and that the generator was online ready to go. Luke could hear the rumbling of the gasoline engine outside. He smiled at Tricia, an attractive brunette, with her hair pulled back in a ponytail. She was wearing a SUNY Stony Brook sweatshirt that hid her athletic figure. A self-professed gym rat, she had maintained her schoolgirl figure into her mid-thirties. She had the olive skin of her Italian father and the delicate features of her French mother. With avocado-green eyes and a pleasant smile, she was one of Luke's favorite people. Unfortunately, thought Luke, they had never found the time in their busy careers to connect. Someday, perhaps.

Surrounded by anxious onlookers, Luke pressed one of the buttons. Nothing. Then he pressed the other button. Silence. Luke brushed away a trickle of perspiration from his eye and tried again. There was a slight pause, then, a shudder and off in the distance, he heard the sound of a hidden mechanism whirring into action. Suddenly, the entire alcove pivoted a crack to reveal a wrought iron spiral staircase. Their mouths dropped open and a collective 'Ahhh' escaped their lips. They spent the next several hours prying open the door.

Luke waited until the dust settled before stepping aside to allow Tricia to enter and climb up. The others followed like hounds catching a scent.

"Don't touch anything!" Tricia admonished, swiping at spider webs that draped the stairway.

With flashlights ablaze, they entered the secret lair. Luke thought, 'we've got you now, Otto, give up your secrets, you old bastard.' The scene before them was a combination bordello and speakeasy. Opposite the entrance was a large bed, now covered with dust and a decaying, once-red duvet. The ceiling over the bed was covered with a pitted mirror. Bed stands, with lamps drooping with cobwebs reminiscent of Spanish moss, bracketed the bed. Across the room was a dusty bar made of ebony and white marble. The flashlights reflected off the mirror, cut glass tumblers and crystal decanters filled with liquors arrayed behind the bar. An area rug so thick with dirt and dust that its provenance could not be discerned, covered the wooden floor of 'Otto's love nest' as Tricia dubbed it. To the right of the opening was a tall, mahogany secretary with glass doors protecting various leather-bound tomes.

After allowing them to assess the scene, Tricia announced that it was time for them to leave her to her task. They reluctantly complied but only after floodlights were carried up the spiral staircase to illuminate the chamber. With a last wistful glance they descended, envious of the archeologist. Jed sneezed from the dust as he exited.

After several hours of cataloguing Otto's nest, Tricia emerged dusty and thirsty. She announced that it was time for lunch. They piled into Jed's SUV and drove to a local eatery. During the ride, Tricia was deadpan. However, once she had freshened up in the ladies room of Cristiano's Restaurant and had two glasses of ice water, she re-animated.

"So far I've taken several hundred photos to capture the state of the site and I've begun cataloguing the books in the secretary."

"When do we get to jump into Otto's stuff?" interrupted Jed as he sipped his iced tea.

"In about a month," Tricia replied matter-of-factly.

Luke watched Jed as he nearly choked from the effort of trying to scream while drinking. Before he could formulate his incredulity at the outrageous length of time, Tricia burst out laughing and said, "Well, more like . . . tomorrow afternoon at the latest."

Luke and Tommy joined in the laughter as Jed sheepishly wiped tea from his chin. Tricia added, "I've brought something to whet your appetites." She reached into her camera bag and removed a single photograph that she displayed on the table. Before them in black and white, slightly curled was an image of three people.

"OK, Luke, do you recognize them?"

"Well, I think the older guy in the center is our man, Otto Kahn. Although I've never seen a picture of him in informal clothes, nor wearing a Russian *ushanka*, the moustache and his bearing make it a safe bet that it's him. The two boys in front of him must be his kids. Look at the way he has his hands on their shoulders. Very paternal."

"The image is from 1919. It's written in pencil on the back," said Jed. "So that fits. Otto had young kids about that time according to the research we've done on him."

"They sure look like twins. I did not realize that he had twins. And what's the one on the right holding?"

"It looks like a matryoshka doll. You know, those Russian folk craft figures that open to reveal a smaller doll that opens to reveal a smaller one and so on. The name is the affectionate form of the name Matryona. But, it's a popular souvenir item from Russia. You know, we all had them as kids. OK, so maybe it was a girl thing. But, I had one as a kid," remarked Tricia.

"No, I had one, too. Except, mine was super heroes. It started with Superman and went down in size to Mighty Mouse," said Luke nostalgically.

"When I was in grad school, I had a professor who was obsessed with the Matryoshka Principle. It's a design paradigm that involves an 'object within an object.' He always challenged us to find the thing within the thing," remarked Tommy.

After lunch, Tricia visited her friend Jeremy, who owned an antique shop in Huntington Village to borrow his ring of several dozen keys that had been collected over the years. Back in the secret room, Tricia focused on the tall, handsomely-carved mahogany secretary. The glass paneled doors to the upper bookcase of the secretary were locked, as was the center slant-top that formed the working surface when open. Typically, when the desk was open there would be interior compartments and open nooks to keep papers sorted. The lower drawers of the piece below the fold-down desk were unlocked; however, to Tricia's disappointment there was nothing inside.

After trying most of the keys on the upper glass doors, Tricia was becoming resigned to the necessity of bringing in a locksmith. The next to last key did the trick and the lock to the upper bookcase clicked open. She adjusted her latex gloves and camera as she gently removed each volume on the shelves. She had already entered the titles into her database. Next, she methodically reviewed each book, adding detailed observations to her list. Each book was leather-bound with gold lettering on the spine. Most were first editions, signed by the author with personalized inscriptions. Tricia particularly marveled at several tomes by her favorite author, Mark Twain. Inside the flap of *The American Claimant*, Twain wrote, "Otto, our protagonist, Colonel Sellers, reminds me of you. Neither of you can refuse requests from the less fortunate among us who then take advantage of your kindness. While I was writing this, I would wake up in the night laughing at its ridiculous situations. I hope you find it humorous, too. All the best, S.L. Clemens."

Tricia's eye fell on another book by an American hero, *The Rough Riders*, by Theodore Roosevelt. As she opened the book a handwritten note on Sagamore Hill letterhead slipped into her lap. It read: *"July 31st, 1919, Dear Kahn, On my return from Pittsburg I found your note. Will you dine here Wednesday next at 7:30? Always yours, Theodore Roosevelt."*[27]

Using the same key as she had used for the bookcase, she quickly opened the desk lock. The top folded down and was supported by struts that opened simultaneously as the desk surface lowered into place. The surface of the desk was a burgundy leather that she found surprisingly supple. Inside the compartment was a series of miniature cubbies atop three drawers. The face panels of the drawers were burled wood with a lighter finish that tastefully complimented the rich, dark red of the rest of the piece. As she opened each of the drawers she felt a slight tug at various intervals as she gently pulled them open. Her examination of the contents yielded nothing exceptional. One of the more interesting documents was a February 1919 report signed by D.S. Beaton, head chauffeur of Kahn's motor fleet, that was prepared for the Dunlop Pneumatic Tyre Company inventorying the motor stable listing all the types and sizes or tires for the four Rolls Royces, one Pierce Arrow, two Hudsons, one Brewster and something called a Dune Rover.

When Tricia was finished, she began to return the materials to their original places. She had just finished the top two shelves and was getting ready to place the books on the lowest shelf when Luke entered. As Tricia turned to greet him, the book she was replacing slipped out of her hand onto the shelf with a hollow thump. She looked up at Luke.

"Did you hear that thump?"

"Yes, do you think there's a hidden compartment?"

"Maybe. Wouldn't it be perfect if we found the old man's diary?"

Tricia removed the book and tapped the shelf surface with her knuckles. There was definitely a hollow reverberation. Excitedly, she began pushing and tapping all around the area, to no avail. There was no give, no hidden button or latch that they could find. Luke approached the piece. Tricia barred his way and held up a pair of latex gloves that he put on reluctantly. Luke pulled out the drawer under the shelf and shined his flashlight into the vacant space. He saw nothing out of the ordinary. Tricia examined the underside of the drawer.

"I think I found something. There are notches on the underside of the drawer. I thought I felt a tug when I opened each of the drawers, but, now, I think the notches might be something more. Let's try opening the drawers in varying degrees to see if there is some pattern that might release whatever is protecting the hollow space."

"Yeah, like a combination."

They spent the next hour gently pulling and adjusting the drawers without any results. Jed, who along with Tommy had joined them, watched with interest after they explained what they were doing. After a few minutes, Jed asked, "How many notches are there?"

"We have not counted them, what are you suggesting?"

"OK," said Jed. "Our ghost is named Otto Hermann Kahn. He named his greatest monument O-he-ka, so we know he is into his initials. Let's count the notches and see if there are twenty six, you know, for the alphabet."

Tricia replaced the drawers and slowly withdrew each, her brows furrowed in concentration and her lips mouthing the numerals as she progressed.

"Thirty. Each drawer has thirty notches. Now what do we do? We just have thirty which probably was the number of notches that would fit on that length of drawer. There could be millions of permutations of three sets of thirty."

"Wait," said Tommy. "Didn't Kahn grow up in Germany?"

"Yes, so what?" questioned Tricia.

"There are thirty letters in the German alphabet."

"I think he's got it!" cried Luke, who was scribbling on his pad. He counted the letters of the initials.

"Try '15-8-11, O-H-K.'"

Tricia gently pulled out the drawers in that order and smiled broadly as an audible click resonated through the area. She pushed on the panel and it levered open. She reached in and withdrew a small ledger.

PART 3

The Great War Rages

December 1914
East of Limanowa, Poland

**Silent night, holy night,
All is calm, all is bright.**

~ Joseph Mohr, 1816

It did not take long for the reality of war to set in. The Russian Army had been outsmarted, out-generaled and outfought from the outset of the war. At the Battle of Tannenburg in August, the Army had been decimated. In early December, the Third Army had been forced to retreat after losing the Battle of Limanowa. Now, as Christmas approached, the Army had been reduced to defensive positions. It seemed like the Germans were always one step ahead of them. Prince Dmitry Pavlovich stood in the rear of the command tent as General Ruzsky outlined their situation and plans to protect the Army until the spring.

Morale was abysmal. The high hopes of the summer had eroded like the diminished sunlight of autumn. Now that winter was upon the Imperial army, it was all the officers could do to maintain morale. Fortunately, they had been able to dig their trenches before the ground froze. Nevertheless, the bitter cold, combined with the relentless noise of German mechanized

215

vehicles moving behind the small tract of territory that separated the two great armies, frayed the nerves of even the most resolute soldiers. Day and night for weeks, the Russian soldiers huddled in their defensive positions while they heard German vehicles and shouts from across the divide.

Prince Dmitry was assigned to the cavalry and his early bravado had succumbed to the painful reality that his forces would be utilizing nineteenth century weapons against the modern twentieth century weaponry and mobility of the German army. He missed the carefree days when he and Felix would debauch their way through life. Now, every minute decision could result in death.

Something was amiss. Then it dawned on him. The mechanized racket from across the front had stopped. There was only blessed silence coming from the German side. When Dmitry deduced that the enemy might be preparing for Christmas Eve, he ordered the Chief Sergeant to provide the soldiers with extra rations of vodka to celebrate the holiday. Soldiers, he mused ruefully; he could barely call them men when he looked at the youthful faces of the teenagers that filled the ranks. Vodka, or Russian courage, as it was called by some of the veterans, was always welcome. Some of the men gathered around fires and gradually Dmitry heard the humming of carols.

As he walked among the soldiers, relishing the quiet, he spotted Corporal Yuri Witowski and Sergeant Vadim Treblinkov scurrying furtively behind one of the command tents carrying a duffel. Both men appeared to be inebriated. Dmitry followed and watched in amazement as Vadim withdrew a costume of Ded Moroz, the Russian Father Christmas. Vadim took off his uniform jacket and quickly replaced it with a heel-length coat that was vibrant blue and trimmed in white fur that matched a round fur hat. He finished the costume by attaching a curly white beard to his cheeks. Yuri handed him a long straight branch to serve as his magical staff. Vadim helped Yuri don a full length golden pelisse that was the traditional costume of Snegurochka, the Snow Maiden and granddaughter, who assists Ded Moroz in dispensing presents.

As the men emerged from behind the tent, Dmitry heard the distinctive melody of Christmas carols being sung by Russian soldiers. Faintly, and a half beat behind, he thought he heard the same melody, but the carols were being sung in German. The effect was angelic. Voices became louder as the two sides played off each other's melodies. After some time, Dmitry watched in astonishment as Vadim tied a white flag to his staff and Yuri lit a torch. Both men clambered up the side of the forward trench and marched singing at full throat into the divide. There was a tension on both sides as Vadim and Yuri continued walking and singing as loudly as they could.

Suddenly, a light appeared on the German side and a stout figure dressed in a red, fur-trimmed suit emerged from the darkness. He, too, sang the carol passionately but in German. It sounded like a heavenly duet; first Vadim and Yuri, then Fritz in German. He approached the Russians and held out a bottle of schnapps. Yuri lifted the torch high to illuminate the scene. Fritz tensed slightly as Vadim reached into his robe. His hand grasped a bottle of vodka that he produced enthusiastically and handed to Fritz. The exchange complete, both men lifted their bottles skyward and cried Merry Christmas in their native tongues. Laughing, they clinked the glass necks of the bottles and drank heartily.

Soon, others ventured out into the divide. Vadim was showing Fritz pictures of his wife and daughter, and Fritz hugged him and nodded admiringly. Along the divide, men were congregating in small groups, exchanging tobacco and chocolate here, a tin of sardines for a small ball there. The singing continued and fellowship abounded. The spell was broken when a German officer ordered the battalion trumpeter to play the retiring of the colors. The soft strains of the end-of-day music drifted over the frozen divide and had its desired effect. Slowly, reluctantly, the men bade each other farewell and trudged back to their respective lines. Dmitry watched sadly at the passing of the miraculous moment when men of good will faced each other as men, not enemies sworn to kill.

Several thousand miles to the south and west, there was real peace in Madrid, the capital of neutral Spain. King Alfonso awoke in his sumptuous chambers covered with a goose down comforter embroidered with his family crest. After a hearty breakfast of Andalusian sausage, poached eggs and biscuits studded with jalapenos, cheddar and chives, he walked into his adjoining study. It was garishly decorated with ribbons and a magnificent Christmas tree replete with new, colored electric lights that were little tubes filled with liquid that bubbled as the lights heated. The smell of pine wafted pleasantly through the area. The King reflected on his fortunate decision to maintain neutrality that had been a stroke of genius.

Dozens of presents wrapped in fancy paper were strewn around the tree. His eyes rested on one gift in particular that sat regally upon his desk. It was a large box wrapped in gold mesh cloth with a bright red and gold card resting atop a similarly-colored bow. With anticipation, Alfonso opened the card and read the handsome calligraphic Christmas wishes and special thanks for his role in securing the release of Vaslav Nijinsky from his friend Otto Kahn. Like a young child, the King attacked the wrapping vigorously to reveal a mahogany case inlaid with mother-of-pearl. There were golden clasps on each side near the base. He unhooked the clasps and lifted the top to uncover a golden typewriter. Every surface, screw and lever was coated with gold. The keys were etched marcasite. Where the nameplate of Remington, the manufacturer would be, there was a bejeweled royal crest of the Spanish monarchy. Normally blasé toward elaborate gifts, Alfonso chortled joyously. He immediately loaded a piece of gold stationery that accompanied the unique typewriter and began typing Christmas greetings to his mistress.

April, 1916
Suitland, Maryland

It may well be doubted whether human ingenuity
can construct an enigma . . . which human ingenuity
may not, by proper application, resolve.

~ EDGAR ALLAN POE

GOING BACK TO HIS DAYS AT SEA, the glare of the bright sun had so irritated his optic nerves that Strafe frequently suffered from debilitating headaches. His new-fangled, green-tinted sun spectacles were a welcome relief from the bright Maryland sun. The promise of modern science tantalized his fertile mind. He was always on the prowl for new methods to conduct the business of intelligence gathering. One thing he knew for certain was that the telegraph and radio had changed the way that spy business was conducted. Although modern communications allowed greater and faster transfer of information than ever before, they also presented greater opportunities for interception. Cable and wireless communication were so new, that security protocols were struggling to keep pace.

Two long years of war in Europe and the accelerated pace of communications meant that greater coordination was critical among countries with aligned interests. In 1914, at the start of the war, Strafe's relative, Admiral Henry Francis Oliver, re-energized the British Department of Naval Intelligence with the appointment of William Reginald Hall to Director of Naval Intelligence. When Strafe shared the 'Ramon' codebook recovered by Chorney in Mexico, the Admiral invited Oliver to Britain for a coordination session. The Ramon codebook was considered the Rosetta Stone for deciphering German communications.

During this trip to London, Strafe worked directly with Commander William Reginald "Blinker" Hall, nicknamed for his incessant eye tic. Blinker and Strafe forged a close personal relationship that was instrumental in creating the best joint intelligence capability in the world. Strafe was one of a handful of non-Brits allowed into the fabled Room 40 where the discipline of cryptanalysis was being applied to modern communications.

His current project was a case in point. The 'Ramon' codebook had enabled them to decipher numerous important dispatches from Berlin and thwart, or deflect many German espionage projects. Recently, however, the pace and intensity of German efforts in the U.S. had accelerated. The arrival in Washington of Count Johann Von Bernstorff, the new German Ambassador, coincided with a dramatic increase in sabotage attempts.

Strafe reviewed the report before him with unease. Something was missing. The interpretation unit had clearly translated the high priority message as "Schwartz Tom approved. Proceed with plans immediately." Tom Schwartz or Thomas Schwartz was clear, but what did the message mean? Their investigation of people with that name had come up empty. There was a Tom Schwartz who lived in Mineola, Long Island, but he was a milkman. There were six Tom Schwartz' in New York City, but they were teachers, or carpenters, or garment district workers. One was a lawyer, who had passed away three years ago. Frustrated, Strafe did the only thing he could do. Start over.

Connections, that's what he was failing to see. His eyes fell on a series of newspaper articles from the Providence Journal from the prior year's summer involving an *expose'* of German espionage. There were reports of German agents fomenting labor unrest at the Remington Arms factory and other New England munitions plants.

The morning coffee was beginning to have its usual effect, so Strafe closed the folder on his desk and took a bathroom break. As he walked down the corridor painted in a sickly, light pea soup green, he glanced out the window and noticed a pregnant woman wheeling a baby carriage along the sidewalk. This was the fifth pregnant woman he had noticed since his daughter-in-law had announced her pregnancy with their first grandchild last week. He mused about the phenomenon whereby once your mind focuses on something, like pregnant women, you saw them everywhere. He tried to come up with a name for this phenomenon. The best he could come up with was ubiqu-awarety, combining ubiquitous + awareness. This phenomenon had served him well in past analyses of masses of disparate information, by drawing his awareness to connections that otherwise might not be made.

On returning to his desk, he noticed that an article had slipped out of the folder and lay next to his chair under the desk. The article was about a German plot to use legislation in Congress, the Ship Purchase bill, to purchase certain merchant marine vessels that had been interned under the Embargo, thereby sending millions of dollars from the United States to replenish the German treasury. Curiously, there was a quote from Otto Kahn "... admitting that the story about the purchase of the ships was true, although '*wrong in part.*'"

The mention of the name Otto Kahn triggered his recollection of an article from The New York Times, the previous summer, about an assassination attempt on financier, J.P. Morgan who was gunned down in his Long Island mansion by a former Cornell German professor. The local papers had reported an unconfirmed rumor that the assailant had spent the night before the attempted murder at Oheka Castle, the home of Otto Kahn. Was there a link between Otto Kahn and the decoded wires?

With his feet on his desk, he re-deciphered the message. He translated it again and again. There must be some speck of evidence that I'm missing, he thought. Maybe he had missed some connection in the files on the personnel in the German embassy in D. C. and their operations in New York City. He scanned the names of the German delegation that had arrived in Washington after the outbreak of the war in Europe: Ambassador Count Johann Von Bernstorff, Dr. Rolfe Albert, "commercial attaché," Dr. Bernhard Dernberg, propagandist, Capt. Franz von Papen, military attaché, Capt. Karl Boy-Ed, naval attaché, and Wolf von Igel.

Nothing.

Strafe stared at the message until it blurred. "Schwartz Tom approved. Proceed with plans immediately." A corollary of the rule that it is hard to prove a negative is that it is hard to see what is not there. What wasn't he seeing? Suddenly, a burst of clarity unraveled the puzzle. There was no comma. In their tidy military thinking, he and his team had assumed that the message referred to a person named Tom Schwartz. What if Schwartz Tom did not refer to a person? What if it meant something else, like a thing, or location? What if Schwartz were an adjective, not a noun? Of course, Schwartz is German for Black. Could the message refer to Tom Black? No, there was no comma. Maybe it meant Black Tom. That had to be it! He recalled seeing a memo about the throughput of munitions shipped to the Allies from Black Tom Island in New York harbor. That must be it; the Krauts were planning something at Black Tom Island.

It made perfect sense . . . but, what and when?

Standing on a landing in the stairwell on the twenty-fifth floor outside the offices of Wolf von Igel located at 60 Wall Street in New York City, Kurt Chorney's stomach was jittery. He was part of a group that was about to conduct a raid on an apparent front for German espionage efforts. He preferred action in the open field, rather than in the confines of an office building. But, there he stood along with three federal agents. Strafe had instructed him to attend the raid as an observer and gather any codebooks that might be present. For reassurance, he squeezed his arm to the Colt M1911 he was wearing under his jacket.

The target of the raid was a German national, who was nominally overseeing Germany's Military Information Bureau in New York City. In actuality, von Igel was running a comprehensive spy and sabotage operation. Since the war had begun, the violence and destruction by German operatives had escalated dramatically. The young lieutenant had read reports attributing to von Igel a witches' brew of clandestine operations on U.S. soil. It ranged from funding the acquisition of explosives to destroy infrastructure and ships, to bankrolling strikes and orchestrating propaganda designed to dispirit workers and erode America's industrial output.

ONI had recently received a tip about a possible plot to sabotage the Welland Canal. This was a strategically located canal that allowed ships travelling along the St. Lawrence River to bypass Niagara Falls, reducing shipping times significantly. The Canal was being re-routed and upgraded by the Canadian government as part of the war effort.

The trail to von Igel was based on information from a Canadian Dominion Police officer, who had observed a 1915 Harvard coupe with porcelain New York license plates loitering around the secure construction site at the Welland Canal. Officer David had observed the occupants leave the car with cameras and climb to a nearby rise to take a multitude of photographs of the access roads and the construction site.

When the car headed for the U.S. border, the Mountie pulled them over and received evasive answers from a huge, blond driver, who spoke with a decidedly German accent. Although their paperwork checked out, his instincts told him that these men were up to no good. His detailed report about their activities and their descriptions included the fact that the car was registered to Plattdeutsche Shipping Company located at 52 William Street, NY, NY.

The reference to the Plattdeutsche Shipping Company piqued Strafe's curiosity. It was a suspected front for von Igel's dynamitism. The organizing papers for Plattdeutsche Shipping listed Otto's bank as agents for receipt of legal process. Could there be the link between von Igel and the Monocle? A raid on von Igel's office might just reveal what von Igel was planning.

Chorney listened to the last minute instructions from Joseph A. Baker, Assistant Superintendent of the New York Division of the Department of Justice, Anti-Espionage Task Force. According to the porter who had just finished cleaning the office suite, there were three men and a woman secretary on the premises. The objective of the agents was to neutralize the occupants and take von Igel into custody, then confiscate all the files and send them for analysis.

Although the three agents were armed with revolvers, Baker cautioned them to use their weapons only as a last resort. Baker had spent his career as a field agent. He came from a family of law enforcement officers, who had served the nation with distinction. He was short and stocky with a no-nonsense demeanor. With clear brown eyes and a jutting jaw, he was the picture of determination. Next to Baker was Rusty Sullivan, a burly Irishman whose face bore the flattened nose and scarred orbitals of the former prizefighter that he was in his early twenties before he joined the force. The last agent was Nick Angelo, a well-built thirty-year-old, on loan to the Justice Department Task Force, from the New York City Police Department. Detective Angelo had fought his way out of New York's Hell's Kitchen to become a proud member of New York's Finest. He was swarthy with strong Roman features and a quick, toothy smile.

The suite consisted of an anteroom where the secretary sat, an office where von Igel and his bodyguard were located, and a small, windowless file room adjoining the office. The outer door had a frosted-glass panel that bore the suite number and no other identifying marks.

Agent Baker checked his watch. Go time. He opened the door and quickly advanced to the reception desk. Rusty and Nick fanned to the sides and Kurt blocked the door behind him. Baker flashed his badge to the secretary, who half-rose to inhibit his entry into the inner office. Baker was too quick for her and threw open the office door and strode into the room.

von Igel was seated behind a large wooden desk. He was in his forties, suave and well-dressed. He had an aristocratic air and his dull, gray, fish-eyes exuded a lifeless, shark-like stare. His dark, chalk-striped suit, slicked back hair and pencil moustache gave him the appearance of a celluloid gangster.

Seated in front of von Igel was George Van Skal, former managing editor of *Statts-Zeitung*, a local newspaper funded by the German government. It specialized in propaganda to German-Americans about invented French and Russian atrocities. Van Skal was in his late thirties. He had a well-scrubbed pink look on his chubby face. The lobe of his left ear was missing as the result of a sword wound inflicted during a training exercise while he was a cavalry officer in the Imperial Army on active duty in the Balkans. He was in the United States under a journalist visa. This was a pretense. His plain, undistinguished features completed the visage of a bland, modern spy, the kind who would go unnoticed in a crowd.

Over by the window was the bodyguard, Fritz Paul Willfuhr. He was a giant of a man, who had competed in the 1912 Olympics in the shot put and wore a perpetual scowl of intimidation. Blond, clean-shaven, with an athlete's crew cut, he reminded Chorney of the Thunder god, Thor, who Kurt had read about in German folklore books as a kid. All he needed was a bearskin toga, a metal helmet with horns and the magical hammer, Mjölnir, to complete the picture. His size made his clothing appear incongruous because it was so ill-fitting. To Kurt, he resembled an over-stuffed sausage.

As Baker advanced across the room, he withdrew a subpoena from his jacket pocket. He presented it to a startled von Igel. The agents followed Baker into the office. Immediately, the bodyguard rose and moved anxiously toward Baker. As von Igel read the document, the bodyguard glared at the agents with a savage stare that might have made lesser men quake but had the opposite effect on this team of experienced law enforcement agents. They were on their toes, poised for action.

von Igel read the document slowly, dragging absently on his Turkish Trophies cigarette. Contemplating the situation, he took a deep breath and then exhaled. In a thick German accent, von Igel sneered at Baker, "Get out of here. You are in German territory. Get out, swine!" Rising to his feet, he tore the subpoena into little pieces and threw them at the agent.

It seemed like time halted as the dismembered subpoena floated in the air. When the pieces had fluttered to the floor, Baker calmly stated, "I'm sorry, Sir, you will have to come with us and your papers will be impounded."

Wolf gave his bodyguard a nod and the big man rushed at Baker. Sullivan stepped in his path and squared off in front of him. Fritz lowered his head and bull-rushed Rusty. The big man had too much momentum to be stopped by a deft combination to the face thrown by Rusty. His nose bloodied, Fritz crashed into Rusty and they tumbled to the floor, fists flailing.

In the meantime, von Igel raced toward the file room. Nick sprang into action, tackling von Igel and bringing him down as he strained toward the door. von Igel screamed and kneed the detective in the jaw. von Igel clawed his way to his feet. Nick tackled him again; this time rolling on top of him, delivering punches in rapid fire. The spy covered his face and cursed, spitting out the epithets through bloody teeth.

While Nick was subduing von Igel, Baker was entangled with Van Skal, who had jumped him from behind and had him in a power half-nelson. Baker winced in pain as Van Skal ground Baker's face into the carpet. After assessing the relative needs of his companions, Kurt sprang onto Van Skal, picked him off Baker and flung the reporter across the room. Van Skal smacked into the bookcase adjoining the door and slid, unconscious, into a heap. A dozen or so books rained onto his motionless body.

In the center of the room, Sullivan and the bodyguard had scrambled to their feet and were duking it out. Both men were bleeding profusely. Acting instinctively, Kurt grabbed a heavy, round crystal paperweight from the desk and threw it at the bodyguard. It struck him in the temple like a good old-fashioned bean ball. The bodyguard staggered. Kurt gathered his weight and launched himself into the big man's ribcage. Chorney heard a distinct crack as he drove the bodyguard into the desk. The big man wheezed as the air rushed out of his lungs. Sullivan finished him off with a right uppercut that lifted him onto the desk with a resounding thud. The desk wobbled briefly, then the legs gave way and it crashed to the floor, kicking up the shards of paper that once were a subpoena.

Kurt winced slightly as he rubbed the side of his face where he had collided with the bodyguard. While Baker and Sullivan disarmed and manacled the Germans, Angelo checked the anteroom. It was vacant; the secretary had skedaddled, leaving the outer door open. The hallway was filling with busybodies gawking into the hitherto anonymous office.

"Move along, folks. Nothing to see here," Officer Angelo admonished.

Kurt approached the file room cautiously. There was a crudely-installed toggle switch on the door jamb. Kurt heard a faint ticking inside the wall. von Igel muttered to Fritz in German to prepare for the delayed blast. When von Igel had rushed toward the file room earlier, Kurt had suspected something sinister. Now, he knew that they would all be blown to smithereens momentarily by a time-delay bomb.

He traced a wire from the toggle switch on the jamb to a panel in the wall. He frantically ripped the panel loose to expose an evil-looking device topped by a large alarm clock. The second hand was inexorably approaching twelve. He had less than a minute before detonation. von Igel laughed derisively and shouted, *"Kaiserreich für immer!"*

Kurt's heart pounded. Through the frosted glass on the file room door, he spied something that might work. Smashing the door open, he grasped a mop handle and rolled a bucket into the office. In one motion, he flung the mop at von Igel and thrust the ticking bomb into the soapy water as the second hand ticked toward twelve. They all braced for the explosion.

The only thing to erupt from the bucket was a smoky sizzle. The Americans breathed a collective sigh of relief, while the Germans unleashed a torrent of profanity that would have made *Teufel* the devil blush.

Judging from the screams of outrage coming from Ambassador Count Bernstorff in Washington, the operation had struck a nerve; these documents must contain a treasure trove of sensitive information. For the intelligence officers, the easy part was over; now, they had to sort through, and decipher thousands of documents. Tedium lay ahead, but there were plots to foil and bad guys to arrest.

The Count had already publicly demanded that Secretary of State Lansing impound the documents to protect their integrity and imprison the agents involved in the criminal assault on German sovereignty. Privately, the German espionage apparatus was in a frenzied panic to redirect its plans. Fortunately, Lansing had been pre-briefed and professed ignorance to Bernstorff's communiqués. At a press conference, the Secretary of State declared that the Department of Justice had acted to thwart enemy *provocateurs* and that there was absolutely nothing to identify von Igel's operation as part of the German delegation.

Count Bernstorff was boxed in. If he linked von Igel's operation officially to the German Consulate, he would implicate his government formally in the espionage activities of von Igel and cause undesirable damage to Germany's objective of keeping the United States out of the war. Based on instructions from Berlin, the Ambassador ceased his public remonstrations. von Igel would have to bear the consequences for the Fatherland, unprotected by its diplomatic shield.

Kurt squeezed himself into the janitor's closet that was adjacent to von Igel's office. Pursuant to a court order, the government had installed a microphone to see if they could capture intelligence about sabotage plans. The installation had been accomplished under the cover of a repair crew that was sent in to fix the damage that had occurred when von Igel was arrested. Kurt shifted on his stool, trying to get comfortable in the cramped space. He was wearing headphones and had a pad on a lapboard to log in and take notes of any conversations he might hear.

There was a distinct crackle in his ears as the door to the inner office slammed. He recognized the voice of von Igel, who was cursing a blue streak in German about the lack of support from the Ambassador. An unrecognized voice cautioned him to calm down and lower his voice. The deep bass voice of the massive bodyguard chimed in with his own string of curses that strained Kurt's linguistic abilities and challenged his imagination as to their anatomical feasibility. After venting, the unrecognized voice resumed in German with a report on the preparations.

"Our operatives are in place now. *Geheimagent Rot, Grun and Blau* ready to proceed when funding is received. *Geheimagent Braun* is working on the guards. We have Kristoff inside, but we are trying to lock in a more senior person."

"Thank you, Rudolph. We will continue our efforts. You will handle the money. We will await your signal when everything is in place."

"*Danke.*"

Strafe congratulated Chorney on discovering the code names for the German operatives, red, green, blue and brown. This information might identify the future saboteurs, or their targets. The commander was most enthused about the new connection to "Rudolph." They did not know whether it was a first name, or a last name, or whether it was an alias, but at least it was a start. Strafe advised Chorney that "Rudolph" had been followed to 52 William Street after the meeting with von Igel. Since it was after hours, the tail broke off contact with the suspect when he entered the nearly-deserted building. His team was in the process of developing the photos that had been taken of Rudolph.

"Kurt, we believe that we may eventually link Rudolph's activities to the Monocle. It was hardly a coincidence that he went to the same building that houses Kahn's banking firm. I've been suspicious of this guy for years, but we've never been able to tie him to any crimes on U.S. soil. We'll just have to keep at it. In the meantime, our sources tell us that the Monocle is heading back to Europe again. We need you to tail him. Here is your packet. The steamship tickets and your encrypted instructions are in there. Any questions?"

Kurt scanned the packet. "Not really, sir. Is Otto going to Petrograd? I just can't get used to the new name for St. Petersburg."

"I suspect that things are about to become unhinged there. Be careful, son."

In his dingy office a few blocks from the Jersey City waterfront, Frank Hague sat pondering his career. Hague was the child of Irish immigrants and grew up in the "Horseshoe" section of the rough-and-tumble Second

Ward of Jersey City. Although his pugnacious attitude led him to consider a career as a professional boxer, it was his silver tongue that provided the way out of the ghetto. Before his attractive nose and lily white skin could be savaged in the ring, he realized that managing a boxer was more profitable than absorbing punishment as a boxer. Using his Irish gift of persuasion, he convinced several gym mates to let him manage their interests. His stable of fighters was so successful that he soon achieved local notoriety.

With the help of a local tavern owner, Hague parlayed his 'from the neighborhood' appeal, to win an election to the office of Constable. He shrewdly used his office to assist the immigrant population and position himself for grander endeavors. Hague made sure that a tidy percentage of all fees collected found its way into his coffers. With his affinity for high-necked, starched collars and pocket handkerchiefs that matched his silk ties, he soon became known for his sartorial splendor. Despite cutting a dandy figure, he was filled with unrequited ambition. He always wanted more.

He thought that his ship had come in when he fortuitously supported a relatively unknown university president in his quest to become the governor of New Jersey. Although Woodrow Wilson was perceived of as cerebral and humorless, he won the governorship handily in 1910 as an anti-machine reform candidate. Two years later, with the help of certain Wall Street interests, Wilson won the Presidency of the United States. Although Frank Hague was an influential early Wilson supporter, his candidate showed no gratitude. Wilson went to Washington and Hague was left behind, stuck in political limbo as the thirty-nine-year-old Commissioner of Public Safety for Jersey City. To make matters worse, he was losing his hair. Hague feared that his ambitions would never be realized. He had little money and fewer prospects. That was all about to change.

There was a timid knock on his door and he was surprised to see one of his constituents. Mrs. Anna Rushnak was a stout woman whose hard life running a boarding house had aged her beyond her forty-five years. Her gray hair was covered with a cheap scarf. As she entered the office, her brown eyes were on the verge of tears.

"I'm sorry to bother you, Mr. Hague. But I'm afraid and do not know where else to turn." Her chapped hands shook as she reached for the chair that Frank offered her.

"Now, now. Don't be upset, Mrs. Rushnak. What is troubling you? Would you like some water?"

"No, no thank you. I'm OK. It's just that I have learned about something terrible. And you are the only person who I believe can help."

"Thank you for your confidence. Tell me about it and I'll see what I can do."

"As you know, I run a respectable boarding house. There is a young man who stays with us. He's tall and thin and in his early twenties. He works somewhere down at the docks. I heard him telling one of the other boarders that they are planning to blow up the docks. They think it's unfair for the United States to send guns to Russia, France and England and not send any to Germany. They want to stop the shipments and they are going to explode the docks."

"By docks, do you mean Black Tom Island? That's terrible. What is the young man's name?"

"Michael Kristoff, his name is Michael Kristoff. He is working with German spies, I'm sure of it."

"Do you know any other names? Names of the spies?"

"No."

"Do you know when they plan to do this?"

"No."

"What else can you tell me?"

"Nothing really, except that I'm scared, really scared, Mr. Hague."

"OK, Mrs. Rushnak. You did the right thing. I'll see what I can do. Don't worry." He ushered her out of the office and thanked her profusely for performing her civic duty. He assured her that without citizens like her the country would be in bad shape.

Hague knew that over the last few years, the Lehigh Valley RR had constructed a terminal at Black Tom Island in the Hudson River to accommodate the shipment of millions of tons of munitions. Nearly half the men in his ward worked for the railroad on Black Tom. Hague knew that the well-being of his community was inextricably linked to the curiously-named place. Legend had it that the island was named after a freed slave named Tom who squatted there. He had endeared himself to the local politicians by bringing them luscious oysters. In return, they let him live there without hassling him.

Hague had toured the island over the years and knew that security was virtually nonexistent. The island was covered completely with sidings and warehouses. There were few lights and it would be easy to approach the island from the water or landside, that's how lax security was. Hague tried to figure out the best way to use this information to his advantage and possibly turn it into a payday.

He travelled to Washington to express concern for the safety of his constituents and perhaps accumulate some goodwill that might prove useful in the future. He met with everyone who would see him. His first approach was to reveal this information to Jimmy Hamill, the Congressman for the 12th District and Joe Tumulty, President Wilson's private secretary. He was flatly rebuffed as a hysteric. Overtures to Senators Martine and Hughes, and, even Assistant Secretary to the Navy Franklin D. Roosevelt, proved fruitless. Disappointed, Hague returned to Jersey City empty-handed.

One pair of ears that did pay attention to Hague's entreaties belonged to Otto Kahn whose sources in the White House advised him that alarms were being sounded about security concerns of property owned by his client, the Lehigh Valley Railroad. Otto sent a message to Hague that he was interested in meeting to discuss a matter of mutual interest. A meeting was set for lunch at *Kenny's*, a local pub that Kahn had heard was the site of many of Hague's accommodations, as he liked to call them.

The meeting was held in early July and was attended by Hague, someone introduced as Benny, Otto, and Rudolph Hecht from Kuhn Loeb, Otto's bank. It was a blazing hot summer day. The sun was so bright it hurt just to open your eyes. Otto's chauffeur expertly wheeled the maroon Rolls Royce into the unpaved lot across from the pub. The restaurant was dark and it took them a few minutes to acclimate to the cool interior.

Hague brought them to a shadowy room that was paneled in knotty pine with a shiny lacquer finish. They sat at a wooden table scarred with dark, brown cigar and cigarette burns, like so many charred remains of the backroom deals made over drinks by the bosses during Frank's tenure.

"Thank you for meeting with us," said Otto, in a manner that lent unwarranted dignity to the proceedings.

"As you know, my client is the LVRR, which employs hundreds of your constituents in the rail yards and support facilities throughout Jersey City. You realize, of course, that any complaints by you about Black Tom Island will put all those jobs in jeopardy." He paused to let that thought sink in.

"Now, Otto, may I call you Otto? The last thing we would want to see is them jobs disappear. But, ya gotta understand that them jobs could disappear if the place goes 'Kaboom.' All's I'm saying is that we're hearing threats about the Krauts, excuse me, I mean Germans, who may want to do harm to the depot. Now, as a true son of the old Sod, I have no kinship with the Tories who are slaughtering my cousins in Dublin. If the Tories don't get any weapons, it's no never mind to me. It's just that with all these competing interests, the key question is 'what's in it for Frankie boy?'"

"We share your concerns and believe we have a solution to allay your fears. After all, you must have the means to care for your constituents in case something horrific happens. My colleague, Mr. Hecht, will present our proposal."

"Yes, thank you, Mr. Kahn," said Rudolph Hecht, with a decidedly German accent. He was a slender, young man with a full moustache whose clothes mirrored the clothes of his boss. Gray pinstripe suit, white shirt and red bowtie. He reached into his briefcase and withdrew some documents.

"Our research has shown that you are the sole owner of the Shamrock Management Company. We, that is, LVRR is prepared to engage Shamrock as employment agent for LVRR's needs at the depot."

"That's a good start. But, my concern, and, I'm sure you share it, is what happens if the depot has an unfortunate accident? The volume of war stuff going through those gates is staggering."

"We address that also. We are prepared to list Shamrock as an additional insured on LVRR's insurance policy. So, if anything should happen at Black Tom, Shamrock would receive recompense."

"That's very generous," said Hague, smiling broadly as he rose to shake hands with Kahn and Hecht. "I believe that we will be able to move forward without any further alarms."

"It's been a pleasure meeting you, Mr. Hague, . . . Benny," replied Otto bowing slightly.

April 1916
Petrograd, Russia

He had a nasty reputation as a cruel dude.
They said he was ruthless, they said he was crude.

~ THE EAGLES, *LIFE IN THE FAST LANE*

IN PETROGRAD, OTTO GAZED INTO the hotel mirror. He was aging well.
Although his hair and moustache had turned gray over the years, it helped him professionally. He recalled with some pain the many occasions early in his career when his advice had been scoffed at because he was a mere youth. He had solved that by nurturing a thick moustache to give him *gravitas*. His habit of waxing the ends of his moustaches came from Margaret, who chided him for looking sour with his drooping walrus 'staches.

Otto adjusted his monocle, clipping the lanyard to his lapel button. He liked to perpetuate the myth that he wore it due to a war wound. Just last week, he had explained to Lady Beverly that a true gentleman does not elicit sympathy for one's afflictions; rather, it is one's duty to soldier on, sparing the more delicate members of society the details of one's sacrifices.

It was a crystal clear day, perfect for his meeting with the Tsar at Catherine's Palace in Tsarskoe Selo. Otto looked through the glass enclosure of the Imperial gymnasium and considered the pristine beauty of the Imperial gardens. The pure, white snow was accented with sparkling icicles like so many stalactites, drooping from the topiary gardens looked like an ethereal, ice cream cake menagerie. The elephants and bears stood in stolid contrast to the gangly giraffes and the proud double-headed eagles that appeared to hover over the domain, fierce and majestic. Contrasted to New York's gray, mushy slush that clogged the streets, this was positively divine. The Boy Mayor John Purroy Mitchel in the City was incapable of clearing the wretched stuff away. Kahn made a mental note to cut his campaign contributions.

During a break in their fencing session, Otto remarked, "Your Excellency, your daily workouts at the front with the sabre have served you well. You nearly decapitated me a few times. Eh."

"I must say that wielding the sabre has strengthened my forearms and legs. My thrust is now the best it's ever been. But enough play. Let's get down to business. Otto, we need locomotives and gondola cars immediately to service the western front."

Despite his innate aversion to banking types, especially those with Hebraic lineage, the Tsar admitted to himself that this one had proven indispensable. Over the years, Kahn's analysis of Mother Russia's need for rolling stock and modern line communication had enabled the effective transportation of its military resources. As a consequence, Russia had fought the bloody war to a standstill.

"Otto, this war has demonstrated that, more than ever, the ability to transport munitions is crucial. Without rapid deployment of ordnance, our brave troops would be defenseless like the babes slaughtered by Herod. The coming year is pivotal."

Otto adopted his most humble pose, "I agree with Your Excellency completely. To answer your question directly, of course we can satisfy your urgent need. I've pre-positioned my suppliers to build and ship the frames and switches to Stockholm, where they will be assembled and brought to your doorstep . . . , provided, of course, the Allies can effectuate safe transit across the waters."

"Yes, most definitely, the U-boats have taken their toll. But after what happened with the *Lusitania* last year, Uncle Willy knows that he must be careful not to arouse the Americans," said the Tsar.

Otto responded, "So true, so true. It would surely bode ill for the Kaiser, if the Americans suffered a grave loss at the hands of the Germans." Kahn paused and cleared his throat.

"Your Highness, there is a matter of some delicacy involving financing for this year. We are all aware that Mother Russia has always paid her debts. However, lately as you might expect, my associates have become apprehensive, due to all the derogatory reports about military matters, Rasputin, and the Duma."

"How dare you question the honor of Mother Russia!" the Tsar exploded. Two brawny attendants moved toward Otto, but a tilt of the Tsar's head froze them in their places.

"You know it's not that at all. My associates remember what happened in 1905. Opening the Royal Vault to the press was unprecedented back then, but it had the desired effect of quelling the opposition. You must admit that pictures in the newspapers of row after row of Imperial gold did much to calm the storm. *Entre nous*, our efforts helped enhance the image," Otto remarked, dryly.

"My associates would like assurances that the Romanov family will secure the financing directly. Before you say *nyet*, consider the fact that the Hanovers have personally backed London's effort, as have the Rothschilds in Paris. The world is changing, and old approaches are no longer acceptable. I'm sorry to say that this is necessary."

Otto knew not to overplay his hand and allowed silence to fill the room. He knew the monarch had no choice and just needed some time to absorb the request.

"We will only do so for materials delivered on Russian soil pursuant to our schedule," replied Nicholas curtly.

"Agreed. I'll have the papers drawn up and presented to Minister Bark, Your Highness."

Nicholas nodded to his secretary who briskly approached. There was a whispered exchange. Momentarily, the chamber door opened and afternoon tea was wheeled in. The steward returned to announce that Monsieur Fabergé had arrived.

In came a short, flabby gentleman, meticulously dressed. His round face was encased in silver ringlets that matched his round, owl spectacles. He was joined by a younger version, no doubt his son, who carried a shiny, mahogany case, inlaid with the ubiquitous Romanov eagle. With a graceful bow and flourish of his arm, Fabergé announced, "Your Highness, I present to you a tribute to Mother Russia's military greatness in the form of an egg to be presented to the Tsarina on the occasion of Easter 1916."

An attendant took the case and placed it on the desk in front of the Tsar. As Nicholas opened the velvet-lined box, his eyes lost their war-weariness for a moment. A beautiful, black enameled egg, adorned with the Tsarina's name, an emblem of St. George slaying the dragon and the double-headed eagle shone before him. Nicholas withdrew the oblong object and placed it upright on his desk. The egg was perched on four, miniature, shiny, steel artillery shells. Quite ingenious, he thought as something nagged at him. He lifted the egg again; there it was — it was extremely light.

As Nicholas pumped the object, Fabergé rose and in an apologetic tone, said, "With our apologies, Your Excellency, this egg is not made of solid gold like the previous ones. We made it out of steel. It's the war, Sir. We cannot get gold for our jewelry business."

"Not even for the Tsar?" Nicholas questioned. Fabergé shrugged helplessly.

"It is so . . . empty," sighed Nicholas, the war-weariness returning to his eyes.

"If I may, Your Highness, pose a solution," interjected Otto. "This Steel Military Egg is a tribute to the armies of Mother Russia and a symbol of the sacrifices of your brave troops and, indeed, of the Royal Family. It may need a little accompaniment to bring it to the standard of excellence established by Monsieur Fabergé. And what would make the Tsarina happier than a picture of her courageous Nicholas at the front? Last month, I was in Paris and saw miniature enamel paintings of the greatest delicacy. I'm sure that the famed Fabergé artists could duplicate those miniatures."

Karl Faberge was not one to miss a cue, "Yes, I can see it now a miniature portrait, no, tableau of the Tsar with the Tsarevich at his side, devising strategy at the front. Our man, Vassily Zuiev, a gifted enamellist, can start tonight. The frame would be gilded," he said.

Nicholas nodded vacantly, having lost his zeal for the project. With that the meeting adjourned, and the Tsar was left alone beneath the portrait of his dear, martyred grandfather and a war still raging.

30

Spring 1916
Vienna, Austria

Similarly, I will not give to a woman a pessary to cause abortion.
I will keep pure and holy both my life and my art.

~ HIPPOCRATES

GOING TO VIENNA STOP HOTEL ALPINE APRIL 24 TO 28 STOP
WANT TO SEE AXEL STOP PLEASE ARRANGE STOP THANKS
MARGARET.

Otto sat quietly at his desk contemplating the telegram. He had not
heard from the mother of his son during the four years since she had abruptly
abandoned them both. He tried to conjure up her face but had difficulty
visualizing the woman who broke his heart. His dreams of domestic bliss
and a new life in London as a Member of Parliament had all been dashed
that one afternoon four years ago. So much had transpired since then.
Suddenly weary, he removed his monocle and closed his eyes. Questions
came flooding into his head. What was behind this request? Had she come

to her senses and realized her mistake? Did she want him back as a lover? Did she want to take Axel back to America to raise him? None of these thoughts made any sense.

After checking through intermediaries, he determined that her request was just 'Margaret being Margaret.' She had no interest in normal domestic life, whatever that was. If anything, she had become more radical and committed to her Eugenics cause. She was becoming quite notorious with her writings, speeches and rabble-rousing. With a sigh of relief, he came to the conclusion that the best course of action was to treat the request as one from a former business associate, akin to asking for a ride on a railroad that they both had constructed. He instructed his secretary to contact his cousin, Rolfe, and ask whether he would accommodate Margaret's request.

The transatlantic trip was harrowing. Not only were the seas rough; there was constant apprehension that they might be attacked by German U-boats. The war was waging in full force and civilians were fair game. She spent most of the trip below decks preparing her materials for her upcoming speaking engagements.

The meeting had been scheduled at the Prater, Vienna's park for the people. The name Prater was derived from the Latin word, partum, meaning 'meadow.' The one-hundred-and-fifty-year-old park was conveniently located between the Danube River and the city center. Among its attractions was the *Wiener Riesenrad,* a world famous Ferris wheel that stood in the Wurstelprater section of the park. It had been built nearly twenty years earlier to celebrate the Golden Jubilee of Emperor Franz Josef I. Reaching a height of two hundred and twelve feet, the giant observation wheel offered outstanding views of the ancient city and dominated the skyline.

Using the *Riesenrad* as a reference point, she walked along the main promenade through the park, the *Hauptallee.* As she searched for the rendezvous point, she fretted about what Axel would call her. Mother or any form of that word was repugnant to her. *Fraülein* Sanger would have to do; it was simple and formal, just the tone she wanted. She wore no make-up and her auburn hair was tied back in a school-marmish bun secured by a marcasite clip that had been given to her by her latest lover, H.G. Wells.

Sitting on a wooden bench across from the *Stadtgasthaus* Eisvogel restaurant, Margaret was surprised at the nervous feeling in her stomach. She wondered whether the request to meet her son four years after disowning him had been prudent. She wondered whether some maternal instinct was motivating her. She recoiled at the thought. Her entire adult life had been dedicated to denying and eradicating maternal instincts. Sanger checked her watch; it was five minutes past the one o'clock rendezvous time. She was about to get up and walk away when she heard a deep masculine voice address her, "*Fraülein* Sanger?"

"Yes, you must be Herr Baer, *ja*?" Standing before her was a heavyset man with a pug nose, florid skin and jutting jaw. He stood before her, uncomfortable in an ill-fitting black suit. A brown, suede Tyrolean hat adorned his head of thick brown hair. To his left was a slender man wearing a military uniform and a dour expression. He had a plain, open, undistinguished face, save the dark circles under his eyes and his clipped black moustache.

"*Ja*. This is my friend, A.J.," answered Rolfe. "And, this is Axel."

His meaty hand raised the thin white hand of a small, four-year-old boy dressed in a junior navy suit replete with a white sailor hat cocked to the left. The boy's freckled skin and dark red hair reminded Margaret of her youngest brother. His upturned face was handsome in a delicate, androgynous way.

"Say *hallo* to *Fraülein* Sanger, Axel," said Rolfe, in an authoritative voice.

"*Hallo*," the small boy responded, waving his right hand in greeting.

Margaret knelt down and pointed to a hot chocolate sign, "*Heisse Schokolade*?"

Axel nodded enthusiastically. As the boy drank his chocolate, Margaret arranged to meet Rolfe at this spot in three hours. Rolfe explained that it was imperative that he return to work, but A. J. would accompany her during the visit.

The reluctant mother sat down with Axel and handed him a small wrapped package. The youngster's eyes opened wide. He mumbled his appreciation and then gaily tore at the wrapping paper. When he saw what was inside the package, his shoulders slumped. Margaret removed the tissue paper covering a bright shiny fountain pen. She lifted it and removed the top, but nothing could dissipate the cloud of disappointment in his eyes. A.J. tried to relieve the mood by ushering Axel over to the miniature train called the *Liliputbahn*. The three boarded the train and rode it to the *Reisenrad*. Margaret eyed the giant wheel with anticipation.

"Come, Axel. Let's ride the Ferris wheel. From the top we will be able to see the entire city," exclaimed Sanger, trying to generate enthusiasm. Axel stared at the towering machine and pulled back from her.

"No. Thank you, *Fraülein* Sanger."

Not to be deterred, Margaret took hold of Axel's hand and tugged him toward the entrance to the Ferris wheel. Axel's feet dug in and he leaned away from Margaret, trying to wriggle his tiny hand from her grasp. His obstinacy made her more determined to pull him along. She tugged harder.

"Come, you'll enjoy it."

"*Nein, nein, nein,*" he cried, collapsing his legs so that he hung like a broken marionette. Tears formed in his eyes as he glared at this stranger, who was dragging him along the ground. The struggle began to attract worried looks from folks walking nearby. Before the scene escalated, A.J. intervened.

"*Fraülein*, let me take him while you go on the *Reisenrad*. He's afraid. Please don't force the child," he said. Realizing the tenuousness of her position, she relented and released Axel. Straightening her blouse, she assented and marched off toward the large wheel.

After an exhilarating ride on the *Reisenrad* with its panoramic views of Vienna and the Danube, Margaret located A.J. and Axel near a pretzel stand sharing a Viennese specialty. A.J. offered Sanger a pretzel and regaled Axel and her with the story of how the pretzel saved Vienna. In the early sixteenth century, Vienna was under siege by the Turkish Army that was sweeping across Europe. Since the city's defenses were impenetrable, the Turks decided to tunnel under the city walls to conquer the city. To avoid detection, they dug their tunnels at night. Unbeknownst to the invaders, the Viennese pretzel makers also worked at night to provide fresh baked pretzels for the citizenry. The diligent bakers heard the Turks tunneling and alerted the authorities, who repelled the subterranean attack, thereby saving Vienna. In gratitude, the King issued a pretzel coat of arms honoring the pretzel makers for their part in the victory. Axel delighted in the story and giggled as he pointed to the pretzel coat of arms on the side of the pretzel stand.

They walked back toward the *Zum Elsvogel*, as the locals called the iconic restaurant. Margaret tried to engage Axel in conversation about his favorite things, but the young boy gave her only monosyllabic answers and he refused to make eye contact with her. She was relieved when she saw

Rolfe waiting at the bench a few minutes early. Axel ran to Rolfe as if he were a life raft in a raging sea. The big man swooped up the boy. Axel gave Sanger a half-hearted thanks and tugged Rolfe toward the exit.

"If you don't mind Rolfe, I would like to escort *Fraülein* Sanger back to her hotel," commented A.J.

"As you like," said Rolfe.

"*Guten tag, Fraülein* Sanger. I will report to Herr Kahn." With that, he performed an about-face and marched away carrying Axel in his sturdy arms.

"Are you hungry? We could have a bite to eat at *Zum Elsvogel*, it's legendary. It's been here since 1805." Sanger regarded the young soldier favorably and consented.

Due to the economic strains of the war, the restaurant was nearly empty. They were seated immediately. The disconsolate look in her eyes revealed her disappointment.

"Don't look so sad, *Fraülein*. You cannot expect a four-year-old boy to warm up during the first visit."

"I'm afraid that it will be the last visit. I am not good with children. No, that's not it. I do not like children. They are selfish and more trouble than they are worth."

The ensuing silence was broken by the waitress arriving with their steins of beer.

"This is the most flavorful beer I've ever tasted," said Margaret, licking the fluffy, white foam from her upper lip.

"*Ja!* Austrians are master brewers. Do you know that only true Austrians are allowed to brew beer for sale?"

"That's interesting. How does the government know who the true Austrians are?"

"If your ancestors haven't been here for at least two hundred years, you cannot qualify."

"In America, we are not that old. We cannot have restrictions like that."

"Then, you need to have other ways to determine who is truly American."

"Well, it's not that simple, but there are new scientific methods that will enable us to tell. Have you heard of the science of Eugenics?"

"*Nein*, what is it?"

Sanger needed little encouragement.

"Eugenics is the science of identifying hereditary traits and using that information to maximize racial stock. By eliminating poor heredity, eugenicists believe we can eliminate many of society's problems. In essence, if we had more children produced by the fit and fewer children produced by the unfit, we would be better off."

"Interesting. How do you identify who is unfit?"

"There are some obvious categories. The handicapped, the feeble-minded and the degenerates are burdens on society. I have personally seen the suffering caused by frequent pregnancies. My own mother, bless her soul, was pregnant eleven times. It ultimately killed her. I have seen women die from self-inflicted abortions because they could not handle another child. I have seen the desperation of the poor. I write a monthly newsletter to educate women about controlling the number and timing of pregnancies. Until women can control pregnancy they will be slaves."

Their waitress arrived with their orders of Weiner schnitzel adorned with the traditional sunny-side up egg and another round of beers.

"What is your magazine called?"

"I call it *The Woman Rebel*. We have the ability to create a better humanity. My mission is to develop 'practical and acceptable ways' to control procreation. Contraception, sterilization and abortion will eradicate the unfit.

"You just have to look at the advances being made in animal husbandry. If you own a cow that produces more milk than the other cows, you make sure that the bull impregnates that cow. If you have a cow that gives birth to blind calves, you eliminate them from your herd. For the first time in human history, we can identify the fit and eliminate the unfit. In my country, we now have laws for mandatory sterilization of the unfit and feeble-minded. The beneficial result will be a race that is free from race pollution."

"Interesting," commented A.J.

"Just look at you. You are a soldier. You have been to war, no?"

"Yes."

"What is that medal you are wearing?"

"It's the Iron Cross. I received it for bravery under fire."

"Quite admirable. Do you know why you are fighting? I'll tell you. The primary cause of this war is the terrific pressure of population in Germany . . . . The German government had to do something to reduce the size of her population."

Sanger continued, "The most urgent problem today is how to limit the over-fertility of the mentally and physically defective. We must stem the tide of race-degeneracy. By encouraging mandatory sterilization and eugenic abortions, the science of Eugenics will be the salvation of humanity. By getting involved in this movement, you can be what we call a race patriot."

"But who decides who should live and who is not worthy of life?"

"Most of the time it's obvious. In time, we could establish a system of Eugenic Boards to make these determinations. Everyone would be required to come before a court or board to justify their existence periodically. If you are unable to show that you contribute more to society than you consume, then you deserve to be eliminated — humanely, of course."

"Where can I learn more?"

"In Germany, two doctors, Alfred Ploetz and Ernst Rüdin established the Society of Race-Hygiene, the *Gesellschaft* for *Rassenhygiene*, about ten years ago. Rüdin is a propagandist for the purity of the 'Germanic people.' He believes that Germany is suffering from race pollution. To reverse this societal disease, he recommends preventive, coercive measures to eliminate the procreation of the mentally ill and other undesirables. We are all working together to educate society on these issues. The first step is to accustom people to birth control. Birth control is the entering wedge for the eugenic educator."

"What are your plans?"

"When I return to America, I am going to open a birth control center and challenge the laws that prevent us from providing contraception to the masses. We will start in the poor neighborhoods in order to stop the blight of unwanted children. *Very early in my childhood I associated poverty, toil, unemployment, drunkenness, cruelty, quarreling, fighting, debts, jail with large families*[28]. If we are not careful, we will drown in a tidal wave of unfit children."

After A.J. picked up the check, they ambled down the *Hauptallee* toward Sanger's hotel.

"You are quite fascinating, Fraulein. Are you married?" asked A. J.

"No, I believe that traditional sexual mores are infantile, archaic and ignorant. I believe in the infinite possibilities of sexual expression. I am free to love whom I choose, when I choose."

"I've never met a woman like you, Margaret. I would very much like to spend more time with you."

"Well, A.J., why don't you come up to my room and we can explore the infinite possibilities of sexual expression," Margaret whispered coyly.

A.J. followed her into the small room. She turned to him, gesturing for him to wait while she entered the water closet. She returned dressed in a filmy negligee and eased herself onto the bed. A.J. unbuttoned his shirt and removed his trousers. They fell into a passionate embrace, with Margaret removing the rest of his apparel while he smothered her breasts with wet kisses. Admonishing him to slow down, she proceeded to explore his body with her tongue. He was mad with lust when he entered her, frantically expressing himself.

1916
Black Tom Island, New York Harbor

I love the smell of napalm in the morning.

~ John Milius, *Apocalpyse Now*

JULY 30TH WAS A STIFLING DAY of unrelenting swelter, followed by a hot, humid night. It was the kind of night where the air was so still and muggy that one sweated and sweated and sweated. Not even the disappearance of the sun brought any meaningful relief. He could feel the heat trapped in the asphalt and metal that covered Black Tom Island, rising treacherously from the ground to meet the hot, stagnant air that hung above them. Mick Chapman's uniform shirt clung to his back like a damp shawl. He was glad that he had brought a clean, dry shirt to change into before he headed for home at the end of his shift. At least he had the next day off and could go swimming to beat the heat. The 'dog days' of summer were forecast to continue without relief.

Mick was a thirty-year-old bachelor, who was glad to be working the graveyard shift as a watchman. As his flattened nose attested, he had spent his youth seeking prize money in the ring. His long black hair was wet with sweat and hung limply over his forehead. His dark eyes were surrounded by scars from too many cuts patched up in the ring so he could keep fighting. Mick was quick to smile, although his jagged teeth detracted from his rugged handsomeness. He owed this job to his former manager, Commissioner Frank Hague. Although Mick had trouble grappling with complex matters, he clearly understood the importance of his job. He and the seven other guards were hired to protect millions of pounds of munitions and dynamite.

Since the war had broken out in Europe a few years earlier, the Black Tom depot had become the busiest pier on the East Coast. Vast quantities of weapons, ammunition and explosives had passed through these gates, loaded on cargo ships and shipped off to Britain, France and Russia.

Mick had just finished his rounds through the complex of warehouses, railroad cars and loading platforms. The facility was secure. It was time for his dinner break. Mick got his sandwich from his locker and joined Greg on one of the barges.

Greg was sitting Indian-style on the bow of the barge, reading a newspaper by the light of a lantern. His short, curly red hair and freckled face were illuminated by its yellowish light. He had muscular arms from his time working in his father's blacksmith shop in Bayonne. He had befriended Mick fifteen years earlier when they battled for the state boxing championship from rival high schools. Mick had won, of course; but the mutual respect coming out of their bouts was a solid foundation for a life-long friendship. Mick never lorded his victory over Greg and admitted that, "Greg had a right hand that felt like a mule kicking your head in."

"How ya' doing tonight, partner? I can't wait to go to the beach tomorrow and swim until this old body is as cool as an icicle," said Mick, as he sat dangling his legs over the side of the barge.

"I wouldn't do that if I were you," replied Greg, laconically.

"Do what?"

"Go swimming or hang your legs over the side of this here tub."

"What in heaven's name are you talking about, Greg?"

"You don't know nothin', do ya? In the last two weeks there have been shark attacks at Jersey beaches. Four people have been killed. Just eaten up by sharks; the water all red with blood. Don't you read the papers? Just a couple of days ago, an eleven-year-old boy was dragged under by a shark at nearby Matawan Creek. He was never seen again. And, yesterday a teenager had his leg bit off by a shark. The only thing that saved him was his brother and another guy got into a tug a war with the shark. That boy is in the hospital with one leg gone. He's lucky to be alive."

"You're pulling my leg, right?" said Mick, playfully punching his friend's arm.

"No, siree. Lookee here," countered Greg holding up the *Jersey Journal*. The headline read:

SHARK RAMPAGE CONTINUES WITH SECOND ATTACK AT MATAWAN CREEK

Boy loses leg in latest of series of deadly shark attacks in Jersey, taken to St. Peter's Hospital

The front page carried two other shark stories. The first about a nine-foot great white shark being caught a few miles from Matawan Creek that had human remains in its stomach. The second told of armed volunteers combing the Jersey coast to snuff out man-eating sharks.

Mick pulled his legs up on to the deck and set down his sandwich saying, "I think I just lost my appetite."

Mick looked across the staging area to where his cousin, Padraic, sat at a picnic table outside the guard building playing cards with four other guards. The men were shrouded in a cloud of smoke from smudge pots they had set out in violation of regulations prohibiting open flames within the depot. Devin Dermotty, the senior man on duty, was sleeping one off in the security booth at the front gate. Devin had reported to work drunk. His girlfriend had abandoned him for a handsome Marine she had met while at a birth control rally in the City. They all knew that Devin was protected and could not be fired because he was first cousin to Commissioner Hague who everyone knew was the king of Jersey City.

Shortly after midnight, Michael Kristoff approached the front gate and peered into the security booth. He worked at the depot during the day with the stevedores who hoisted the crates of ammunitions onto the decks of the cargo ships. Kristoff knew the layout of the depot like the back of his hand. He had immigrated to the United States when he was fourteen. His natural shyness coupled with his inability to pick up English readily, left him isolated and outcast in school. He gravitated toward the other foreigners in his school and soon came under the influence of a boy named Anton Sokol whose family came from that portion of Czechoslovakia that belonged to the Austrian Empire. They shared a common language and a disdain for anything English. Anton had introduced Kristoff to *Geheimagent Braun*, the German spy in charge of the plan to detonate the munitions at Black Tom Island. Now, they were the land contingent of the sabotage team.

The plan was elegant in its simplicity. The land contingent was to plant "pencil" bombs throughout the facility. These were small explosives the size of a pencil that had delayed ignition. The pencil bombs were copper cylinders containing incompatible acids. When the cylinders corroded and the acids mingled, an intense flame erupted. These devices had been perfected by von Igel's team and had been planted by German agents on ships carrying munitions from New York harbor. They ignited several days later after the ships were well out to sea, with devastating consequences. By varying the thickness of the copper chambers, the devices could be calibrated to ignite at varying time intervals. The devices for Black Tom were set to go off one hour after they were placed among the over one hundred boxcars filled with gun powder, ammunition and firearms.

The marine contingent, *Geheimagenten Rot, Grun and Blau*, all operatives experienced at sabotage, was to enter the river upstream of the facility and drift down to a barge moored at the pier. The barge, the *Johnson No. 17*, had been illegally berthed at the pier in violation of safety restrictions that forbade loaded barges from mooring at the pier. On this night, the barge was loaded with over four hundred cases of detonating fuses and fifty tons of dynamite. The plan was for the marine contingent to board the barge from the Manhattan side, plant pencil bombs around the cargo and slip away in the darkness.

When Kristoff saw that Devin Dermotty was sound asleep at the front gate, he signaled the 'All Clear' for Anton and *Braun*. Taking care to stay in the shadows, they scurried into the depot carrying their backpacks of incendiary devices. Michael led them past the boxcars brimming with explosives and firearms that had been manufactured at the Remington Arms Factory in Bridgeport, Connecticut and the DuPont gunpowder plant in the Brandywine Valley, Delaware. The team went past the switching engines that were still hot seven hours after their workday had ended. The saboteurs sweated profusely in the intense heat. As they exhaled from the exertion of their stealthy advance through the yard, it seemed like millions of mosquitoes had sensed their presence and had descended on them in swarms. Trying not to slap the attacking mosquitoes, the men plowed ahead toward the warehouses.

When they reached the last railroad car, they had to cross an open staging area to get to the warehouses. The guard building was in this area and they could hear the sounds of the men bantering as they played poker. The saboteurs were unable to see the guards because of the smoke from smudge pots that the guards had lit to keep the voracious mosquitoes at bay.

As Padraic roared in triumph at winning a hand by pulling an inside straight, the land team slipped past the guards into the shadows of the warehouses. *Geheimagent Braun* assumed command and directed Kristoff and Sokol to disperse and plant the incendiary devices strategically throughout the buildings. They moved swiftly and silently, reminding themselves of the great good that would come from this night. With each twist of the timing caps, the clock to detonation ran down.

Over on the barge, Mick cocked his head. He thought he heard a splash, maybe of an oar. Then, he heard a thump, followed by a scratching noise. He turned away from the river and saw a large shape crawling up the mooring line extending from the barge to the bollard on the pier. Mick focused in on a large rat that was prowling up the rope. He grabbed a large bolt from the deck and tossed it at the shape. It struck with a thud. The rat squealed and fell with a splash into the river. Mick and Greg both laughed. On the other side of the barge, the saboteurs froze.

After a few minutes, *Rot* and *Grun* clambered onto the deck, while *Blau* steadied the row boat. They dispersed and quickly stuffed pencil bombs into any opening they could find. Greg caught a glimpse of a shadow on the deck and rose to investigate. *Rot* pressed himself against the cabin and unsheathed his knife. As Greg cautiously turned the corner, *Rot* clamped a hand over the shorter man's mouth and plunged the knife through his back into his heart. Greg eyes widened as he struggled, and then, stiffened as the metal drove home. *Rot* slid the body to the deck quietly and ran aft toward his escape.

Mick, hearing a scuffle, moved quickly toward where Greg was lying gasping his last breath. It took Mick a few seconds to process the horrific scene before him. Just then he heard a voice call out, "*Grun, schnell.*" Mick glanced to his right and saw a shadowy figure moving aft. Mick hurdled some gear and pounced onto the fleeing figure, fists flying. If it had been a fight, the referee would have stopped it and declared Mick the victor by TKO.

But it was not a prize fight and Mick continued to pummel the unconscious saboteur with super-human rage. He did not even hear the rowboat push off, nor the sound of oars frantically distancing the craft from the barge.

Finally, Mick's rage was satisfied. He searched the dead man's satchel and found the remaining pencil bombs. Mick did not recognize the devices, but knew they were sinister. He sprang to his feet, lifted Greg over his shoulder and ran toward the guard building screaming "Fire" at the top of his lungs.

Padraic reacted first and ran to the emergency phone and called the fire department. He reported a fire at the Black Tom munitions depot. As the operator was asking his name, Padraic hollered, "Sorry, gotta go! This place is getting ready to blow."

Declan ran to the evacuation alarm and pulled the cord. Suddenly, a siren pierced the night and all the guards and the land contingent instinctively began sprinting toward the gate house. As Declan ran past the gate house, he saw Dermotty raise his head uncomprehendingly. Declan screamed, "Devin, get your arse out of there. This place is going to explode!"

Mick lagged behind the other guards and watched in amazement as three saboteurs emerged from the shadows and joined the frantic retreat. As he crossed the causeway heading for safety, he saw the three men flee into the woods. Moments later, he watched an automobile with a distinctive grill, speed down the road, its headlights bouncing in the darkness. Mick could do nothing but keep running, his friend's blood spilling down his uniform.

Angela Libelluia was sleeping soundly in a bunk bed in the Main Building on Ellis Island when she was tossed to the floor by a tremendous explosion. Windows shattered, sending shards of glass raining down on the sleeping immigrants in the huge hall. She heard screaming metal slam into Lady Liberty. The night sky lit up like Mount Vesuvius erupting. The ground shook with each successive blast. The explosive concussions rattled the foundation of the building. She feared that the end of the world was upon them.

Over in Jersey City, shrapnel propelled by the explosions crashed into the fabled clock tower, forever freezing the time at 2:12 AM. The Black Tom Island disaster was the largest explosion ever caused by man. When the pencil bombs detonated, between two and four million pounds of munitions exploded. Streaks of light and whistling bullets pierced the darkness. Several blazing barges broke from their moorings and floated adrift spewing their deadly pyrotechnics in the harbor.

The *Jersey Journal* best captured the devastation in its headline:

BIG MUNITIONS EXPLOSION AT BLACK TOM; 50 BELIEVED DEAD; 21 HURT, IN CITY HOSPITAL

The shock from the attack was felt in Philadelphia, 90 miles away. Glass was shattered in buildings as far as 25 miles away. It was reported that heat and debris from the fire and explosions damaged buildings in lower Manhattan from the Battery all the way up to Times Square. Tremors from the explosions were felt on the monumental Brooklyn Bridge. The Hudson Tubes connecting Manhattan to Jersey City began leaking. Engineers from the Jersey City Public Works Department reported serious cracks in the outer wall of City Hall. Tombstones and monuments at area cemeteries toppled.

Despite the magnitude of the explosions and the loss of life and property, the authorities offered no explanation of the cause. The stabbing death of one of the guards, the statement of Mick Chapman to the police, and reports of saboteurs fleeing the scene in a late model Mercedes, did not appear in the papers.

Among the articles appearing in the *Journal*, was an interview with Commissioner Frank Hague. After commending the bravery of the police and fire departments, Mr. Hague reported that the Johnson Barge Company would be fined for illegally mooring barge No. 17 at the depot because it tried to *"avoid a twenty-five dollar towing charge — a false economy indeed."*[29]

1916
Petrograd, Russia

The fair weather of opportunity will not wait.

~ Otto Kahn, Financier

Nicholas stood in his office peering through the large, semicircular window. Bluish smoke from a cigarette in his hand curled up around his head. He looked at his reflection and studied the puffiness under his eyes with disgust. His mood darkened with his sense that winter had come early this year. Outside the clouds were low and steel blue with menacing black undertones. The relentless wind moved the thick clouds rapidly across his vista, bringing more and thicker clouds. The forecast was dire.

He felt a darkness pressing at the glass, straining to enter and devour him. For a moment, he thought that to be buried in the darkness might be a relief from the grim situation he faced. The destruction at Black Tom Island in New York harbor had dealt a severe blow to the war effort. His troops needed American munitions desperately.

If only the Starets could perform a miracle to save Mother Russia. Bah! He thought, that monk is a mad degenerate who causes more trouble every day. The Tsarina is aware of his dissoluteness, but she excuses it. She says,

"If he really does these awful things, then it is with a special purpose — to temper himself morally."[30]

Nicholas considered her rationalization as a mother's weakness. Yet, could he deprive her of the only person who stood between Alexei and death? Like a tapeworm, Rasputin preys on her dependence. He knows that as long as he can keep our Sunbeam from the clutches of that damned disease, that we will tolerate his degenerate behavior. But, at what price?

He quickly chided himself for even considering that his son, his heir, was measurable in earthly terms. Alexei brought him immeasurable joy with his funny faces and irreverent remarks about his ministers. The lad can perceive that they are fools, scurrying in their self-aggrandizing ways and flapping their gums without saying anything of consequence. But what alternatives are there?

There was a knock at the door. Without turning, the Tsar checked his wristwatch; it was time for his next appointment. Otto Kahn stood before him with a look of excited expectation like he could not wait to share good news. Well, thought the Tsar, maybe the clever banker possesses a way out of this tangle.

"Ah, Otto, let's sit by the fire. Sergei, bring us some tea."

"Good afternoon. How is Your Excellency today?"

The Tsar, as his mood dictated, ignored the attempt at pleasantries. He got right to the point. Mother Russia was in desperate need for munitions and the Supreme Ruler could not let his people down. What was Kahn going to do about this disaster?

"I have met personally with Newton Baker, the new Secretary of War, who assured me that he would personally see to it that munitions would be shipped before the cold weather."

"Do you have any idea of how vulnerable we are!" shouted Nicholas. "That is not acceptable. All could be lost by then! I am pursuing other sources in the Orient to supply our brave men. I will not allow them to be slaughtered by those German butchers."

The Tsar was bluffing. China simply did not have the capacity to produce the quantities of munitions needed. Kahn knew it, and Nicholas knew that he knew it. Otto was glad to alter the direction of the conversation.

"Your Excellency, I believe that preservation of the wealth of the realm should be the highest priority."

The monarch snapped his head toward the banker.

"What do you mean?"

"We are hearing from our sources that the German High Command has targeted the gold in the Imperial Vault as their prime objective in 1917. Apparently, they believe that capture of the Imperial Treasury is within reach. At that point, they will be able to fund their evil ambitions. That is what we are hearing."

Nicholas staggered back into his chair as if he had just heard something that was inconceivable moments earlier. His eyebrows knotted and the side of his face convulsed rapidly. Kahn turned away so as not to add to the Tsar's discomfort.

"Your Highness, I have a proposal for you to consider — Operation Diaspora."

"What? What?" asked the Tsar irascibly.

"When Russia's fortune is stored in one place, it becomes, as they say in America, a sitting duck; extremely vulnerable. The best way to thwart the Kaiser's designs on your gold would be to disperse it. The treasure should be sent in four equal tranches to Moscow, Vladivostok and Stockholm for ultimate shipment to New York. The remaining tranche would travel with Your Excellency. In this fashion, Mother Russia has immediate access for operational needs and the Treasury would be in secure locations thereby limiting the potential for disastrous loss. Basically, it's the counsel we provide all of our clients — spread the risk. As they say in America, don't put all your eggs in one basket."

Nicholas pondered what Kahn proposed. He thought that maybe the gift of clairvoyance might help him evaluate this proposal. The Tsar picked up the phone and spoke softly into it. A few minutes later, Rasputin entered the room. He bowed awkwardly toward the Tsar.

"Grigory, please sit. We would like you to listen to Herr Kahn's Operation Diaspora and give us your thoughts. Otto, explain your proposal," directed the Tsar.

Rasputin's countenance darkened as Otto presented his plan and its rationale.

"Your Excellency, I strongly oppose this so-called Operation. I think that moving the Treasury invites disaster. While the gold is in motion, it will be vulnerable and when it gets to its destination, it will be in a less secure place than it is now. If Your Excellency is considering moving the Treasury, I would suggest using some natural fortress, like the Borschevsk Caves near the Antonovo Lake, or the Sosnovy Bor cavern, or, even the Oreshek Fortress situated on Lake Ladoga. All are close by and can be made impregnable."

Otto stifled a laugh. Rasputin shot him a murderous stare. Nicholas' scar twitched. He covered it self-consciously. An awkward silence ensued.

"Your Highness, the contention that the Treasury is vulnerable while it is in motion, is simplistic. It has been said, that war is deception. There are ways to disguise the nature of the gold. The use of deception and multiple conveyances would be effective in hiding the gold while it is in motion.

"The idea that natural formations can be made impregnable is also silly. Quite honestly, Your Highness does not have the time or manpower to turn a cave into a bunker. The gold should be near proven defensive positions that are already impregnable."

"*Nyet*, Your Excellency. I smell a trick. Do not accept this crazy scheme from this . . . this *German!*" shouted Rasputin.

Nicholas sat dumbfounded as Rasputin stormed out of the room. The Tsar's cheek jittered furiously like it had been jolted by electricity.

The following morning, Otto mused that, despite the evident deprivations caused by the war, the Hotel Europa was still as grand as ever. His shoes tapped a brisk cadence as he strode across the marble floor of the lobby, down the vermilion rug to the private dining chamber. His nurturing of Antoine over the years had been a worthy investment. The French-trained concierge had actually been born on the Alsatian border. His grandfather had been arrested with Otto's father in Mannheim in 1848 when the bourgeoisie had unsuccessfully rebelled against autocratic rule. Both had been sentenced to death; but Otto's father had been fortunate to escape to America. Antoine's father had not been so lucky.

Antoine had made the arrangements for a lavish breakfast meeting with the leaders of the *camarilla*. Otto greeted Grand Dukes Mikhail, Nikolai, Pavel and Kyril, and General Nikolai Ivanov. Kahn took the opportunity to disseminate news about the horrible explosion in New York harbor. They all appreciated his insight and assurances as to how quickly the munitions could be replaced and delivered. As they digested Otto's optimistic predictions, he changed the subject to affairs of state. Each shared his own story of Rasputin's interference and how the Tsar had dismissed honorable, competent men merely at the whim of Rasputin. The *camarilla* voiced their concerns about the damage the Tsar and Rasputin would continue to inflict on the war-stressed government.

"Our dilemma is that the Tsarina protects Rasputin. Nikki is weak and relents to the wishes of the Teutonic princess and the muhjik half-breed," said Pavel bitingly.

"The mad monk lives a charmed life. Agents under the Tsarina's direction guard the degenerate day and night," added Mikhail. "I have warned my brother, Nicholas, about the damage that Rasputin's actions are causing to the dynasty. In his heart, he knows the truth; I can see it in his eyes. But he is insistent about protecting Rasputin because he believes that the Starets is the only one who can keep Alexei alive. Nicholas is adamant and refuses to entertain any discussion about removing Rasputin. Nicholas has lost the ability to rule effectively."

"The war effort suffers, too, from the distraction Rasputin presents to the high command. The rank-and-file soldiers, of course, have other worries, but their morale is low due to the rumors of degeneracy. They wonder why they fight while the Tsar allows others to commit acts that disgrace the throne. They call Nicholas the 'Bloody Tsar' because of all the casualties we have endured," grumbled General Ivanov.

"Gentlemen, I share your concerns. I have a plan to eliminate this problem once and for all. The code name is the Keystone Imperative. My only hesitancy comes from uncertainty as to whether the *camarilla* will support my plan to rid this pestilence from the halls of power. We need only your approval to finalize the details and the plan will be implemented. What do you say?" questioned Otto.

The five men exchanged glances, nodding to each other; half in relief that someone was willing to step up, and half in anticipation about the consequences.

"On behalf of the *camarilla*, I give you our blessing and undying support on your success," said Mikhail solemnly.

"Gentlemen, on my sacred honor, I will purge the vile rot from the Imperial family!"

The portents of an early winter descended on Petrograd, as if in punishment for some grave national sin. Bitter wind whipped snow through the alleys of the gloomy city. Chorney departed the steamer, his duffel slung across his back. The guard at the entry gate eyed him warily as he limped down the gangplank. The atmosphere at the checkpoint was tense and Kurt could tell that one false move could land him in jail or worse, back in uniform as cannon fodder at the front. The wooden brace he wore stretched from his ankle to his hip. It chafed the skin on his lower leg and he could feel the sticky coagulation of blood seeping into his sock. The guard, a surly man in his forties, stomped his feet to stay warm as Chorney awkwardly withdrew his papers from inside his greatcoat. He avoided direct eye contact so as not to antagonize the agent.

"Are you injured? How did it happen?" asked the guard in a dialect that Kurt had difficulty grasping.

"Yes," he replied, knocking on the wooden leg and raising his trouser leg to display the bloody sock. "I was hit by shrapnel during the Battle of Tannenburg last August. Now, I come to Petrograd because my family has been killed by the German pigs when they overran Vistula. I was at the army hospital in Dvinsk when they attacked. Captain Beriev forbade me to return. Given my inability to walk, the only safe transport was by this supply ship to Stockholm. We picked up food there, and now I am free to search for relatives here in Petrograd."

Although the guard would have enjoyed intimidating the wounded veteran, he had more pressing duties. The guard reluctantly thrust Kurt's papers at him and motioned for Chorney to pass. Kurt glanced back to see the guard pushing and clubbing his way through the cowering crowd.

Pain radiated up his leg as he trudged through the packed snow. It was afternoon and the sun was dimming in the steel gray sky. He was shocked at the deterioration of conditions since the war began. Petrograd was on the verge of chaos. He had heard about the severe food shortages, but he was not prepared for the thousands of refugees from rural areas on the streets.

A band of a half-dozen boys ranging in age from nine to twelve, eyed him hungrily as he limped past. They were dressed in frayed, thin coats; their pale faces were stained with grimy smears of dirt, vestiges of time spent rummaging through refuse. Kurt loosened the buttons of his coat with his left hand. As he entered a side street about a block from his rooming house, he felt the thump of an ice ball strike him in the back. When he turned, a barrage of ice balls pelted him and the boys charged him. He swatted the first two assailants aside, using their momentum to push them past. He deftly grabbed hold of the next boy, who appeared to be the leader of the pack and had a shiny Bowie knife at his throat before any of the boys could blink. With wide eyes, they backed away and ran down the street. Kurt pushed the young ruffian in his grip away and rewarded him with a kick in the rump that sent him sprawling into the grimy snow.

"If you ever come near me again, I'll cut your balls off," Chorney barked.

Chorney entered the rooming house, greeting the proprietress. The widow Asanoff, a short round woman with a cheery smile, returned his greeting.

"Did I just hear a disturbance outside? No? It is good to see you again, Herr Chorney. I received your message and readied your room. Oh, and, yes, there is a package for you upstairs."

"It's good to be back. But I see that things are not good here. The war has taken its toll. The city appears destitute and desperate," Kurt opined.

"That it is, that it is. But, ... Oh my God, you're hurt. What happened?"

"Oh, it's nothing, my leg stiffened up after a fall from a train platform. Just a clumsy fall; nothing to worry about. It will loosen up once I rest a bit."

He limped up the stairs with Mrs. Asanoff clucking her concern behind him. Once in his room, he tossed his bag onto the bed and removed his trousers. With great relief, he unhinged the wooden brace. He snagged the envelope from the dresser and lay on the bed, flexing his leg. Tearing open the package, he slowly read the encrypted report, scribbling notes along the margins.

The report identified a grave threat called the Keystone Imperative. There were whispers inside the Imperial Palace about an impending attempt to destabilize the Russian government through assassination. The authority of Nicholas' rule had been eroding rapidly since he had fired the Grand Duke Nikolai as chief commander of the military and assumed the position himself. As Chief Commander, the Tsar was blamed for every defeat and casualty suffered by Russian forces. With the Tsar absent at the front, the Tsarina had increasingly injected herself into governmental affairs by unceremoniously dismissing ministers and department heads, often at the acrimonious insistence of Rasputin. The royal palace was wracked by dissension and bitterness.

Apparently, the Tsar had been targeted for assassination by members of the *camarilla*. The attack was to take place before Christmas. According to sources at the Palace (probably Pasha, he thought), the Tsar was scheduled to leave Petrograd to return to headquarters at the front in two days. There he would be murdered. Arrangements had been made for Kurt to join the cooking crew that accompanied the Imperial Party. He was to report to Tsarkoe Selo the next morning and see the chamberlain for assignment to Chief Daniko Solvanovich. His job was to keep his eyes on the Tsar as much as possible and try to thwart any assassination attempt. Due to Nicholas' steadfast refusal to entertain a separate peace with Germany, American interests required a continuation of his leadership. Kurt used the report to kindle a fire in the cold fireplace opposite the window.

Late 1916
New York City, New York

I cannot forecast to you the action of Russia.
It is a riddle wrapped in a mystery inside an enigma . . . .

~ WINSTON CHURCHILL

THE STRAIN OF THE LAST FEW YEARS had turned his once-black crew cut to salt and pepper, with a predominance of salt. Espionage, sabotage, propaganda and the relentless probing of U.S. defenses had left him weary but determined to protect American interests wherever they were threatened. Captain Oliver considered the shrapnel that had gouged Lady Liberty a personal affront. He knew that events were accelerating rapidly and that he would have to force the issue.

It was a brisk December day and the dry, brown leaves filled the sidewalks and covered the curbs outside the St. Regis Hotel in midtown Manhattan. As Rudolph Hecht walked toward the subway on his way to work at his office at Kuhn Loeb, he was thinking that the desiccated crunch of the fallen leaves reminded him of the bones of all the dead and dying soldiers in Europe. Suddenly, two husky men in dark suits and gray fedoras unceremoniously thrust him into a waiting sedan. They blindfolded him and drove to a water conveyance that brought him to the place where he now sat on a metal chair in a room without windows.

Rudolph Hecht was middle-aged, early forties, perhaps. He had light brown hair that fell limply over his high forehead. As Strafe Oliver looked at Hecht through the two-way mirror, the suspect's anxiety-filled eyes darted around the room searching for some clue about his predicament. Right now, the officer was separated by five inches of wood and plaster from a member of the German spy ring that had taken out Black Tom Island in New York Harbor. So far, the German spy had smugly resisted questioning, only repeating his demands to speak to the German consulate.

"You are in no position to make demands, Herr Hecht," said Strafe biting out the last two words. "We have evidence that establishes your role as the money courier in the Black Tom explosion last summer."

"That's ridiculous," stammered Hecht.

"Not according to Dr. Albert. You know, . . . Dr. Rolfe Albert, a commercial attaché with the German Embassy in Washington. He says that you and your cousin, Otto Kahn, were the principal sources of money for the sabotage. Letters and phone conversations with Kristoff put the explosion right at your doorstep."

"For the hundredth time, I do not know what you are talking about," protested Hecht.

Strafe suppressed a smile at how his office had "acquired" the Albert documents that provided the basis for his questions. On a steamy, late summer day, Chorney had been assigned to a routine tail of Dr. Rolfe Albert. The German had attended a luncheon at a restaurant on the Lower East Side where he had had a couple of beers. Kurt followed him from the restaurant onto the Lexington Avenue subway. As the train left the Thirty-Third Street station, Dr. Albert's head nodded forward in a doze. Chorney waited as the rocking of the train lulled Dr. Albert into a deeper nap. When the subway pulled into the Fifty-First Street Station, Chorney impulsively grabbed the briefcase from Albert's limp hand and raced out of the car just as the doors closed. The young officer's description of the startled Albert's face pressed against the subway car door screaming 'Stop thief' was, as they say, priceless.

"I'm just a businessman. I work at Kuhn Loeb. You can check with Otto Kahn. He will vouch for me," whined Hecht.

"Really? Is that so? Maybe this picture of you with Michael Kristoff in a diner near the pier will help you remember? It sure looks like a money drop before the Black Tom Island explosions," said Strafe. "Do you know the penalty for sabotage that kills innocent American civilians? I do, it's hanging by the neck until dead."

The gloomy Petrograd weather had seeped into Otto's mood. Events were outpacing his planning. Keeping the United States on the sidelines was becoming more difficult every day. Germany's quandary was simple: to prevent the United States from supplying the *Entente* with weapons and munitions, Germany had to engage in extensive sabotage on American soil and soon would have to resort to unrestricted U-boat warfare. The more successful these measures were, the greater the likelihood America would enter the war. It was the proverbial rock and a hard place.

Just as Germany's margin of error was shrinking, so was his; if America entered the war, the achievement of his goal would become impossible. Elimination of the Imperial Russian Government and the ensuing chaos were critical to his plans.

A knock on his hotel room door disrupted his train of thought. He adjusted his silk kimono and answered the door. An alert-looking young man in hotel livery stood at attention.

"Sorry to disturb you so early in the morning, Sir. This telegram marked 'Urgent' just arrived from the United States. We thought you might want to see it as soon as possible."

"Thank you," said Otto, slipping a bill into the bellhop's hand. Once the door closed, the banker tore open the telegram.

RUDOLPH VANISHED STOP PLEASE HELP STOP MARJORIE HECHT

Otto walked over to an easy chair with a view overlooking the city. The twinkling lights from the street lamps created a magical panorama. His mind churned with questions that could only be answered in a direct conversation. He tried to conjure up Marjorie's face. He had not seen her since Rudolph's wedding several years ago. He just could not see her face.

Anyway that did not matter. Rudolph was his confederate at Kuhn Loeb, his detail man. Dare he risk calling his cousin's wife? Dare he not risk calling his cousin's wife? He decided on an alternative course of action.

Strafe entered the cinderblock room to find Hecht sleeping on the floor in the corner.

"Wake up, Hecht. I have something to show you. And, you better be straight with me," growled Oliver. Hecht blinked rapidly, disoriented. In the sound-proof, windowless room he was losing track of time, place and day.

Strafe pulled up a chair and placed several surveillance photos of an athletic-looking, middle-aged man in a dark, tailored suit waiting outside an elevator door bearing the stylized emblem of the St. Regis Hotel.

"Who is this man?"

"It's Hard."

"Listen, Hecht, if you don't cooperate . . . ."

"I am cooperating. This man is Hard Scrapple. He's one of Mr. Kahn's associates."

"What is his business?" asked Strafe.

"He operates the foundry called the Serpentine Rail Company and his father-in-law owns the Lehigh Valley Railroad," replied Hecht. Interesting, thought Strafe, Lehigh Valley RR ran the depot at Black Tom.

"What does Serpentine make?"

"They make a lot of things out of molded metal, like rails, locomotives . . . train stuff. And . . . oh yeah, they work for you."

"What the heck does that mean?" questioned Strafe.

"They have a contract with Fort Knox to mold gold bullion for the Treasury. No kidding. With all the gold coming into the United States from the Europeans, the government re-forges the gold into U.S. bars. They use iron nest molds to pour molten gold into. The nest molds bear the seal of the United States and the foundry adds a serial number."

Interesting, thought Strafe, but it's not helping to reveal the target of the Keystone Imperative.

"Why is he meeting with your wife?"

"I don't know, I don't know," replied Hecht in an exasperated tone.

Oliver was frustrated at the lack of confirmatory intelligence regarding the Keystone Imperative. He must figure out a way to discover the target. Strafe knew that it was time to ratchet up the interrogation. An agent knocked at the door and beckoned to Oliver. After a whispered conversation, he returned to the prisoner.

"So, Herr Hecht, I have just heard from our agents that your wife, Marjorie, is now in custody. We will do our utmost to make your pregnant wife comfortable."

"This is outrageous. She has nothing to do with my business. You must release her at once." His German accent became more prominent as he became agitated.

"Listen, this is your last chance. If you do not help us, you will be executed for sabotage and your fatherless child will be born in prison."

"My wife is innocent and I don't want my child raised without a father. If I help you, will you get me immunity?" Hecht pleaded, his defiant façade crumbling.

"Look, I can't make any promises. I have to clear it with higher-ups. Just tell me something to show my bosses that you really want to help and that you have valuable information worth immunity."

"What?"

"Tell me who Keystone is. We must know if it is the Tsar."

Hecht hesitated, calculated the odds; then, said, "Keystone is not the Tsar."

December 1916
Petrograd

. . . and the goat shall bear all their iniquities.

~ Genesis 27:11

H E STOMPED HIS FEET to remove the snow from his boots. Heavy snows had blanketed Petrograd. The lobby of the Hotel Europa was bedecked with pine rope, red and green ribbons and bright lights to celebrate the impending Christmas holiday. Otto rather liked the new electric lights; they reminded him of the festival of lights from his youth in Mannheim. His thoughts drifted to his childhood pledge, *Auri Sacra Fames* and how close to fruition it was.

His reverie was broken by Antoine who greeted him warmly, no doubt, in anticipation of a generous, holiday gratuity. Otto had spent more time than usual in Petrograd this year and certain members of the staff at the hotel had performed above and beyond the call of duty by flawlessly and discreetly executing his plans. Whether it was transportation to Tsarskoe Selo, or a late night dalliance with Anna Pavlova, he knew that he could rely on Antoine to make the arrangements. None were more critical to his success than tonight's meeting.

His steel-gray eyes squinted slightly as Antoine escorted him through the main dining area to a private salon. Judging from their dress, the clientele at the hotel were still obviously wealthy personages, yet Otto detected a decided absence of Russian nobility. Many of the royalty were engaged in the war as officers in the Tsar's military. He also noticed that there were fewer women of the aristocracy in the public areas of the hotel, probably due to the strains of the war. The ladies of the court had been replaced by the ladies of the night — gorgeous young women who serviced the foreign visitors, while the young men of Russia bled and died on the battlefield for Mother Russia. Antoine, the once-haughty concierge, adapted to his new role with pragmatism, rationalizing that the war had simply changed the strata of his procurements.

"Here we are, Herr Kahn," Antoine announced.

"Thank you, Antoine," said Otto, as he slipped a few pounds into the man's discreetly-poised hand. "Please hold dinner service until seven o'clock."

He walked toward the table where two men were huddled together, lost in conversation. Their hands were intertwined and they were gazing longingly into each other's eyes.

"Excuse me, gentlemen. We have work to do. When we have finished, you can go play whatever games you play."

"Good evening, Herr Kahn," said Nijinsky mimicking Antoine. He was dressed in a maroon, velvet sports jacket, white shirt and checkered cravat at his throat. A thin, black line had been traced around his eyes, and there was the slightest hint of rouge on his cheeks. His broad sallow face was alight with a silly smile like he was laughing inwardly at some unknown jest. Otto regarded him warily. The star *danseur* had behaved erratically since his detainment in Vienna several years ago. His relationship with Serge Daighiliev, the director of the Ballet Russe and Vaslav's former lover, had so deteriorated that the only communications were hissy fits reported in the tabloids. Good for business at the box office but suspect for his extracurricular activities.

"It is good to see you, Otto," said Felix, who was dressed in full military garb, complete with braided gold rope on his left shoulder and several brightly-colored medals on his chest. The medals were the result of family prerogatives, not from any acts of valor on the battlefield. Due to his mother's intercession on behalf of her only surviving son, and, a generous donation to the Tsar's war effort, the Prince was exempt from combat duty and served in the ceremonial branch of the Imperial Guard. After all, the

Russian nobility loved to parade around in their uniforms, while the peasants struggled and died in muddy trenches.

"Otto, as you know, the war has taken a heavy toll in blood and suffering. Father Winter has arrived early this year and there have been food shortages in the cities. Some of the peasants are desperate and they have resorted to rioting," reported Felix. "But I have very good news. Today, I attended a session of the Duma and heard Vladimir Mitrofanovich Purishkevich speak out against Rasputin. He really blasted the rogue. The Duma gave him a rousing ovation. When his speech was over, I approached him about joining us. He agreed without hesitation."

"That is very good news. Purishkevich will be able to stifle any outcry in the Duma when the deed is done. Now, all we have to do is set the trap and do the deed," offered Otto.

"Dmitry and I have been developing a plan. Do you know Munya Golovina? Anyway, she loved my dear deceased brother and, now carries a torch for me. She is also a devotee of Rasputin. We know that Rasputin fancies himself a healer. So, I have complained to Munya about chest pains. She suggested seeking the monk to cure my pains, as I knew she would. She has agreed to broker reconciliation with the Grishka. I am meeting him at her mansion tomorrow. Remember when he slapped me at the *Troika*? I should have slain him on the spot. We would not have this problem if I had acted then . . . ."

"Do you think he will believe that you want to reconcile?"

Felix brought his hands to his open mouth and feigned surprise. Vaslav started to giggle hysterically.

"Otto, my little friend here is a consummate actor. He could masquerade as a woman and convince his own mother that she had a daughter. If anyone can fool that fool, it is this one," said Vaslav slapping Felix on the shoulder jocularly.

"OK," replied Otto. "After he trusts you, how will we get him in a vulnerable situation? The Tsarina has her agents guarding him day and night."

"No problem. We will lure him to my palace under the guise of meeting my wife, Irina. He has told Munya that he would love to meet my Irina. She is the Tsar's favorite niece and Rasputin is always looking for ways to curry favor with the Tsar. After I regain his confidence, we will invite him to my palace to meet Irina. Once he is in my place, he will be like a Christmas suckling."

"How long do you think it will take?" Otto asked.

"I will meet with him tomorrow. Irina is in Crimea and will return for Christmas. We will be able to accomplish our objective by Christmas."

"Christmas? I love Christmas," whooped Nijinsky, with childlike glee.

Felix was beside himself. His wife, Irina, had sent him a telegram expressing extreme anxiety about the plot. Worse, she declared that she would not come to Petrograd to act as "bait" for Rasputin to lure him to his murder. Felix called his co-conspirator Dmitry to advise him of the collapse of their carefully orchestrated plans. Dmitry paused briefly, then, said calmly, "This changes nothing. We proceed as planned. Don't worry; we improvise. The Holy Fool will never see the bait. He just has to think that the bait is there."

Dr. Stanislaus de Lazovert had been recruited by Purishkevich to help prepare the poison and assist with the driving. Pulling on rubber gloves, Dr. Lazovert pulverized potassium cyanide crystals and mixed the powder into the icing on the Russian teacakes with the pink icing. Additional cyanide powder was hydrolyzed in order to line several wine goblets designated for Rasputin exclusively.

Dr. Lazovert steered the Russo-Buire touring car down Nevsky Prospekt to Rasputin's apartment at 12 Kiroch Street. The bitter temperature had abated somewhat and it was at the freezing point. A wet snow had fallen and it gave the city a surreal aura. The moon was in the second phase and shone brightly through the disappearing clouds. With a pointing motion, Prince Felix directed the big car to the building and sprang out when the car stopped. As he approached the building, an agent stepped out of the shadows and questioned him. Felix stifled a gag at the smell of the guard.

"I'm here to visit the Father." Felix responded. Since the agent was used to admitting important people to visit Rasputin at all hours of the day or night, he swallowed a yawn while reviewing the credentials Felix had displayed.

"Is he expecting you, Prince Yusopov?"

"Yes."

"Proceed."

Felix strode past the stocky officer and went around to the side entrance and knocked. A curtain on the door was pushed aside and Rasputin's face appeared. The door opened with the unlocking of several latches. Rasputin was wearing a black, silk poet shirt, embroidered with blue cornflowers that overlapped his black velvet trousers. A wide raspberry-colored sash encircled his waist. His long hair was neatly brushed back into a ponytail. The scent of cheap cologne suffused the air around the monk.

"Well, Grigory Efimovich, it's time to go; it's past midnight. You don't want to keep Irina waiting."

"OK, Little One," Grigory whispered, "I'll get my coat."

As Felix glanced nervously after the retreating Rasputin, a curtain rustled off to his left and he thought that he saw a pair of eyes slip into the darkness behind the curtain.

"Let's go, Grishka. Without a shepherd, sheep are not a flock. The novices are waiting."

"As we say in Siberia, 'Even the best shepherd loses a sheep to the wolf.' But we also say, 'The wolf eats, the bear protects'," responded Rasputin.

Rasputin followed the Prince to the car and murmured a greeting to Dr. Lazovert. The powerful vehicle propelled them to their destiny. During the short car ride, Felix described the exclusive ballet performance earlier that evening in the fifty-seat theater in the Yusopov Palace that was built in perfect scale of the Mariinsky Theater.

"Grishka, wait until you partake of the delicious 'rinas we have waiting for you."

Rasputin grunted in anticipation. The big vehicle pulled into the courtyard adjacent to the side entrance to Yusupov Palace.

"We're remodeling the south wing for Irina and me to live in; so you'll have to excuse the disarray. Irina is freshening up and will be down shortly. But, do come in and make yourself at home."

Rasputin walked up the steps to his left and entered the grand foyer. There was a spectacular curving balustrade before him and a matching one behind him. They converged at a landing on the second floor. In the center of the space hung a multi-tiered chandelier illuminated by hundreds of small incandescent bulbs that were reflected by Venetian cristallo pendants. Each acted like a prism and sprinkled rainbows across the walls and onto the ceiling that was thirty feet above the awestruck peasant. His eyes then tracked to the room before him and he observed the canvas-covered furniture and scaffolding along the walls in the large receiving room. The room was unlit, save for the light coming from the chandelier.

"Isn't it magnificent?" gestured the Prince. "This chandelier has been in our family for centuries. It was a gift to Prince Dmitry Yusupov from Tsar Feodor I when he bestowed the title of Prince on our family. We replaced the candles with light bulbs. It's quite valuable. But come, I have a surprise for you."

Felix wrapped his arm around the peasant's arm and pulled him into the Green Room where a gramophone was being cranked to life by none other than Anna Pavlova, the prima ballerina. The room was dimly lit by a series of candelabras on one side, casting eerie verdigris-tinted shadows.

"Anna, this is the esteemed Father Grigory Rasputin, who I'm sure you've seen in the papers. Isn't he just darling? Much cuter in person, than his photos, eh?"

Anna picked up a glass, "Pleased to make your acquaintance. May I pour you some Madeira? Oh, excuse me, how rude. This is my dear friend and colleague Bronislava Nijinsky. You can call her Roni. Over there, that's Nadya and, of course, you know Roni's brother, Vaslav, and Prince Dmitry."

Anna was wearing a stylish, silver gown that displayed her lithe body to perfection. Thin straps graced her shoulders and widened into the bodice, which was covered with red rhinestones on a field of silver brocade. Beneath the bodice, the gown flowed like a waterfall to her ankles, revealing the barest hint of her ruby red sandals. Rasputin nodded, half bowing.

He turned to Nadya, a sultry beauty whom he recognized from the *Mad Monk* several years ago. She was tall and wore an elegant black dress that was cut in a deep V that accentuated her *décolletage*. She greeted him with a kiss on each cheek.

Rasputin sat down on a bench covered with a tarp and next to a table set with delicacies. He ate the sumptuous food with his fingers. While she poured wine, Nadya leaned forward, giving Grigory a delightful view of her breasts. She winked at him and handed him a goblet of wine and saluted, "na zdorovje!" They all echoed her toast and swallowed deeply.

More wine was poured and the guests began dancing to the pulsating rhythms coming from the gramophone. Before long, he found himself sitting with Roni explaining his principles of love and repentance. She had large, soulful eyes in a shade of green that almost glowed in the soft light. Like Nadya, Roni was wearing a black gown; however, her dress had a demure neckline and billowing sleeves of sheer fabric that evoked the peasant blouses of his native Pokrovskoe. Roni studied his face intently as he expounded on his belief that joy comes only through repentance, and repentance could only be experienced truly through sin. The greater the sin, the deeper the repentance and the more satisfying the joy. He was facing her, holding her hands and penetrating her eyes with his hypnotic stare. Rasputin sensed a flicker of doubt flash through her eyes for a moment, then disappear.

"Is something wrong?"

"*Nyet, nyet*," she stammered, "I just need something to drink."

Nadya walked seductively over to the monk carrying a silver tray of pastries and cakes. "Come, eat," she whispered. "They're decadent."

"No, *Nadiuscha*, since the attack on me several years ago, I do not contaminate this temple of the Holy Ghost with sweets," he responded, gesturing stiffly toward his abdomen.

"Whatever you say, Grishka. Let's have some more wine." She filled his glass and entwined her arm in his and lifted her glass to her red lips and drained her glass. Rasputin followed suit, laughing as Nadya slipped a tablet into her mouth and kissed Rasputin passionately, transferring the tablet. They imbibed more wine.

"Grigory, tell them about the Khylst."

"In my native Siberia, they are a sect of believers that practice asceticism and by doing so achieve divine grace. One of the ways the community, called an Ark, can collectively purge itself of sin is to perform the ecstatic ritual of *radeniye*."

When Roni looked perplexed and started to question further, Rasputin said, "It's time to stop bloviating. Let's dance the *Barynya*. It's time to remove our masks and let our feelings pour through our movements and grace will flow. Will you dance with me?"

He spun and whirled, first with Roni, then Nadya, and then with Anna. They danced in a rhythmic circle. Off to the side, a figure in the shadows switched the disk on the gramophone. The tempo increased and the dancers flashed about rapturously. Standing partially obscured by draperies, a dark figure sipped a cognac as he watched the scene unfold. The phantasmic figures reflected off the monocle that dangled from his lapel.

While Rasputin was dancing, an arm reached for Roni and guided her from the dancing area. Another figure, also dressed in a black dress, entered the dance. The figures whirled gaily and Nadya was whisked away, replaced by another black-clad dancer. Grishka whooped and clapped as if possessed by a dervish. Anna, who had not taken any wine, caught the eye of the dark figure by the gramophone and whirled off in his direction.

"Leave with Roni and Nadya quietly. We have some business with the Holy Fool."

A frightened look of resigned understanding crossed her brow and she nodded assent. The ladies bundled into their furs, leaving the revelry behind them. Roni glanced back over her shoulder and saw the ominous black figures whirling feverishly to the hypnotic rhythm of the music from the gramophone. Nadya casually swooped down and hooked Rasputin's satchel with her arm. Soon, the ladies were with Dr. Lazovert in the Russo-Buire heading to the Hotel Europa to spend the fateful night.

Rasputin was breathing heavily and whirling for all he was worth, when the gramophone started to slow. His arms were interlocked with the black figures as the threesome twirled and turned. The music wound down and the arms tightened on Rasputin's and pulled him backwards toward the stairwell by the side entrance. The monk laughed and lifted his heels in exaltation. Then, he looked to both sides and saw no gaiety. The mood had turned venomous.

"Unhand me. I need the water closet."

There was no response and the dark figures continued to pull him downstairs. The basement room was furnished as a dining room with a broad wooden table encircled by stout chairs. The floor was covered with a large brown bearskin rug, with a large head and ferocious-looking teeth. On the far wall, opposite the stairs, was a granite hearth and a dark, wooden door. Logs wet from the snow hissed ominously as the fire blazed and was reflected in the life-like bear eyes. The walls were whitewashed and candles provided a seductive glow. Trays of teacakes and wine bottles and glasses covered the table.

Rasputin could feel his new patent leather boots thumping down the stairs. He resigned himself to this new game and resolved to play along with the infamous trickster, Felix. Rasputin had heard of the wild bacchanalias of the ruling class, with Felix and Dmitry leading the festivities. Grigory's head was still spinning and he closed his eyes and anticipated the new levels of debauchery that he was about to experience. He let out a huge guffaw. The two black clad figures kissed him and caressed him. In his inebriated state, he did not hear the soft clank of manacles that were placed on his wrists and ankles. Each appendage was attached to an arm or leg of the chair. His attention shifted from his groin to his head where alarms started to blare.

"Wait . . . what's going on? Roni, Nadya, where are you?"

A harsh voice whispered in his ear, "Your time is over, Grishka."

In his other ear he heard, "Prepare yourself, Grigory. Final retribution is nigh."

He could not rise; his ankles were strapped to the chair. The manacles imprisoning his hands were firmly bolted to the arms of the chair. As his head cleared and he began to assess his dire situation, Grigory's survival instincts activated. There were two black clad figures in gowns near him and he heard at least two other voices on the stairway. If he could get to the door at the landing and get outside, he would have a chance. He readied his body for action.

When the taller of the black figures was behind him, Rasputin exploded into an upright position. The chair splintered, giving him freedom to move. He whirled and smashed his forehead into the face of the nearest black figure, who crumpled in a heap. The other leaped on him from behind and caught him in a stranglehold. Rasputin tried to reach over his head, but the hold tightened and his knees buckled as he began to lose consciousness. As he fell to the ground, he felt a sharp kick to his left temple. Rasputin's eyes flickered as he saw several pairs of boots enter the room.

The shock of spirits of hartshorn placed under his nose, startled him awake. The left side of his head throbbed and he tried to focus his eyes on his tormentors. From his vantage point on the floor, he counted the feet of five people.

"You muhjik bastard, you broke my nose!" screamed a voice that he recognized as Prince Felix. A swift kick to Rasputin's ribcage jolted him off the floor. He hunched over in agony. Hands pulled him upright and he was bludgeoned across his forehead by Felix wielding a broken chair leg. Rasputin momentarily blacked out. When he regained consciousness, he was upright and Felix was standing in front of him pointing a revolver at him.

"Grigory Efimovich Rasputin, you have debased the Imperial Court, you have committed crimes of treason and corruption and betrayed the Romanov Dynasty by your high crimes, you are hereby sentenced to death," said Prince Felix, who along with Grand Duke Dmitry Pavlovich were now wearing their dress military uniforms.

"Do you understand the charges?"

Rasputin stared fiercely and murmured, "You know not of what you speak."

"Silence, you insolent pig!" screeched Felix, "Now you will see how the Aristocracy deals with peasant usurpers."

He unholstered his service revolver and turned out the cylinder. After emptying all the bullets, he placed one round in the chamber, flipped the weapon shut and spun the cylinder. He pointed the weapon at Rasputin's chest and squeezed the trigger. Rasputin gasped at the audible click. A trace of a mocking smile creased his face. The Prince turned to his right and handed the revolver to Prince Dmitry.

Rising to his full height, Dmitry adopted a marksman's stance and, after spinning the cylinder, he barked, "For Mother Russia." He pulled the trigger and the hammer slammed into an empty chamber.

The Prince rigidly brought his gun hand toward his face and pivoting the weapon on the trigger guard, he presented the weapon to Vladimir Purishkevich. The Duma member nervously took the weapon with two hands. He clumsily spun the cylinder and pointed the gun unsteadily at the monk. He yanked the trigger. There was a resounding blast as the weapon fired. Rasputin stared uncomprehendingly at Purishkevich, then laughed in the realization that the drunken legist had missed.

Rasputin bellowed, "You fools. Don't you know that I am protected?"

An enraged Felix slapped the monk with the back of his hand.

"Silence! Next."

Purishkevich sighed with relief and passed the weapon to Prince Felix, who again loaded a round in the cylinder, deftly snapped the cylinder, and spun it.

"Vaslav, it's your turn. Take the gun." The dancer, who was still wearing the black gown, wore a wicked smile, as he brought the gun to his lips and licked the rim of the barrel lasciviously.

"Ah, Grigory, we could have made such wonderful music together." He sidled up to Rasputin and caressed his ear with the barrel of the gun. He worked the gun down Rasputin's chest, past his waist and forced the gun inside his waistband, stopping at the Starets' groin. "How about we make the Father a eunuch?" He pulled the trigger and once more Rasputin gasped audibly as the room filled with an empty click.

"Enough," shouted Felix as he grabbed the loaded gun from Vaslav.

The agitated Prince stepped back two paces, spun the cylinder and pointed the gun at Rasputin, shouting "Die, filth." The explosion of the charge startled them all and the echo reverberated through the small room.

The bullet tore into Rasputin's chest and he dropped to the rug in a puddle of blood. Dmitry bent over Rasputin, placing two fingers on his neck.

"No pulse. It's done."

Prince Felix was shaking as he put the gun into his holster. "I need a drink. Let's get one upstairs before we get rid of this peasant scum."

Back in the Green Room, Prince Dmitry poured drinks for all and put his arm around Felix and said, "Felix, the family is proud of you. The warrior Khans have again defended the honor of the Tsars. To Prince Felix!"

"Here, here," echoed Purishkevich.

Prince Felix followed by Vladimir, walked down the narrow staircase to the basement dining room where Rasputin lay. When Felix reached the bottom step, he stopped. The body was gone. Before his mind could comprehend what was happening, he saw a blur of the white curtain to his right and powerful hands gripped his throat. As Rasputin lunged at him, a primal roar echoed in the narrow space. Felix fell backwards, knocking Vladimir down. Rasputin climbed over them. He struggled up the stairs, threw open the side door and staggered out into the courtyard. Desperate, he whirled left and right. His eyes fastened on a large bulky object next to the door.

Rasputin launched himself at the wooden box and heaved. Agitated voices filled the cold, night air as his pursuers scrambled up the stairs. The throbbing in his head and the searing pain in his chest faded, as primal fear consumed him, providing super-human strength. The door began to swing open as Rasputin grunted and toppled the heavy wooden crate across the door, trapping his pursuers on the basement landing. As shouts, curses and bullets rained on the door, Rasputin stumbled away.

His mind was racing as he crossed the snow-covered courtyard. His eyes fixated on the open gate and the street beyond. He urged himself forward as blood dripped down his left arm onto the pristine snow that covered the car tracks. He expelled huge clouds of frosty air with each breath. He thought how strange it was that he did not feel the cold. His next thought was one of silence. The racket behind him had subsided. Hope of escape welled in his breast as Rasputin approached the opening to the street.

He lurched into the street that ran along the canal. Headlights strained through the thickening snowflakes to illuminate the road. A car was bouncing through the ruts, coming in his direction. He positioned himself in the middle of the road. The blood from a gash over one eye clouded his vision. He raised his good arm in a stopping gesture.

The automobile skidded to a stop on the packed ice beneath the surface. Rasputin slumped over the passenger-side bumper and slid along toward the running board. To his left, he heard excited voices emerging from the courtyard. He knew that his life depended on getting into the car. Rasputin used the chrome door handle as leverage to pull himself up to the window. As he lifted his head, he stared uncomprehendingly at the driver.

"*Nyet,*" his minded screamed as he focused on the murderous eyes of his nemesis.

Otto Kahn sat behind the wheel pointing a Browning semi-automatic at him.

"*Nicht mehr, blutdreck.*"

The words uttered by Kahn were drowned out by the blast of the weapon. The flash from the muzzle burned Rasputin's skin as the bullet entered his forehead.

1916

The Great Petrovski Bridge,
Petrograd, Russia

You can kill the body, but not the spirit.

~ ROBERT LOUIS STEVENSON

"COME ON, LIFT!" cried Dmitry as they struggled with the bulky rug containing Rasputin's inert body. The wind had driven the clouds away and moonlight streamed a ghostly light into the courtyard. The three men struggled with the unwieldy bear rug that wrapped the corpse. Dmitry led the way carrying the rug in the crook of his arm. Otto carried the middle with two hands shuffling his feet to keep up. Vaslav brought up the rear. Nijinsky was wearing a knee-length overcoat over his black gown. His bare white legs shone eerily in the moonlight.

As they approached the Prince's Russo-Buire touring car, Dmitry hefted the rug onto his shoulder in order to free a hand to open the trunk. When he did so, the shorter men holding the other end struggled with the burden. Suddenly, the body slid halfway out of the rug and crunched onto the snowy gravel. Rasputin's face, distorted from the blows inflicted by the Prince, glared at Vaslav. The terrible eyes were open, staring dully at him.

"*B'lyad*," cursed Vaslav. Dmitry dropped his end and walked toward the body. With a grunt of effort, he yanked the edge of the bearskin rug and the body spun out onto the snow-crusted pavement.

"*Eto piz'dets*," he said. "Let's just put the body into the trunk." They abandoned the blood-soaked bearskin on the ground, devoid of life or use.

Grasping Rasputin under his armpits, Dmitry instructed Vaslav to lift the feet. Together they swung the body and heaved it into the open trunk. Otto slipped into the driver's seat and cranked the powerful car to life.

Behind them, Dr. Lazovert unlocked Dmitry's highly-polished black, six cylinder Lessner-90 limousine and got behind the wheel. The plan was to make it appear that Rasputin returned home late that night. Purishkevich, wearing Rasputin's overcoat and beaver hat got into the passenger seat. The conspirators planned to have the doctor drive to Rasputin's home and then, Purishkevich, disguised as the monk, would exit the car and walk toward the back entrance. Purishkevich would then go through the alleyway and meet the Doctor on the opposite street and make their escape. Felix remained behind, sanitizing the scene as best he could.

Driving the Prince's car, Otto turned out of the courtyard and headed along the Moika Canal toward Great Petrovski Bridge where they intended to dispose of Rasputin's body by pushing it through the ice. The windows of the car fogged up as the overheated men sat in silence breathing heavily. As Otto drove over the street rutted with packed ice, the body in the trunk thumped ominously.

After what seemed like forever, he spied the bridge. It was desolate and ill-lit. He eased off the accelerator and coasted to a stop. Dmitry and Vaslav got out and walked over to the railing on the roadside. They peered into the river and assured themselves that the ice was broken below them. The drop to the river was about ten feet and they heard the frigid water rushing under the bridge.

Dmitry grabbed the body behind the knees while Vaslav took Rasputin under the armpits. They carried the corpse to the bridge railing and swung it to gain momentum. As they flung the body, Nijinsky felt the hands of Rasputin tighten around his upper arms. As the body flew over the railing, Vaslav went with it. His scream was stifled by the ice-cold water. Both Rasputin and Nijinsky disappeared below the surface.

Otto and Dmitry watched in horror as Vaslav floundered in the frigid water trying to extricate himself from Rasputin's grasp. The two splashed in the scant light. Vaslav kicked off his coat and clawed his way to the surface. He grasped the edge of the ice and used his powerful legs to kick Rasputin away.

The current forced Rasputin under the ice. Vaslav pulled himself over the edge of the ice and lay shivering while he heard the monk thrash beneath him. He watched through the ice that separated them as life departed from Rasputin. His eyes pierced Vaslav's soul as they turned from fierce intensity to opaque dullness.

Dmitry edged his way along the ice toward Nijinsky, who was shivering uncontrollably. Otto ran to get the big car and a blanket. As Dmitry reached for Vaslav, the ice creaked ominously. The tall officer immediately dropped to his stomach to spread his weight out. With his lengthy reach, he grabbed Vaslav by the wrist and began sliding him toward the river bank. Nijinsky was muttering incoherently about ghostly eyes and the cold grasp of death.

Dmitry unsheathed a long, thin knife with a curved blade, and in a single motion, slashed the dress from Vaslav's shivering body. As Otto raced from the limo, he caught the sight of the naked Vaslav in the headlights. His skin had turned a chalky blue, like marble. Kahn marveled at the perfectly-proportioned, muscular body of the dancer, thinking that it was worthy of Michelangelo's chisels. The image was marred only by the uncontrollable shaking of Nijinsky and the frantic actions of Dmitry, who was rubbing Vaslav vigorously. Finally, Otto reached them with the heavy, wool blanket.

"He's going into shock and may be suffering from hypothermia," shouted Dmitry. He was in the back seat with Vaslav, massaging the dancer's extremities. From the driver's seat, Otto half-turned and handed a vacuum flask to Dmitry.

"Here is hot coffee. That should help."

Dmitry took the flask and carefully tried to get Vaslav to drink some of the hot liquid. When they neared the Prince's palace, Otto steered the limo to a motorcar that was waiting down the street and across the canal from Yusopov palace. A chauffeur alighted from the motorcar and helped Dmitry and Otto half-carry Vaslav into the back seat. Otto turned toward Dmitry, who snapped to attention and saluted smartly.

The ring of the phone was insistent. She blinked herself awake. It was still dark outside. She wondered who could be calling at this early hour. She grasped the candlestick phone and lifted the receiver.

"Hello. Who is it?"

"Anya, I'm sorry to wake you. This is Matronya, Father Grigory's daughter. Do you know where my father is? He never came home last night. I'm scared."

"Slow down, child. Tell me when you last saw him?"

"He left the house last night around midnight with Prince Felix."

"Prince Felix? I can't believe it. Why would he go anywhere with that degenerate?"

"I saw him myself. In our kitchen. He came to the back door and Father let him in. I watched from behind the curtain that separates my room. Felix had an evil look in his eyes when Father left the room to get his coat. It made my skin crawl. Then, when Father returned, Felix was all smiles and jokes. Father put on his coat, took his satchel and they left together. I'm scared."

"Did you hear anything they said?"

"Not really. Just something about the Prince's palace and Grand Duchess Irina . . . , but nothing specific."

"That's strange. Irina is in Crimea. I was with the Tsarina yesterday when she spoke to Irina who said she was staying in Crimea for Christmas. Matronya, stay home until I call you. I will get the Tsarina to help us. Be strong, my child."

She hung up and immediately dialed the Palace.

"May I speak to Pasha, please. It's urgent."

"Good morning. How may I be of service?"

"This is Anya. I'm sorry to bother you, but I must see the Tsarina as quickly as possible. I'm afraid that we may be facing a disaster. Would you come and get me and bring me to the Tsarina?"

"Most assuredly. I will be there shortly. Shall I notify Her Imperial Highness's chambermaid?"

"Oh, yes, of course. I'm so distraught that I did not even think. Of course, yes, please do."

In a short time, Anya was dressed and ready to go. Pasha knocked on her door. Pasha guided her wheelchair across the way to the palace and the Tsarina's chambers. Alix was wearing a silk robe with a collar made of soft white fur. Her face was clenched in worry.

"Anya, please tell me what is going on. You have never scared me like this before. What is it?"

"My Lady, I apologize, but I fear the worst has happened." She proceeded to relate the conversation with Matryona.

"What? She must be mistaken. Our Friend would never go with Prince Felix! I know that Father Grigory mentioned his desire to meet Irina on several occasions. But, Irina is in Crimea . . . ." Suddenly, the Tsarina hesitated; her countenance darkened.

"No, no. Felix would not be so diabolical."

"Your Highness, I fear that he would be . . . especially with encouragement from the *camarilla*," replied Anya.

Alix reached for the phone and barked to the operator to get the police chief on the phone immediately. Anya watched as the Tsarina listened, nodding her head wearily.

"Please do. Come without delay. Thank you."

As she hung up the phone, her shoulders sagged and her face went blank as she digested the information she just heard. Her eyes filled with tears and she sobbed into her handkerchief.

"It is almost too terrible for me to tell you. The police found the Yusupov house in the most ghastly state of blood and — ugh!" she exclaimed, "it made me sick to hear them describe it, and it makes me sick just to remember it. They've murdered him. Murdered him like an animal. Oh, Anya. What will we do . . . what will we do now?" Anya reached for the Tsarina and hugged her. Alix collapsed into her arms.

1916

Tsarskoe Selo, Russia

A rule of thumb for the warrior is that he makes his decisions
so carefully that nothing that may happen as a result of
them can surprise him, much less drain his power.

~ CARLOS CASTENADA

THE BIG VEHICLE EASILY NEGOTIATED the curves and ruts of the
snow-covered roads from St. Petersburg to Tsarskoe Selo in good time.
The black limousine cruised admirably. Otto sat pensively in the plush,
gray suede bench seat. He had to admit that the Russian coach builders
certainly knew how to make sturdy carriages that could withstand the
rigors of Russian winters. The bouncing reduced perceptibly once they
reached the Imperial grounds. He adjusted his gloves, straightened his
homburg and checked his face in the mirror that he rotated open from
the pear wood panel on the vanity located on the back of the seat in front
of him. He could not resist smiling and winking at the debonair countenance before him.

Otto studied the façade of the impressive building. The renowned
formal garden in front of the palace was hidden under a blanket of snow.

282

Otto was reminded of Nijinsky's description of the palace as Mother Russia's 'whipped cream.' As Kahn admired the grand edifice, he was almost giddy. After all, he mused, if he succeeded in his mission today, he would need ideas for his own castle. So, it was with juvenile anticipation that he walked spritely up the wide steps to the main entrance.

Standing inside the oaken door was a large, dark-skinned man in a uniform of Tsar-teal, his waist encircled by a red and gold sash. Kahn vaguely recognized him as a member of the Tsarina's security detail.

"Otto Kahn. I have an appointment with the Tsarina."

"Yes, I know. Follow me, Sir," replied Pasha stiffly.

Otto followed the bodyguard up the marble staircase. At the top of the stairs, they turned right and entered the Great Hall, or Hall of Light, with its chandeliered brilliance and mirrored walls. There were a half-dozen servants polishing the gilded doors and cleaning the crystal fixtures. They continued through the Cavaliers Dining Room and the Portrait Hall before entering a series of smaller rooms and parlors known as the Golden Enfilade.

"Please have a seat," said the big man, who gestured toward a delicate Chippendale chair.

Otto stared in wonder at the wall panels that glowed with a soft, honey luminescence. Each surface of the room was clad in amber, prized since antiquity for its translucent beauty and reputed healing qualities. Each wall contained eight amber panels stacked vertically. Otto touched the cool surfaces tenderly. The amber ranged in color from molasses brown to marigold yellow. Each amber segment shone as if illuminated from within. Interwoven among the panels were marvelous bas relief pastoral scenes, sculpted cameo-like in the amber. Alternating between the panels were long, thin, gilt-framed mirrors.

On close examination, he discovered stunning mosaics of semi-precious stones that were created by Florentine artists during the Renaissance. The stones formed marvelous images relating to the five senses. An ethereal glow suffused the room, so overwhelming the senses that the presence of masterful oil paintings and a ceiling plafond in the *trompe d'oeil* style were hardly noticeable. The paintings on the walls were framed with amber, meticulously carved with designs. The effect was one of immeasurable luxury and honeycomb-like security.

"It's quite the marvel, isn't it?" a soft, feminine voice asked.

"Oh, Your Highness," Otto stammered. "This is the most wondrous room that I've ever had the privilege to enter. I can see now why it has been called 'the eighth wonder of the world.'"

"It's quite ironic that two centuries ago, it was a gift from Kaiser Frederick Wilhelm to Tsar Peter the Great. Now, our German relatives would ravage Mother Russia and strip her of her grandeur, if they could."

"Oh, Tsarina, do not torture yourself worrying about such unthinkable atrocities," said Otto in his most consoling tone.

Somehow she appeared more diminutive than he had remembered. Her movements were deliberate, her shoulders slumped from an invisible weight. Crumpled in her left hand was a monogrammed silk handkerchief. The rims of her eyes were red, and, there were dark circles that hastily-applied makeup could not conceal. Otto studied her face and the spidery lines that seemed to have etched her countenance since he last had an audience with her. She shuffled over to a chair next to Otto as if lifting her feet were an unbearable effort.

"Herr Kahn, I fear that our Friend has been murdered."

"No, no, Your Highness, he is just missing, probably sleeping off his latest binge in some tart's bedchamber. You know that he consorts with the gypsies, and always turns up none the worse for wear."

"I wish it were so, but we have received reports that great evil has befallen our Friend. The chief of police just left. He told us that one of the officers, Policeman Vlassiyev, patrolling near Yusopov palace, entered the courtyard after hearing gunshots. There, he encountered Vladimir Purishkevich, who was in an agitated state. According to the officer, Purishkevich boldly stated that they had killed the usurper Rasputin, and that if the officer were a true Russian patriot, he would keep his silence. At the end of his shift, the officer reported the conversation to his commanding officer, who immediately reported it to the police chief."

Otto gasped incredulously. "Who is 'they' who supposedly killed the Father? They must be punished."

"The police believe that Purishkevich, Prince Felix and Prince Dmitry were involved. It's really not difficult to trace. The Yusopov Palace was awash in blood. That silly boy denied it, making up some story that the blood was from a dog that had to be killed. Does that deplorable boy think the police are so stupid? They slaughtered Rasputin like a dog. How dreadful!"

"That seems preposterous. They are noblemen, not murderers. Was there anyone else at the palace last night?"

"Oh, the usual party-goers were at Felix's last night, but the police reported that all the motor coaches left by midnight. The courtyard was empty when the officer arrived at 3 AM to investigate the gunshots. The police recounted no other comings or goings at the palace between midnight and 5 AM. The only people observed in the vicinity were two men and a woman who entered a waiting motorcar after 5 AM."

"The police are at the palace now, taking Prince Felix and Prince Dmitry into custody. They have denied the murder but appeared not to have slept at all last night."

"Well, then, the police will get to the bottom of it, and justice will be done."

"It's no use. If they killed our Friend, they will not be punished. As part of the Imperial Family, they have immunity from prosecution for killing a mere peasant like the Starets," she spat out the last words bitterly.

"Nikki has been trying to modernize the feudal penal code that he inherited, but with the war and everything, it has fallen by the wayside. Oh, what have we come to? What will become of the Tsarevich? Our Friend's healing is the only thing that has saved him."

Otto leaned forward in his chair, gave her a look of sincere compassion, and said, "Your Highness, now may be the time for the plan we spoke about last year, Operation Diaspora. The Tsar has already taken his tranche with him to headquarters. We have everything else in place and just need your assistance to go ahead. We can have the Romanov gold safe in Moscow and New York before year's end."

She studied his face carefully. Her gaze bore into his steel gray eyes for a long moment. Seeing no guile, she whispered, "You can do this? Tell me how."

Otto proceeded to tell her that the Tsar's "luggage" would be divided to minimize potential disruption. There would be four main shipments: one to the Tsar at the front, another to London, via Stockholm, the third south to Moscow for safekeeping in the Kremlin and the fourth on the Trans-Siberian Railroad to Yokohama, then by ship to the United States. There will be multiple real and decoy shipments. The shipment south will be under the protection of General Abram Mikhailovich Dragomirov. The shipment east will be under the protection of Vice Admiral Kolchak.

"Finance Minister Bark is aware of our plans and just needs a signed directive from Your Highness to move the 'luggage.' I have taken the liberty of having Minister Bark prepare an official directive for you to sign."

Otto reached into his portfolio and presented a document. Alexandra took a pen from the desk and scribbled her signature on the parchment.

"Wait here while the girl gets my seal." Alix reached over to a wide sash and pulled the servant's bell.

As the Tsarina slowly walked to the door, she was framed in the doorway. Otto thought that she projected the essence of sadness and defeat. The loss of Rasputin had devastated her and sapped her will. She was caught in the vortex of descent into chaos and despair. The fight she had been waging over Alexei's health, the corrosive Imperial family, the impertinent Duma, the dishonest press and thousands of other woes that had afflicted her and her beloved Nikki had pushed her beyond hope.

Otto beamed inwardly as he tucked the sealed order into his portfolio. He bowed and assured the Tsarina that all would be well. With a dull, grief-ridden countenance, she waved him off dismissively. Her face was drawn, her eyes bloodshot from tears, strain and grief.

Kahn strode purposefully out of the Amber Room. The Araby guard eyed him coldly then escorted him to the exit. Otto directed the driver to go to the Winter Palace to rendezvous with Minister Bark. When Kahn met Bark, he could barely contain his glee. Waving the order bearing Alexandra's seal, he gushed,

"Pyotr, we have to work quickly, before chaos descends."

⌒❧⌒

1916
Petrograd, Russia

When money speaks, the truth is silent.

~ RUSSIAN PROVERB

W HEN OTTO RETURNED TO HIS hotel late that night, the front-desk clerk handed him an urgent message bearing the seal of the Ministry of Finance. A handwritten note tersely requested that he come to Bark's house immediately. Putting aside his fatigue, Otto did an about-face and exited the lobby. The hotel doorman gave him a double-take as if to say *you just got here*; nonetheless, he whistled to the next cab in line.

During the ride, Otto reviewed a mental checklist of the details of Operation Diaspora. He could not identify any issues that might have prompted Bark's cryptic message. The Minister lived in a large Victorian mansion on Petrogradsky Island. Before he could lift the brass knocker on the door, Bark appeared and ushered him into the house while checking up and down the street to see if anyone had followed Otto.

They settled into the library. The fireplace was aglow with a crackling fire that sent a comforting radiance through the room.

"May I offer you some Christmas cheer?"

"Please, dispense with the pleasantries. You called me here in the middle of the night. I'm tired and want to handle whatever problem has arisen. Then, I want to get a good night's sleep," replied Otto, in an irritated tone.

"OK, I know that you are tired, but this 'opportunity' is too good to waste while we rest."

"Well, come out with it, man."

"Do you believe in *Ded Moroz*, the Russian Father Christmas?" asked Pyotr.

Otto started to rise. "No, I don't, and, I don't have time for Russian fairy tales," he sputtered abruptly.

"Please sit. I only ask about *Ded Moroz* because he has come early to us this year."

"Stop with the riddles. Tell me why you dragged me here!"

"This is why," said Bark, handing Otto a sheaf of bills of lading with a flourish. "This shipment arrived from Bucharest at the Imperial Mint today."

Otto read with interest. The Romanian government was under severe pressure from the German army and had just shipped the royal treasury to the Tsar for safekeeping until the end of the German invasion of Romania. Kahn's mind went into overdrive trying to calculate all the angles.

"There is a skeletal staff at the Mint. I know the functionary in charge and he is always looking for ways to avoid work," commented Bark. "If we can figure out a way to come up with an authorization before the shipment is unpacked and entered into inventory, we can have the shipment redirected per our instructions."

"I have a way. We will have to work fast . . ." said Otto.

Oleg Mitrokov was rather tall, and wore *pince nez* glasses through which he condescended to greet his guests. His face was angular and pockmarked from a bout of variola minor as a young adult. With dark Slavic eyes and prominent cheekbones, he exuded the practiced indifference of a career bureaucrat. The Ukrainian was the first assistant to the Sergeant of the Exchequer, Boris Witte, son of the recently-deceased Prime Minister, who had responsibility for the Imperial Mint that was located in the Fortress of Peter and Paul.

Oleg had gotten his job supervising at the Mint by virtue of the fact that his mother had been a lady-in-waiting for the Dowager Empress, who had vouched for young Oleg. Now, twenty years later, he was in charge of incoming and outgoing shipments. He was a functionary who had survived in his post at the Mint by placidly accepting orders without examining them critically. The staff, which had already been depleted by the war, was skeletal due to the religious holiday. Usually, nothing of importance occurred during Christmas time.

It was with some annoyance that he accepted a rail shipment from Romania the previous afternoon. He had no qualms about leaving the unexpected shipment of crates, totaling over ninety tons, on the gloomy, cavernous loading dock until after Christmas. Mitrokov consoled himself with the thought that although the loading dock was completely jammed with crates, at least, the new shipment would help block the blustery north winds that swept across Neva Bay in the winter and went through the back wall of the old building like a sieve.

Two figures bundled in long, fur greatcoats and kalpaks, approached the entrance to the Mint. Mitrokov stirred, listlessly.

"Good day, Minister Bark," he wheezed in a nasal voice. "Achoo!" he sneezed.

"Given all the demands of the military to pursue this blasted war, we just cannot keep this place habitable. Please come into my office. It's a little warmer there."

They followed him into a small office with stone walls and two tiny, narrow windows. The poorly-glazed glass rattled like chattering teeth in the wind that whipped through the ancient fortress. A small brazier lit bright with orange coals, struggled against the encroaching chill. ·

"What can I do for you, Minister Bark?"

"As you know, the Tsar has departed for the Mogilev military headquarters at the front." Oleg was flattered at the thought that the Minister would believe that a lowly functionary like him would be privy to such knowledge.

"Before His Excellency departed, he directed me to have the shipment from Romania diverted to the cargo ship, the *Velikogo Aagtedyk*. Here are His Excellency's instructions," said Bark, handing a document to Mitrokov.

Imperial Mint
Petropavlovskaya fortress, 6
Petrograd
Attention: Sergeant of the Exchequer
Count Boris Sergeivich Witte

Re: Iasi Shipment/Romania
Rom/Iasi BOL #51637-1916 — Rom/Iasi BOL #51784-1916

Whereas, the capital of Romania Bucharest is under imminent threat by the Central Powers; and,

Whereas, at the behest of our good friend and ally, King Ferdinand I of Romania, we have undertaken to protect the treasures of the sovereign State of Romania, which is currently at war with our enemies; and,

Whereas, this material was shipped from Iasi station, Romania pursuant to Bills of Lading: Rom/Iasi BOL #51637-1916 through Rom/Iasi BOL #51784 ("*the Romanian Treasures*"); and,

Whereas, there is currently civil unrest in Petrograd,

Therefore, We have determined that *the Romanian Treasures* would be more secure at sea under the protection of the Baltic Fleet.

Accordingly, We order the aforementioned *Romanian Treasures* to be transferred forthwith to the cargo vessel, the *Velikogo Aagtedyk,* presently anchored at Kronstadt.

Signed and sealed this 24th day of December in the year of Our Lord 1916

Mitrkov studied the document. He held it up to the light. Taking off his glasses, he said,

"This is definitely the Tsar's stationery and signature. However, performance of this order is quite out of the question. Herr Bark, you, of all people, should understand the manpower needed to transfer this volume of material onto a cargo ship. We simply do not have the resources."

"Not to worry. This is the *highest* priority. You know how volatile the streets in the city are. Striking workers are everywhere. There has been a breakdown of civil order in several quarters. The crew of the *Aurora* has organized its own soviet. It would be a catastrophe of international proportions, if the Romanian treasure were lost to the mobs. I do not want to disappoint the Tsar; that would not be a wise career move. I have already diverted resources from throughout the system. We have stevedores and yard men ready for the loading. Your job is to prepare the manifests. I will take full responsibility."

"Yes, sir," exclaimed a visibly relieved Mitrokov.

It was a cold winter day in Berlin as she entered the *Prater Garten* in the *Prenzlauer Berg* neighborhood. The interior of the beer garden was welcoming, sending a steamy sauerkraut and beer smell to her nostrils. She found a table near the back so that she could survey the incoming diners. This was her first time in Berlin since the war had begun. She noticed that the streets were less crowded and there were more men in military uniforms than there were civilians. A strong atmosphere of malaise permeated almost every social interaction she observed.

Before the war, the populace was buoyant, even cheerful. Now, the faces of the people were dour and weary-looking. Even though it was late afternoon, there were few, if any, children on the streets. A buxom, middle-aged waitress approached her, and with a sullen push, delivered pickles and sauerkraut in a standard white china bowl that sloshed precipitously before coming to a halt. Nonplussed, the young brunette looked at the waitress blankly.

"I'll have a draft pilsner, please, while I wait for my friend," said Nadya in flawless German.

She removed her heavy coat from her shoulders, resting it on the back of her sturdy, wooden chair. She surveyed the white stucco and dark wooden beams of the restaurant and breathed a sigh of relief. Since she had departed from Petrograd two days earlier after a tension-filled night at the Yusopov Palace, she had traveled nonstop. Her Dutch passport had been invaluable in allowing her to travel through the war zone from Russia to Germany, albeit ponderously. Using the requisite encryption, she had requested a meeting with her handler in Berlin. The reply cable had designated the *Prater* as the meeting place. She reflectively clutched her bag tightly to her side, reassuring herself that the valuable package was secure.

As the waitress returned with her pilsner, a man slipped into the chair beside her.

"It's a cold day for a beer, isn't it?"

"Not if you've been shopping in hot stores all day," she replied, according to script. He was short, balding, with a no-nonsense demeanor. With a neatly-clipped moustache on his upper lip to cover his slightly buckteeth, he reminded her of a ferret. He placed his ebony cane on the chair next to him. She admired the ivory handle that was delicately carved in the form of a screaming eagle. Directing her attention to the waitress, Nadya ordered *schnitzel, gurken salat und kartoffel salat.*

"I'm famished from all that traveling. Would you like to order?" she asked, passing him the menu.

"I'll have the bratwurst and a *Berliner Weisse.*" The waitress scribbled the order down and departed.

"It's good to see you, Herr Schmidlin."

"Thank you, H-21. Tell me about the demise of the mad monk."

Nadya recounted the events at Yusopov Palace up to her departure with the other women. She waited to disclose her prize until after the waitress had delivered their food. They ate in silence. When they were through with their plates, she lifted her bag onto the table and removed a simple wooden box with strange symbols on the cover.

"This, my friend, is a bonus prize for you. This box contains the special crystals that the Starets used to heal. They are quite remarkable. According to Rasputin, these crystals were delivered from heaven in 1908 when the massive devastation occurred in Tunguska, Siberia. Remember the unexplained explosion that destroyed thousands of acres of forests in a remote area of Siberia? The monk told me that these crystals were produced by that blast. They were given to him by the Monk Makariy, a legendary, Siberian cleric, with the belief that they possessed special healing properties. Rasputin's ability to heal the Tsarevich of hemophilia was due to his use of these crystals. I'm sure that these crystals will be of great use to the Fatherland."

"I see. Thank you," said Schmidlin matter-of-factly. "What else do you have to report?"

Nadya stared at him with her mouth open and her eyebrows raised. "Excuse me. You don't seem to understand. This box contains one of the great gifts of our time. Please don't slough it off. I know that you think that Rasputin was a charlatan; but I saw him perform miracles firsthand. Whatever you do, don't just hide this away in some warehouse."

Glaring through his gold wire-rimmed glasses, Schmidlin hissed, "It is you, *fraülein*, who does not understand. My superiors are interested in winning this war. We will do that by eliminating the Eastern front. We must get Russia out of the war. All else is superfluous. Now if you please, what else do you have to report?"

"OK. After the deed was completed, Otto Kahn returned to the Hotel Europa and came to my room and shared my bed. Afterward, we spoke about his plans. He told me of an operation that was in motion. It involved the dispersal of the Imperial treasury. He told me to pass this message to you and that you would understand it." She took a theatrical pause.

"Well, what is the message, *fraülein*?" Max hissed impatiently.

"He said that two companies from the Preobrajensky Regiment will depart from Petrograd for Moscow. One will travel by a heavily guarded riverboat convoy and the second will travel by train from Petrograd. Then he used a term I did not understand. He said the 'Moscow tranche' would travel by rail in a train with no military markings. It will leave Petrograd on the morning before Christmas and is scheduled to arrive in Moscow on Christmas Eve. The plan is to deliver the tranche when everyone will be preparing for the sacred day. He observed that a commando force of about thirty men could easily overpower the guard contingent assigned to the train. The trick will be to then move the cargo out of Russia."

"I will leave the logistics to those trained in this sort of operation. Thank you. Your remittance has been deposited in your Dutch account.

We will send your next assignment through the usual channels to you in Paris. Good evening."

Schmidlin stood and walked away empty handed. Nadya thought for a second that she should let him leave without taking the wooden box. It would serve him right, she thought. I will be able to collect a generous price for these crystals in Paris. Just as he reached the exit, Herr Schmidlin reversed course and walked by the table swooping up the crystals like a bald eagle snatching a salmon from a stream, with nary a nod to a perplexed Nadya.

On the third day after the events at Yusopov Palace, Kurt awoke in his cramped quarters to the sound of a newsboy hawking his papers with the announcement that,

Grigory Rasputin has ceased to exist!

Chorney quickly threw on his clothes and raced outside to purchase a newspaper. On the front page, below the headline was a gruesome picture of the dead body that had been retrieved from the Neva River near the Great Petrovsky Bridge. The face was distorted almost beyond recognition. A ragged, dark splotch, an apparent bullet entry wound, marred his forehead. The monk's trademark hair and beard appeared matted with blood. His lower body was entangled with rope. The arms were raised, grasping upward in a grotesque frozen pose. It was a picture that would forever mark the tragic end of Rasputin.

Articles detailing the discovery of the body and the rumors surrounding Rasputin's murder filled the paper. There was the obligatory regurgitation of all the scandalous stories of the monk's time as a healer in the capital. After reading the gruesome details, Chorney had no appetite for breakfast. He thought of his colleague Pasha and wondered how the Imperial family was handling the horrendous news. Kurt also thought about how the change would affect the likelihood of the United States entering the war.

Chorney went to his commo-post to see if he had any orders. He was gratified to see that he was to attend a meeting with a confidential informant. Too much was happening in the capital for him to be twiddling his thumbs.

He relished the opportunity to get back into action. The only concern he had was the person he was to meet. Unless he had decoded the message incorrectly, he was to make contact with the Marmot.

Since he had time before the arranged meeting, he walked aimlessly, doubling back frequently and modulating his pace to ascertain whether he was being followed. When he was sure that his movements were not being tracked, he made his way to an obscure tea room near the university. The walk and the delicious smell of fresh brewed spiced tea had stimulated his appetite. While Kurt was washing down his breakfast of Tsar's eggs, two soft boiled eggs served with salmon roe and blini, the Marmot entered. After exchanging the all-clear signal, Iliodor joined him.

The cleric licked his lips nervously and cast his eyes downward as he eased into the booth. Chorney regarded him warily, recalling their last encounter in Pokrovskoe. He could still hear the deranged Guseva shrieking gleefully, "I will kill the anti-Christ." Fortunately, she was wrong; but, the *camarilla* was relentless and finally assassinated the one person in the Imperial court who had the strength to hold the royal family together.

"So, I have vital news. The Romanov fortune is being shipped out of Petrograd."

Kurt marveled at the cold-bloodedness of the Marmot, who acted like nothing happened the last time they saw each other. The young officer could still see the maniac waving the knife murderously at him as he shielded Rasputin. Back to business.

"Tell me where and when."

"One tranche has already gone with the Tsar at the front, one tranche by the ship *Velikogo Aagtedyk* to Stockholm, another to Moscow by train, and, the last by train to Vladivostok. Here is a schedule of departures."

Kurt reviewed the paper, which set forth tracks, piers and times.

"How did you learn this?"

"I am confessor to Grand Duke Michael who is a member of the *camarilla*. He asked me to advise him about the religious implications concerning the death of Rasputin. I memorized this information from a paper I saw on his desk. Reading upside down is one of my talents."

"What do you know about the murder of Rasputin?"

"Nothing, except that it was orchestrated by the *camarilla* and the bankers."

"Names?"

"He did not deny the rumors that Princes Felix and Dmitry committed the murder. The question presented to me was whether the killing of a peasant by a nobleman, or, in this case, noblemen, in defense of the crown was justified before God and man."

"And your answer?"

"I told the Grand Duke that the murder was perfectly justifiable. The life of a peasant is nothing compared to the sanctity of the throne."

"Was there anyone in the Imperial family who held a different view?"

The Marmot looked at Kurt quizzically as if the question was unfathomable and the answer self-evident.

"Well, if you mean was there anyone who felt that the persons who perpetrated the elimination of the threat to the throne should be punished, the Emperor and Empress were distraught at Rasputin's death and believed that the princes should be severely punished. However, the grand dukes and the whole family stood as one against the Emperor and Empress. They declared that no one should be punished for that purging. They did not consider it a crime."

"Doesn't the Tsar have supreme power in such questions?"

"The Tsar and the Tsarina are in a perilous position. The Tsar's dismissal of Grand Duke Nicholas Nichailivich from the post of commander of the armies tore the family apart. There is little sympathy for the Tsar and the problems he has with the war. Further, the Tsarina has enemies in court for many reasons; primarily her German relatives and the embarrassment of a son that she produced."

"What does that mean?"

"You know the Tsarevich is weak and sickly. He is a hemophiliac just like others in the Tsarina's family. They blame her for the contamination of the Imperial Romanov bloodline. When you add in the scandalous, depraved conduct of the 'Starets,' you see the *camarilla* has ample grounds to support the young princes, who defended the honor of the family and are the rightful heirs."

"So the princes are to be congratulated for murdering Rasputin and they will go unpunished?"

"Precisely, the *camarilla* wields so much leverage over the Tsar that he succumbed to its demands that the only punishment for Rasputin's death should be that the two princes be banished to their Crimean estates, and the other plotters should be left unpunished. The Tsar had no choice but to acquiesce, his throne depends on the support of the *camarilla*."

1917
Petrograd, Russia

My dear Martyr, give me thy blessing that it may follow me always on the sad and dreary path I have yet to follow here below. And remember us from high on your holy prayers.

~ Tsarina Alexandra, note placed in Rasputin's casket

THE DREADED PHONE RANG. It was Director of Police Beletsky, who informed the Tsarina that the autopsy of Father Grigory was complete. He suffered numerous gunshot wounds and broken bones from blows delivered by various blunt instruments. The most shocking aspect of the autopsy was that Rasputin was alive when he was dumped into the river. Alix gasped at the horror; *Our Friend* shot, beaten, tied up, mortally wounded and thrown into the dark, frigid waters of the Neva by villains, was an abomination beyond description. Alix fell to her knees heaving dryly, her face ashen, her eyes dull and pained.

Anya, who was in the next room, limped in at the sounds coming from the Tsarina's chamber. She suffered painfully from injuries that she had sustained in a train derailment while traveling from Tsarskoe Selo to Petrograd. She would have been paralyzed from the waist down had it not been for the miraculous healing of Rasputin. The phone jangled. Vyrubova lifted the receiver and advised that the Tsarina was indisposed. Director Beletsky asked her to tell the Tsarina that the body was available for burial. Anya choked at the finality of the announcement.

Count Benckendorff, head of the Imperial Chancery, arranged for the body of Rasputin to be brought to a *chapelle ardent* where it was prepared for burial. Intimates of Father Grigory assembled to pay their respects. Rasputin's wife and children accepted condolences from many members of the aristocracy and clergy. The Tsarina arrived, shrouded in black with a thick veil shielding her tear-stained face. She was accompanied by the four Grand Duchesses. Next, came the two who would miss the monk the most; Anya and Alexei limped into the chapel together. After Alix paid her respects to the wooden coffin that contained Rasputin, she staggered to a seat next to the family. Matryona leaned over and whispered, "This is from my Father for you." She handed her a letter written in the monk's characteristic, uncultured handwriting.

> *Dear batiushka-Tsar* and *matiushka-Tsarina* ('Father-Tsar' and 'Mother-Tsarina')
>
> *I write and leave behind me this letter at St. Petersburg. I feel that I shall leave life before January 1st. I wish to make known to the Russian people, to Papa (the Tsar), to the Russian Mother (the Tsarina) and to the Children of the land of Russia, what they must understand.*
>
> *If I am killed by common assassins, and especially by my brothers the Russian peasants, you, the Tsar of Russia, will have nothing to fear for your children for they will reign for hundreds of years in Russia. But if I am murdered by boyars, nobles, and if they shed my blood, their hands will remain soiled with my blood, for twenty-five years they will not wash their hands from my blood.*
>
> *They will leave Russia. Brothers will kill brothers, and they will kill each other and hate each other, and for twenty-five years there will no peace in the country. Tsar of the land of Russia, if you hear the sound of the bell which will tell you that Grigory*

has been killed, you must know this: if it was your relations who have wrought my death, then no one in the family, that is to say, none of your children or relations, will remain alive for more than two years. They will be killed by the Russian people.

I go, and I feel in me the divine command to tell the Russian Tsar how he must live if I have disappeared. You must reflect and act prudently. Think of your safety and tell your relations that I have paid for them with my blood.

And if they do, they will beg for death as they will see the shame and disgrace of Russia, see the coming of the Antichrist, plague, poverty, destroyed churches, and desecrated sanctuaries where everyone would be dead. Russian Tsar, you will be killed by the Russian people and the people will be cursed and will serve as the devil's weapon killing each other everywhere. Three times 25 years they will destroy the Russian people and the Orthodox faith and the Russian land will die. I shall be killed. I am no longer among the living. Pray, pray, be strong, and think of your blessed family."

Faithfully always,

Rasputin[31]

Alexandra read the missive again and again. She despaired for the lives of her children. She prayed that his final prophecy was wrong. The Tsarina shivered uncontrollably as the chill hand of death reached for her from beyond the grave.

February 1917
Paris, France

**Death lies on her, like an untimely frost
Upon the sweetest flower of all the field.**

~ WILLIAM SHAKESPEARE

IF ONE COULD NOT BE HOME for the holidays, the Elysée Palace Hotel on the Champs-Elysées in Paris, was not such a shabby alternative, thought Otto. After checking in, he had spent the afternoon strolling around the Eiffel Tower. Standing more than 1,000 feet tall, the Eiffel Tower had eclipsed the Washington Monument as the world's tallest man-made structure when it opened in 1889. As he stood beneath the iconic tower, the banker, who was used to financing monumental projects, appreciated this triumph of the human spirit. It was built by Gustave Eiffel as the gateway to the 1889 *Exposition Universelle* that commemorated the one-hundredth anniversary of the French Revolution. At the turn of the twentieth century, the gaslights were replaced with 3,200 electric spotlights that were installed in its latticework superstructure and arches. Wartime France took advantage of the Tower's height by installing a radiotelegraph antenna at the top of the edifice. This pragmatic decision was to have significant, unforeseen consequences.

As he waited for his *après* dinner engagement, Otto absently drank a Campari and soda. The alcove adjacent to the lobby overlooked the courtyard of the Elysée Palace. Although he had done everything in his power to assure success, a profound dread flowed through him. All the negativity that engulfed Petrograd that winter seemed to permeate him.

The situation back in America was perilous. Hecht was still missing. von Igel had been arrested. The noose was tightening. He stretched his collar nervously.

Despite his confidence that he could not be linked to the sabotage from the German side, he was terrified by the disappearance of Hecht. All could be lost if Hecht was in the custody of the Americans and he decided to cooperate. Hecht knew everything about the planning and financing of the Black Tom Island explosion. Moreover, Hecht was vulnerable. Otto stared vacantly at the floor. Just as he was on the verge of committing one of the most audacious and lucrative achievements of all time — it was truly a masterpiece — he faced unthinkable danger. He was as close to losing everything as he was to having everything.

Kahn sat despondent. He must conjure a way to neutralize Hecht. But, how? He had no idea where he was, what he was doing, or what his captors knew. Otto wondered morbidly what it would feel like to be tortured, or left to rot in a dark, dank prison . . . alone. Why should he expect Hecht to withstand such treatment, when Otto himself did not think he could withstand pain and torture?

To what depths would utter disgrace, loss of power and status drive him? Would he be able to withstand the slings and arrows of torture? Would he be reduced to abysmal despair? Would he be able to end it all? What method would be best? Otto shuddered. He ordered another drink.

Otto tried to distract himself while waiting for his associate to arrive from Switzerland. A gentleman sitting across from him was reading the *International Herald Tribune*. Otto noticed a small headline on the folded-back paper that read, "**Margaret Sanger Sentenced to Jail.**" Kahn quickly walked to the lobby newsstand and purchased his own copy. He riffled through the paper for the article. According to the report, Sanger was arrested for dispensing contraception at a clinic in Brooklyn without a medical professional in attendance.

At her trial, the judge offered her the highest degree of leniency along with an arrangement that would allow her to appeal her conviction, thereby preserving her challenge to the law while avoiding incarceration. She defiantly refused the court's "extreme clemency" saying that she was indifferent to a sentence of personal imprisonment. An exasperated judge sentenced her to thirty days confinement in the workhouse.

When Otto turned to that page, his jaw dropped. There was a picture of Sanger in the grip of two bailiffs. Standing in the first row of the gallery behind Sanger, was his wife Addie, her fist raised toward the judge and her face twisted in rage. Beneath the photo was the caption, "Socialite Mrs. Otto Kahn screams 'Shame!' at Judge." He wondered what else could go wrong.

A flash of lavender caught his eye, and an exotic scent reached his nose. He turned to behold the stunning figure of Nadya in a full-length gown that lacked the usual structure of ladies' apparel of the day. Her tall, lithe body moved gracefully toward him. He rose, half out of habit, and half in tribute. Her radiance and sensual carriage attracted the attention of all the men in the lobby; the women looked warily at the social and moral threat that she posed. Nadya glided over to him and kissed him on both cheeks. The sight of her erased the trepidation that had been tormenting him.

"*Bon jour, mademoiselle.* May I get you something?" queried a waiter.

"I'll have champagne, thanks."

"Are we celebrating?" asked Otto.

"Yes, my dear, I have just negotiated a fabulous new contract with the *Follies Bergeres.* I will perform *Salome* and the climax of the performance will be my veil dance. We open in the spring. It's so exciting!"

The waiter returned with the frosted bottle of champagne and popped the cork. Nadya laughed girlishly. Otto smiled at her infectious *joie de vivre.* Her eyes shone violet in the golden illumination from the crystal chandeliers. With a flourish, the waiter deposited a ruby-red raspberry into each crystal flute. The plop of the berry sent a rush of effervescence to the surface. Otto lifted his glass to Nadya to toast. Nadya giggled as the bubbles tickled her nose.

"Pardon me. Are you the famous exotic dancer?"

"Why, yes," Nadya replied, with a gracious air of one used to celebrity.

"May I please have your autograph? My friends would never forgive me if I didn't ask," said a gentleman proffering a pad.

Nadya took the pad and waited expectantly.

"Excuse me," the flustered man stammered, "Of course, here is a pen. Sorry."

Nadya accepted the pen with a nod and slowly signed her name:

Mata Hari, Child of the Dawn

The man stared at the page appreciatively, mumbling his thanks as he walked away.

"How is Vaslav? I hear that he is in terrible shape," asked Nadya.

"Yes, I think the poor fellow has lost his mind. After the events at the river, he was treated for hypothermia. He also became delusional. I have told his wife Romola that he must be institutionalized and that I would provide the necessary funds."

"How tragic!"

"I know. He has been a bit unstable since the ordeal he suffered in Vienna at the start of the war. And now, of course, with the events at the river; I think it's more than the poor man can bear. Imagine staring into those dreadful eyes through the ice . . . ."

"I'm sorry I asked. Please let's talk about less depressing matters."

Otto asked her how her travels to Berlin had gone. She engaged his eyes with a seductive stare as she related her encounter with Herr Schmidlin.

"I expected to get at least a bonus for services above and beyond. But, the heartless bastard treated the crystals as an afterthought."

"What crystals?"

"Don't you know? I pilfered the monk's healing crystals from the palace. I thought that our Teutonic friends would place a high value on them, given the war and everything. But the cold creep just snatched them up like he was doing me a favor by removing the trash."

"Really," said Otto. "Perhaps his nonchalance was to deceive you into thinking the crystals lacked value. If he acted otherwise, you would have rightfully expected a sizeable reward."

"You're probably right," Nadya sighed.

She withdrew a cigarette from a gilded cigarette case inlaid with mother-of-pearl. Otto responded by deftly producing a shiny gold lighter that he flicked into action. Nadya leaned forward and watched as Otto's eyes devoured her cleavage. He felt her bare foot caress his shin. He began calculating the logistics of a dalliance with the sultry charmer. Her reputation

as a courtesan was well-known and Otto's mind began to wander in anticipation of the night's pleasures. Nadya lowered her eyelids demurely and
nodded toward the elevator. Otto eagerly took the hint and rose, dropping
some bills on the table. Nadya slipped her elbow through his and pressed
her breast to his arm warmly.

She was whispering in his ear as they approached the elevator, oblivious
to their surroundings. Otto pressed the elevator call button impatiently. Just
as the doors opened, a firm hand settled on Nadya's shoulder.

"Margaretha Gertruda Zelle?"

Nadya hesitated and looked at the stern young man, who continued to
hold her by the shoulder. His dark brown eyes were serious and implacable.
The elevator doors closed. Nadya allowed herself to be steered to the side.

"Who are you and what do you want?" she demanded, her playful mood
evaporating in an instant. He reached into his jacket pocket and withdrew
a small leather case that flipped open to display a badge of the *Deuxieme
Bureau*, the counterintelligence branch of the French military.

"I am Roget Lafontaine of French security and I'm afraid that I'm going
to have to detain you for questioning."

"My dear fellow, you must be mistaken. This young lady's name is
Nadya Roggents," protested Otto.

"Sir, I'm going to have to ask you to step back. Mademoiselle, are you
Margaretha Gertruda Zelle?" Sensing the officer's determination and that
a lie might make matters worse, Nadya responded, "Yes, sir. My birth name
is Margaretha Gertruda Zelle."

"Please come with us. We have questions for you." Lafontaine gently
took her elbow and led her through the lobby to a waiting sedan.

Otto stood with his mouth agape. He felt as if the walls of his carefully
constructed safety bubble were collapsing on to his head. He must escape.
But, to where? The world was on fire and he was next on the stoking pile.

March 1917
Tsarskoe Selo

Caught like a mouse in a trap.

~ Tsarina Alexandra in letter to Tsar Nicholas

Major Boris Kracilnikov was the commanding officer of the elite unit of His Imperial Highness's Cossack Convoy that was responsible for the defense of the "Tsar's Village" and its invaluable residents, the Imperial family. He came from a noble lineage of military professionals, who had served the Romanovs with distinction for generations.

His great grandfather, Gavril Kracilnikov had sacrificed his life in a vain attempt to thwart the assassination of Tsar Alexander II. He had been a Major General in command of the Imperial Guard in 1856 when a bomb planted by terrorists decimated the royal entourage and mortally wounded the Tsar. The evening before the assassination, Kracilnikov had learned of the plot from an undercover operative that he had assigned to infiltrate the *Narodnaya Volya*, *The People's Will* or *The People's Freedom*. The encoded message from his spy had identified the site of the planned attack. Unfortunately, despite extreme precautions, the plot succeeded due to a traitorous mole in the Cossack detachment guarding the Tsar. The assassin strapped the explosives to his chest and detonated the bomb just as Kracilnikov was closing in to arrest him. The blast was so powerful it killed Kracilnikov instantly and literally cut the Tsar in half.

The young Cossack officer's grandfather served Tsar Alexander III with distinction and his father, Tikhon Kracilnikov, had attended Officers' Candidate School with Nicholas II. Presently, General Tihkon Kracilnikov was one of the Army's most valued Generals serving at the Dvinsk front.

Attired in his field commander's uniform complete with riding crop tucked under his right arm, the Tsar was inspecting the Cossack detachment assigned to protect the Imperial family at Alexander's Palace. Passing in review of the elite soldiers, the Tsar stopped in front of Major Kracilnikov.

"Major, it is with a heavy heart that we leave, but duty calls us to the front. We are getting excellent reports from your father. We will give him your best regards. We are confident that you will carry on the proud tradition of the Cossacks and your family. May the spirits of your ancestors and the previous Tsars guide you to glory. Please protect Tsarskoe Selo and our family with every ounce of strength at your disposal."

"Yes, Your Excellency. Thank you, sir!"

Nicholas took a last look at the Cossacks and nodded approvingly. As he wheeled toward his vehicle, he caught a glimpse of his beloved Alix with the Tsarevich standing inside an upper window waving to him. The gray reflection of the early morning sky made them appear as apparitions. A shudder of foreboding rippled through him as he thought of how in times past, his forebears must have left this charmed place to confront their enemies.

Refocusing on the young Major, the Tsar took his mind off the ghosts of the past and the perils at hand to recollect a happier time, the marriage of Major Boris in the chapel at Tsarskoe Selo, the previous summer. He envisioned the officer in dress uniform, standing at rigid attention as he watched his bride gracefully approach the nuptial altar. The bride, Yelena Pushkin, a descendant of the legendary poet, Alexander Pushkin, was quite a beauty. Nicholas recalled thinking at the time that the blissful couple was the flower of Russian youth and its future.

The Marines at the gates to Tsarskoe Selo saluted sharply at the Tsar's Izorski-Fiat armored car as it gained speed and headed east toward headquarters. The armored car program was one of Nicholas' innovations. The Imperial Army purchased touring car chassis' from Fiat, reinforced the frames and outfitted the bodies with 6mm thick armor plating. The vehicle had a crew of five, a driver and two gunnery crews to man machine guns in its dual revolving turrets. One of the turrets was open to permit firing at aerial targets. The giant armored vehicle, dubbed the *Tsar*, had pneumatic tires which were doubled in the rear to handle its weight, and was capable of speeds of sixty kilometers per hour. This behemoth could be converted to a light track system for off-road travel. The system had been designed especially for the *Tsar* by Francis Kegresse, the Director of the Tsar's mechanized garage at Tsarskoe Selo. The *Tsar* was painted with alternating freeform patterns of grayish brown and black. In addition, a white camouflage canvas skin that could be lashed onto the exterior in snowy conditions was stowed.

As the Imperial convoy by-passed Petrograd, the smell of burning wood mixed with the acrid smell of combusting diesel fuel caught at the back of his throat. Nicholas was thrust back to the reality that confronted him. He had spent the last two days with Duma Chairman Rodzianko and Prime Minister Golitsyn, who both warned of increased rioting in the capital due to increased brutality of the secret police.

The Tsar deluded himself into believing reports from his secret police that radical elements in the workers' councils had stoked anti-government fervor against the Duma primarily. These reports stressed that the soviets viewed the legislators in the Duma as the betrayers of Mother Russia. Nicholas chose to believe the portions of these reports that the citizens still revered the Tsar and despised the legislators. This made sense to him. Most of them were low-born and blatantly corrupt without exhibiting even the slightest pretense of integrity.

The task before him required a delicate balance of defending the homeland against the German onslaught, while squelching worker unrest and restoring order to the capital. He planned to bring several regiments that were currently deployed in the northern edge of the front, back to Petrograd to impose martial law.

Once order had been restored and the spring thaw had come, many of the rebellious workers would return to their agrarian pursuits and the troops could return to the war. A collateral benefit would be that service in the city would be a restorative for the soldiers, a welcome break from action at the front. This would serve the Army well in meeting the expected spring offensive from Uncle Willy's forces. Of course, his British cousins assured him that the Americans would provide a much-needed surge by then.

The royal convoy traveled toward the front, stopping only at various communication checkpoints to receive wire updates of events at the front and in Petrograd. Headquarters was mobile and agile in order to provide the latest intelligence to his commanders. He was quite proud of the operation that had been developed and implemented under the war college instituted by Otto Kahn. The war college had helped to modernize the Army's capabilities and the mobile command center was his favorite innovation. Of particular value had been the construction of railway sidings throughout the upgraded system that allowed for decentralized storage of materiel that could be used for rapid deployment as needed.

It was early morning when they arrived at Dno, the location of the new headquarters. He focused momentarily on the irony that Dno was the Russian word for bottom. As Father Grigory, rest his soul, had taught him, Nicholas banished any negative thoughts. He wondered what Alix was doing at this moment. She was so distraught when he informed her of his decision to return to the front. She begged him to bring Alexei but that had been out of the question — much too dangerous for their Sunbeam; better he be safe and warm at the palace.

Back at Tsarskoe Selo, the Tsarina had spent a sleepless night caring for her sick children and bolstering the flagging confidence of her military guardians. At that very moment, in the pre-dawn light, she was reviewing the readiness of the Imperial Cossacks, dressed in their scarlet, knee-length *beshmets* with narrow, long sleeves and stand-up collars. They were girded by thick leather saber belts with swords at the ready. Their chests were crisscrossed by bandoliers filled with live rounds. They wore blue visor caps swathed with a broad red band, bearing an oval silver-ridged badge. The shoulders of the officers bore epaulets bearing the Tsar's initial under an Imperial crown and fastened by gilded double-eagle buttons.

Her fur-lined boots crunched in the snow that covered the courtyard where she and her only healthy child, Grand Duchess Marie, walked in front of the formation of young men standing at attention, each with their weapons loaded and a full supply of ammunition in their packs. The Empress pulled her thick, Tsar-green pelisse more tightly around her as the sable trim dragged through the snow dirtied by the booted footsteps of so many soldiers. She longed to return to the peace and serenity of her home and sanctuary that had turned into a military encampment in the wake of the rebellion in Petrograd.

Noticing that the formation was considerably smaller than the day before, she questioned Major Kracilnikov. Without making eye contact, he informed her that a few hours earlier the Marines under the command of Grand Duke Kyril, the Tsar's cousin, had abandoned Tsarskoe Selo and had marched to the Tauride Palace in Petrograd with the intent of pledging their allegiance to the Duma.

Other than a visible tightening of her jaw muscles, the Tsarina gave no reaction. She realized that the only barrier between her family and the rebel mob was the two companies of Cossacks standing before her.

In Dno, Nicholas peered through the dense morning fog. He could barely see the massive armored train that was their destination. The train was parked in a secret siding that did not appear on any maps. This, too, had been one of the innovations suggested by the banker, Kahn. The powerful engine idled, releasing jets of steam and exhaust, reminding him of a giant, snorting warhorse raring for battle.

Nicholas was greeted warmly by his old friend, General Tikhon Kracilnikov. Tikhon had been one of Nicholas' companions on the young heir's world tour to become, as his stern father half-joked, 'more worldly and manly.' Tikhon was the first to administer to Nicholas as he cowered in the doorway after the dreadful machete attack in Kyoto. They both had watched as cousin George had used his cane to thrash the assailant senseless. Tikhon had stanched the bleeding from the side of the future Tsar's head with a beautifully embroidered silk scarf that he had just purchased for his new wife. That day had truly been the end of innocence, reflected the Tsar.

The situation in Russia was indeed dire. There were food shortages and riots in Petrograd, Moscow and Kiev. Those damned soviets were growing bolder and more impudent by the day. The Army was pinned down across the front and the harsh winter had decimated morale. Just when he thought that matters could not get worse, he read a communiqué that shocked him. General Ruzsky, the commander of forces along the northwest front, reported that his forces were under siege by thousands of ravenous wolves. Ruzsky explained that the situation was so dangerous that he had negotiated a truce with German General Von Hindenburg so that both armies could concentrate on eradicating the wolves. Ruzsky reported that the joint operation had succeeded. He was compelled to mention lingering superstitious rumors of supernatural forces haunting the forests.

Nicholas settled in his comfortable armchair in his customized railcar that doubled as his war room. Seated before him at the conference table was his senior command staff. He was certain of the loyalties of Kracilnikov, Brusilov and Ruzsky. Nicholas was less certain that he could rely on Ivanov and Tremenko. Nicholas listened to their grim reports as the bottles of vodka were passed around the table. The Tsar proceeded to outline his plan to send troops under General Ivanov to occupy the Duma and quell unrest in the capital. The plan was greeted with unenthusiastic resignation. Ivanov and Tremenko conferred on the details, while Nicholas socialized with the other generals. When Nicholas rose to leave, he was interrupted by the stocky general.

"Haven't you forgotten something, Your Excellency?" croaked General Ivanov.

"We don't think so. What?"

"The gold payments for our continued service. Generals have expenses too, Your Highness." The latter statement brought a chuckle from the men. Ivanov elbowed Tremenko and refilled their glasses with vodka. The two men clinked glasses and greedily gulped down the clear liquid.

"Oh, you're quite right, Nikalai Iudovich," responded the Tsar. Then, addressing his assistant he said, "Alexeyev, produce the bullion archive ledger."

Alexeyev opened the red leather-bound volume entitled "Mobile Vault, 1917." The ledger showed entries starting on January first of all gold bullion by serial number carried in the vault car. According to the accreditation of Finance Minister Bark, five sections of bullion, each section worth fifteen million dollars, had been loaded into the vault car on the first of the year. To date, the ledger showed that Section Fifteen had been almost depleted, with about six bars left. By agreement, each General was to receive ten gold bars until the Ides of March.

The men left the warmth of the Tsar's office car and stepped out into a stiff, northeast wind. They quickly closed their collars and bundled up as they trudged through the drifting snow to the vault car. There were pairs of sentinels at each end of the car, who gave way when they recognized the Tsar. Alexeyev, followed by Nicholas, and the others climbed the steps to the platform of the railway car. Nicholas and Alexeyev both removed keys from around their necks and simultaneously unlocked the two keyholes in the thick, heavy lock. The tumblers of the lock rotated with audible metallic clicks that reverberated in the soundless forest.

To Alexeyev's dismay, the solid metal door was frozen shut, and only gave way with a loud noise of ice cracking when Alexeyev and two of the guards forced it open. Alexeyev entered through the door and lit a lantern which he handed to the Tsar who entered the anteroom of the vault car alone. He approached the inner door before him and spun the dial to the combination lock that was in the middle of the door. After several twists and turns on the dial, he cranked the latch on the door, which swung open with well-oiled ease. He held the lantern up chest high and entered the vault.

The yellowish light reflected off the gilded bars that rested in their iron-reinforced cradles, emitting an eerie glow. Alexeyev walked to the center of the car and he and the Tsar repeated the lock opening procedure until a sliding cargo door appeared. Alexeyev released the safety bolts and slid the door open. On the ground before him were the enlisted men of General Ivanov. Alexeyev proceeded to hand them the remaining gold bars from Section Fifteen, which they carefully deposited into the storage compartment of the General's Russo-Balto armored car. Alexeyev marked the ledger accordingly.

He then went to Section Sixteen and started to unload the bars. He sensed that something was wrong. These bars were significantly lighter. General Ivanov noticed the change in Alexeyev's demeanor and bellowed, "Is something wrong, Alexeyev?"

"Well. Sir, I'm not sure, Sir."

"What do you mean?"

"Well, it's just that the bars from Section Sixteen are lighter. They are not as heavy as the others."

General Ivanov clambered up into the vault. As he did so, he dislodged one of the bars that Alexeyev had placed on the ledge. It clanged onto the edge of the armored vehicle and landed with a thud. There was an awkward silence as General Tremenko turned his flashlight onto the fallen bar. It lay broken with gray metallic surfaces exposed at the fissure. Tremenko kicked the bar with his boot and gold flakes speckled the toe. A flash of recognition crossed Ivanov's face. He turned toward the Section Sixteen rack and started heaving bars at his armored car. They clanged and fell in a metallic heap of chipped gold flecks and jagged iron edges.

"What are you trying to pull here, Nicholas?"

The look on the Tsar's face was a mixture of startled confusion and despair. His upper lip quivered as he tried to stifle back the tears that were forming in his shocked eyes. His shoulders slumped in dazed disbelief. Alexeyev was manically racing through the vault randomly lifting bars in a vain effort to find a heavy gold one.

"*Mene, Mene, Tekel, Parsin.* You have been weighed, measured and found wanting. You are a disgrace. The Tsar is dead!" shouted Ivanov who shook the Tsar by the shoulders. One by one, the Generals walked by Nicholas with expressions of disgust, disappointment and good riddance. Only Kracilnikov offered kind words, imploring Nicholas to escape in the hi-powered armored *Tsar*. Nicholas looked at him vacantly and shook his head from side to side.

"We cannot abandon the war effort. We cannot abandon our family," he spoke in a barely audible tone.

He had been dispatched to Petrograd to assess the situation. What he observed confirmed his worst fears. As he walked from the train station toward the Winter Palace, he came upon a barricade in the street. A voice from behind the overturned wagons and barrels ordered him to halt. Pasha complied. Two men carrying rifles approached him.

"Who are you, and what is your purpose here, Comrade?"

"My name is Pasha Kelly. I am a sailor on the Cruiser *Aurora*. I am going to the *Troika* to meet Captain Aleksandr Belyshev of the ship's revolutionary committee."

"Show us your identification," ordered the taller of the two men.

Pasha slowly reached into his greatcoat and produced a leather billfold and displayed his identification card. A grubby hand snatched the wallet from Pasha and gaped at the document blankly. Pasha wondered whether the man was literate. He grunted approval. Before handing the wallet back, the man removed several bills.

"That's your toll. Now move on!" he blurted.

Pasha spent several hours walking through the city. Although he frequently encountered barricades manned by revolutionaries, he saw no policemen or soldiers maintaining order. He saw four different police stations engulfed in flames. Jails and prisons had been overrun. Criminals in ragged striped uniforms roamed the streets voraciously. Frequent gunshots punctuated the air, providing aural proof of the chaos evident by the smell of charred and burning wood. The only Imperial flags he saw were smoldering heaps on the steps of government buildings. Makeshift flags of red calico flapped on every available post and pole. The only government building that appeared to be operational was Tauride Palace, the home of the Duma. The site of the new Provisional Government was barricaded and fortified by military units that had deserted the Imperial government.

Kelly retreated back to Tsarskoe Selo with a heavy heart for what his observations portended for the Imperial Family. As his train pulled into Alexander Station, a rumor spread among the passengers that the revolutionaries had taken over the station. Pasha quickly moved to the rear of the train. Seeing the telltale glow of fires ahead, the big man jumped from the moving train, tumbling roughly on the rocks, ice and snow. He was cut and bruised, but thankful to be free.

Back at Tsarskoe Selo, he reported immediately to Count Benckendorff, the Grand Marshall of the Imperial court. The Count eyed Pasha gravely.

"What do you think should be done?"

"I recommend immediate evacuation. This compound is indefensible. The Imperial family is in mortal jeopardy if they stay here." Kelly replied.

"Out of the question. The children are sick with the measles . . . ."

"When a house is on fire, the sick children are carried to safety. The revolutionary beast has tasted blood. It will become insatiable and devour everyone in its path," answered Pasha passionately.

"I will submit your report and recommendation to the Tsarina. Thank you."

Pasha knew that the Tsarina would never leave the Palace without her husband. Her daily cables to Nikki were returned marked "Place of residence unknown." The Tsar was still at Headquarters refining the wording of his Abdication Manifesto. He gulped down a tumbler of vodka and cursed his fate as he penned the last important document of the Romanov dynasty.

At an adjoining desk, Alexeyev was negotiating the terms of the Imperial family's departure from Russia with the leader of the Provisional Government. The expectation was that the Imperial family would depart through Murmansk and proceed to London. However, there were dark forces at work that would impact these expectations dramatically.

March 1917

New York City, New York

If we drove out a medieval tyranny only to make room for savage anarchy, we had better not have begun the task at all.

~ TEDDY ROOSEVELT, *THE STRENUOUS LIFE*

A S HE READ THROUGH THE DETAILS, Otto thought that the request for immunity for Hecht was extremely well-documented. Copies of the government's files had cost him dearly. Never had he spent so much money for something spewing so much grief and *tsuris*. The wheels of justice were grinding inexorably toward him and would eventually crush him.

It was imperative that he find a way to stop the process. His lawyer had told him that unless the government got testimony from Hecht, the other evidence was circumstantial and insufficient. With the alacrity and ferocity of a pit bull, his lawyer had filed a writ of *habeas corpus*, demanding the production of Hecht. Privately, he conceded to Kahn that, given Hecht's alien status, the suspicion of his involvement with the Black Tom Island sabotage and the precedent established by Lincoln during the Civil War, the writ for Hecht was a long shot. Kahn pondered the dilemma and knew that he must use every weapon at his command. The stakes were too great.

"This way, Mr. Kahn, your private salon is ready," said the somber *maître d'* Pierre who always displayed a dour countenance to his customers. He and his brother, Mateo, had emigrated to the United States from Paris at the end of the last century and still felt nothing but disdain for the barbaric Americans. True, their restaurant, *l'Escargot*, was one of the most successful in New York City, but he was appalled on a daily basis at the lack of sophistication of his clientele. Why just the evening before last, he had watched in horror as a customer from Duluth smothered his *escargot* with ketchup. Pierre's master chef at *Le Cordon Bleu* would have ripped off his apron and unleashed a string of profanities as he stormed out the door. In contrast, Pierre simply applied an Old World technique on the unsuspecting rube for his culinary effrontery by using his pencil to inflate the bill.

Otto arrived early so that he could escape the clamor of his office. The abdication of the Tsar had caused an uproar in the markets, to say the least, and his clients were beseeching him with incessant urgency for his sage advice. As he sat in the plush armchair looking vacantly out the window at the rush of worker-bees scurrying home, he tried to suppress the encroaching sense of dread that threatened him since Hecht's disappearance and Nadya's arrest. Otto thought wryly that but for . . . , his plans had worked to perfection; well, almost to perfection.

The Tsar's luggage with its Romanian appendage had arrived in New York and was safely ensconced in Kahn's Manhattan mansion for now. Minister Bark was positioned at the Anglo-International Bank in London in case the Tsar somehow escaped from Russia. Kahn was doing all he could on the Hecht front. Otto concluded that he had no choice but to resolve the last few loose ends that needed attention and let the Hecht matter take its course. If all else failed, there was always the Browning — a messy, but efficient solution.

"Your guests have arrived, sir. Shall I show them in?" queried Pierre.

"But, of course," said Otto, closing the drapes so that the room took on a conspiratorial illumination.

"Leon, it's so good to see you again. How has your stay in the Bronx been?" said Otto, alluding to Trotsky's residence on Vyse Avenue in the Bronx since he had arrived in New York some six weeks earlier.

Otto shook the hand of his guest enthusiastically, placing his left hand on the taller man's elbow. He was several inches taller than Otto and wore a rough suit of Eastern European cut that contrasted sharply with the finely tailored silk wool blend suit worn by the host. Leon Trotsky had a severe demeanor that made him appear much older than his thirty-eight years. He wore thick eyeglasses that were too small for his beady raven eyes and massive head. His high forehead and thick mane of unruly black hair gave him the look of a scientist, who obsessively spent too much time in his laboratory. Otto knew enough not to judge a book by its cover; he had read enough of Trotsky's writings to know that he possessed a first-class intellect and that his ideas were fueling the revolution.

"It is good location. Easy to subway. But, *I do not expect my stay here to be very long, however, for a revolution is bound to break out in Russia in a short time, and as soon as that happens I shall hasten to my home country and help in the work of Russia's liberation,*"[32] responded Trotsky in a heavy Russian accent.

"The Socialist Party met at the Lenox Casino in Harlem last night. Unfortunately, our resolution declaring war to be immoral failed to carry. Can you imagine that? We are the Mensheviks, from the Russian word *menshinstvo* meaning 'minority.' Our counterparts are the Bolsheviks from the Russian word *bol'shinstvo* meaning 'majority.'"

Kahn was not really interested in internecine politics. He interrupted Trotsky.

"Let's get down to business. Events in Russia are accelerating and our opportunity is here at long last. The Tsar has abdicated. A Provisional Government of those fools in the Duma is running the country. The people are sick and tired. They do not want more of the same leaders. The soviet workers committees have mobilized. These committees are elected by the workers, soldiers and peasants. They represent the true Russia. People are in the streets. We must act before the Provisional Government can stabilize the situation." stressed Otto.

"I am hearing same thing," said Leon laconically.

"My partners are working hard to support the cause. They are working with the Germans to transport Lenin and his comrades to Petrograd."

"The Romanov pigs have caused much suffering among the proletariat and the Jews," commented Trotsky.

"Whatever terms we agree to must include elimination of the so-called *camarilla*. The cancer of the Romanov Grand Dukes and Duchesses should be eradicated once and for all. Terminated with extreme prejudice, as they say in spy circles," said Otto ominously.

"Do I detect a personal agenda, Herr Kahn?" questioned Trotsky.

"You do. We do not want anyone making claims once the government of the Soviets is in control."

"On that we agree. We do not want them in exile plotting to return. The takeover of government must be final and forever. There will be no Romanov survivors."

They ate in silence for a few minutes, as if the enormity of their mutual assertions had exhausted them. Trotsky broke the ice.

"We are in good position. My brother-in-law, Lev Kamenev, is running our organization in Petrograd. We have smuggled enough ink and paper into that city to stop a German assault division. The printing presses are working day and night, inciting the people with details of the excesses and atrocities of the aristocracy."

"OK, sounds very effective. Let's get down to brass tacks. When can you leave for Russia? What do you need to fund this revolution? We are prepared to provide ten million dollars through 1917," offered Otto, somewhat impatiently.

"Herr Kahn, your firm made that much profit from the war. We will need at least three times that amount, deposited immediately with Nya Bank in Stockholm. You know my cousin Abram Givatovzo. He will be the exclusive signatory. Plus, I will need $50,000 in cash to make my crossing to Petrograd."

"You drive a hard bargain, Leon. Here's what we will do. Ten million will be deposited immediately per your instructions. Another ten million will be deposited when you tell us that your forces are ready, but no later than six months from now. The last ten million will be deposited when you take over complete control of the government and grant us concessions over the national bank, the railroads and the oil fields at Baku. The fifty thousan in cash will be delivered tomorrow."

"You have deal, Otto. I will leave as soon as I hear from Abram that the first ten million has been deposited." Trotsky's white napkin fell from his lap as he rose to shake hands with Kahn to seal the deal. It fluttered like the vagaries of fate.

Quite some time had passed since Oliver had submitted his request for immunity for Rudolph Hecht to his superiors. In the interim, Chorney had been recalled from the Tsar's mess detail too late to thwart the Keystone Imperative. Conditions had deteriorated gravely in the aftermath of the murder of Rasputin and the Tsar's abdication. The Empire was teetering and Strafe had been coordinating with the American ambassador on contingency plans should the government fall. They had been formulating plans for American forces to move to Archangel in case they were needed.

There were reports of a total breakdown of civil order in the cities. Heavy snows had interrupted food deliveries to Petrograd and there were strikes by workers everywhere. Rumors of cannibalism and anti-Semitic vigilantes roaming the streets were rampant.

Strafe's immunity request had presented detailed evidence of the Monocle's involvement with the Black Tom bombing, including pictures of briefcase money transfers. The only thing missing was testimony explaining the transactions photographed. There was no doubt in Oliver's mind that Hecht would be able to provide the necessary evidence. The naval officer knew that he could not hold Hecht *incommunicado* forever. The State Department had already made inquiry of ONI, as to whether it had any information about a missing German national named Rudolph Hecht. So far, Strafe had deflected the inquiry, but now the Justice Department had officially requested production of Hecht.

A high-priced lawyer from New York had filed a writ of *habeas corpus* against the government, seeking production of Hecht in court. Legal action had been forestalled only by the horrendous events in Europe. In a matter of days, the issue would come to a head. Granting immunity was his best hope to nail Kahn for treason, and in nautical terms, hang him from the yardarm.

Strafe sat nervously in the anteroom of the Assistant Secretary's office. He was always awed by the pervasive sense of history and honor of the Navy when he visited the Navy yard in southeast Washington, D.C. He had been summoned by Franklin Delano Roosevelt with a cryptic command. Oliver knew that such commands usually meant trouble.

Roosevelt's rise to the position of Assistant Secretary of the Navy seemed pre-ordained. Not only did he follow the footsteps of his illustrious cousin, Theodore, who had served in the same position, Franklin came from a family of mariners on his mother's side, the Delanos. He was an accomplished swimmer and sailor. A well-placed call to the White House from certain Wall Street donors clinched the deal. It was hardly a surprise when President Wilson plucked him from relative obscurity as a New York State Senator to become the Assistant Secretary.

As Oliver rehearsed his justifications for the detention of Hecht, the door to the inner office opened and Theodore Roosevelt emerged.

"Oliver, it is so good to see you. How are things over at ONI?" asked T.R., shaking Strafe's hand firmly. Before the officer could respond, the former President said brusquely, "I see that Franklin is waiting. You mustn't keep the Secretary waiting. Take good care."

Franklin Roosevelt beckoned to him to enter. Roosevelt was tall and handsome, with an obvious patrician bearing. He had short, wavy black hair and was clean shaven. His movements were athletic and he had a healthy, windblown suntan, no doubt developed during weekends of sailing on DC waterways.

Oliver settled into a stiff-backed chair, as his superior moved behind his desk where there were three files. Strafe recognized his thick investigative file and immunity request report. He also recognized his personnel file. The third file was bright red and was unknown to him. Could it be a court martial folder, he wondered?

"Oliver," intoned FDR. "I have studied this file carefully," tapping the investigative file lightly.

"I find it most disturbing."

Then, picking up the thinner personnel file, "I find this personnel file most exemplary, except for that *Culgoa* business," he said, alluding to the incident that led to the charge against Strafe for dereliction of duty. Oliver exhaled. The past always follows you. He tensed waiting for the boom to be lowered. Ever the politician, Roosevelt paused to let the tension build.

FDR then fingered the third, red file, carefully as if touching it might burn his hand.

"Now, this file is dangerous, combustible," he said flipping it open. "This is a top secret report from Blinker Hall containing a decrypted telegram from Germany's Foreign Secretary Zimmermann to Mexican President Huerta offering United States territory to Mexico, if it joins in hostilities against the United States. President Wilson has advised me that he is going before Congress to seek a declaration of war against Germany and the Central Powers."

Another pause. Strafe was a skilled chess player, who thought many moves ahead. The confluence of the files confused him.

"It is my job to reconcile these files. As you know, war is here. Goddammit, we're already at war. The Professor just hasn't declared it yet. But, even that technicality will soon be remedied. We are going to have to put certain, er, distractions behind us and be singularly focused on defeating the enemy. Can you do that, Oliver?"

"Yes, sir," responded Oliver, unsure over the direction of the conversation.

"Good! In that case, I would like to congratulate you on your new position as Rear Admiral of the Atlantic Fleet, effective immediately. My cousin, Theodore, will be thrilled; he told me that you are a true patriot. My adjutant will brief you on all the details," said Roosevelt who had come from behind the desk and was shaking Strafe's hand vigorously as he steered him out the door.

By the time Strafe had returned to his office, Hecht had been released and the Black Tom Island investigative files had been sent to storage. The only papers left on his desk were his commission to Admiral and his deployment orders.

42

1917
Petrograd, Russia

When living with the wolves, howl like the wolves.

~ Vladimir Lenin

The long white nights and cooling breezes off the Gulf of Finland gave Petrograd a refreshing aura in summer. Not so during the turmoil of 1917, quite the opposite. It was as if nature itself conspired against Mother Russia. The early summer weather was stiflingly hot. The extended daylight served only to expose the degradation and destruction in the once-proud capital. Anarchy and mob rule were the order of the day.

Chorney had successfully infiltrated a soviet or workers committee comprised of naval veterans affiliated with the Cruiser *Aurora*. He had been chosen by his new comrades to attend a meeting at the complex known as the Smolny Ensemble. It was located along the Neva River and had previously been the location of a tar processing facility, known as the *Smolyanoi* (Tar) Yard. Although Smolny was only a few miles from the Winter Palace as the crow flies, it took him many hours to get there. Strikes, wartime shortages and sabotage had obliterated the once-efficient municipal transit system.

As he approached the complex, he recalled a description of the cathedral as like a blue-and-white "confectioner's cake with arches, pediments and columns." In the bright summer sunlight, the effect of the cathedral in the center, balanced on both sides by complementary buildings, was stunning. Before the war, the Smolny Ensemble had been known as the Institution *des Demoiselles Nobles*, a finishing school for Russian noblewomen. The cathedral's central dome rose to a height of over one hundred yards and the local residents remarked that it "scraped heaven."

Lenin had ripped out the cathedral's main and side altars, and used the commodious interior as his headquarters. Chorney joined the hundreds of workers gathered in that vast open space to hear their leader's vision. Lenin was less than five-and-a-half feet tall. His distinguishing feature was his bald dome of a forehead that shone with sweat when he mounted his orator's box and railed about the struggle against oppression.

"Comrades, I have been in exile for many years. Recently, I was under house arrest in Zurich, Switzerland. It was only through the intercession of mighty international forces that my comrades and I were able to travel home to Russia. But, how were we treated? Like dumb animals, like cattle; we were herded into a railroad car that was sealed and guarded. The oppressors fear us! We traveled for days locked in a carriage with no windows. Under guard, we traveled through Germany, then to Sweden, and finally to the sacred soil of Mother Russia. On April 17th, we arrived at Finland Station in Petrograd and you welcomed us bearing red flags and singing *La Marseillaise*. I must confess that tears of joy ran down my face that night, like never before. We all know in our hearts that our time has come at last."

Lenin continued to speak for hours and hours until even the sun got bored and receded, which was quite a feat in the land of white nights. He explained his hatred of the Romanovs, who executed his brother simply because he sought justice for the oppressed. Lenin's voice rose as he condemned the Russian Orthodox Church as a pawn of the oppressors. He believed, as his intellectual predecessor, Karl Marx, that religion was the "opium of the people," invented in response to their impotence.

The diminutive orator then turned to his vision for a new form of government based on democracy implemented through workers' councils. Outlining his plan for constructing a revolutionary government parallel to the Provisional Government that operated out of the Winter Palace, Lenin exhorted their support. The avowed Marxist intended to use force if necessary to fill the vacuum of power while the loyalists, separatists and monarchists squabbled. At the conclusion of his speech, he and the audience were thoroughly exhausted. The men drifted out to find the nearest drinking hole.

As Kurt was walking out of the cathedral along the sidewalk to the main street, he observed Lenin enter one of the side buildings. Through the window he saw Lenin shaking hands with a well-dressed figure about the same height as Lenin. Kurt rubbed his eyes in disbelief. Could it really be the Monocle?

When he reached the corner of the building by the street, Chorney slipped into the shadows and crept along the building until he was under the window where he approximated seeing Lenin and Kahn. The window was open in to let the night air in.

"It's good to see you Vladimir. I trust that your journey was satisfactory. You know, we paid the Swiss extra for those luxury coaches that you and your two dozen comrades were transported in," commented Otto in his unmistakable voice that was a mixture of arrogance and condescension.

"Yes, that was a nice touch. Most appreciated. What is the status of my friend Trotsky?" Lenin asked.

"His journey has been much more arduous than yours, but he should arrive in Petrograd any day now. I thought that he would travel easily once we got President Wilson to push through an American passport for him. He was sailing for Europe when everything went wrong. When his ship, the S.S. *Kristianiafjord*, stopped in Halifax, Nova Scotia, he and his party were detained by an over-zealous military secret service official on the grounds that he was a German spy. Trotsky's party was interned with other German prisoners in a facility in Amherst, Nova Scotia.

"Leon cabled me for assistance. I immediately called Wilson and threatened to unleash hell if he did not get Trotsky released. The Professor instructed the State Department to communicate the extreme displeasure of the United States at the detention of a passenger with an American passport. Shortly after that, the Canadians received a counter-order from the British Embassy in Washington to release Leon and his compatriots. They should arrive any day now."

"What about the money? Revolutions are not inexpensive," said Lenin.

"We have supported Trotsky with ample funds, with the proviso that when you are successful we receive a return on our investment in the form of resource concessions and control of the national bank," replied Kahn.

"That's all well and good for Trotsky, but what about me?" queried the Marxist.

"OK, I understand your point. The American Congress has granted Wilson a Special War Fund. I will personally instruct my lawyer, Elihu Root, the former Secretary of State, to secure additional funds from Wilson for you."

In the wake of his report on the Smolny Cathedral meeting and the deteriorating situation in Petrograd, Chorney was ordered to evacuate the Marmot and himself to a secure facility in Stockholm. It was October and there were riots in the streets. Chorney knew that there was insufficient time to use the normal protocols for contacting the confidential informant. He donned his deflective body suit that Suitland had developed to protect the torso from mortal injury. Although it was heavy and bulky, he knew that his "chain mail armor" was definitely warranted, given the malignant violence in the streets.

Random gunfire punctuated the early morning stillness. He double-checked the compartments of his rucksack that contained various currencies, gold coins, citizenship papers of several countries, ammo and his evasion kit. Last, he rechecked his personal weapons and mentally reviewed his operational priorities. Satisfied, he threw the rest of his belongings into the fireplace. With one last look around, he bade farewell to the 'Chorney Operations HQ.'

Emerging on to the street in the pre-dawn darkness, he detected a malevolent blood-red cast on the eastern horizon. He could not tell whether it was due to meteorological conditions or from fires that burned throughout the city. Either way, he acknowledged the proverbial sailor's warning.

He hustled to the rectory adjoining the Cathedral of St. Vladimir where Iliodor resided. As Chorney approached the rectory on Blokhin Street, he heard a commotion and saw two hefty Okhrana agents dragging the Marmot into a waiting car. Chorney quickly positioned himself. He unhooked the top of his pack and unzipped the weapons compartment and removed what he needed.

As the Okhrana vehicle pulled away from the curb, Chorney pulled the pin and sprang into action. He jumped onto the running board and shattered the driver's side window with his elbow and deposited the smoke grenade into the front seat. The car immediately filled with smoke. Chorney yanked the steering wheel, sending the vehicle careening into a lamppost. Throwing open the back door, he seized the coughing Marmot by the arm and dragged him down the alley.

Picking up his rucksack, Chorney raced with the cleric to a wooden barrier at the end of the alley and fairly threw Iliodor over the top, quickly following. He heard shouts and whistles behind them, but he knew that the agents would be dazed and confused by the attack and unable to respond coherently.

After navigating several back alleys at full speed, they turned left onto Dobrolyubova Prospekt. The venerable Fortress of Peter and Paul loomed before them. It had been built in 1703 by Tsar Peter the Great when he first decided to build his capital on a series of islands on the Neva River. It was notable for the sacred and for the profane. The Peter and Paul Cathedral in the center of the Fortress, with its spire rising over four hundred feet, housed the crypts of every Tsar and Tsarina in Russian history. The garrison was also notorious for its role as a jail for high-profile political prisoners starting with the imprisonment of Peter's treasonous son, up to, and including Trotsky and Lenin's older brother, Alexander.

From where they stood, the rendezvous point with the extraction craft was across the plaza that fronted on the Neva River. He knew that he had a short window of time before the boat would leave. He briefed the disheveled Marmot on the situation. They were preparing to sprint to safety when they heard the angry growl of a mob heading toward the Kronversky Bridge that led directly to the gates of the Fortress. Chorney looked at his watch and assessed the progress of the mob that was roiling toward the Fortress. He calculated that they could melt into the rear of the mob and traverse the plaza with it. Once across, they could easily slip onto the escape vessel.

His plan was working perfectly until he heard the all-hands-on-deck alarm blaring. That could only mean one thing. Suddenly there was gunfire from the Fortress. Panic ensued and Chorney and Iliodor were buffeted back across the plaza. Worse yet, Chorney saw the crew untying the extraction vessel that was in the line of fire from the Fortress. Like the pulse of a wave, the pressure of the retreating mob hit them and the slender cleric fell backwards.

Chorney grabbed Iliodor's forearm and pulled. Miraculously, the thin man lurched toward him. Chorney bent and caught him at the waist and slung him over his shoulder. Getting his legs under him, Chorney plowed through the crowd like Jim Thorpe running for the end zone, knocking away anyone in his path. He only stumbled once and he reached the fishing boat as it was pulling away from the dock. With a powerful thrust, he launched himself toward the boat and sprawled onto the deck before the awestruck crew. The skipper recognized Chorney and promptly moved him and the dazed cleric below decks to safety. The next stop across the Bay of Finland was Stockholm.

1917
Tsarskoe Selo to Ekaterinburg

Like a band of gypsies we go down the highway . . .
Insisting that the world keep turning our way.

~ WILLIE NELSON

THE ABDICATION DEVASTATED THE FAMILY. Nicholas returned from Dno a broken man. As best he could, he tried to maintain a brave exterior. However, as the weeks of captivity passed, the disrespect and contempt for the Tsar and his family grew. The deposed leader bore the brunt of the derision. When the Tsar first arrived at Tsarskoe Selo, the guards were deferential toward Nicholas. However, over time, the soldiers were replaced by workingmen, who were still respectful, but resented the privileged family. By the time the royal family was transferred to Ekaterinburg, the contingent in charge of the royal family was comprised of thugs and rabble. They held the first family in the lowest regard.

Even at the zenith of his power, Nicholas was never a sturdy man; but, during his humiliation and captivity he appeared to shrink. His pallor was sickly and great, dark circles hung under his eyes like hangman's nooses. The twitches on his face were almost constant and he stammered when he spoke even the simplest sentences. Ashamed and frustrated, he withdrew to sullen silences. Not even Alexei's mimicry of the most buffoonish of their captors could rouse a smile from Nicholas. Looking at the shell of a man before him, Pasha was reminded of Dante's warning at the gates of hell: "Abandon hope, all ye who enter here."

While Chief-of-Staff Alexeyev was negotiating with Kerensky's Provisional Government in March 1917 for the safe passage of the Imperial family to London, the Petrograd Soviet voted to arrest Tsar Nicholas. Kerensky had no choice but to obey the workers' councils. Kerensky ordered a special commission of inquiry to determine whether either of the sovereigns had committed treason. According to Alexeyev, once the special commission finished, the Imperial family would be allowed to travel to England. While Nicholas accepted this explanation with dull fatalism, Alexandra threw a fit.

The family was systematically isolated from friends and allies. When Anya Vyrubova protested the ill-treatment of the Imperial family to the Provisional Government, she was arrested and imprisoned at the Fortress of Peter and Paul. When Major Boris Kracilnikov objected to Kerensky, he was re-assigned to VladivostokVladivostok, thousands of miles away.

Months later Kerensky informed Nicholas that he and his family would be relocated. The family was excited about the prospect of rebuilding their lives. Unbeknownst to the Imperial family, the destination was not sunny Livadia Palace on the Crimea, but Tobolsk, Siberia. Pasha and a handful of servants and tutors traveled with the royal family to Tobolsk on trains marked "CRC, the International Committee of the Red Cross."

In October, the Bolsheviks toppled the Provisional Government and the new soviet rulers ordered the royal family to be moved from Tobolsk to Ekaterinburg, the capital of a soviet stronghold in the Red Urals. The royal family was housed in a modest residence previously inhabited by an engineer named Ipatiev. Conditions for the Tsar's family continued to degrade. Perhaps the greatest humiliation of all came when the commissar-in-charge issued a military rations card to the Tsar limiting the family's food consumption to the amount granted a common soldier.

When the Bolsheviks ousted the Provisional Government, they controlled the major cities. However, there were significant segments of the country that opposed the Bolsheviks. The opposition included rogue groups like the Czech Legions that had been stranded in Russia while fighting against the Germans.

Admiral Kolchak commanded the White Russian Army, which presented a formidable obstacle to the Red Army of the Soviets. The Kolchak divisions had experienced military leadership, the sympathy of the civilian population and, most important, over $325 million in Romanov gold. This was the eastern tranche of Operation Diaspora that had been destined for San Francisco. Otto had failed to account for the chaos following the abdication and Kolchak's loyalty.

As the winter of 1918 waned, tendrils of green shoots poked from their earthen beds as if testing the air and light to determine whether it was safe to emerge. Trotsky stood in his office staring at a map of Russia dotted with red and white pins denoting the location of the opposing forces. The Red Army in Siberia was failing miserably. Every day, there was news of another defeat and more territory coming under the control of the Whites. The ragtag Army of the Soviets was no match for the seasoned troops under the command of Admiral Kolchak. Now that the Czech Legions had combined with the White Army, Soviet control of the Red Urals was in jeopardy. Kolchak's forces had captured Tyumen and liberated Kyshtym, Miass, Zlatoust, and ShadrinskIt. The regional capital of Ekaterinburg, where the Imperial family was imprisoned, was encircled.

Trotsky held a communiqué from General Reinhold Iosifovich Berzin, who the Central Committee had sent to the Urals to confirm whether the Tsar and his family were still alive. In light of the deteriorating military situation, Trotsky was increasingly concerned that the Tsar might be liberated. Berzin reported that the Imperial family was alive and in custody in Ekaterinburg.

Restrictions on the royal family tightened. One night, during the changing of the guards at midnight Pasha escaped. He assured the family that he would return as soon as possible. Pasha followed a path into the woods to a creek that he followed for hours. He was determined to find friendly forces and return to rescue Nicholas and his family.

The Central Committee appointed Yakov Yurovsky as commandant of the contingent guarding the royal family. Born Jewish, he harbored a fierce animosity toward the Tsar on account of the anti-Semitic pogroms during his reign. He was dangerous and devious. When he first arrived at the Ipatiev House, he posed as a physician and examined Alexei's injured leg. When Commandant Yurovsky took charge of their prison the following day, the Imperial family was shaken by the deception.

Yakov sat with an unlabeled bottle of vodka in the small pub in the Hotel Amerika in Ekaterinburg. He poured himself another shot into a chipped shot glass to quell his frustration at waiting for Aleksandr Georgievich Beloborodov, chairman of the Executive Committee of the Ural Region Soviet. The bottle was half-empty when Beloborodov came down to the bar from the meeting of the Soviet Executive Committee. Beloborodov signaled for the waitress to bring an additional glass. He poured a healthy shot and chugged it down, wiping his mouth with the back of his wrist.

At twenty-seven years of age, Beloborodov had risen quickly up the chain of command of the regional soviet because of his well-deserved reputation for ruthless violence. It was said that he used his knowledge of electricity to extract information from reluctant witnesses with great efficiency.

"Comrade Yakov, we have a decision. Since Ekaterinburg is surrounded and will likely fall in a matter of days, the Central Committee has approved our recommendation to eradicate the Imperial vermin."

"What about the civilians? What is to happen to them?"

"By civilians, do you mean the wife and daughters?" Yurovsky nodded.

"They all must be executed," spat Belorodov. Yakov flinched at the vehemence of the short man. Yurovsky had killed many enemies of the people, but he had never killed innocent women and defenseless children. He poured himself another drink and quaffed it in one gulp. 'Liquid courage' as his mentor in the Cheka often said.

"What about the servants? Kill them, too?" Belorodov nodded solemnly.

"Here's the decree," the electrician said, sliding a smudged handwritten paper across the table.

Decree of the Ural Executive Committee of the Soviet of Worker, Peasant, and Red Army Deputies.

Possessing information that Czechoslovak bands are threatening the Red capital of Urals,

Ekaterinburg, and bearing in mind that the crowned hangman could hide and escape the people's tribunals, the Executive Committee, carrying out the will of the people, has decreed to execute the former tsar, Nicholas Romanov, guilty of countless bloody crimes.

16 July 1918   Aleksandr Georgievich Beloborodov

44

July, 1918
Ekaterinburg, Siberia

When I die, it will be a shipwreck, and as when a huge ship sinks, many people all around will be sucked down with it.

~ PABLO PICASSO

THE SUMMER SUN HEATED the metal barrel of the rifle that Pasha wore slung across his back. After months of inaction, he was relieved to be involved in the campaign to drive the Reds out of the Ural region. Riding in the lead armored vehicle of the White Army with Admiral Kolchak as the column took control of Ekaterinburg was exhilarating. Pasha hoped that they were not too late to save Nicholas and his family. He directed the driver to the Ipatiev house. The American's shoulders slumped when he saw the vacant building.

Pasha raced into the abandoned house and ran up the stairs three at a time. The rooms on the top floor were deserted. He searched each floor with growing dismay. When he finally got to the basement, he was hesitant to enter. The stench of death was palpable. Peering through the grimy window of the cellar, he cringed at the sight of the blood-splattered walls. Despite his experience, he retched on the parched dirt.

"Excuse me, sir. We found this man behind the fence. We were going to throw him into the prisoner wagons, when he saw you and started screaming that he knew you. He is in sorry shape, and probably suffering from shell-shock, but we thought you might know him," reported Sergeant Birdla. Before him, groveling in the dust was one of the guards that Pasha knew only as Moshnik. His Red Army uniform was two sizes too big and draped comically over his emaciated frame. He had a large, beak-like nose and his cheeks were covered with about ten-days' stubble.

"Yes, I do know him. Bring him over to that table and let me speak with him," said Pasha.

"Here drink some water, Moshnik." The factory worker-turned-guard gulped water from Pasha's canteen appreciatively.

"Now, tell me what happened to the Tsar and his family," said the big man, in a coaxing voice.

"When the Whites attacked Ekaterinburg, the Reds fled in trucks. There was no room for me. They kicked me off," he explained, lifting his shirt to display a boot-sized bruise on his ribcage.

"Tell me what happened to the Tsar."

"Exactly one week ago, Commandant Yukovsky returned from the hotel and went to Dr. Botkin's room. Since my shift had just ended, I went to the shed to change. It was very hot that night and some of the windows were open. I heard Yukovsky tell Botkin to wake the family, because he expected an attack by the White artillery and it would dangerous for them to stay on the third floor. It would be safer for them in the basement.

"A few minutes later, they all came down the stairs. In addition to Nicholas, Alexandra, the four Grand Duchesses, the Tsarevich, there was the physician, Demidova, the ladies maid, Trupp, the butler, and Khartonov, the chef. The Tsar was carrying his son. You know, the boy has trouble walking. The right side of the Tsar's face was twitching violently when Yukovsky, Nikulin and Yermakov herded them into the cellar.

"I crept over to the window to see. I heard Yukovsky pronounce the death decree from the Soviet. The Tsar screamed, 'What? What?,' his face twitching for the last time. Suddenly, Yukovsky shot him in the head. Nikulin and Yermakov started shooting wildly at the others. There were screams and wailing. The shooting continued for at least a minute. The three were cursing as they shot the women. The bastards even shot the little spaniel that Alexei called Joy.

"I ran back behind the shed before they discovered me.

"When they emerged from the basement, I heard Yukovsky say, 'That's why the women were so hard to kill, their clothes were stuffed with so much gold and jewels that the bullets couldn't get through.' The other two laughed like blood-crazed banshees."

Kolchak's forces lingered in Ekaterinburg in a vain effort to locate the bodies of the slaughtered royal family. They followed every rumor concerning abandoned mine shafts, lake bottoms and unmarked pits to no avail. Kolchak was obsessed. He believed that finding the bodies of the former rulers was essential to upholding the dignity of Mother Russia. He also thought that evidence of the brutality of the Reds would constitute a rallying cry for his forces. While he lingered, the Third Red Army under General Berzin was consolidating for an all-out counterattack.

General Reinhold Iosifovich Berzin, the Commander-in-Chief of the Northern Ural-Siberian Front, was born in Livonia, Latvia, to a family of peasant-workers. He was a large-framed, imperious man with piercing brown eyes. Despite being only thirty-six, he was a veteran of twenty years of anti-Tsarist guerilla activity.

As a teenager he had joined the *Jaunā strāva*, New Current, an organization of militant Latvian nationalists that resisted the yoke of the Tsar. In 1905, he organized a raid on an Imperial armory to steal weapons and ammunition. Unfortunately for Berzin, a double agent had notified the Imperial commandant of the plan. Berzin's group walked into a trap.

Berzin was convicted of revolutionary treason. Due to his youth, his death sentence was commuted, and he was sentenced to hard labor in Siberia. There, he befriended a fellow prisoner with the *nom d'plume* of Leon Trotsky. They both escaped in a deer-pulled sleigh through the frozen landscape of Siberia in February 1907. Berzin spent the next ten years as a fugitive. When the Tsar abdicated, Berzin was recruited by Trotsky, and soon rose to his current position as leader of the Third Red Army.

In a peaceful meadow not far from Lake Baikal, Admiral Kolchak explained the situation to his general staff. Pasha sat in the command tent listening intently. What had started promisingly as a mission to rescue the Tsar and his family had degenerated into a desperate flight for survival of his army. Only his superior tactical training and the discipline of his troops had enabled them to avoid the clever trap set by the Soviet forces. He had two major obstacles to overcome. Both had started as assets, but were now grave liabilities.

"My grandmother used to repeat an old saying that her grandmother taught her. Roughly translated it says, '*Hidden inside every blessing is a curse.*' We have been blessed to have the Czechoslovak Legions as comrades-in-arms. This group of almost sixty thousand soldiers has been with the Russian Army since the beginning of the war. These patriots hope that their homeland will become a sovereign state after the Germans and Austro-Hungarian curs are defeated. We drink to Czechoslovakia!" he exclaimed, raising a glass of vodka.

"Although the Czechoslovak Legions have fought courageously at our side, I fear that the Bolshevik overthrow of the Provisional Government could result in a shift in the Legions' allegiance. This is not their fight. Their fight is with the Central Powers, not the Reds."

"But the Soviets' insistence on peace at any price with Germany makes it their fight, no?" interrupted Major Koyla Kalashnikov.

"That may be true in a way," said the Admiral. "But can we be sure? We should assume the worst, and pray for the best. I just want you to consider the possibility of the Czechs altering their allegiance and the effect that would have on our efforts."

Kolchak let his senior officers mull over this problem while he outlined the second obstacle.

"We are fortunate to have ample amounts of Romanov gold to fund our operations. That has served us in good stead. However, the gold is cumbersome to transport and it is greatly coveted by our adversaries. Because the precious cargo is stored in armored railcars, we have been forced to conduct our operations within proximity of the Trans-Siberian Railroad. This has constrained our maneuverability. A case could be made that by restricting our mobility, it has increased our vulnerability.

"Gentlemen, the time has come to resolve these two issues. I have devised a plan. The utmost secrecy is needed, but we have a unique set of circumstances in our favor. Lake Baikal lies thirty versts to our east. We can be there by the end of day tomorrow and we will execute Operation Trident."

A day's march behind Kolchak's White Army, General Berzin was also meeting with his general staff. Berzin had force-marched his troops in pursuit, in hopes of trapping Kolchak against the lake. Now, he was on the cusp of obliterating the greatest threat to the soviet takeover of Russia.

"Comrade General, Avi Kuriansky, the leader of the scout patrol has returned, and is ready to make his report. Shall I bring him in?" said Lieutenant Vulganin.

He was anxious to hear the report in order to learn how Kolchak planned to counter the Red Army's lightning offensive. Kolchak and his forces were encumbered by the slow-moving armored trains containing the Tsar's gold. He corrected himself — the people's gold. His intelligence had informed him that the tracks of the Circumbaikal Loop around the lake had been sabotaged and, in any event, were not designed to handle the weight of the armored train carrying the gold. Furthermore, there was insufficient capacity to ferry a force the size of Kolchak's army across Lake Baikal.

He believed that Kolchak would have to fight along the lowlands bordering the lake in order to defend the gold. His only other choice would be to abandon the gold to save his army. Berzin salivated at the prospect of positioning his artillery on the hills overlooking the lakeshore and pounding Kolchak's army into submission. He afforded himself the luxury of imagining the gratitude of his mentor Trotsky and the Central Committee, when he reported the news of Kolchak's defeat and the delivery of hundreds of millions of dollars worth of gold to Moscow.

"Good afternoon, Comrade General," saluted Lt. Kuriansky.

"Be seated, Avi. Tell me what that Old Salt is up to."

"Well, sir, it is safe to say that he is not preparing to fight."

"Really?" asked Berzin in a surprised tone.

"That's right, Sir. He has disregarded convention and is dividing his forces into three parts."

"Interesting," remarked Berzin.

"The Czech Legions are moving *en masse* north along the lakeshore road. The White Army is marching south toward China."

"What about the armored train cars?" questioned a surprised General.

"That is the puzzling aspect of the maneuvers, sir. The cargo, the people's gold, is being loaded from the armored railcars onto the ferry. It appears that the loading is almost complete."

"What is that rascal up to?" wondered Berzin.

Conditions around Lake Baikal presented significant challenges to the engineers building this section of the Trans-Siberian Railroad. Since the shoreline was marshy and unstable, the Circumbaikal Loop around the lake was susceptible to track failure. A series of disastrous train wrecks had limited the traffic on the Circumbaikal to light railcars. The use of conventional ferries to cross the lake had proven ineffectual due to the thick ice that formed on the lake during the harsh winters. To solve the problem, the Tsar commissioned the construction of a large icebreaker, the *Baikal,* that would be able to smash its way through the ice.

The *Baikal* was a tall, broad vessel with a conventional ferry shape. She was painted white and had a black hull. Four huge black stacks defined her profile. On this voyage the main deck was weighed down with row after row of shiny gold bars bearing the emblem of the Romanov dynasty.

Kolchak personally selected the team for the mission on the *Baikal.* When forming the team, Kolchak remembered that when the American had joined them, he had told Kolchak of his experience with submarines. The General added Pasha to the *Baikal* team, along with fourteen Russian seamen and Captain Mikhail Lebedev, Kolchak's trusted son-in-law. Under the watchful eyes of a stern petty officer, pairs of sailors manned each of the four large, steam engines of the powerful vessel. Lebedev and Sergeant Beryl Chapayev manned the bridge. Pasha and the remaining seamen installed tripod-mounted machine guns, fore and aft, in the unlikely event that they were attacked while on the lake.

With a long blast of the steam whistle that resonated throughout the harbor, the *Baikal* left the pier. She sat low in the water. Massive columns of thick, black smoke, punctuated with fiery sparks, bellowed from the stacks as she accelerated toward open water. The early morning sky was gray and tinged with high wispy white clouds. The air was crisp and the cold lake water sprayed the bow as they steamed forward.

Pasha wore a Russian sailor's uniform that he had received earlier that morning. The traditional hat was too large and kept sliding off his head. In addition to the carbine he received from Kolchak's armory, he wore a Bowie knife strapped to his calf and a derringer on his ankle. He had a Mauser C96 'broomhandle' pistol in a holster at the flat of his back.

On a hill not far from Port Baikal, Reinhold Brezin stood with his aide d'camp with a pair of powerful binoculars watching the Baikal as it steamed from port. Brezin was puzzled by the paucity of soldiers on board.

After an hour, Brezin noticed something that perplexed him further. The trailing billows of black smoke seemed to stop. What could be happening, he wondered, as he removed the field glasses from his eyes.

"Here, Vulganin, you look. Am I crazy, or did the *Baikal* stop?" The lieutenant took the glasses and squinted toward the water. The sun had risen and the glare off the water made it difficult to see the large white object on the horizon. But, the constant stream of trailing smoke had stopped. The smoke rose vertically from the ship.

"Yes, Comrade General, the *Baikal* is motionless. Maybe the engines have failed," he opined.

"I doubt it. The stacks are still spewing black smoke. The engines are definitely operational. What are they doing?"

On the *Baikal*, Captain Lebedev mustered his men to reveal their mission. Two men were assigned to the Captain, who ordered them to disassemble the weapons and load them onto the lifeboats. The other men were assigned to the gruff sergeant and they followed him to the engine room. One man was ordered to crank up the steam engines, while Pasha, the sergeant and the remaining men broke into four three-man teams. The sergeant and his men proceeded to the starboard side and Pasha and his teams took the port side. One team on each side went toward the bow and another went toward the stern.

With one man to handle the watertight compartment doors, the others were to open all valves and hatches in that compartment. Once done, they were to escape through the compartment doors that were to be closed behind them. The starboard and port teams were to work toward amidships where the ladders topside were located. The plan was to coordinate the scuttling, fore and aft, and bow and stern, in order to maintain the roll and yaw of the ship. The last thing they wanted was for the ship to lose orientation of the centerline and be thrown off-kilter.

Kolchak's men performed well. The engine man was already topside, when the four teams converged at the topside ladders. The experienced sailors shimmied up the ladders with an alacrity that only a sinking ship could inspire.

The *Baikal* was taking on water rapidly. Kelly heard the water beginning to lap at the boilers when he and the sergeant approached the ladder. The sergeant was a beefy man with large, tattooed arms and a gristled face that bore the degradations of twenty years of military service. With the lake water rising to his ankles, Pasha mounted the ladder after Chapayev started climbing. Suddenly, the big man kicked at Pasha with his heavy boot, shouting, "Not you, Yankee."

The kick struck Pasha flush in the face, breaking his nose. He was knocked back down the ladder. He quickly regained his balance and re-climbed the ladder. When Beryl attempted to kick him again, Pasha was ready and grabbed his leg and twisted manically. The sergeant came crashing down the hole on top of Pasha.

He quickly maneuvered from under the Russian and began punching him with all his might. Beryl reached behind his back and pulled out a sap. Beryl struck Pasha in the neck with the weapon, knocking him back. The sergeant was on his feet and grabbed the ladder with both hands. He vaulted himself toward Pasha and kicked him in the chest with both feet. Pasha fell backward heavily into the rising water. The sergeant stood over him menacingly. A huge explosion rocked the ship. Chapayev smashed into a ledge of the ship's structure. Pasha cringed as he heard the gruesome sound of his assailant's neck snapping.

The explosion breached the *Baikal's* hull. The ship was sinking rapidly. Pasha scrambled up the ladder unsteadily. The structure was breaking apart. Kelly reached topside and ran across the deck to the railing. His heart sank as he saw the lifeboats pulling away rapidly. He reached for his knife and slashed at ropes holding a life preserver. Pasha realized that he had to get off the ship; otherwise, he would be sucked under when the ship sank. He ran as fast as he could with the preserver on his arm and dove into the frigid lake. As he jumped, he screamed "Geronimo!"

On a distant hill, General Berzin watched helplessly as the Tsar's gold sank to the bottom of Lake Baikal.

1994

Cold Spring Harbor, New York

Gold is a treasure, and he who possesses it, does all he wishes
to in this world, and succeeds in helping souls into paradise.

~ CHRISTOPHER COLUMBUS

Date	B/L	S#	%	Troy dwt.	USD	GBP	Comm	OHK	RBS	Total

These were the columns in the hidden ledger that they discovered in
Otto's Love Nest. The pages were filled with Otto's chicken-scratch, handwritten notations, dating from 1917 until well into the 1930s. The notations
were in different inks, some were in pencil. Jed suggested that "B/L" stood
for Bills of Lading and no one had a better guess. They made inquiries
regarding the location of records that might shed light on the issue. It did
not take long to make arrangements to view Otto Kahn's papers at Princeton
University where the papers had been donated.

Luke stretched his legs and shifted uncomfortably in the wooden armchair. He was at a table in the Rare Books and Special Collections reading
room at the Firestone Library of Princeton University, reviewing boxes

341

and boxes of records from the late, great Otto Kahn. He had been there for several days and had gained great insight into the life and times of Otto. Luke was amazed at the personages that Otto interacted with; it seemed like he was intimate with every prominent figure of the early twentieth century. Whether it was a note from Winston Churchill, or a hand-written investment proposal from Enrico Caruso for Opera Stars throat lozenges, it was undeniable that Otto was connected with a capital "C."

While perusing Otto's business records, something caught Luke's eye and bolted him to attention. From a faded manila folder, he carefully removed bills of lading pertaining to iron shipments from Gothenberg to New York on the *SS Stockholm*. Luke recognized the masthead of the Rederiaktiebolaget Sverige-Nordamerika, Shipping corporation Sweden-North America. The shipments occurred in the spring of 1917.

As he studied these documents, he wondered about the nature of these transactions. Otto was a banker. What was he doing shipping iron from Sweden to the United States? Luke was aware of Otto's business relationship with R.B. Scrapple, the iron magnate who partnered on many railroad deals with Otto's clients. Luke checked his watch and realized that the hour was getting late. After receiving approval, he photographed the documents.

Back at his motel room, Luke emailed the images of the bills of lading to the team, along with his observation regarding the incongruity of the iron shipments. While he waited for a reply, Luke compared the timing of the shipments to the events occurring in Europe at that time. Woodrow Wilson had just delivered his war message to Congress, seeking a Declaration of War against Germany. British air forces suffered horrible losses in the month known as Bloody April. The Tsar had abdicated and Russia was being ruled by the Provisional Government.

Tommy, the team geek, responded first with his analysis. He opined that the documents were erroneous because the weights listed did not correspond to the amount of iron shipped. Luke found this comment incomprehensible, so he called Tommy for an explanation.

"It's really simple, Luke. A bar of iron weighs eight pounds. When you look at these bills and calculate the numbers of bars and compare it to the weight declared, it is way off. Probably, by a factor of three. I don't know what was going on, but something is not right with these bills of lading."

"Tommy, these are original documents that I held in my own hands. How could they be bogus?"

"I'm not saying that they are bogus. What I am saying is that the weights do not correspond to the weights you would expect for iron bars."

"So, could there be a typographical mistake?"

"I doubt it. Even a hundred years ago, they knew that they had to get paid based on the weight of the cargo shipped."

"Essentially, you are saying that the shipper did not care if you were shipping iron or wood, as long as you paid for the weight shipped, you were good."

"There are other factors, but weight is most determinative of shipping cost, yeah."

"Let me see if I have this correct? If I'm shipping iron or lead, the shipper does not care because I'm paying for the weight shipped."

"That's about right."

"So, what would weigh three times as much as iron?"

"Let me see. One possibility would be . . . no, he couldn't have. Could he?"

"What?"

"Luke, I think the wily old bastard was shipping gold disguised as iron!"

1919

Cold Spring Harbor, New York

If you want to be joyful and happy, then, just be that!

~ Leo Tolstoy

THE GREAT WAR WAS OVER. The Treaty of Versailles was signed on the fifth anniversary of the assassination of the Archduke Ferdinand, ending the most devastating war ever. Over sixteen million lives had been lost and billions of dollars of property had been destroyed. For Otto Kahn, it was the best of times. The world was his oyster. Operation Diaspora had gone exceptionally well; three of the four shipments had reached the intended destinations. Only Admiral Kolchak had prevented perfect execution of his plan.

The construction of his castle was nearing completion. No expense had been spared to make it the most magnificent residence in the country, if not the world. The golf course, airstrip, greenhouses and indoor pool were above and beyond the usual Gold Coast mansion, if there was such a thing. But, the *piece'd'resistance* was the elevation. Thanks to innumerable railroad car loads of rock and soil that had been deposited at the site, Oheka was now the highest location on Long Island. In military terms, he held the

344

command view, the unassailable high ground. Oheka was the culmination of his *Auri Sacra Fames.*

Fast forward seventy-five years. The location was the same, but the mood was quite different. Luke had just come from a meeting with Jed and their bankers. Perhaps, they had underestimated the enormity of the task of resuscitating the castle. The latest estimates for renovations were astronomical. Jed complained that his head was about to split open from counting zeroes. When all was said and done, Otto had spent untold millions building Oheka and living like he was the 'King of New York.' Luke and Jed were just a couple of guys from Long Island whose closest connection to royalty was that they liked to eat at Burger King. The harsh reality was that they just did not have the resources to restore Oheka. They both conceded defeat. The dream was over. Maybe, just maybe, some things were better left buried. The reality of lives of quiet desperation beckoned.

Luke pulled into the courtyard and saw Tommy's truck. He did not relish telling Tommy that they had decided that it was time to cut bait. They had planned to enter the Iron Bunker and look around. Not wanting to go into the rusty chamber again, he resolved to tell the scientist and be done with it.

Tommy greeted him with a smile like they were on some archeological dig. He stood at the entrance to the shaft with his gear already on.

"Hurry, Luke, there is something we have to decipher."

"Look, Tom, it's over. We can't keep chasing ghosts."

"I know that you and Jed are discouraged, but we have not explained the anomaly that registered on my magnetometer when I first surveyed the site. Come on, I need your help. It won't take long. I promise."

"OK. One hour, I'll give you one hour," Luke assented, reluctantly.

Using the winch control, they lowered themselves to the bunker and swung in. Once they had removed their harnesses, Tommy unpacked the magnetometer while Luke examined the workbench. There were various chisels and mallets covered with dust. Tricia had catalogued everything when they first found the room. Jed had made creepy jokes that it was Otto's torture chamber and threatened to bring the subcontractors here to negotiate less expensive bids.

"Hey, check this out," said Tommy. "There's a section over here that Maggie is saying is not metal."

Luke went to the corner where Tommy was working and peered at the patch. Taking out his pocket knife, he scraped at the area. Maggie was right. Under the dust and accumulated rust, his knife stuck plaster. He dug in further and removed a sizeable chunk of plaster.

"Bring the light closer," he said to Tommy.

They peered into the hole and were able to see an edge. Luke scraped and scraped until he saw that the object he was scraping was the outline of a metal bar. He wedged a crow bar behind the bar for leverage and yanked. It refused to budge.

"Here, come help me pry this out," he rasped to Tommy, rust sticking in his throat.

They both pushed as hard as they could. Rust-stained sweat formed on their foreheads. The lever moved ever-so-slightly.

"Ok, let's give it all we've got."

Suddenly, the crowbar fell as the bar toppled loose and fell to the floor with a clang. An iron bar lay at their feet. Luke nudged it with the toe of his work boot. The top of the iron bar separated from the bottom and they stared in disbelief at what lay before them. They gathered their things and scrambled back to the surface and raced to Luke's portable phone.

"Jed, you are not going to believe it. We pried an iron bar out of the wall in the Iron Bunker. Turns out, it was actually a nesting mold, you know, like those used in a foundry to make different shaped metal objects? Well, inside this iron nesting mold, we found a gold bar with the Tsar's symbol on the top of it. We think the Iron Bunker is lined with these suckers. That's right. I don't think that we'll have a problem resurrecting the old lady now!" he whooped.

TO BE CONTINUED

Additional material relating to Otto Kahn and the next volume in the *Oheka Chronicles, "The Lone Saboteur,"* can be found at www.BehindEveryGreatFortune.com

Acknowledgements

NUMEROUS PEOPLE have contributed to making this work a reality. Special thanks to Robert Kuncio-Raleigh whose superb editing and incessant support were an inspiration. Rhonda, Louis, Valerie and Jenna Amoroso also worked hard to improve, check and design the manuscript. Friends and colleagues too numerous to mention provided insight and encouragement throughout the gestation of this book. Jeff Schulz of Menagerie Company and Christy Meares lent their design expertise to this production. I would be remiss if I did not extend kudos to Lisa Mercurio for her excellent guidance.

All that being said, any mistakes or missteps in *Behind Every Great Fortune*™ are mine alone.

End Notes

1 Yannick Murphy, *Signed, Mata Hari* (Little, Brown and Company 2007), 276.
2 Gert Jonkers, "Gore Vidal, the Fantastic Man," *Butt*, No. 20 (7 April 2007)
3 Edward Radzinsky, *The Last Tsar: The Life and Death of Nicholas II* (Anchor Books Doubleday, 1992), 29.
4 Edward Radzinsky, *The Last Tsar: The Life and Death of Nicholas II* (Anchor Books Doubleday, 1992), 44.
5 Rasputin, Grigori Jefimovich http://www.propheties.it/rasputin.htm (July 2013).
6 The Travels of Marco Polo. ISBN 978-0-14-044057-7
7 "Kahn Buys More Land," *Long Islander,* 13 March 1914, 5.
8 "The 'Hereditary Commission,'" *New York Times*, 20 May 1906.
9 H. W. Crocker III, *Don't Tread on Me.* (New York: Crown Forum, 2006), 57.
10 Theodore Roosevelt, *Citizenship in a Republic, The Man in the Arena*, speech delivered at the Sorbonne Paris, France, April 23, 1910.
11 A.J. Balfour, principal speaker at opening banquet, FIRST INTERNATIONAL EUGENICS CONGRESS. Delivered at the Cecil Hotel, London, Great Britain, July 24, 1912.
12 Thomas R. Malthus. *An Essay on the Principle of Population.* (Oxford World's Classics reprint 1798), iv.v.1.

[13] George Bernard Shaw, interview *Listener* Feb 7, 1934. Despite chronological disparity, there is no question that Shaw was an avowed Eugenicist. *See* George Bernard Shaw, Lecture to the Eugenics Education Society, Reported in *The Daily Express*, March 4, 1910.

[14] Emma Goldman, *Living My Life, Volume 1*, (Readaclassic.com, 2010), 55–56.

[15] Edward Radzinsky, *Rasputin The Last Word*, (Phoenix, 2000), 211.

[16] Anon., *Spala: Letter from Nicholas II to his mother the Dowager Empress Marie, October 20, 1912*, http://www.livadia.org/otmaa/spala.htm (July 2013).

[17] Anon., *Spala: Alexei Nicolaievich*, http://www.livadia.org/otmaa/spala.htm (July 2013).

[18] Robert Massie, *Nicholas and Alexandra*, (Atheneum Publishers 1967), 185. Although Rasputin communicated these words by telegram, there is a greater dramatic effect by having him deliver them in person to Alexandra.

[19] Edward Radzinsky, *Rasputin The Last Word*, (Phoenix, 2000), 135.

[20] Edward Radzinsky, *Rasputin The Last Word*, (Phoenix, 2000), 139, referencing Felix Yusopov, *Lost Splendor*, "The idea that I would one day be one of the richest men in Russia went like wine to my head." http://www.alexanderpalace.org/lostsplendor/xii.html.

[21] Edward Radzinsky, *Rasputin The Last Word*, (Phoenix, 2000), 340.

[22] Alpha History, *The Nicky and Willy Telegrams* (1914) http://alphahistory.com/worldwar1/nicky-and-willy-telegrams-1914/ (July 2013).

[23] David Fromkin: *Europe's Last Summer: Why the World Went to War in 1914*, (William Heinemann Ltd, 2004), 218.

[24] Mina Curtiss, *Other People's Letters*, (Boston, Houghton Mifflin Company, 1978).

[25] Account by Borijove Jevtic, one of the leaders of the Narodna Odbrana of fate of Gavrilo Princip, http://wwi.lib.byu.edu/index.php/The_Assassination_of_Archduke_Franz_Ferdinand(July 2013).

[26] Vaslav Nijinsky, *The Diary of Vaslav Nijinsky*, ed. Joan Acocella (New York: Farrar, Strauss and Giroux, 1995), 14.

[27] Theodore Roosevelt, Note to Otto H. Kahn, July 28, 1919, Otto H. Kahn Papers, Princeton University, Department of Rare Books and Special Collections, Firestone Library, Princeton, New Jersey.

[28] Margaret Sanger, *My Fight for Birth Control* (New York: Farrar & Rinehart, 1931), ch. 1

[29] Jules Witcover, *Sabotage at Black Tom: Imperial Germany's Secret War in America — 1914–1917* (Algonquin Books of Chapel Hill 1989), 22.

[30] Radzinsky, *The Last Tsar: The Life and Death of Nicholas II* (Anchor Books Doubleday, 1992), 110, attributed to Maria "Munya" Golovina in conversation with Felix Yusopov. Here attributed to Tsarina Alexandra for dramatic effect.

[31] The authenticity of Rasputin's prediction of his own demise has been soundly rejected by expert historians. Edward Radzinsky, *Rasputin The Last Word*, (Phoenix, 2000), 647. However, there appears to be support among contemporaneous witnesses to Rasputin's prediction of death to the royal family if he were murdered. *Id.*, at 648.

[32] *A Revolutionist's Career*, by Leon Trotsky, *St. Louis Labor*, Feb. 1918.